The Sinner
Copyright © 2023
by Shantel Tessier All rights reserved.

For more information about the author and her books, visit her website— https://shanteltessier.com/
You can join her reader group. It's the only place to get exclusive teasers, first to know about current projects and release dates. And also have chances to win some amazing giveaways- https://www.facebook.com/groups/TheSinfulSide

Editor: Amanda Rash & Rumi Khan
Formatter: Melissa Cunningham (To.All.The.Books.I.Love)
Cover model: Jayme and Tony Rivera
Photographer: KayLa Ruiz Photography
Cover and interior designer: Melissa Cunningham (To.All.The.Books.I.Love)

# PLAYLIST

"Sick" by Adelitas Way

"Gasoline" by Halsey

"Thank You for Hating Me" by Citizen Soldier

"DARKSIDE" by Neoni

"I Hate everything About You" by Three Days Grace

"Lilith" by Ellise

"Pray" by Xana

"Battle Born" by Five Finger Death Punch

# WARNING

Things to know about *The Sinner*

Stalker

Forced proximity

Secret society

It is MF (no sharing the h)

J/P (jealous/possessive) H

OTT (over the top) H

**The Sinner** is set in the Lords' world introduced in **The Ritual**. They can both be read as standalones in no particular order.

Easton Bradley Sinnett—Sin—does not give a fuck about anyone or anything. He takes what he wants when he wants it. No questions asked. If this is not the kind of H you want in a dark romance, then you won't like this book.

# THE SINNER

USA TODAY & WALL STREET JOURNAL BESTSELLING AUTHOR

## SHANTEL TESSIER

*To all the dark romance readers whose minds are as fucked up as mine, this is for you. Embrace the darkness, for it is there that a light gets its chance to shine. And you are a motherfucking star, so don't ever be afraid to light up the night.*

# PROLOGUE
## L.O.R.D.

A Lord takes his oath seriously. Only blood will solidify their commitment to serve those who demand their complete devotion.

He is a **Leader**, believes in **Order**, knows when to **Rule**, and is a **Deity**.

A Lord must be initiated in order to become a member but can be removed at any time for any reason. If he makes it past the three trials of initiation, he will forever know power and wealth. But not all Lords are built the same. Some are stronger, smarter, hungrier than others.

They are challenged just to see how far their **loyalty** will go.

They are pushed to their limits in order to prove their **devotion**.

They are willing to show their **commitment**.

Nothing except their life will suffice.

Limits will be tested, and morals forgotten.

A Lord can be a judge, jury, and executioner. He holds power that is unmatched by anyone other than his brother.

**Chosen one:**

*A Lord must remain celibate during his first three years at Barrington University. Once he is initiated into the Lords, he is gifted a chosen for his senior year.*

### *A Lady:*

*After they graduate from Barrington, they are to marry a Lady— a wife to serve him. If he shall die before her, she is then gifted to another Lord to ensure the secrets are kept within the secret society.*

# ONE

## SIN

### INITIATION

Loyalty

Freshman year at Barrington University

I sit straight up as I hear my bedroom door bang against the wall. The lights are flipped on, making me squint at the harsh brightness. Men's voices are screaming at the top of their lungs, but the words they're saying don't register in my foggy mind.

Hands grab at my body, and my adrenaline immediately kicks in. I punch aimlessly, my body now wide awake and aware that men are in my room. I hit a face, making one of them grunt. I hit another body part, making another curse.

But there are too many of them. I'm yanked off my bed and fall face-first onto the floor. A knee is shoved into my back, and my arms are yanked behind me. "Get the fuck off me," I shout before something is shoved over my head, effectively taking away my sight.

My heavy breathing fills the hot and heavy hood.

I roll over onto my back. Kicking my feet aimlessly, I try to make contact with anything I can. But something heavy presses down on my chest, and I feel a prick in my neck. My body instantly betrays me as it goes limp on my floor. The last thing I feel is something being wrapped around my ankles when my eyes roll into the back of my head.

———

I OPEN MY HEAVY EYES, HAVING TO BLINK SEVERAL TIMES before they focus. My head is foggy, my body sluggish. They drugged me. It takes me a few seconds to see I'm in a room with other men—fellow Lords who are being initiated.

I only count three. The rest must have been taken somewhere else for a different type of initiation. Rumors are, they like to break us up. That way we're not all aware of what goes on. What we're expected to do. Some are challenged more than others. It's to weed out the weak from the strong.

This is a part of our journey to rule the world. *If you want to be a man, then you take one's life.* My father once told me that when he came home covered in blood, pistol in hand.

Growing up, I always thought we were different. But that night solidified my suspicions. I was twelve when I found out he was a Lord, and I'd one day get the chance to be one as well.

*You'd be surprised what a man will do to survive, Easton,* he added when I questioned how he could take a man's life and then go about his day like it didn't happen.

"Welcome, brothers," Lincoln calls out from behind me. "This is the beginning of your journey. Your first assignment, gentlemen. If you do not complete it, you will not receive another."

Translation—if we don't kill our target, we're out. And you don't want to be stripped of your Lord title. They won't kill you, but you'll always be looking over your shoulder with the possibility.

The point of being a Lord is to do their dirty work for them. There are millions of us throughout the world. You become a Lord after three years of initiation, and if you go against your oath, you're killed.

A man is shoved into the room with his hands tied behind his back and a hood over his head. His dirty clothes are covered in blood and filth.

"Gentlemen." Lincoln comes up behind him. "Who would like to show us how it's done?" he asks.

"I'll do it," I say without thought. This is not the time to be afraid. It's the chance to show what you're made of. You can't rule the world and be afraid to sacrifice others.

Linc walks over to me and nods. "Go ahead, Sin." He calls me by my nickname. "Pick your poison."

I stand on shaky legs, my mind still sluggish, but I can do this. I walk over to a table where there's a rope, gun, and pocketknife.

*Pick your poison.*

I grab the knife and turn back to the man kneeling in the center of the room. He's shaking his head, but the hood prevents us from seeing his true identity. Doesn't matter. If I don't kill him, someone else here will. I can tell by his muffled screams that he's gagged.

Before I can reach him, he falls facedown and tries to wiggle his way across the floor. If I were levelheaded, I'd laugh. I kick him in the side, knocking him to his back. Straddling his bare chest, I see the Lords' crest on it—a circle with three horizontal lines running through it. It's not old by any means but also not new. Probably a couple of years.

I feel all eyes on me. I take in a deep breath and crouch down, opening the pocketknife and shoving the blade into his neck.

Yanking it out, I watch the blood squirt all over both of us. His body now convulsing before movement ceases completely.

Standing to my feet, I hold out the knife to Lincoln and he smiles at me. "You keep it."

# TWO

# SIN

## INITIATION

Devotion
Sophomore year at Barrington University

I'm straddling my motorcycle, my earbuds blaring "Sick" by Adelitas Way when the song pauses, alerting me of an incoming message. Unzipping the pocket of my leather jacket, I remove my cell and read the text.

> UNKNOWN: You have thirty minutes.

I put it away and pull my leather gloves on, followed by my helmet, fastening the buckle under my chin. Starting up my blacked-out R1, I feel the engine rev between my legs and kick it into gear. I tear out of the parking lot, squealing the back tire. Taking the back way, I lean into the curves, practically dragging my knee as I wind up the hill on the Pennsylvanian road.

As I ascend, my headlights shine on the two lanes. There is no shoulder here. It goes from road to tree line. One wrong move and I'd be in the hospital or dead. No one is on this road at this time of night, so if I were to crash and it didn't kill me, who knows how long I'd lie there before I got help. Neither one sounds appealing tonight.

Approaching my destination, I slow down and take the last curve before stopping at the top of the hill. Placing both of my feet on either side of the blacktop to hold up the bike, I look over the house, now in full view.

Nothing but a glass four-story front. The lights are so bright that if I wasn't wearing the darkened face shield on my helmet, my eyes would hurt.

I've been here before. A lot of times, actually, over my twenty years of existence. This will be my first time for business.

Cars line the cobblestone circle drive. He's having a party. I'm not surprised. A man of his stature must keep up appearances for all intents and purposes. He's a respected Lord. But he's done something they don't agree with.

Usually, I wouldn't give a fuck what a man has done—Lord or not. An order is an order. But him? This house? Why? I've obviously missed something right in front of my face all these years. Maybe I've been too blinded with big tits and bleach-blond hair to pay much attention to anything else that lives inside the mansion.

Picking up my foot, I put the bike in gear once again and take off, making my way down the hill via the hidden road. None of his guests would use this way to access the house, so I'm able to remain unseen.

Coming to the bottom of the hill, I continue past the house before bringing my bike to a stop on the side of the road. I push it right into the tree line to hide it in the darkness. I remove my helmet, leather gloves, backpack off my shoulders, and jacket to have better mobility with my arms. I yank the earbuds out of my ears and shove them into my jeans pocket. Then I place my backpack on the seat and unzip it. I grab what I need and screw the suppressor onto the end of the barrel. I shove the gun into the back of my jeans, securing it for the time being. Then I remove the hoodie, pulling it over my head, along with the mask, before I place the backpack on my back, just in case, and make my way across the street toward the house.

My combat boots crush the leaves and branches under the soles once I hit the other side. The house lights up the woods in the middle of the night. As if any partygoer could miss the twenty-million-dollar mansion.

Making my way up to the house, I smile that the idiot doesn't even have security at the front gate tonight. That's how fucking cocky he is. Stupid motherfucker. He is not untouchable.

I stay low, crouching down behind the trimmed bushes lining the side of the property. Every now and then, I peek to watch the guests get out of their cars and limos to be escorted inside by men dressed in white tuxedos.

Not a single guy who resembles security is to be seen. He feels safe here. Making my way to the side of the house, I see the wooden lattice that I know she uses to get in and out of the house when she's snuck out in the past. I start to climb it until I get to the second floor, where I jump the railing to the balcony. Wrapping my leather-covered hand around the knob, I turn it to find it unlocked.

Slipping into the bedroom, I look around and see it's empty, like I knew it would be. She's downstairs partying with the others. It's been going on for hours. I'm sure she's drunk and bored as shit by now.

The room is spotless. Not a single thing out of place. Her king-size four-post bed sits against the wall to the left. The white duvet covers it along with an obsessive number of pillows. The bench at the end has her favorite throw blanket that she prefers to wrap up in when watching a movie. I gave it to her for her birthday a few years ago.

Slowly walking through the room, I inhale the scent of vanilla.

It makes me groan, thinking of grabbing her hair and burying my face in her neck. My fingers digging into her creamy thighs while my cock fucks her cunt.

I'm so fucking hard that it hurts. I dream about her when I'm asleep and awake. She's consuming me to the point I'm suffocating.

Shaking my head, I adjust my dick and make my way to the door. I don't have time for that right now. I leave the bedroom door open as I step out of the room and into a lit hallway. Large, expensive artwork hangs on the walls that he paid millions for from well-known artists.

Music filters up from the lower level as I wrap my gloved fingers around the wooden banister to see the people below.

Everyone is dressed to the nines, like they always are. But my eyes catch sight of a bleached blonde. Ellington Jade Asher. She stands over in the corner by a bar. Her back leans against it while she looks over the crowd with an expressionless look on her gorgeous face, and she's holding a glass of champagne in her hand. I wonder how many she's had.

*My little demon.* She's always been the one. She doesn't know it, but when the time is right, I'll let her know.

Her mother walks up to her, and Elli gives her a fake smile.

Soon, Elli. Soon you'll worship me like the devil worships his hell.

A man walks up the stairs, and I smile when I see who it is. *Jackpot.*

I push away from the banister and quickly make my way to the end of the hallway to the master suite. I hide behind the open door in the shadows and wait.

The sound of his feet approaching has my heart racing. I remove the gun from my jeans and slowly cock it, trying to make as little noise as possible.

He enters the room, and I watch him make his way past the

Alaskan king bed and into the adjoining bathroom, all while he whistles. The light shines under the shut door, and I make my way over to it, softly turning the door handle and poking my head inside. I see him at the sink, opening a bottle of pills. Viagra.

Fuck, I hope someone shoots me when I have to take medication to get hard.

Popping the pill in his mouth, he throws back his glass of scotch, swallowing it. Not sure what the fuck he's going to do with a hard dick while in the middle of a party, but it doesn't matter.

When he turns to exit, I step inside the bathroom, raising my gun to aim at his head. He doesn't even have time to register what's about to happen when I pull the trigger.

The bullet hits him right between the eyes. Blood runs down his face and onto his shirt, and I watch his blue eyes turn black. A smile tugs at my lips while the life slowly drains out of him. I like the rush of killing. I know that's what a serial killer would say. And although I do kill people, I do it because I'm ordered to. Not because I choose random people to torture. My assignments come from a higher-up. And you never say no. A Lord lives in a kill-or-be-killed world. And I don't know about you, but I'd do anything to survive. Even if that means taking someone else's life.

He drops to his knees before falling face-first onto the white marble floor.

I bend down next to his body and remove his cell phone from the pocket of his William Westmancott suit. Then I take the bolt cutters from my backpack and put his right pointer finger between the two blades before snapping it off. Dropping his hand, a fresh pool of blood flows from his now severed finger.

"I'm going to need this," I say, opening up my backpack once again and pulling out the small lunch box. I place the finger inside, securing it with the ice pack, and then unzip my jacket pocket before placing the cell inside for safekeeping. He's got a lock on it.

Note to self: never use a body part to unlock your phone. It can easily be removed and used. Even an eye.

My head snaps up when I hear a sharp intake of breath. She sees the man lying facedown, and her red lips part to scream. The champagne flute in her hand falls to the floor, shattering at her heels. "Daddy—"

I'm slamming her up against the wall next to the open door before she can finish. My hand slaps over her mouth, and I pin her in place.

Big ice-blue eyes look up at the mask covering my face. I've never seen anything more beautiful. I could stare at them every second of every day. They've never been so large; she's terrified of what she sees. Me. I can feel her small body trembling against mine, and tears start to fill her eyes. They're gorgeous.

She blinks, quickly looking at the man's body and then back to me. I remove the gun from my waistband and press it into the side of her ribs with my free hand. She whimpers, her legs buckling. But I remove my hand from her mouth to move it around her neck, holding her up and restricting her air.

Her now smeared lips part, and I hold the gun in place. "This is our little secret," I whisper, not giving my voice away. *She knows me.*

Nodding, she grips my forearm, and I hate the fact that I wore gloves because I've dreamed of my hands on her skin like this. Of course, my cock was fucking her cunt at the same time.

"I'd hate to have to kill you too." I push the gun farther into her ribs with my words, hoping she'll take me seriously. I'd never kill her, but I sure as fuck would make her regret being alive.

Tears spill over her bottom lashes and run down her cheeks while her lips start to turn blue. Her body fights me, but not as much as I'd expect. I tilt my head to the side when she pushes her hips forward into mine, and I know she can feel how hard I am.

I bite my tongue to keep from moaning. Fuck, I knew she'd be this way. A part of me has always known she'd be my dirty little whore once I got the chance to make her mine.

I let go and take a step back. She falls to her knees, coughing and choking out a sob. I crouch in front of her, using the gun to push the bleach-blond hair from her tear-streaked face. She looks up at me through her watery lashes, and I imagine shoving my cock down her tight throat. Or in her pussy from behind. Making her come while she stares at the man I just killed lying on the floor. I want him to know she'll be my filthy little slut one day, and I'm going to do things to her that will make her disgusted with herself. I'll control her like a puppet on a string.

"Please ..."

I stand, grabbing a handful of her hair and yanking her to her feet. She goes to cry out, but I slap my free hand over her mouth, pulling her back to my front. The backpack is already on my shoulder, so I hold the gun to her ribs and order through clenched teeth, "Walk."

She does as she's told with her arms up and out to the side, and we silently make our way through the bathroom, out of the master suite, and down the hall past all the guests on the lower level to her bedroom.

Shutting the door behind me with my boot, I let go and shove her farther into the room before locking us in. Alone.

"Pl-ease," she begs, turning to face me. I like that she wants to look at me. That she's not going to turn and hide. Those big blue eyes look me up and down, taking in my size and weighing her options. When she realizes she has no chance of winning in a fight, she licks her wet lips and decides to bargain. "Money—"

"Facedown on the floor. Hands behind your back," I order as quietly but as sternly as I can, interrupting her. The moment I step out of the window, she'll run for help. And that's just unacceptable.

She places her hands up in surrender, the movement pulling

her already short black cocktail dress up a little more, exposing the top of her thighs. My eyes linger on them for a second, wondering what she tastes like. I just want to spread them wide while I bury my tongue so deep inside her she's screaming for me to stop.

Sniffing, she goes on, getting my attention. "I won't—"

I hold my gun up to her chest, and a sob breaks loose, causing her shoulders to shake. Her knees give out, and she falls to the pristine white carpet like the good girl she is, positioning herself on her stomach.

Removing my backpack, I unzip it and grab what I want. Then I straddle her hips, placing my gun in the back of my jeans. Pulling her hands behind her back, I secure them with a zip tie, making her sob once more.

I stand and look over her lying there, tied and ready to be used. Fuck, how many times have I imagined this? It's like the Lords are rewarding me and torturing me at the same time.

As a show of our loyalty, we can't fuck anyone for the first three years of our initiation. Not until our senior year. I'm only a sophomore. But right here, right now, I feel like this is an opportunity I can't pass up. Checking my watch, I see I've got eight minutes before my time is up. Technically, the job is done, so I've already passed this initiation.

"Spread your legs. Ass up in the air," I command.

Burying her face in the carpet, she does as she's told. She understands she has no leverage here. If she wants to walk out of this room alive, she'll give me what I want.

Ever so slowly, she spreads her knees, the movement lifting her ass up in the air, forcing the hem of her dress to rise up in the process. I crouch down between her legs, looking over the wet spot in her nude-colored thong. "What turned you on the most? Your *daddy* lying dead on the floor? Or my gun pressed into your side?"

A shrill scream comes from her when she realizes she's been

caught. The bitch is turned on by it. I knew she was. The adrenaline of danger can be arousing for some.

Grabbing her hair, I yank her to her feet and shove her back into one of the corner posts of her king-size bed. I start removing my belt.

"Please!" She sobs, trying to run from me, but I hold her in place with my body.

The leather is yanked through my belt loops, and I shove it into her mouth. Bringing it behind her head, I secure it around the back of the post where I buckle it in place as tight as it will go.

I move back to stand in front of her, my heavy breathing filling the inside of my mask. The only thing she can see are my eyes, and I'm wearing contacts. They're as red as the blood pouring out of the guy I killed in the room down the hall.

Hers swim in tears while drool runs down her chin. Her straight white teeth bite into the leather. I remove my gun once again and lift it. She whimpers, closing her eyes. I unscrew the suppressor and press the end of the barrel to her upper thigh, slowly raising her dress to expose her underwear.

I cup her pussy, and she flinches, her eyes popping open to meet mine once again. "One with no voice, can't say no," I say simply.

She blinks, fresh tears spilling over her bottom lashes to run down her cheeks.

I wish I could lick them off her face, but my mask covers my mouth. "But you wouldn't tell me no, would you?" Pulling her thong to the side, I run my glove-covered fingers over her cunt. Looking down, I rub my fingers together, smearing her wetness. The underwear didn't lie.

She sniffs, but her hips push forward. I smile behind my mask. She fights the belt in her mouth while her tied hands are smashed between her back and the post I've secured her head to.

"What is one person's heaven is another's hell," I state and then reach up and yank on her dress, pulling the thin straps down over her arms to expose her breasts to me. She's sobbing uncontrollably, but her pretty pink nipples are hard, and I run the barrel over them while she mumbles unintelligible noises around the makeshift gag.

Lowering the gun down her shaking body, I kick her legs open, and she blinks rapidly. I lean into her neck, inhaling her scent, and my cock jerks inside my jeans. "You're my heaven, and I'm your hell," I whisper, making sure she understands her current situation.

Pulling back, I watch her eyes fall closed, and fresh tears roll down her once-done-up face. Her flawless makeup is ruined. I like it. All it's missing is cum smeared all over it.

Lowering the gun between her legs, I shove a finger into her, making her cry out. I'm running out of time, so this isn't going to be slow. It's going to be rough.

I enter a second one, and she rises up on her tiptoes in her Dior heels. I then remove them, running the gun over her cunt, and her breathing turns erratic. I watch her eyes grow heavy as I work my fingers into her over and over, adding a third and then a fourth. She's crying, body shaking while she sobs, and I slip the tip of the barrel into her before removing it and doing it again. Her pussy opens up for me, and her eyes close. Once the barrel is wet enough to enter on its own, my fingers abandoned her cunt and slap her breasts.

Her body leans into mine, and I smile behind my mask. I knew she'd be this way. Desperate. She's been trained for years—groomed to be a Lord's whore by her mother and her father. Even if they didn't mean to, it's just a part of our world. You serve regardless of whether you have a dick or a pussy. A dick just has more power in this scenario.

As I pump the gun in and out of her, she thrashes against the bedpost but never closes her legs. I'm not even holding them open anymore.

I pinch her nipple, pulling on it, slapping her breasts and face. She's sobbing, drool running down her open mouth and onto her chin and chest to where her dress is bunched up around her pierced belly button.

When I remove the gun, she sags in her heels, and I slap her cunt, making her cry out. I shove two fingers into her. "Fuck, you're soaked," I growl through gritted teeth, looking at her juices smeared all over my glove-covered fingers. I have to remind myself to hide my true voice. I want to tell her who I am and see that look in her eyes. I know she likes me because we've been dancing around the idea for years. It just never worked out, and then I started initiation, blowing any chance I had with her. A woman like Ellington Asher needs sex. She needs to know she's wanted. And the way she's getting off on fucking my gun shows me just how fucking twisted she'll be in bed when I finally make her mine.

I push the gun back into her cunt, and this time, I don't let up. I fuck her with it until she's a sobbing, drooling mess. When I pull it out, I hold it up to her face. "Look at that cum," I praise, running it against her cheek and down her neck. She tries to pull her face away, but the belt holds her in place, the leather pinching her cheeks.

"What we did tonight is our little secret," I say, and she nods the best she can. "What I did tonight is our little secret, understand?" She nods again, sniffing as snot runs from her nose that is red from her crying.

I leave her there for a few seconds while I load everything in my backpack on the floor. After putting it on, I remove my belt from her mouth, and she softly cries out. I can't help but run my leather glove over the indentions the belt left on her cheeks. "Open," I order, and it doesn't surprise me one bit that she parts her swollen lips. I place the small pocketknife between her perfectly white teeth, and she holds it in her mouth. "You'll need that to get your hands free."

Her eyes widen at my words, understanding that I'm leaving her here. Just in case she decides to talk, it'll take her at least a couple of minutes to cut through the zip tie before she runs off and tells everyone about the dead body in her parents' bathroom and how the murderer fucked her with his gun.

I make my way down the side of the house and across the street to my motorcycle. I go to start it up but stop myself. Curiosity getting the best of me. Something she said is eating at me.

Unzipping the pocket of my leather jacket, I pull out the cell and the severed finger from the backpack. I scan it to unlock the device. I scroll through his incoming and outgoing texts and phone calls. Nothing really looks out of place. I open his email and go through it. Nothing.

I'm about to close it when I see another folder. Opening it, I plan on scrolling through the emails, but there are none. Odd. But there are multiple folders. Each one is labeled by year. I open one up.

My heart accelerates at what I see. My finger scrolls through them so fast that my mind has a hard time keeping up with the images. My hands start to shake, my chest heaving as I try to catch my breath. The blood is rushing in my ears, and I start pulling on my hoodie's collar.

Glancing up at the balcony, I see her standing outside on it. Her hands hold the railing as she looks out into the dark night. She can't see me because I'm too far hidden behind the tree line. She didn't run to get help immediately after I killed James. I know my secret is safe with her. And I know why.

# THREE

## SIN

### INITIATION

Commitment
Junior year at Barrington University

I sit tucked back in the corner on the terrace when I hear the glass doors open and close, alerting me that the homeowner has finally arrived.

I wait, sitting perfectly still. I have my cell phone off and tucked into my pocket so no one calls or texts and gives me away.

"Yeah, I'll call him tomorrow." I hear his voice travel as he walks over to the wet and dry sauna, removing his black silk robe. "Right, it's like taking candy from fucking babies," he goes on, talking on his cell. "He won't know what fucking hit him after we're done."

I smile. Ironic, considering he has no idea I broke into his house over an hour ago and have been waiting out here for him to sit in the sauna as part of his nightly routine.

Remaining still in the darkly lit corner, I watch him say his goodbyes before removing the robe and entering the sauna.

It's an octagon shape, with benches on each side and a round heating element in the center. Reaching over, he picks up the ladle that's in the bucket and pours what he thinks is water over the heating element.

Steam rises and a shrill scream comes from his mouth as the steam hits his face and chest.

The man has done something to piss off the Lords. I don't know the specifics. It doesn't matter. He's betrayed his oath and must pay the consequences. I've been watching him for a week and his routine never faltered. Idiot.

"Burns, doesn't it?" I say, coming to stand in front of the glass door, placing my hands in the pockets of my jeans.

"What the fuck?" he barks, looking around aimlessly, eyes tightly shut. "Who ... what the...?"

"I replaced the water with acid," I inform him.

His screams grow louder and he begins to wipe his eyes, once again blinking rapidly as he tries to open them.

He's gasping, grabbing his neck, his skin already starting to bubble. He's panicking instead of thinking clearly. He stumbles backward and trips over the heating element in the middle, falling on top of it.

The high-pitched scream that follows makes me smile. He manages to roll over off the side of it and I see the burn marks already on his skin.

"A third-degree chemical burn is no joke," I add. "You fucked up, Lance."

"No, no. No," he rushes out, eyes tightly closed and getting to his feet. He can't see shit so he walks around aimlessly, running into the walls. His skin bubbling to the point it's starting to fall off. "I didn't mean to..."

"What's done is done. By my oath, you are a brother. But you betrayed us. Therefore, you must be terminated."

"Noooooo."

I wrap a zip tie around the wooden door handles to ensure he can't get out if he manages to find them. I watch through the glass as he very slowly turns to nothing but bones as his skin falls off his body along with his hair.

Another initiation completed.

It's time to go see my little demon. It's become a reward. After I finish an initiation, I go and get her off. It's the best part of becoming a Lord.

# FOUR

## SIN

### INITIATION

ONE OF THEM
SENIOR YEAR AT BARRINGTON UNIVERSITY

I 'm on my knees, hands cuffed behind my back. I'm kneeling beside fourteen other brothers. There were twenty-five of us during my freshman year, but not all of us made it. A fellow Lord by the name of Ryat kneels to my right. My friend Jayce to my left.

Lincoln stands in front of us, hands behind his back, chest bowed and a smile on his face.

This is it. What we've trained for. What we were bred for. A Lord is a machine. He does not fail at any task, no matter how big or small.

I can feel the power that surrounds the room. Men dressed in suits that cost more than most make in a year. It's like electricity. It excites me more.

My breathing picks up when I hear the singe of Ryat's skin to my right as he gets his brand. I'm next.

One by one, we will each take our oath and become a Lord

tonight. We start our senior year at Barrington in five weeks, and we are all very aware that this is just the beginning. The past three years of initiation are nothing compared to what's to come.

Lincoln comes to stand in front of me, and I look up at him through my lashes. "Easton Bradley Sinnett, you have completed all trials of initiation. Do you wish to proceed?" he asks me.

"Yes, sir." Without a doubt in my mind. This is just another step toward getting who I want—a gorgeous blonde who has no idea who I really am. I can't wait to show her.

"Remove his shirt," he orders someone behind me.

The fabric is yanked behind my head, exposing my chest and stomach to the room. I take in a deep breath, knowing what's to come. The next second, the chain wraps around my neck from behind. A boot presses into my back, pulling it tight to restrict my air but not suffocate me. It's so we can't fight them. No matter how much we are willing to go through to get to this point, a man's fight or flight will kick in during situations like this.

"A Lord must be willing to go above and beyond for his title. He must show strength and have what it takes." He dips the end of the hot iron into the fire at his feet, slowly turning it over. I try to fight the chain wrapped around my neck, my cuffed hands clenching and unclenching. "If you shall fail your position as a Lord, we will take what was earned." He looks at the guy who stands next to him. "Silence him."

The chain is pulled tighter, taking away what little breath I had left while the guy shoves a cloth into my mouth. I fight harder, but the guy with the chain shoves his boot into my back, holding me in place.

"Easton Bradley Sinnett, welcome to the Lords. For you shall reap the benefits of your sacrifice," Lincoln states before I feel the hot searing pain in my chest and smell my own flesh burning.

# FIVE

# SIN

Three years of celibacy can make a man go crazy. Just ask any Lord. We are to show just how far we will go to prove ourselves. We have to be initiated into the secret society our freshman, sophomore, and junior years at Barrington University—only the elite attend from all around the world. But not every male student at Barrington is a Lord. Some don't even know we exist, and we prefer it that way. It's easier to attack when you jump out from the shadows.

We've officially been Lords for seven weeks now. We're two weeks into our classes at the university. Our senior year, we get pussy. A chosen is given to us. She is offered on a silver platter to use however we want.

For someone who hasn't had his dick sucked in three years, I'm not all that excited about accepting a chosen. Nothing about that process appeals to me. I like the chase. The hunt. A challenge.

It's funny how the Lords teach us to take what we want, including a life, but we're supposed to accept the pussy they offer us. Where is the excitement in that?

I sit at the round poker table at the house of Lords—we're

required to live here while attending Barrington—looking over the cards in my hand with a cigar in my mouth. I can't stand them but thought *what the hell* when Jasper—a fellow Lord—opened the box that sat on the table. His father gave them to him in celebration that he gets some pussy tomorrow.

"Pick a name, dude. You're taking forever."

I look over my shoulder to see a few guys standing at the pool table. A black vase in the middle full of folded-up pieces of paper.

"What's the point in picking names again?" I ask curiously. "You've already decided on your chosens." They've been talking about *drawing* all day, but I'm not sure why. The vow ceremony for our chosen is tomorrow night, and we already know who we're getting. Some of us get who we want, and others don't. I only want one woman, but unfortunately, she wasn't on the list.

"Pussy," Jasper answers, looking up at me. "Want to draw?"

I shake my head. "No thanks," I say, turning back to my game.

"Ryat, how about you, man?" I hear Jasper ask.

I look at Ryat, who sits across from me at the table. He, too, stares at his cards. "No."

"Come on, Ryat." Jasper whines like a chick, and Ryat's green eyes snap to glare at him, getting his attention. "What if she doesn't show?" Jasper asks.

"She will," Ryat says matter-of-factly.

"Dude, why are you putting all your eggs in one basket when you can have six baskets?" Larson jokes from my right, listening in.

"You mean, why is he putting his cock in one cunt when he can have twelve?" Jake mumbles around his cigar. "Seriously, man. I wouldn't waste your time on Blakely. She'll never be over Matt."

Ryat tenses but doesn't acknowledge that statement.

"Well, I'll be nice." Jasper goes on from behind me at Ryat's silence, "When she doesn't show up tomorrow at the vow ceremony to be your chosen, I'll share my pussy with you. Hell, I'll even be nice enough and give you her ass."

Ryat tosses his cards down and gets up from the table, leaving the room without another word. I can't tell if he's mad or just tired. We're not close. Over a hundred men of all grades live in this house right now. Only fifteen of us made it to be seniors this year. His two best friends, Prickett and Gunner, who sat on either side of him, also get up and silently exit the room.

"Hey, Sin, you sure you don't want to draw?" Jasper asks again.

"Positive," I answer with a sigh. The guy is relentless. Ryat had the right idea by leaving the room.

"I bet you'll change your mind when you see who I just got," he adds with a dark laugh.

It's not like women volunteered for their cocks. They just wrote down the names of girls who attend Barrington that they want a piece of and threw them in a vase to draw from. Then they'll do whatever it takes to fuck them. They've got a bet going on who can fuck the girl they draw first. I think the pot is up to fifty thousand dollars. They're bored as fuck, if you ask me.

"Oh yeah?" I ask, not giving a flying fuck whose name is written on his piece of paper.

"Two words," he calls out, and my body tenses when he speaks again. "Ellington Asher."

"Damn." Nate sighs. "I'll trade you." He holds up his folded piece of paper with a frown. "Elli's a freak in bed. Lets you do whatever the fuck you want."

"How the fuck would you know that?" Jacob shoves his shoulder.

"Rumors, man. She's the best kind of slut."

My hand tightens on the cards, crinkling them. *That's a lie.* She's not sleeping with anyone that I know of. And I would know. I've been sneaking into her bedroom for the past two years. I've kept her satisfied as much as I can without breaking my oath to the Lords.

Chance, another Lord, raises his hand from my left. "Pick one for me," he mumbles around his cigar. "Go ahead and pick me two. Better my odds."

Jacob laughs, dipping his hand into the vase. "You have to fuck them both at the same time, Becks." He calls him by his nickname, pulling out two pieces of paper.

"I can do that." Chance smiles.

The door opens, and Lincoln steps inside the room, his eyes on mine. "Sin, may I speak to you for a moment?"

Dropping my cards, I exit the room and follow him down the hall to his office. He holds the door open for me, and I step inside, falling into his chair. "Everything okay?" I ask, trying to ignore the voice in the back of my head that tells me one of my fellow Lords is going to be fucking the girl I've wanted since I realized what sex is. I've come too close to just hand her over to someone else. Put too many hours into getting her where I want her.

He sits at his desk. "I've got your first assignment for your senior year."

I smile. Thank fuck. Life has been boring lately.

He slaps down an envelope, and I open it. My body tenses at the four pictures I see. *What the fuck is this shit?*

"Get me as much information as you can." He points at the man who is in all of them. "And, Sin...?"

My narrowed eyes slowly rise to meet his, the blood rushing in my ears, but I try to keep my breathing calm, not wanting him to notice.

"I want more than just notes." With that, he looks at his computer, dismissing me.

I grab the envelope, exit the room, and head right back to the game room. Walking over to Jasper, I snatch the piece of paper out of his hand and storm out, ignoring the sounds of their laughter carrying down the hall.

Entering my bedroom, I slam the door shut and stomp into my

adjoining bathroom. Senior year we get our own suites. I turn on the water and get undressed, needing a cold shower.

I've been seeing Elli for the past two years. Since that night I fulfilled my assignment and forced her to come on the barrel of my gun. But she has no idea it's me, and I've never fucked her. I make her come while wearing a mask, and I always tie her up. The second time I met with her was just as good as the first.

*I gently shove the door open from her balcony, the soft wind pushing the dark curtains around me. I push them away as I enter her room to find her asleep in bed with the duvet pulled up to her neck. I make my way over to her and pull it back to expose her naked body. It's as if she was expecting me.*

*It's been two weeks since I was at this house, in this room, and she was coming on my gun. She's on her side, one leg bent, the other out straight. I see her left hand holds my knife. She's expecting me to come back, thinking she'll stab me. Sorry to disappoint her.*

*I remove my handcuffs from my backpack and gently push her onto her stomach. She starts to stir, and I pause, waiting for her to relax into the mattress.*

*When she's softly snoring, I grab her arms and bring them behind her back, then quickly wrap each cuff around her dainty wrists and crawl in next to her.*

*Now on her stomach, her heavy eyes open and meet mine. She gasps, but like I expected, she doesn't scream. Realization takes a few seconds to sink in before she notices her hands are cuffed behind her back.*

*"You left your door unlocked," I whisper, reaching out and pushing her bleach-blond hair off the side of her face. I was just here four hours ago with my parents to join her and her mother for dinner. I never left. I sat outside in my car around the corner just waiting for her to go to sleep. "That's not smart, Elli."*

*Her dark brows pull together. "How do you know me?" she asks, her voice full of curiosity. I'm sure she's lost sleep trying to figure out who I am. I once again wear my mask, black jeans, and matching hoodie with my red contacts and leather gloves. She can't see a single part of my skin.*

*"Why does it matter?" I ask my own question.*

*She wiggles, rocking her body side to side, and I push on her shoulder, guiding her onto her back. I get up and straddle her narrow hips, my eyes dropping to her exposed chest. I smile as I watch her nipples harden for me.*

*"Ow," she whines, arching her back, her arms now pinned underneath her. "I need—"*

*Slapping my glove-covered hand over her mouth, I stop whatever demand she was going to order me. It won't happen no matter what it is.*

*My free hand grabs the knife that lies next to her. Opening it up, I hold it to the side of her face, and she whimpers, those gorgeous eyes widening. Her hips arch underneath me, and I smile behind my mask.*

*Removing my hand from her lips, I let the tip of my finger trace them. She sucks in a deep breath, her chest rising. I adjust myself between her legs and lower the tip of the knife down her chest bone, over her stomach, and to her pussy. I flip it in my hand, the handle running up and down her cunt, spreading her pussy lips for me.*

*She moans, her eyes falling closed, and I slide the handle into her. She arches her back and neck, her legs opening wider for me to have better access. I pump it in and out, watching her juices cover the black handle.*

*Her body rocks back and forth, her breathing getting heavier, and my free hand reaches out, slapping the side of her breast. She gasps, so I do it again, and she's moaning.*

*I drop my hand to her cunt and rub over her clit. My thumb plays with her piercing. It's so hot. I want to pull on it with my teeth. Suck it into my mouth and watch her back arch while she screams.*

"Oh God..." She trails off, licking her lips.

I hate that she doesn't know who I am. That she can't call out my name when I make her take what I give her. One day, she will. And when that day comes, she'll realize there is no God in our world. There's nothing holy in a world full of sinners.

My eyes drop back to the knife, and I hold the blade while I get more forceful with the handle. Her legs spread wide to make sure she doesn't cut herself. Pity. A part of me would like to see her bleed for me. I'd lick it clean off her body like an offering.

"Oh my God." She's gasping, her neck arched, and I reach up and wrap my free hand around her throat, restricting her air while I position myself on my knees, hovering over her while I fuck her cunt with the handle of the knife.

I lower my face to hers, watching her ice-blue eyes go heavy. Her plump lips part on an attempt to get in air, but I don't allow it. She stiffens under me, and her eyes fall closed as she comes like the good whore I knew she'd be.

Sitting up, I pull the knife out while letting go of her neck. Her body sags into the mattress, sucking in a breath. I hold out the knife to her face, and her heavy eyes open to meet mine. She parts her lips and sticks her tongue out. I run the handle along it, watching her lick it clean.

Fuck, I want to taste it. Not yet. Soon, I'll get to have her however I want her, whenever I want her.

I shut off the water, pulling myself from that memory. It's only one of many. Getting out of the shower, I see the envelope on the counter. I open it up again and look over the photos in my hand. My heart races at the fact that she's spreading her legs for someone else.

When did he come into her life? How had I missed it? It's been a few weeks since I visited her. I've been busy with the Lords and unable to get away to see her. We've been so close to the vow ceremony that I thought I'd just wait. I was tired of torturing myself, getting her off but unable to get a taste. As of tomorrow, that will no longer be a problem.

Slamming it down, I place my hands on the edge of the counter and bow my head. It doesn't matter. He won't stop me from getting what I want. Lifting my eyes, I smile at myself. I love a challenge. And this will be my greatest one yet.

# SIX

# SIN

The following night, I'm sitting in my Zenvo TSR-S, lights off and tucked back behind the tree line off the two-lane road.

The guy in my passenger seat is counting out the stack of hundred-dollar bills I gave him.

"No offense," he mumbles.

"None taken." I'd count that shit too. You can't trust anyone these days.

He takes a few from the stack and hands them through the cracked window to the friend he brought standing outside the car. "Get ready," he orders the guy.

"Nice doing business with you." The kid laughs at me before walking around the front of my car and getting into his, parked next to me.

We wait silently. Adjusting in my seat, I feel the gun tucked into the back of my jeans. Like I said, you can't trust anyone these days. I went to a hole-in-the-wall bar, made an offer to some men I knew wouldn't refuse some cash, and struck a deal.

Here we are.

Sitting up straighter, I watch headlights come toward us. When the headlights pass us, we remain still, hidden by the tree line. The car sitting to my left turns theirs on and pulls out onto the road, following it.

About time, I turn on my lights and pull out onto the road, going in the opposite direction.

The house comes into view at the end of the road, and I pull into the driveway. It's a white cottage tucked back into the woods of Pennsylvania. Secluded. Perfect place to hide bodies. There's an old wives' tale that these woods are haunted. That the Lords have buried so many men in the ground that if we ever had a flood, the bodies would rise and cover the street.

I wouldn't be surprised if it happened. At twenty-two, my body count is five, and it's only going to go up from there.

Coming to a stop, I see a car I recognize in the driveway. I expected it to be here. We sat tucked back in the trees when it drove by two hours ago on its way to this house.

Rolling my car to a stop, I pull the spare set of keys out of my pocket. "Take it straight there," I order the man in my passenger seat.

He nods, taking them from me. Getting out of my car, he gets into the other, starts it up, and I watch it drive off just as my cell starts vibrating in my pocket.

"Hello?" I answer, turning toward the house.

"Dude, where the fuck are you?" my best friend Jayce barks into my ear. "The vow ceremony is about to start. Your chosen—"

"You can have her," I interrupt him, knowing where this conversation is going and not caring.

He starts laughing, and I end the call when I make it to the back door. Just as I suspected, it's unlocked. I gently push it open to step inside, holding my breath that it doesn't squeak and alert anyone in the house of my presence. Closing it behind me, I tiptoe across the tile floor and quickly scan the room. It's dark. The clock that hangs on the wall to my left tells me it's a little after midnight.

I have an assignment. Get in, get a list together, and report the information that I document back to the Lords. Making my way down the hallway, I stop to take a look in the kitchen. Using my flashlight, I see a bottle of wine on the white counter. It's empty along with two wineglasses. One has a very distinctive pink lipstick stain. I'd know it anywhere.

Turning away from the kitchen, I head toward the master suite. I've spent the past twenty-four hours studying the blueprints of this house, so I know where everything is.

Pushing open the bedroom door, I shine my light to see it's empty. That means there's only one other place to look. I make my way back to where I entered the house, but instead of going outside, I take a right down another hallway. There's a door at the end with two locks on it. Both are deadbolts, but they lock from the outside. They are designed to keep something in on the other side. Not to keep someone out.

Turning both to unlock, I step inside, knowing it leads to the basement. My boots are heavy on the wooden stairs. Coming to the last step, I lift my light to see the room. It's what anyone would call a dungeon. Whips, chains, and leather belts hang on the back wall in various shapes and sizes. Some would use them to destroy flesh. He uses them to make women come. Handcuffs, chains, and rope also hang from hooks and sit on shelves with masks and gags.

*This is a sex dungeon.*

I can't say that I'm not jealous because I am. One day, I'll have my own, but until then, I'll just borrow his.

Shining my light over to the single bed in the center of the concrete room, I see what I came for. She lies there in the middle of the mattress, on her back, arms and legs spread wide open. She's naked.

She's got a blindfold over her eyes and a gag in her mouth—a clear piece of tape over her lips, but I can see what looks to be her underwear inside her mouth, filling out her cheeks.

Knowing she can't see me, I flip on the light to get a better view. She's not moving in her restraints, and by the look of the second empty bottle of wine I spot down here, I'd say she's passed out due to having too much to drink. Or maybe he drugged her. Either way, she willingly drove her car here, knowing he would tie her up and leave her. He plans to use her when he returns. That's what I've found from the research I've done so far anyway. He likes them to sit and wonder when he'll return to use them. They get off on the anticipation.

This explains why she hasn't messaged me to ask where I've been since I haven't been over to visit her. She found someone who can give her what she wants. Actual dick. Well, it's her lucky night. I'm officially a Lord and can stick my cock wherever I want.

Walking over to stand at the end of the bed, I look over her. The bed has an iron rail headboard and matching footboard. Vertical bars run up and down on both ends. Gives him something to tie them to. It's a twin-size. Doesn't need to be big or comfortable, for that matter. It's not meant to sleep on.

Rope wraps around each wrist and ankle, then are tied off to the corners of the bed, securing her to it. No covers or pillows. Just her on a bare mattress spread wide open and ready to be used. My hard cock presses painfully against my jeans. I've seen her naked before. I've tied her down and gotten her off more times than I can count over the last two years, but this time, it's different. She's here for me to use. However I want.

Unable to stop myself, I reach down and undo my jeans, pulling out my cock. I stroke it a few times, my fingers feeling the piercings that run along my shaft.

When you're told you can't fuck, you find other ways to get off. Porn got old really fast. One of mine is pain—giving and receiving.

A mumbled cry comes from her taped lips, and she arches her

back. She's awake, after all. I make my way over to the headboard and look down at her. Reaching out, I run my fingertips along the tape over her pretty lips. The once pink lipstick is smeared all over it.

She yanks on the rope harder, her hips thrusting so hard that the bed rattles when she slams them back down onto the mattress. My heart pounds in my chest at the fact that she was going to fuck another man tonight. That I'm not the only one to get to use her. I've watched her in her room. I've followed her everywhere. When did she have the chance to meet him? To even have the conversation to make herself so vulnerable to him?

I slap her. Not hard enough to leave a print but enough to sting. She winces, but I love the way her nipples harden. She's just like me. Pain gets us off. Leaning over the headboard, I grip both of her full breasts in my hands and massage them. Then move to her nipples, and I twist them between my fingers before pulling on them, making her scream into the tape, and I let go. Her body sags into the bed, and she breathes deeply through her nose.

Making my way back down to the foot of the bed, I lightly touch her ankle. Soft as a feather, I run the tips of my fingers along her smooth leg and up her inner thigh. The woman is five-four and doesn't weigh more than a hundred and ten pounds. She moves once more, her back arching, her arms and legs pulling on her restraints.

I smile, my hand stopping on the inside of her thigh, just inches from her smooth cunt. She twists her narrow hips, trying to get my hand to go where she wants it. I want to deny her. Rip off the blindfold and see the shocked look in her pretty eyes. See fear that I've found her here so helpless. Embarrassed that she's tied up for another man, but I'm the one who's going to make her a whore.

My hand moves upward, and I slide two fingers over her cunt. Unable to help myself, I spread her pussy open wide for me to look at how wet she is. She whimpers, her neck arching, and my free hand reaches out, wrapping around her delicate throat and holding it down to the bed. She goes frantic, her hips bucking while she mumbles nonsense into her gag.

I push a finger into her, biting my bottom lip to keep from making a noise. She thinks I'm someone else, and I don't want her to know it's not him. I push a second one in, moving them in and out a couple of times before adding a third. She sucks in a deep breath through her nose, and I feel her throat work as she swallows against my hand wrapped around it.

Pulling them out, I watch as she sags against the bed. I climb between her open legs and shove my knees into her thighs, pulling the rope around her ankles taut at this angle. I could untie her legs, knowing she won't fight me, but I'd rather have her like this. I don't even bother removing my jeans.

Leaning over, I spit on her cunt, making sure she hears it, and then slap the side of her breast like I did her face. She whimpers, body jerking, but her nipples harden. Fuck, her tits are perfect. I'm not an expert, but I know she's a thirty-two C cup. I've checked her bra sizes before. When I say I'm obsessed with this woman, I mean it. I know everything there is to know about her.

The fact that she's tied up in another man's basement reminds me that I only thought I did.

Getting her off over the past couple of years as a stranger has just made my obsession ten times worse. Do you know how hard it is to keep your true identity a secret when you know they want you? It's a new level of fucking torture.

My hand comes down, slapping her cunt, and she cries out into her gag. I do it again, and the metal bedframe rattles at her useless attempt to free herself. Looking over her pussy, I see it's now red, and I start to massage her clit. She still has it pierced, and I still crave to taste it. But not now. I'll get my chance. Tonight is just the beginning of the rest of her life being mine and serving me.

I might not be fucking my chosen right now in front of my fellow Lords, but I no longer have to be celibate. I can fuck whoever I want. I've waited years for this—for her—and I'm not going to pass up the opportunity. No matter how wrong some may think it is.

I grab my wallet out of my back pocket and pull out the condom. I don't want to use one, but I know *he* would. I'm not sure if she'll feel the difference, but I want to make sure she doesn't question it. I've never fucked her with my cock, and she's never seen it. So she has no idea that it's pierced, and by the looks of the empty wine bottles, I'm not even sure she'll remember this night.

Ripping open the package, I remove my knife from my other pocket and poke a hole in the end. I might be using one, but I sure as fuck want my cum leaking out of her pussy afterward. She may not know it's mine, but I will.

Taking my dick in my hand, I slowly push into her waiting cunt. I bite my lip to keep from making any sound once again as she sucks me in like I belong there.

*Goddamn.* It's been too long since I've been inside a woman. So tight and warm. My breath catches, and my eyes fall closed. She's what I imagine heaven is like. If I thought it existed. Men like me only know hell. Kill, take, bleed. It's a system branded into our brains.

I shove my hips forward, making the bed rattle, and I watch her tied hands fist, her black-painted nails digging into her palms. I pull out and slam forward again, forcing her tight cunt to take my dick. Unintelligible noises come from her taped lips.

My fingers dig into both of her hips, and I pin her down while I fuck her as if she was left here for me to find and use while watching my cock move in and out, covered in her wetness.

Letting go of her hips, I slap her across the face, and her pussy clenches down on me. My little demon likes that. I do it again, and she arches her back, sucking in a deep breath while her pussy pulses around my dick.

Leaning forward, I wrap my hands around her throat, cutting off her air, and fuck her into the mattress like I'll never get this chance again, when I know I will. No matter what, she belongs to me now—always has—and she's about to find out too.

My eyes scan her face, what little I can see of it anyway. My lips are so close, I pucker them and kiss her taped lips. Pulling back to just look at her, I spit on her face. She can't feel it, but she heard it, making her buck her hips, my cock still deep inside her. I watch it run down the clear tape, and I reach out and lick it off.

The sound of my heavy breathing fills the room while she fights me. I can't wait for her to watch me fuck her. To see her cry for me while I'm inside her. It'll be fucking perfect.

Her pussy clenches while she arches her back. Letting go of her neck, she breathes heavily through her nose. My eyes drop to her cunt and watch my cock slide in and out, now covered in her cum.

*That's my little demon.* That's what I've been waiting for all these years. Pulling out, I run my hand up and down my shaft, then slap her face again. Her body arches. I reach up and grab a handful of her hair at the crown of her head, careful not to pull the blindfold off, and lift her head from the bed and fuck her.

Sinking my teeth into my bottom lip, I come with a groan. Goddamn. Placing my hands on either side of her chest, I feel my cock pulsing while buried deep inside her. I'm light-headed. The room spins like I've been the one drinking.

Three years is a long time, especially when you've spent the last two teasing yourself.

I pull out, and her body relaxes into the bed, totally spent while she remains shaking. Getting up, I remove the condom and grab my backpack. I pull out what I need and go back over to the bed. Grabbing the edge of the tape, I rip it off her lips. Then I reach into her mouth and remove her thong, shoving it into my jeans pocket.

She licks her lips, raising her hips off the mattress.

Kneeling next to her, I slide my hand underneath her head and lift it off the bed as much as I can with her arms tied down. Then I place the tip of the small tube at the edge of her lips. She opens up for me, thinking I'm giving her water.

Tilting it up, I watch the liquid slide into her mouth. She coughs, some flying out and onto her chest, but she doesn't need it all since she's been drinking tonight.

Laying her head back down, I place the now empty vial in my backpack and remove my hoodie that I had shoved in there, knowing I'd need it.

I wait a few minutes and then untie her legs. She pulls them up, bending her knees, and they fall to the side. Going to the head of the bed, I untie the rope from the two corners but not from her wrists. Rolling her over onto her stomach, I pull her hands behind her back, tying the two ropes together to secure her arms behind her. Then I take the hoodie I brought and shove it over her head to cover her nakedness.

My cell vibrates in my pocket, and I pull it out to see the text.

**Done.**

I smile, then bend over and pick her up in my arms, carrying her from his house. I'm officially allowed to have whoever I want now, and I want her. She's mine, and no one touches what's mine.

# SEVEN

# ELLINGTON

I stand in the middle of the dimly lit room facing the door. The only way out. I feel them at my back. My body vibrates like electric currents are running through my veins.

Laughter fills the room, making me shiver, but I don't run. No. That would be stupid. They'll find me. It'll be better for me to stay where I am. Take what they give me, and then they'll leave.

I'm their toy. And tonight, they want to play.

"Gasoline" by Halsey shakes the walls that hold me captive with the monsters. The partygoers on the other side of the door have no clue that we're in here.

Something slips over my eyes from behind, and my breathing hitches.

I fist my hands—my nails digging into my palms—to keep from lifting them and pushing the blindfold off. I don't resist. Well, not unless they want me to. That's another game we like to play.

"See no evil," a voice whispers in my right ear, making a shiver run up my spine.

My lips part to help accommodate my accelerated breathing.

"Speak no evil." Those words come from directly in front of me before something is shoved into my mouth. The force pushes my head back in the process.

I taste metal. It holds my mouth open, and I start salivating at the thought of not being able to scream for help.

"Hear no evil," another voice says before soft leather is slid over my ears, taking away any sound of the outside world.

My legs shake, my heart pounds, and I try to swallow but drool runs down my chin.

What started from the Three Wise Monkeys has evolved into three fucking psychos that I hand myself over to.

Something hard and thick wraps around my neck, forcing me to lift my chin—a collar. Seconds later, I'm yanked forward, tripping over my Chanel heels. I stumble into a hard body, my hands landing on the chest of one of my captors. He's shirtless. My nails dig into his skin as the base of my neck is grabbed underneath the collar. The pain from his fingers digging into my skin forces me to the floor. My hands and knees slap the concrete. I suck in a ragged breath through my open mouth. Then I'm being dragged across it by the collar.

I'm their pet. Crawling on my hands and knees by a leash, I'm pulled to a stop, and hands grab at my body. I'm tossed onto what feels like a mattress. It's hard and unforgiving and smells of BO and cheap Axe body spray.

I'm rolled onto my stomach, and my arms are yanked behind my back. A rope is wrapped around my wrists, securing them together. They're lifted, pulling on my shoulders, shoving my face farther into the nasty-smelling mattress. A cry is forced from my open mouth. Fresh drool runs from my lips.

Hands grab my legs, spreading them wide before rope is wrapped around them, keeping me spread open for their convenience.

I'm panting, my heart racing, and my pussy throbs.

"That's all we have time for today." My professor interrupts my story.

I close my notebook, looking up from the podium. My eyes scan the large classroom that isn't even half full of students. If you're afraid of public speaking, this isn't the class for you. Ninety percent of our grade comes from our participation to come up with different sexual scenarios and share them with everyone.

A few eyes I meet are already on me. Others are busy doing anything else but listening. One guy has his head back and mouth open while softly snoring. The guy next to him is doodling in his notebook. The girl beside him is popping her gum.

"Nice work, Ellington. You'll get to go first tomorrow to finish," Mr. Hamilton announces.

I gather my things and exit the class.

"Damn, girl, that was hot." My best friend nudges my shoulder as we enter the hall. Kira sat in on the class today. My professor lets outsiders join to get as much attention to his class as possible. Not many want to stand in front of a room full of people and tell your deepest, darkest desires.

I roll my eyes. "Whatever."

"I'm serious. I honestly don't know how Mr. Hamilton doesn't get a boner every time someone is up there sharing their assignment. I mean"—she steps in front of me and walks backward, her blue eyes wide with excitement—"I'm fucking wet after that."

I throw my head back, laughing. "You're a virgin," I remind her.

"Not anymore," she sings before biting down on her bottom lip.

"What?" I gasp. "Since when?"

"So, Ellington." Mack comes up to us, and Kira rolls her eyes at him. I narrow mine on hers, wanting to know when and who she lost her virginity to, but it'll have to wait because he goes on. "That story—" He clears his throat and adjusts his jeans. She gives me a pointed look as to say *told you so.* "That was descriptive." He runs his hand over his head nervously.

"That was the assignment." I shrug.

"Geez, Mack, haven't you ever watched porn before?" Kira asks him with another eye roll.

My best friend may have never fucked a dick until recently, but the girl has been starving for years. Her parents are very strict. It's amazing that they even let her be my friend.

"Yeah, but not like that," he responds softly.

"It's called gang bang with BDSM," she informs him. "Tie me up and line them up."

His cheeks redden, and he drops his dark eyes to look at his unlaced Timberlands.

She grabs my arm and yanks me toward the doors and shoves them open. "Seriously, though. I need a night out after that. Possibly a cigarette."

"You don't smoke," I add, still laughing at her.

"If I was fucked like that, I'd start."

Her words have me nibbling on my lip in thought. I've had a guy like that. One who makes you need a fucking hit afterward. He's dark, mysterious, and a complete stranger. I've never seen his face, but I don't need to. In a way, he saved me. He just doesn't know it. And I'll never tell him, but my life would be very different if he hadn't shown up that night at my parents' house.

Two years he's been in my life. But over the past couple of months, he's been silent. I haven't reached out, and he hasn't surprised me in the middle of the night. I leave my French doors unlocked just in case. Yet every morning, I wake up feeling disappointed.

Deciding to be the one to reach out, I pull my other cell phone from my backpack and open the app that we use to communicate and send a quick text.

Me: Tonight?

He reads it immediately, but after a few minutes, I realize I'm not going to get a response. I hate that I've relied on him for so long. He's no longer interested in me. It's crushing. Like a breakup to a relationship that I never even had.

A part of me hoped that he'd just ignore the text. Fuck, for all I know, he's married, moved, or died. But he's obviously still alive and just doesn't want me.

Pocketing the cell, I try to ignore the pain in my chest. It's for the best. I'm not the kind of girl you stay around to be with. I'm the kind a man calls at two o'clock in the morning because he wants his dick sucked. And I accepted that a long time ago.

## SIN

I TURN MY CAR OFF AND GET OUT, WALKING DOWN THE ROAD. It's the second night in a row that I've parked and waited in the shadows for my chance to see her.

Making my way up to the gate, I climb the fence and jump over it. I've got my black hoodie up and over my head, my mask in place with my gloves on. Like always, all she'll see is my red contacts.

Walking up to the white Victorian mansion, I climb the lattice and push open the French double doors to enter her room from the balcony.

I never responded to her message today. I was surprised she had reached out to me to begin with. I thought it would be harder than that to take her from her new fuck buddy. Her message just tells me that she won't put up much of a fight when I tell her that she now belongs to me and no one else. Her message also told me that she's growing bored with him and wants more. He's not fulfilling her needs.

I accept that challenge.

Last night after I carried her out of his house, I took her home and placed her in her bed. After removing her blindfold and untying her wrists, I left. She was out from the alcohol and GHB I gave her. She probably doesn't even remember going to his house, let alone how she drove home. When I had arrived with her, her car was parked exactly where I told the guy to put it. He was worth the money.

I step inside her bedroom when I see it's empty. My eyes immediately look over at the open door to her adjoining bathroom. She's in the shower. I can hear the water running. We never agree on a time.

Elli has had my personal cell number since I got my first phone when we were kids. So I went and bought an extra phone for her after my second visit as the masked man. I wanted her to have some sort of communication with me without knowing it was the real me. I downloaded an untraceable app for us to use that I had put on that specific device to contact me—the guy who gets her off.

Sometimes I'd show up when she would message me. Other times, I would show up unannounced. That's what makes it so much fun.

She has the light off in the bedroom. The large room is bathed in her scent—vanilla. Just the thought has my hard cock jerking inside my jeans. I know how good her pussy feels now, and I want more. My mouth salivates at the thought of spreading those soft thighs and getting a taste. Making her come knowing that it's me. I want her begging with fucking tears in her eyes while I tease her.

Listening to the water shut off, I make my way to the far corner. She's got long, thick curtains that cover the double glass doors to her balcony. I open them, stepping behind, making sure they shield me from being seen. I'm not normally the type of guy who hides, but I like catching her off guard.

Peeking around the edge, I watch her exit the bathroom into the bedroom. She's got a fluffy white towel wrapped around her body underneath her arms while holding her cell in one hand. She sits on the side of her bed, her wet blond hair draped over her shoulder. She types away, and it begins to ring seconds later.

"Hello?" she answers it on speakerphone.

"Hey, honey, I didn't expect you to still be awake." Her mother's voice comes from the other end of the line.

"I was out late with Kira."

*Lie.* She wasn't with my sister. I just saw her at our parents' house before I left to come over here.

"I got your text and just wanted to call and tell you good night and that I love you. I'll be back home on Monday."

"Love you too." She hangs up.

I go to step out but decide to wait another second to see what she does. She sets her cell down and picks up the remote to her TV. The screen lights up the room, and she opens the top drawer to her nightstand by her bed.

My heart accelerates as she retrieves the items she wants and lays them on the bed next to her. Then she flips through the channels on her TV until she finds what she is looking for.

A woman's voice comes through the speakers, and I can't help but look over at it. She's watching porn. The woman is in the middle of a living room. Tied to a black bench. She's on her back, her head hangs off one end, her arms pulled down to her sides and taped to both front wooden legs. Her knees are bent, shoved into her chest, and ropes are wrapped around the inside of her knees and the bench, tying them in place. Her ass hangs off the other end. So her mouth, ass, and pussy are easily accessible to the four naked men who stand around her.

The woman is moving, her body fighting the uncomfortable position they've got her tied up in.

My eyes go back to my little demon, and she's got her back up against a stack of pillows, her legs spread wide and her hand between her legs. She's slowly rubbing her clit, her eyes fixated on the TV. I no longer give a shit what the men are about to do to the woman on the screen.

I'm engrossed in her. The way her eyes get heavy, her lips part, and she licks them. Sucking in a deep breath, she begins to push a finger in and out of her cunt, fucking herself. Her moans fill the room to match the lady on the TV.

Her free hand reaches up and grips her hair, her hips rocking back and forth when she starts to pant.

*Come on, little demon. Come all over yourself.*

She watches the woman get fucked by four men on the TV as if she wishes it was her. The thought makes me want to rip this curtain down and wrap them around her face while I show her that my cock is all she'll ever need.

The pace of her fingers picks up, and her eyes fall closed. I watch, fascinated as she moans and comes on them. Slumping back against the pillows, she opens her eyes and looks down at her hand. She angrily wipes it on one of her many accent pillows and frowns. She's unsatisfied.

The four men are taking turns with the woman on the TV, and Elli watches it for a few minutes. Her head is tilted to the side, and she wears a soft frown. Then she starts to play with herself again. This time, she massages her breasts, then pinches her nipples so hard that she cries out. Then she reaches over and grabs a pair of nipple clamps. She puts one on at a time, inhaling sharply at the bite of the serrated teeth. The thought of putting them on her pussy lips makes my breath quicken. I'd love to see her cry while I fuck her cunt, pulling on the clamps.

Reaching out, she grabs a black leather belt and bends over, wrapping it around her ankles to tie them together.

She lies on her back, pulling her knees up so she can spread her legs a little. She places her wand between her parted thighs and closes them, stretching her legs out straight in front of her before placing another belt around her upper thighs, pulling it tight enough to pinch her skin, making it impossible to separate them. Reaching above her head, she throws a few pillows underneath her to the floor. She then picks up a zip tie and crosses her wrists. She manages to thread it and then pulls it tight with her teeth, making it as snug as the belts around her legs, and then places the blindfold over her eyes.

Reaching out in front of her between her legs, she turns the knob on the vibrator, bringing it to life. The buzzing sound now fills the room.

Lying back again flat, she listens to the girl get fucked on the TV while the vibrator rests against her cunt.

I step out from behind the curtains and walk over to the side of the bed. I pull out my cock and quietly spit in my hand.

I came here tonight to get her off one last time as the masked man she knows. But this is way better. I want to watch her do it. See what she thinks she needs. I watch her hips lift off the bed while she grabs the headboard as if her wrists are tied to it.

God, I want to straddle her neck and force my cock down her throat. It takes all of my restraint not to—the masked man doesn't fuck her—when she starts moaning. Her breathing accelerates and so does my hand.

Her body twists and turns, her chest rising and falling fast with each sharp intake of breath. She comes with a cry, and I have a moment of panic that she's going to rip off the blindfold and see me, expect me to get her off, but she doesn't. She remains where she is, needing more.

Fuck, I love that she's never satisfied. This is what I want. A challenge. I'll fuck her until she forgets who she is, leaving a tally of her orgasms on her chest as a reminder that only I can give her what she needs.

I continue to jack off, watching her tits bounce from her heavy breathing while the chains of her nipple clamps rattle from her harsh movements. She takes in a deep breath, her stomach caving in, and I look over her prominent ribs, imagining my handprints on them. I sink my teeth into my bottom lip when I really want it to be her neck.

Arching her back, she comes again, and I can't help it. My balls tighten, and I hold my breath as I come all over the decorative pillow she wiped herself on earlier.

Her body sags only for a second while the vibrator is still between her legs. Her cunt now sensitive, she starts panting again. Closing her mouth, she swallows, and I slowly make my way back behind the curtain to watch the rest of the show.

She continues for another five minutes but doesn't get off this time. Instead, she raises her tied hands and rips off the blindfold, throwing it to the floor. Angrily, she undoes the belts around her legs, grabs the wand, and turns it off before tossing it away as well. Then she reaches over to grab the knife she placed on the bed and manages to cut her wrists free. I like to think I taught her that the first time I was in here with her.

She whimpers, removing her nipple clamps, and then shuts her TV off. Rolling over, she gives me her back, and I hear her huff. But just when I think she's about to fall asleep, she opens up her drawer again and removes the other cell phone I gave her and angrily types away on it. Then she puts it back, shutting the drawer.

I wait impatiently while listening to her heavy breathing even out, and she falls asleep.

Quietly, I step out from behind the curtain and walk over to her side of the bed. I open the top drawer of her nightstand and look over to see what else she has left in there. A ball gag, a bag of zip ties, and a paddle that says SLUT across it. A choker that reads *whore*.

My cock is hard again, begging me to use everything on her at once. A part of me wants to take advantage of this situation right now, but I have to wait.

Closing her balcony doors behind me, I pull out my cell to see she had sent me a message on the app. Thankfully, I had it on silent.

Little Demon: Never mind. I did it myself.

I smile. She thinks she's going to get a rise out of me—the masked man who makes her come—but she has no fucking clue what's about to come her way.

# EIGHT

## ELLINGTON

The following morning, I run up the stone steps and enter my best friend's house without even knocking. I'm like her parents' adopted child. Our parents are best friends. We grew up together.

"Good morning, Elli." Mrs. Sinnett smiles at me softly, picking up her Louis Vuitton off the round glass table that sits in the middle of their grand foyer.

"Morning, Janice. Is Kira ready?"

She gives a little laugh, heading for the door, and I hold it open for her while her red Dior heels clap on their marble floor. "Is she ever on time, honey?"

I throw my head back and sigh. *We're already late.*

"Thanks, darling." She exits the house. "Have a great day," she calls out as I shut it behind her.

"Kira?" I holler, entering their kitchen. I slam my backpack on the island and open the fridge. "Kira, let's go. We're late." Grabbing a bottle of water, I shut the fridge and scream when I see that her brother was standing behind the door. "Jesus, Sin." I place my hand on my chest and meet his cold blue-eyed stare.

Easton Bradley Sinnett is the most annoying, self-absorbed asshole I have ever met. With that hot, I don't give a fuck what I look like look. Plus, the tattoos he has. Damn, he's like a walking red flag that makes me wet. His dark hair is a disheveled mess like he just crawled out of bed. Which he probably did. Or he hasn't even slept yet. His chiseled face is covered in stubble, telling me he also hasn't shaved. He's shirtless, showing off his extremely hard body. All he wears is a pair of gray sweatpants. The ones that every girl drools over. They hang low on his narrow hips. So low I can tell he doesn't have a pair of boxers underneath. My eyes drop to get a quick look, and sure enough, you can see the outline of his flaccid dick. I swallow, getting a very good visual of how big he is. It makes my thighs clench. Lifting my eyes to him, I hope he didn't catch me, but he arches a dark brow.

*Fuck.*

"Thought I heard a bird screeching." Jayce enters, thankfully helping me avoid an awkward conversation with Sin. Their other friend Corbin enters behind him.

"Don't you guys have somewhere to be? Like class?"

They're Lords. If I didn't grow up around them, the matching brands on their chests would give them away. They're all members of a secret society that rule the world by whatever means necessary. My father was one, just like their fathers are. You have to be born into it. Not just anyone can become a Lord. I hate the society. What they stand for, and how they think they can do whatever they want and get away with it.

"I can think of something to do," Sin says in that deep and sexy voice. He's been teasing me with it for years. We both know that he'll never follow through with it. He just likes to make me squirm.

I swallow nervously when his eyes drop to my chest, and my nipples harden against the soft fabric of my bra, making my breath quicken. Thankfully, Kira enters. "About time. Let's go."

"Shit." She pats down the pockets of her jean shorts. "I forgot my phone." Then she turns, her brown hair slapping Corbin in the face as she runs out of the room.

"Seriously?" I sigh and plop down at the island, waiting for her, doing anything I can to avoid Sin. The older we get, the more I don't know how to act around him. I avoid him as much as I can. Which is hard since his sister is my best friend, but I always try my best.

Thankfully my cell goes off, and I pull it out of my pocket. The masked man never did show up last night. And when I woke up this morning, I left the other phone he gave me at home, in my nightstand, turned off. I'm hoping that will keep me from reaching out and looking desperate.

Opening up the text, I read over it.

> We still on for tonight?

> Sure.

I find myself typing back, needing to get laid. And this guy is actually interested. He's been my backup for a couple of months now. Not as good as my mystery man, but reliable.

> I'm going to a party, but I'll be over afterward. It won't be until after two, though. Is that okay?

> That's fine. I'll leave the front door unlocked.

I inform him. He's been to my house before but never to fuck me. My parents always used to throw parties, and it was full of Lords—the elite only associate with the elite.

I watch the three dots bounce around and then stop before they start again. It vibrates with an incoming message.

See you then.

"Oh, little demon has a boyfriend."

I close the screen and stand, reaching out to push Sin away. The bastard was standing over my shoulder, watching me. Fuck, I hate him. I try to ignore the feel of his muscular chest under my hand. And wipe my palm on my jeans as if the bastard has cooties. "Who I fuck is none of your damn business," I snap defensively.

"If you need a real man—"

I narrow my eyes on Jayce, and he starts laughing, cutting himself off.

Sin steps into me, and my breathing becomes labored while my eyes slowly look up into his. I have to fist my hands down by my sides so I don't touch him. We've tolerated each other for years, but if I was ever given the chance ...

"I'm ready," Kira announces, running into the kitchen. "Let's go. We're late," she adds as if I didn't already know that.

"Thank God," I mumble to myself. Stepping back from him, I grab my backpack off the island. I throw it over my shoulder, ignoring the feel of Sin's eyes on my back.

# SIN

I WATCH THE SEXY BLONDE TURN AND PRACTICALLY RUN OUT of the house with my sister. She doesn't have a clue what I've done to her. And I'm not sure if I'll ever tell her, either. I don't feel guilty or ashamed. A Lord is taught that he can have whatever he wants, even if that means they have to take it. That's exactly what I've done with her, and she gets off on it.

Her little boy toy can't compare to what I can do to her. Plus, he shouldn't have left her so vulnerable the other night in his basement. And last night in her room? Well, she'll learn to lock those doors. The masked man who comes in and gets her off will be no more. She'll know it's my cock, my mouth, and my hands that violate her.

I'll teach her that she can be easily taken by anyone. When I decide to tie her to a bed, I sure as fuck won't be leaving her alone like that dipshit did in his basement. No. I'll sit there and watch her squirm until I decide to fuck her. And I promise you, blindfolded or not, she'll know it's my cock she's coming for.

"Sin, I can't believe you didn't make it to the vow ceremony," Jayce starts, eating his granola bar. He's been talking about it nonstop for the past two days. "It was wild. Ryat yelled at Matt—"

"Here you go." Corbin hands me a notebook, ignoring Jayce like me.

I open it up, and a smile tugs at my lips as I scan over a random page. "I—" The feel of my phone vibrating in my pocket has me setting the notebook on the counter to pull it free. I unlock the screen to see a message from Sandy, a forty-year-old friend of my mother's, and I open it up. It's a picture of her sticking her tongue out while looking up at the camera with a text.

> I got my tongue pierced.

I write out a reply.

> Cool. Maybe it'll help you suck dick better.

It's been a while—the summer before my freshman year at Barrington—since I had my cock down her throat, but I doubt she's gotten any better.

She reads it and sends three crying laugh emojis.

You always make me laugh, Sin. I'll be back Sunday. You've had your vow ceremony, right? Now we can get back to where we were…"

I quit reading over it and pocket my cell. She's away with her third husband celebrating their tenth wedding anniversary. Call me whatever you want, but I don't have a commitment to her husband. Not my fault she can't stay faithful. I'm also aware that I'm not the only one. She fucked Jayce one night before our first initiation at his parents' cabin. She was more than willing to give us one last ride before we had to take a vow of celibacy.

I pick up the notebook on the counter when I see my father enter the kitchen. "Easton?"

"Yeah?" I ask, meeting his stare. He's got a briefcase in one hand and his cell in the other.

"How is your assignment coming along?"

My hands tighten on the notebook. "Good," I answer.

"Will you be able to complete it?" he asks, worry evident in his tone. I'm officially a Lord now, meaning if I don't do what I've been ordered to do, then I'm no use to them. Termination is the only way out from here.

I snort. "Without a doubt."

"May I speak to you in my study for a second?" he asks.

I groan. Not in the mood, knowing exactly what he wants to talk about. My chosen, my Lady, my future. I don't have time right now. Plus, it doesn't matter what he wants for my future. It's not what I want. And I'm not going to let anyone dictate it.

"I have to make some important phone calls," I lie and exit the kitchen, avoiding him, and head to my room. I've got some research to do. My little demon just gave me the key to everything I need to make her mine.

# NINE

# ELLINGTON

I've been around sex all my life. My mother is a sex therapist. My father built her an office on the fourth floor of our house so she could work from home. He even put in an elevator that bypassed the other floors so her clients could have direct access to her office.

I was nine when I started listening in. By age ten, I knew more about sex than most adults ever will. One time when I was twelve, I snuck upstairs and listened in like I usually did.

*I slowly walk down the hallway, stepping as softly as I can to avoid giving myself away.*

*If so, I'll get in trouble. She always tells me, "These are adult conversations, Elli. And unethical of me if you overheard them."*

*I push my back against the wall and slide down to my butt, straining my ears to hear.*

*A woman is softly crying, followed by a man's voice. "I'm sorry, I thought you'd like it."*

*Mr. and Mrs. Taylor. I've listened to a few of their sessions before.*

*"You can't be serious."* The woman begins to sob. *"How... could you...?"*

Mr. Taylor had a kink for watching other men get his wife off —known as cuckolding. His wife didn't but still had the occasional bottle of wine and allowed her husband to take her to a swingers' club or party where he would choose a man for her, and he'd sit back and watch the man fuck her.

She hated it.

The fact that she was able to get off with the stranger made her feel dirty. But that was the only sex she was having. He hadn't fucked her in years.

This particular session was about the night before. Mr. Taylor had two of his best friends over who just so happen to also be his business partners in his multibillion-dollar company. He had slipped something in his wife's wine that night, drugging her to the point she passed out. He then let his two friends tie him up in a chair, naked, facing their bed where they tied up his wife and raped her. He had set up a recorder earlier that day, and he could not understand why she didn't want to watch it the following morning with him. He figured since she had willingly let other men fuck her before that she would be okay with letting his two business partners have their turns with her. He cried and begged her to forgive him.

Instead, she ran out screaming that she was filing for divorce. I had never sat so still in my life, praying she wouldn't see me. Thankfully, she didn't.

Then I heard him beg my mother to fix him. To give him drugs. Do whatever she could do to make him "normal." She reported the rape to the police. By law, she had to.

I saw it on the news the following week. His two business partners being dragged out of their downtown office building and shoved into cop cars. They were both married with children.

I wondered why Mr. Taylor hadn't been arrested along with

them, though. I couldn't ask my mom because then she'd know I had listened in on her session. Two months later, I got my answer. Mrs. Taylor was back, and I sat in that same spot and listened to her cry to my mother once again.

Her husband had committed suicide. Went home after their last session and shot himself in the head on their bed where he had given her up like an offering to a cult. He could not live with himself after what he did to her. He was so disgusted that, at the time, he hadn't realized that what he liked was wrong. Until he understood he betrayed his wife. A twenty-five-year marriage down the drain for a kink.

For three hours, I sat there listening to her cry, and she felt guilty. Her husband was the one who betrayed her, yet she felt responsible for his death.

She was pregnant. She'd found out that morning, and that was the reason for her emergency session. For ten years, they tried to have a baby. They wanted kids later in life. They were both focused on their careers, and once they decided to start, it was too late. Or so they thought, and he had stopped sleeping with her altogether.

I'll never forget the words she told my mother when I peeked into the cracked door and saw her on the couch crying. "He gave me the one thing I always wanted. I'm pregnant, and he's no longer here. Because of me. Because I couldn't love him for who he was." She said she didn't care which man who raped her was the father. She was keeping the baby and would raise it to know her late husband as the dad.

She sobbed. My mother sobbed for her own personal reasons. It was traumatic for both of them. And me?

I learned two things listening to the Taylors' sessions. First, love is utterly fucking bullshit. Who in the fuck allows their friends or anyone else to rape their wife? Let alone record it and expect her to be okay with it?

And second, I learned that just because your body craves something doesn't mean you should give it what it wants. So I pushed everything my body begged for to the back of my mind. But that didn't last very long.

I was young when I realized I wasn't like other women. When I was eighteen, Sin cornered me at a party and told me I was pretty. I knew he was lying. A way to fuck with me. Hell, a friend probably dared him or something. But then he told me that my eyes were so beautiful that he wanted to cut them out and place them in a jar in his room so he could look at them every day.

It made me wet. It also made me realize that I'm more fucked up than any patient my mother had ever seen. What would have made any woman cower made me lean into him. I convinced myself it was the two lines of cocaine I had just snorted too, but that was a lie. Deep down, I knew I'd never have a healthy relationship with a man because I'd never be happy with what society would call normal.

I want toxic. I want madness. I want someone who makes me question my sanity. And I know I won't be happy until the masked man decides to make me his forever. I'm perfectly fine spending the rest of my life not knowing who he is as long as he continues to come see me.

# TEN

# ELLINGTON

I t's almost two in the afternoon when I walk into my psychology of human sexuality class. This is my last class of the day, thankfully. I have big plans to walk in my mother's footsteps regarding my career choice. I have my own reasons, but she doesn't have to know that.

I'm only a junior at Barrington University this year. Sex has always made me curious. And I think the fact that I learned so much at such a young age played a big role in that. I now understand why she didn't want me to hear what was said inside the walls of her office. Put the fact that it was unethical to the side. Just the words of her clients gave me nightmares at times.

I was thirteen when I started getting curious. I'd hear words being used and google their meaning or look up images. If I'm being honest, I'd say I need therapy now. Pretty sure I can diagnose myself as a sex addict. But it's an amazing thing to take your body to the next level. Let alone someone else doing it to you. Sex is like anything else—an act that can be used, bought, or sold. It's addictive. It's that high you're constantly chasing. If you ask me, it's the most dangerous drug out there. It makes you irrational, desperate, and a little psycho.

People look down on women who have multiple partners, but it's acceptable to have a tobacco addiction that can kill you. In a world of everything costing a fortune, an orgasm can cost you fucking nothing. Except maybe a little bit of dignity, but I don't care about that.

Sitting down in my seat in the front row, I open my backpack to pull out my notebook, but it's not there. "What the ...?" I unzip the front pocket and look inside. My heart starts pounding as I think about where I had it last. It was in this class yesterday. I didn't work on it last night at home because it was finished.

"Elli, you're up," Mr. Hamilton states, getting my attention.

"Shit," I hiss to myself.

"Something wrong?" he asks.

My eyes lift to his, and he arches a brow. His hands are on the hips of his Armani slacks. Pretty sure he teaches this class for shits and giggles since he lives off his daddy's money. He's got some Fortune 500 company based out of New York. He's a Lord. Barrington University is for the one-percenters. You can't escape them here.

His dark brown eyes stare at me expectantly.

"I, uh ... no." I rip my bag open again and drop my eyes to look inside it once more as if it will appear like magic. It's not that I don't remember it by heart. It's just that if I don't have it on me, then where the fuck is it? "It's just—"

The door swings open, and all the air rushes out of my lungs when I see three guys enter the room. Three men who do not have this class. My eyes shoot to the professor, and his brows crease. "What can I do for you, gentlemen?" Mr. Hamilton asks. He allows outside spectators, but these three would never willingly want to be in here.

"We're going to join your class for the day," Sin answers.

He looks even better than he did this morning in the kitchen, if that's possible. He's got on a black T-shirt and a pair of jeans and tennis shoes. That's it. But I can't help but notice the way his shirt pulls against his broad shoulders, and his abs are visible through the thin fabric. The jeans fit snugly on his thighs, and I look lower to see if I get the same visual as I did this morning in the sweatpants. I do.

My heart beats wildly in my chest. So loud that it makes it hard to breathe.

"Uh, I'm not sure—"

"That's not a problem, is it?" Corbin interrupts the professor.

"No. No problem." Mr. Hamilton shakes his head, running his hand down his button-up. A clear sign he doesn't approve, but he's also not going to turn them away.

No one turns away these men. They are what you call royalty at Barrington University. Get straight *A*'s even though they never show up to their classes. A Lord can do as minimal as possible and graduate with honors. As long as they complete their assignments and survive, they're rewarded.

I sit frozen in my seat as the three of them walk toward me. They come to a stop in front of my desk, and I look up at them through my lashes, my lips parted, trying to calm my breathing. *What the fuck are they doing?*

A part of me knows. I just refuse to believe it.

The corners of Sin's lips tilt up, and my pulse races at his silent threat.

"You're in my seat," Corbin barks at the guy to my right, making us both jump.

The kid gets up and scrambles away, not even bothering to take his things. Corbin takes the seat next to me, shoving the guy's stuff to the floor, and sits back, getting comfortable by spreading his legs. With his hands interlocked behind his head, his head falls to the side to look at me. His unruly dark hair flopping across his eyes.

I avoid his stare.

"Move," Jayce demands the girl to my left.

*Fuck!*

She does as she's told but much slower with a smile on her face. I'm pretty sure she tells him to call her later as she walks away, making sure to run her hand across his upper chest and winking at him. Her intentions are very clear. She leaves the room altogether, obviously having something better to do for now.

"I'll take your seat, Elli," Sin tells me. His voice instantly has my pussy wet, my thighs clenching.

I swallow nervously. "I—"

"You have a story to read," Sin adds and then pulls a notebook out of the backpack that hangs on one shoulder, slapping it down on my desk.

My heart stops when I see my name written in black marker across the top. How did he get this? Where the hell did he get this? Blood rushes in my ears and sweat beads across my forehead. I never get nervous when reading my stories. They're more like fantasies. As far as the class is concerned, it's sexual scenarios. Mr. Hamilton says reading sex scenes out loud will prepare us to be comfortable hearing couples talk about their sexual experiences once we're seeing clients. What they want and what they're lacking in their relationships.

Why am I anxious now? Is it because I've had a crush on him since as far back as I can remember?

I'm not sure why I care if I have to read it in front of him and his friends. They've already read it, I'm sure.

"Ellington?" my professor snaps, and I look up at him. He straightens his already straight tie and nods to the podium. "You're up. And we are now running behind schedule."

Numbly, I reach out and grab the notebook and get to my

shaky legs. Ever so slowly, I make my way to the front of the room. I turn to face the audience, my eyes on the notebook. My nose is running, and I rub the back of my hand across it.

"Um ..." Licking my lips, I open the book and take a deep breath, knowing I can't escape it. This is my worst nightmare come true.

*The hem of my black minidress is shoved up my back to expose my ass to them. My fishnets are being ripped, and my thong is shoved to the side.*

*Fingers enter me, not even bothering to check if I'm wet, and I shift on the bed at the discomfort, mumbling unintelligible words around the metal gag that rests behind my teeth, keeping my mouth open.*

*They pump in and out of me so hard that it forces my body to rock back and forth on the bed. The rope wrapped around my wrists pulls on me even more.*

*I can't move or fight. This is how they prefer me—tied up and helpless. Forced to take whatever they want to give me.*

*The leash connected to my collar is pulled on, lifting my head, and I know what's coming. The head of a cock enters my mouth next, pushing saliva out of the corners.*

*I can't hear due to the headphones over my ears. I can't speak, and I can't see because of the blindfold. I'm a sex doll. A toy to be fucked.*

*This is what I signed up for.*

*The fingers are removed from my cunt and replaced with a dick. Hands grip my hips, his knees rest against my tied legs, and he shoves into me, holding me in place while the other cock fills my mouth.*

*Over and over, they each fuck me before the one fucking my pussy stiffens and comes inside me. Pulling out of my cunt, I whimper around the cock fucking my mouth. I didn't come. But it's never about me. Just them.*

*He pulls on the collar, taking what little breath I had left away, and shoves himself down my throat. I gag, and he pulls out, coming all over my face. I taste some on my tongue and feel it slide down my chin before he slaps me. When he lets go of me, my head falls onto the bed once again, and I'm lying in sweat and cum.*

*A fresh set of knees hit the back of mine and then a finger is in my ass. I moan, tears running from my covered eyes. Someone grabs underneath my neck, lifting it. The cock that just fucked my cunt is shoved into my mouth because I can taste myself on him. He's rough and pinches my nose. If I could see, I'm sure my vision would go black.*

*I lie here as they each take my ass, pussy, and throat. I never get to come. It's all about them. And I'm the dumb toy who lets them do it over and over.*

I close the notebook and stare at it, refusing to look up at the classroom. I read over my words on autopilot. Knowing them by heart. My voice was shaking as bad as my knees are right now. And my breathing is erratic. My heart pounds so hard that my chest aches.

Someone starts clapping, slow and loud. It's Sin. I know it. But I refuse to look at him. Then someone follows, along with another —his two best friends.

They might as well be laughing at me.

"Good job... as always, Ellington," my professor says, clearing his throat. "Millie, you're up."

"No."

My eyes snap up at the sound of Sin talking to the professor.

"No?" Mr. Hamilton questions.

Sin slowly rises to his feet and turns to the room. "Class is over for the day."

Kids jump to their feet, grab their belongings, and practically run out of the room. Students take this class for a filler. It's for an easy grade. They fuck off and get in their daily nap. So if they can go home and do that instead, they'll take it.

"Wait a minute," Professor says. "Get back here," he orders, but half the class is already gone. Which is quite a bit, considering how small it is to begin with. We don't even have twenty students in this class.

"You too." Corbin jumps up from his seat. "Out."

"This is my classroom," Mr. Hamilton argues.

"Not today," Sin informs him with a smile.

My eyes go back and forth while standing at the podium, my head turning to look between the two, trying to figure out just what in the fuck is going on. But I know whatever the guys have planned, the professor can't fight it. They always win. The professor might be a Lord, but the fact that he works at Barrington tells me he doesn't have as much power as other Lords.

My parents didn't shield me from the ways of the Lords. I wouldn't say I know everything about them, but I know enough.

Corbin walks over to his desk, grabs Mr. Hamilton's Armani button-up, and drags him out of the room. He tosses him out and locks the door.

A quick look around tells me what I already feared. It's just the three of them and me.

"Have a seat, Elli," Sin demands, pointing at my chair like I'm a dog he can command.

My feet move on their own, walking me across the floor. I fall into my seat, my hands on the desk and my eyes straight ahead, trying to calm my breathing. I'm sweating, panting, and about to pass the fuck out. Is this what a panic attack feels like? The room is spinning, my tongue feels heavy, and my mouth is dry.

Sin comes to stand in front of my chair, and his crotch is at eye level. I can see the outline of his hard dick, and I swallow. He reaches down and slowly undoes his black leather belt.

The small movement pulls me out of whatever trance I was in.

71

"Sin—" I go to stand, but a hand grabs my hair and yanks it back, forcing me to look up at the white-tiled ceiling and keeping me in place. I cry out at the sting on my scalp. My breathing accelerates, making my chest rise and fall quickly.

I hear the sound of his belt slap through the loops before he grabs my hands and yanks them across my desk. He crosses my wrists, and I close my eyes when he wraps the leather around them, tying them together. Then my hair is let go, and instead, they grab the belt and pull it up, forcing my tied hands behind my head.

Corbin sits down in the seat behind me. The pressure of his boot presses into the back of my chair, holding my hands in place.

I lower my head since he released my hair and come face-to-face with Sin. He's got his hands on my desk, leaning into my face. "Is that what you dream of, little demon?" he asks, his head tilting to the side, calling me by my nickname. He's been using it since I was ten. My family was on a camping trip with his. Kira set his tent on fire because he wouldn't play Barbies with us. When Kira got in trouble, I took the fall, knowing Sin would destroy her to get even.

Even then, a part of me wanted to get his attention. To see just how far I could push the devil.

A whimper escapes my lips, but I'm unable to answer.

"Hmm?" He reaches up and runs his thumb over my parted lips before pushing it into my mouth. Without thought, I close my lips around it and suck on it. "That's what I thought." His pretty blue eyes harden for a brief second before pulling it out and then he reaches between me and the desk, grabbing the hem of my shirt. "You want to be a toy?" Pulling my shirt up to expose my plain white bra, he slides his hand down my waist.

The thought crosses my mind that I'm not wearing anything sexually appealing under my clothes and I quickly abandon that stupid thought.

72

I fight the restraints, but I can't go anywhere. Corbin has my hands tied behind my head, and the desk makes it hard for me to get away from Sin's touch.

He undoes my jeans and then my zipper. "Sin," I breathe, and he smirks at me. It's soft yet devious at the same time.

Kneeling before my desk, he reaches underneath and grabs my jeans at the thighs and yanks them down my legs, all the way to my ankles, and then stands. He might as well have just tied them together since I still have my shoes on. I can't kick anyone anyway.

"Let's have a feel, shall we?" He slides a hand between my legs, forcing them through the material of my cotton underwear.

I arch my back, my hips lifting up off the cold chair. A cry rips from my lips when he roughly shoves a finger into me.

"Fucking soaked," he praises. Pulling out, I slump in the chair, and he runs the pad of his wet finger over my clit. "Oh, such a naughty little demon. You've got a piercing." He tugs on the bar, and my ass lifts off the seat once again as I suck in a breath at the sting and pleasure the pain brings me.

I got it years ago. Another friend of mine had hers done. Said it made her so sensitive that she got off every time she drove over railroad tracks. I, however, did not get the same experience that she did. But it does feel good sometimes.

Corbin yanks harder on the belt wrapped around my wrists, and it pinches my shoulders together. "Ple-ease?" I beg through a gasp.

"What me to make you come, Elli?" Sin asks, his hand sliding back into my underwear. This time, he pushes two fingers into my pussy, and I rock my hips. The desk rattles at my struggle.

He adds a third, and I scream out. A hand slaps over my mouth, and I look up to see Jayce standing beside me, his hand silencing me. My eyes widen when Sin shoves a fourth into me, spreading me wide open. It's painful in this position. I need to spread my legs, but I don't have that option. My jeans around my ankles prevent that.

"Fuck, Elli, this cunt is tight." He removes them only to push them back in. The desk continues to rattle, and I breathe heavily through my nose while my pussy clamps down around his fingers fucking me. "It's going to feel so good on my cock."

I whimper, tears burning my eyes from the pleasure and the pain he's creating.

"Take her air away," he orders to Jayce, and before I can fight him, he repositions his hand over my mouth so he can pinch off my nose.

I fight in the chair, my legs kicking the best they can, which is not much, as Sin picks up his pace on my pussy. I buck my hips, but all it does is cause more friction over my clit as I rub up against the palm of his hand in this position.

Dots start to take over my vision. My lungs burn, and my eyes water. My entire body stiffens, my legs kicking out as my body convulses, fighting for air. My pussy clenches. His fingers fuck hard and rough. My eyes roll back into my head, and my body goes slack as that burning sensation takes over. Just when I'm about to come, he removes his fingers. The hand is gone from my mouth, and I'm gasping for air when my wrists are let go. I slump in the chair, gasping, crying, and shaking.

Sin grabs my hair, yanking my head back, and places his face in front of mine. His eyes search my now tear-streaked face with satisfaction as if he likes seeing me like this. "If you want to come, you'll show up tonight." Then with that, he and his two best friends exit the classroom.

# ELEVEN

# ELLINGTON

The Freak Show. Ten o'clock. Wear your
Halloween costume from last year.

I read over the text for the hundredth time. Sin sent it to me
an hour ago. I stand in the parking lot by my car. I just
arrived, and it's a quarter to ten. After I managed to get
myself together, I exited the classroom and went straight home. I
took a shower and woke up a few hours later in my bed. I didn't
mean to take a nap, but I was exhausted. Then like an idiot, I got
out of bed and started getting ready for *him*.

Why the fuck am I here?

Why not?

I'm the one using him, right? I have always had darker
thoughts when it came to sex, and I always believed that what I
wanted was wrong. No one has ever told me that. I just know it
from overhearing my mother's sessions with her clients. She never
judged them. They did enough of that themselves. Who wants to
be choked, slapped, and treated like a piece of meat? We're

supposed to be treated like queens, not cheap whores. Maybe that's what I am. What I'll always be.

The *Freak Show* is the old fairgrounds tucked back deep into the woods of Pennsylvania. Once abandoned, they reopened it about five years ago. It's here all year round. Every day is like Halloween. Hence the name *Freak Show*. People come from all around to visit.

My phone vibrates, and I look down to see it's a new text from Sin.

> You have three options: pick one.
>
> Trick or treat
>
> Run to hide
>
> Bleed and die.

I read over the message a couple of times, trying to decipher his riddle. I have no clue what it means.

> Trick or treat.

I answer, thinking that sounds the most self-explanatory.

> Sinful, sinful, little demon. You are my light like the devil is to freedom.

My frown deepens. Light? Devil? What the fuck is he talking about? Another message comes through, and I open it up to see it's a picture of me standing in the middle of the parking lot.

I look up to see where the picture came from, and it's the *house of mirrors*. Swallowing nervously, I start to make my way in that direction and almost trip over my heels in the rocky parking lot. This is what I wore to the guys' Halloween party last year that they had at the house of Lords, which included heels. I should have switched them out for tennis shoes.

Making my way through the crowd of people, I enter the crooked house. I haven't been here in years. The last time was with Kira. I was rolling my ass off, and she was my designated driver.

I grip the metal railing and walk up the stairs inside. The sounds of clown laughter fill my ears, making the hairs on the back of my neck rise. I know it's fake, but it's no different than sitting down and watching a scary movie, knowing damn well it's not real. You can't control how your body reacts.

Misattribution of arousal is physiological confusion. My body confuses itself as to why it's being aroused. For example, fear. When I experience a massive overload of adrenaline, I get turned on. I get off on the unknown.

There's a hallway to the left and another to the right. I take the one on my right, slowly walking down the narrow pathway. My arms are out to my sides, running my fingers along the floor-length mirrors. Red and blue lights flash from above, making it hard to see. It's as if the walls are closing in on me, but it's just an illusion. I stumble in my heels, my breath coming faster and faster by the second while "Thank You for Hating Me" by Citizen Soldier comes from the speakers lined along the ceiling.

I come to the end of the hall and look at myself in the mirror. I've got black leather bunny ears on. They cover the top half of my face; all you can see are my eyes. I've got them done smoky with black eye shadow, eyeliner, and mascara. My lips are blood red to match my nails. I wear a strapless black leotard that has a built-in bra to push up my large breasts, and I top it off with fishnet tights. It's a slutty Halloween outfit at its finest.

Reaching out to touch the mirror, I fall forward but manage to stay standing. There isn't a mirror there. *What?* What the hell was I looking at, then?

I catch sight of something behind me, and I spin around, only to see nothing. The lights turn red and start to flicker. It looks like I'm blinking rapidly, but my eyes are wide open, staring ahead and just waiting for something to jump out at me.

My pulse accelerates, and I take a step back, only to hit something. I scream and turn around to see it's a mirror.

"Fuck," I hiss to myself.

I turn to my left and run down the hallway, pushing a door open at the end, hoping it's the exit, but find a circular room lined with nothing but mirrors. And I'm alone. There's no way out, it's a dead end. I go to turn around, but before I can go back the way I came, the door slams shut on my face. There's no door handle or lever to open it. Just another fucking mirror staring back at me.

Swallowing nervously, I take a step back and turn back to face the room. Chains hang from the black ceiling in various links. Some all the way to the floor, and some so high I can't even reach them.

The lights are so bright in here. I lift my right arm to try to block them from shining down on me to get a better look at the room, but it doesn't work. The warmth from the lights makes me start to sweat.

"You know what they call a devoted demon?" a voice whispers in my ear.

I spin around, only to find I'm alone. My hand goes to my chest, and I feel my heart pounding against it.

"The devil's pet," another voice answers.

Laughter follows.

"What the fuck?" I growl more to myself than them. Making my way over to where I know the door was, I try to open it again and nothing. Fisting my hands, I pound them both on the mirror. "Hello?" I call out. "Hello!" I raise my voice to a scream.

"Save your energy. You're going to need it."

I spin back around to yell once again, but my breath is taken away when I see three men standing at the opposite end of the circular room. All dressed in black jeans, combat boots, black hoodies, and masks. They're not overly terrifying, but something about them has my skin tingling and breath hitching.

The one on the far right is a clown. It's got oversized teeth with what looks like blood dripping from them. Big black eyes and a white face with red cheeks. The one in the middle wears a mirror-like mask. It's got black holes for eyes and is so long that it dips into his black hoodie so you can't see a single inch of skin. It doesn't have a mouth of any kind. The one on the far left looks like a human face that has had all the skin removed, showing all the veins and tendons.

"Sin," I breathe his name, placing my hands out in front of me in defense as if it'll keep them away. "What are you doing?" I ask, licking my lips nervously.

None of them answer, and my knees threaten to buckle. My heart is in my throat, and the blood rushes in my ears. The lights turn off, and I suck in a deep breath. They come back on, and they're gone.

"What?" I spin around in a circle but see nothing but myself in the mirrors. Were they even actually in here? Or was it an illusion of the mirrors?

The lights start flashing red and blue, just like in the halls, and a hand grabs my neck. I try to scream, but my air is cut off when the fingers tighten on either side of my throat. I'm lifted off my feet and shoved backward. A new set of hands grabs me, and my arms are lifted above my head. Something is wrapped around them, and I'm lifted to where I'm dangling from. My heels barely touch the floor.

The hand is removed from my neck, and my head sags forward as I try to catch my breath.

I struggle in the restraints. My body turns from side to side, knowing they've secured me to the chains hanging from the ceiling. The sound of them clanking from my movements echoes in the room.

"S-in?" I choke, still trying to slow my racing heart.

I look around, but the damn lights are still flashing and restricting my vision. I feel like I'm going to get sick, so I close my eyes.

Hands grip my legs, and they are spread wide open. Something wraps around them too, just like my wrists, and seconds later, I can't close them.

"Please?" I whimper, my body shaking.

"But this is what you want, Elli," he whispers in my ear. I shiver when I feel his hand on my shoulder, pulling my hair off my neck to lay down the length of my back. "I just want to make your fantasies come true."

I open my eyes as everything goes black. Then the bright lights are on again, making me blink. All three stand in front of me. The one on the far right holds a belt in his hand. It's not a normal-looking one. It's so long that it puddles on the floor at his feet. The one in the middle has a chain around the back of his neck, draping over his shoulders. Both hands fisting it on either side. The one on the left has a backpack at his feet. And that scares me the most because I can't see what's inside.

The one in the middle with the chain walks toward me. He wears the skinless face mask. I throw my head back and scream so loud, my throat burns.

He walks behind me, and he wraps the chain around my neck from behind. He pulls on it, cutting me off, and places his lips by my ear. "You'll scream when we tell you to."

He hasn't taken my air away completely, but he's restricted it.

The guy with the belt walks up to me. His mirrored mask is broken with cracks all through it as if someone hit it with a baseball bat. It shows my reflection in broken pieces. I can see my makeup smeared from my tears. He tilts his head to the side, not saying anything. Then without warning, he takes the belt and slaps the leather across the inside of my thigh just as the one behind me tightens the chain, taking away my air and restricting my ability to scream out at the pain.

He lets go of the chain, and my head hangs while I suck in a breath. My thigh is now on fire as if someone just held a lighter to it. It throbs, and so does my pussy.

My shoulders scream at the position my body hangs from the ceiling. My feet hurt from my heels barely touching, and my legs spread wide. But my clit is pulsing, and my nipples are erect. My breathing labored.

A hand is between my legs the next second, and the snaps of my leotard are being unfastened. It pops open, and it's yanked up to my waist. I moan, my head falling back, eyes closing.

My fishnets are lowered enough to rip off my underwear, making me whimper at the feel of the material stinging my hips. Something is placed on my pussy. It starts to vibrate.

I start to convulse, my mouth falling open when my entire body stiffens. I'm going to come so quickly. The fear, the adrenaline, the vibration. Fuck, this will be a record. It stops, and I curse them under my breath.

My bunny ears are yanked off my head before they're replaced with a hood, taking my vision away, and the chain tightens around my neck, pinching my skin. The chains that I'm secured to rattle as the sweetheart top of my leotard is yanked down to expose my chest to the room.

Hands grab at my breasts. They're not rough. Mostly soft. Slowly, they massage them. Caressing them with just enough pressure to have my head spinning. Or maybe it's the room. I can't see anything, so I close my eyes. My hot breath inside the hood falling on my face makes me sweat.

A tongue licks my nipple, and I find myself leaning into it.

"Oh God," I moan when his teeth sink into it just enough to make my thighs tighten in anticipation.

Then they're gone, and I groan in frustration. Something clamps down on my right nipple, taking my breath away. My shoulders cave in to try to cover my chest, but it's useless. The chains around my wrists make it impossible and open for their convenience.

"This is when you scream." I hear the voice at my ear again right before pain slices through my nipple. And I do exactly what he says.

I scream into the hood, my body thrashing in the chains that hold me captive. Hot fire runs through me, and my chest tightens. Then like it never happened, it's gone, and I sag once again, now crying.

I swallow my tears, sweat, and snot while I hang here in the middle of a room for them to play with. And I hate how wet I am right now. That I try to rub my thighs together to get some friction.

I tense when I feel a hand on my other breast. It's the same as before. His mouth on it, then his teeth. I take a deep breath when something pinches it, and then that fire again makes me scream like I've never screamed before.


## SIN

Fuck. She's so goddamn gorgeous. I've been so fucking hard since she read her journal in class today. If I had known she had those kinds of fantasies, I would have sat in on that class every day with her.

But it's probably better I didn't. The temptation of getting her off the last two years without fucking her have been hard enough on me.

She hangs before me, her breasts and pussy exposed, and all I want to do is mark her. Carve my name into her body so every damn man knows she belongs to me and that I've waited all of my life for this. For her.

Corbin and Jayce had to help me tonight, and although I don't mind them seeing her naked, I'd never let them fuck her. No one is allowed to touch what's mine. Not unless they want to lose an arm.

"S-in," she sobs into the hood, and I cup her cunt. Her body jerks in surprise, and I spread her pussy open wide, feeling how wet she is.

"Such a good little demon," I praise her, making her hips rock back and forth. The rattling of the chains from her harsh movements makes me smile.

"Please?" she begs so fucking sweetly. I imagine her doing it while crawling to me with her mouth open wide, waiting for me to use it.

I shove two fingers into her, my thumb massaging her piercing, and her breathing hitches. I look over her shoulder at Corbin and nod. He yanks on the chain, tightening it around her neck, and she goes wild when he takes away her air while I fuck her cunt with my fingers. I bring her as close to orgasm as I can, and when her pussy clenches on my fingers, I stop and remove them.

The chain loosens, and she sags once again, her cries filling the room.

"We've just begun, little demon."

# TWELVE

# ELLINGTON

They dress me back in my Halloween costume and release me from the chains. The hood is removed.

My legs shake, and one of the guys—the one in the mirrored mask—bends down, placing one hand behind my back and the other under my knees. He picks me up, and I lie limp in his arms while I watch through hooded eyes. The other two shove everything into the backpack.

We quietly exit the room and out of the hall of mirrors into the fresh night air. I shiver at the breeze even though it feels good on my burning skin. It can get pretty chilly at night in Pennsylvania.

Closing my eyes, I don't even care that my body shakes in his arms. It's begging for a release, and right now, I'd do just about anything to get that. I hear voices here and there, but again, I don't care who sees me like this. I couldn't walk if he forced me. And I'd rather be carried than crawl.

I feel him walking up a new set of stairs, and I open my eyes just in time to see a devil's mouth wide open with red horns and orange teeth. *Devil's Path* is written across the top in big letters.

Off in the distance, I hear the faint noise of screams and the sound of grinding metal.

*It's a roller coaster.*

My eyes open once again when I'm set on a cold and unforgiving surface. I look around to see it's a single cart with three seats. I'm sitting between the mirrored face and the guy with the skinless face mask.

The one with the mirror mask pulls the backpack around the front and unzips it. A hand grips the back of my already sore neck, and I'm shoved forward, my cheek resting on the cold metal bar running across the front of our cart.

Hands grab my arms and pull them behind my back. Handcuffs are wrapped around them, making me suck in a breath. I'm brought back to a sitting position. My legs are spread wide by both of them. They use their boots to hold me open. A blindfold is slipped over my eyes, and blood starts rushing in my ears.

The buttons of my leotard are undone again, and a finger runs up and down my soaked pussy. I moan, my hips trying to rock against it.

"So fucking greedy," the guy to my left says, and my mind is still too foggy to know who is who.

My pussy lips are spread open wide, and then something cold slides inside me. The unknown object isn't large, but it feels a little uncomfortable due to how I'm sitting. I start panting, and I lick my lips in anticipation.

"Don't worry, little demon. You're about to get your wish," one of them says to me. It has to be Sin. Only he calls me that.

They release my legs, and I close them, trying to rub them together to get the friction I need. A hand lands on my chest, holding me in place, my back to the uncomfortable seat as it smashes my cuffed hands behind me. Then I feel something on my chest and stomach, followed by a click. They just locked me into my seat with the overhead harness.

I thrash around, unable to move, and I hear a loud ringing before we jolt forward. My heart gets stuck in my throat. I can't see, and I can't hang on.

I feel us climbing. Hear the click as it takes us higher and higher before it drops us off the edge. I wait for the inevitable fall. My body tenses, my thighs trying to clench, but the overhead restraints latched between my legs prevents that.

The car comes to a stop, and I hold my breath. My pussy vibrates right as it drops us from the peak. I scream, my body falling, the car and my cunt vibrating. It falls on deaf ears, though, over the roaring sound of the wind around us. My breath gets caught in my lungs as we plunge to what I can only guess is our death since I can't see or hang on.

It jerks us to the right, and I fist my cuffed hands, sucking in a breath as my stomach clenches and unclenches. The wind rushes through my hair, and I can feel it whipping across my face. The blood is pumping in my veins as it takes a few dips—up and down, up and down. I can't see, so I'm left with feeling and hearing. My insides are pushed around, my pussy clenching, forcing the vibrator up against my G-spot. Along with the adrenaline rush, I feel an orgasm coming on. It's the danger, the unknown. The lack of control. I've never experienced anything like it.

The restraints are so tight that I can't move. Each sharp turn makes my breath hitch. Each climb makes my pulse race. And each fall has my pussy clenching.

And just like that, stars dance across my covered eyes, my body lifts off the seat, pressing my already sensitive nipples into the overhead restraints, and I come with a scream on my lips as we make a drop that seems to go on forever. I feel like I'm floating, reaching the clouds high in the sky.

My breath is taken away as if someone is choking me. I feel light-headed. Every inch of my skin tingles. I can't tell if we're still falling or if we're climbing once again. All I know is that I never want to come down.

## SIN

THE GUYS AND I ENTER HER BEDROOM BACK AT HER HOUSE, and I hold her unconscious body in my arms. She passed out before I could even get her off the roller coaster. It's funny how little a carny will accept if you've got cash on hand to look the other way. Pretty sure we could have committed murder tonight, and he'd have kept his mouth shut for a hundred dollars.

"Rip off the duvet and top sheet," I order Jayce and Corbin.

They each grab a corner and yank off the white duvet and matching silk sheet.

"Pillows too," I add.

They remove all ten pillows that she insists she needs and toss them over to the side. I lay her on the bed as Corbin throws her bunny ears/mask onto her desk in the corner. I yank the black leotard, pulling it down her body and from her legs. I grab the top of the fishnet tights and pull them down too. She doesn't even move. Jayce drops her heels at the end of her bed, and I roll her onto her stomach. Corbin tosses me his backpack. I unzip it, pulling out the roll of duct tape.

He comes over to bring her arms behind her back, and I wrap it around her wrists, running it up her forearms a little bit to make sure there's no way she can wiggle them free. Duct tape is effective but only when used correctly. Always use more than you think you need.

I push her onto her back so her arms are underneath her. I sit beside her and run my thumbs over her freshly pierced nipples. I thought she'd like that. I wanted to see what they would look like. They're fucking gorgeous, just like I knew they'd be. I can't wait for them to heal so I can change them out with chains. She'll look so fucking beautiful with tears running down her face while I pull on them, hearing her scream.

I rip two more pieces of duct tape off and cross them over her mouth in an X before adding a longer piece across the middle. Making sure it goes from ear to ear. Again, always use more than you think you need. Getting up, I go to her legs, and he holds them in place while I duct-tape them together at her ankles, making it impossible for her to get free.

I stand and throw Jayce the tape just as he tosses me something. "What's this?" I ask, catching it in my hands.

"Something you're going to want to see," he mumbles. "It was sitting on her desk."

I sit down on the bench with my back to her and open the notebook. To see it's dated earlier this month.

*Dear Diary,*

*Aug 15th*

*I saw David again. He rented us a hotel. I arrived first and got ready. I met him at the door dressed in nothing. Just like he had told me to do.*

*I felt stupid. I don't know why but I don't feel what he does. He thinks this is real. But that's not what it is for me. He's something to pass the time.*

*I've tried to date guys, but they just can't give me what I want. They either think I'm fucked up in the head or testing their loyalty.*

*What's wrong with a woman wanting a man to use them? Maybe they're right. I see sex as pleasure. And it should be more of a commitment. That's what he says anyway.*

No matter how hard he fucks me, I'm left feeling hollow afterward. Unsatisfied.

Maybe it's him, but I think it's me. He tells me that I'm a whore for wanting more. That when I'm with him —only him—I'm an honest woman. He fucks up my head better than he does my body. That should tell you all you need to know, but what other option do I have?

It's not the best sex, but it's better than fucking random men who might skin me alive and toss me into a lake where I'd never be found.

He's reliable, and I'm his dirty little secret. So I'll continue to do what he wants even if that means not getting what I want. I'm used to being a secret.

I flip back toward the beginning of the book and see another entry from last summer.

Dear Diary,

May 10th

Sin hates me. Has since we were kids. Too bad I dream about him in the most inappropriate situations. When I started getting myself off, I'd close my eyes and think of him. I'd imagine it was him doing all the nasty and depraved things to me. But I had to stop that. It was just tainting my expectations of what I thought Sin could be capable of if ever given the chance. I'd rather never know that kind of letdown if I'm being honest with myself.

That's all I have—myself. There's no one I can talk

*to about what I've done, or who I want. Kira would be so mad at me if she knew I imagined her brother treating me like a piece of meat to use however he wanted. Sin would think I'm crazy, possibly pathetic.*

*So I'll keep writing down my thoughts and fantasies as if they were their stories. My fictional characters might as well enjoy themselves.*

I close the notebook and look over at her. She's still sound asleep, tied up with duct tape on her bed.

"Here's another one. Looks older," Jayce states, closing a drawer to her desk.

I hold out my hand and he throws it to me. I open the first page. My heart starts to race when I see it's dated two years ago. The night I was assigned to kill for the Lords.

*Dear Diary,*
*August 12th*
*A man killed Daddy last night. I think he thought I was going to rat him out. But that wasn't going to happen. I'm glad he's dead. He was a sorry son of a bitch who deserved a horrible death. A bullet to the head was kind.*

*I let the man fuck me with his gun. It was dirty, raw, and therapeutic in a way. Even though it sounds fucked up, I got off on it. I had never come so hard. I hope he knows that I'm not going to say anything and that he comes back to visit me again. Even if it is to kidnap and take me away from here. This life is boring.*

*I've always fantasized about wanting more. And I think the masked man can give it to me.*

"It's one thirty," Jayce announces to the room, getting my attention.

Closing the diary, I stand and walk over to the door, turning her light off. Then I sit down in the seat in the far corner and wait.

# THIRTEEN

# SIN

I t's two o'clock on the dot when I hear the front doors open and close. The house is so quiet the sound echoes. There was a reason we had to cut our playtime short at the *Freak Show*. While in my parents' kitchen, she had been texting David this morning about coming over tonight. Over my dead body will I allow this dipshit to continue to touch what's mine. I've had my suspicions but wasn't sure until I saw the pictures that Lincoln gave me. Then to see her tied up in his basement the other night? I couldn't do anything about it then without giving myself away. I don't want her knowing it was my cock she came all over.

I sit silently still as I count each step of his boots on the stairs. He pushes her door open with a creak and enters. He doesn't turn on the light. Instead, he walks over to her bed and chooses the lamp. I smile to myself.

"My girl is already ready for me," he muses, looking over her exposed body. Her chest rising and falling with each breath she inhales through her nose. She hasn't moved an inch since I brought her home thirty minutes ago. "Oh, I like these." He reaches out and runs his knuckles over her pierced nipple, and I fist my hands, rage crawling up my spine like a fire engulfs a wall. Reaching up, he grips the back of his shirt and lifts it over his head.

I stand. "She's no longer for you."

He spins around, hands up, and gasps. "Easton?" he breathes my first name. I've always gone by Sin because it fits my personality. Only my parents call me by my first name. "What the fuck are you doing here?" His brown eyes widen.

"I'm here for her," I inform him.

He frowns, turning back to Elli. Then looks at me once again. "I don't understand."

I step into him. "You are to stay the fuck away from her," I warn, causing his eyes to narrow.

"I will not..."

"Tomorrow morning, you will drop her from your class." This son of a bitch sits at his desk while she stands in front of his class reading off her deepest, darkest desires, and then he fucks her in secret. He uses his students, exploits them. Elli isn't the only student he's been fucking, and the Lords have found out.

When she was distracted reading over her text messages this morning, I had Jayce get into her backpack on the island and pull out her notebook for class. Everyone knows what goes on inside Mr. Hamilton's classes, but Barrington University allows it. Like the Lords, it has its own rules.

I saw her texts and made some phone calls of my own after I spoke to my father. That's why the guys and I showed up during his class. We were to make a point. I was claiming my girl. Guess I should have made him stay and watch what I did to her.

His shoulders stiffen. "Now, Easton—"

I punch him in the face, knocking his head back. "You'll do what I fucking tell you to do. Otherwise, you'll lose your fucking job," I shout, that fire growing again. My skin breaks out in a cold sweat. "And I'll take her to the cops and have her file a rape charge against you." His father may be a powerful Lord, but I can still take him down. It'll just mean I have to get dirty. My father is a Lord too. And the Lords don't like it when you jeopardize their existence.

He rubs his face, blood running from his nose. Then a smirk appears on his busted lips. "You'll never be able to prove it."

"Boys," I call out. Jayce and Corbin both step out of the dark corner, and he takes a step back. "I'll do whatever needs to be done to get you the fuck away from her. Even if that means forcing you to fuck her with a gun to your head." As jealous as I feel over my little demon, I'm nothing but determined to do whatever needs to be done to get him out of her life.

His lips thin, and he growls. "You're a sick fucking bastard."

"I can be. It's up to you how far I'll go." I shrug carelessly. There are two guns in Jayce's backpack right now along with a few knives. I'll carve him up like a fucking pumpkin before I pump some bullets into his chest and then throw him on the front porch like a Halloween decoration left out to rot.

"I've got cameras in my classroom." His words make my muscles tense. Even though I expected it. "Just last week, she willingly crawled underneath my desk so I could fuck her mouth. No one believes a whore who cries rape."

I punch him again. This time, his body hits her nightstand, making it rattle, and she stirs, but her eyes remain closed.

"Take him to Barrington," I order Jayce and Corbin. "Then his house. I want every tape and USB drive." I turn to face them. "Get me every recording he has. Destroy every laptop, computer, and cell phone."

"No, wait—" He raises his hands, and I punch him again in the side of his face this time, knocking him to the floor.

I reach out my left hand, and Jayce tosses me his backpack. I catch it and unzip it, pulling out the Glock 19 9mm. I cock it as I crouch down, pushing the end of the barrel to his head, making him whimper. "If I so much as see you look her way, I'll chop off both of your hands and make you watch me set them on fire so you have no hope of reattaching them." Pushing the gun farther into his skull, it forces him to roll onto his back. "Making sure you never get the chance to jack your worthless dick off to the thought of her again."

He closes his eyes tightly. "Easton—"

"Do you understand me?" I ask calmly.

"Yes ... yes, I understand you," he rushes out.

Removing the gun from his head, I stand and nod to Jayce and Corbin. "Go."

They walk over to him, pick him up by his arms, and drag him out of her room, leaving me alone with my girl. Now it's time to wake her up and tell her the good news.

The devil is here to claim his little demon. *She's all mine.*

## ELLINGTON

I OPEN MY HEAVY EYES AND MOAN BUT REALIZE I CAN'T speak. Panic makes my heart race, and I go to sit up, but I can't do that either. I'm on my back with my arms underneath me. At least, I think they are. They're numb.

Turning my head from side to side, I see I'm in my room. My lamp is on, giving the room a soft glow. I try to move my feet, but I turn to my side and look down to see my ankles duct-taped together. I start screaming into the tape that I now know is over my mouth.

"Well, hello, my little demon."

My eyes snap to my left, and I see Sin standing by my bed. He's dressed in a pair of black jeans and a matching hoodie, but his mask from the Freak Show is long gone. I blink, my breathing becoming erratic.

He sits down on the side of the bed, and I arch my neck, trying to relieve the tension in my back. His fingers caress my tender skin where one of them wrapped the chain around it. I whimper.

"I'm not going to hurt you, Elli. Quite the opposite." His fingers move to wrap around my throat, and I feel my pussy clench, my thighs tightening. "I'm going to make every dark fantasy you have come true," he says simply.

Tears spring to my eyes, and I suck in a deep breath through my nose.

"Isn't that what you want?" he asks, his hand leaving my neck and running softly up and down my chest. Light as a feather, making my skin break out in goose bumps.

I nod, unable to answer, realizing I'm naked.

He removes his hand, and I find myself leaning toward him, hoping for his touch, but he stands. I watch with blurry vision from the tears that have yet to fall as he removes his hoodie and shirt and unbuttons his jeans. Pushing them down, he then takes off his boxer briefs. He's hard. His dick standing to attention.

My pulse races at his large size and the piercings that run along his shaft and the head of his dick. I count at least six barbells and one ring.

"See, little demon." He crawls onto the bed and grabs my tied legs. Pushing them to the left, I roll onto my side, and he shoves them to my chest, restricting my breathing even more.

His hand goes to my soaked cunt. "This belongs to me now." He pushes a finger into it. "And so does this." He removes it to slide it to my ass, pushing his finger in there as well, making me tense and scream out into the tape. Shaking my head the best I can, I try to straighten my legs out to push him away.

He laughs, holding my legs out of the way with his free hand. His fingers dig into my skin to hold them in place while I fight him. "Never been fucked in the ass? That's a surprise." He pulls it out, and I sag against my bed. "But I like the idea of being the first cock to take it. I'm going to be your first for a lot of things, Elli." He spits on his finger and then rubs it over my ass again, making me tense. "You'll love it. My cock in your ass while I fuck your throat with a dildo covered in your cum." I moan at that thought. "I'll make you walk around with a skirt and no underwear on. Just so I can lift it whenever I want to see my cum running out of your ass."

He removes his finger and then slips it in again. I rock against it, my body starting to like the pressure it provides. "That's it, Elli. Get that cunt wet for me. You'll be begging for me to fuck this ass in no time."

I feel his cock push against my pussy, and I suck in a breath through my nose as the head stretches my sore cunt.

I cry out when he pushes into me. His size takes my breath away for a moment. He pulls out and then pushes in again, his piercings hitting all the right places. I want to tell him to put on a condom even though I'm on birth control, but he's taken away my option to speak.

"Fuck." He groans, and my heart beats wildly in my chest at the sound. "I've always dreamed of fucking you, little demon."

My breath hitches. "Every time you wore a short skirt or a pair of tight jeans." His fingers dig into my skin so hard they're going to leave bruises. I love it. "I imagined ripping them off you. Bending you over and fucking you like my own little toy."

I whimper, my body rocking back and forth. The silk fitted sheet sticks to my tear-streaked face.

His free hand reaches up to grip my hair and he yanks my head back. His other hand slides behind my knees, pushing them into my chest. He picks up his pace, his cock ramming into my soaking cunt.

"You belong to me now..." He growls in my ear, my scalp stinging from his tight grip. "You will beg me. You will cry for me." His tongue runs along my cheeks, licking my tears. "You will crawl on your hands and knees for me."

I close my eyes as they roll into the back of my head while my toes start to curl.

"You are my treat, little demon." He kisses the tape that's over my mouth as if they are my lips. "And you will do as I say." He pulls back and slams into me. The sound of our bodies slapping fills the room. "Do you understand?"

If I could talk, I'd say yes, but that's impossible. So instead, I mumble into the tape that sticks to my face.

Just when I think I'm about to come, he pulls out and lets go of me. I cry, my body shaking with need.

He flips me over onto my stomach. My knees are crammed underneath me, and my ass is up in the air, but my arms are thankful now that they're not pinned underneath me. I turn my head to the side so I don't suffocate.

His cock slides against my pussy, slowly pushing into me once again. Then I hear him spit before I feel it land on my ass. He pushes a finger into me, and I start to fight him. His hand goes to my head once again, gripping my hair, holding the side of my wet face to the bed.

"I'm going to fuck that ass, little demon. Tonight. The question is, are you going to give it to me, or am I going to take it?" he asks. His finger slowly runs up and down from my ass to my pussy.

I inhale a deep breath and relax my body. "That's it. Such a good girl," he says, pushing that finger into me again. "And good girls get rewarded."

# FOURTEEN

# SIN

I reach over and grab the lube I already had lying on the bed. I pop it open and pour it along her ass. So much that it runs down to cover her pussy and my cock. I continue to fuck her cunt while I work my finger in and out of her ass. Adding a second one and then a third. She's still fighting me. Her body struggles, and I smile, loving it. This is what I've wanted—her. I have no problem giving her what she wants, even if that means taking it from her. She just thinks that something's wrong with her. I'll show her just how fucked up a head can be. How dark a mind can go. She'll bleed for me, come for me, and beg. She will crave to please me.

I push three fingers inside her, twisting them around, watching her ass open for me. Usually, anal takes a little more preparation, stretching and some sort of an enema to clean her out, but I'm too impatient for that right now. So she'll just have to take it. If I make her bleed, then so be it. And I couldn't care less about her making a mess on my dick.

I pull out of her cunt, then grab my dick. I remove my fingers from her ass and slowly rub the tip of my cock along her puckered hole. The ring from my Prince Albert pushes into her. I close my eyes, a groan of pleasure escaping my lips. "Fuck, little demon." My breath catches when I go a little deeper, feeling my cock force its way inside where no man has ever been.

She screams out into the tape and tries to wiggle away from me. Readjusting myself, I place my right foot on the bed next to her, bending my knee. It gives me better control while still kneeling on my left one. My left hand presses down on her back, lowering the angle of her ass, crushing her legs underneath her. "Stay still," I order, my heart beating wildly in my chest. Fuck, I'm going to fill her with my cum tonight.

I push into her ass again. She cries, but I ignore it. The pressure takes my breath away when the head of my cock disappears inside her. "That's it, Elli," I say breathlessly. "Good girl." Her body shakes under mine, and I push farther into her before pulling out altogether. "Feel that?" I enter her again. "Your ass is sucking me in, little demon." I let go of her back long enough to slap her ass cheek. So hard it leaves a perfect handprint. I do it again, and her body convulses. "Fuck, you're doing so good. That's it." I push farther in, but I'm not even halfway yet. "Take my cock, little demon." I thrust harder, getting a little more forceful. "You're doing so good for me." I can feel her resistance, and I must admit it feels incredible. "Open for me, and let me take it," I add, sucking in a breath and going even deeper.

My hand slips across her back from the sweat that covers her perfect skin. So I dig my fingers into her hip, getting a better grip.

I take a shaky breath, pulling out and pushing forward, her ass now opening up for me like I fucking belong. I'll remind her of this every chance I get too. "That's it." I throw my head back, closing my eyes, and I just feel her ass swallow me as I go deeper and deeper with each thrust, no longer giving her a chance to adjust to me. "Goddamn," I moan, sinking my teeth into my bottom lip.

Her cries are muffled, and she's shaking uncontrollably. I've imagined her like this so many times, but nothing compares to the real thing. Holding her down, I'm taking what I want. "Such a good girl. You're doing so fucking good, Elli." I continue praising her while I take her sweet ass, making her mine in every way I can.

I pull out completely and then push back inside her, loving the way she struggles. As if she's going to get away from me. Like she has the power to stop me.

Her ass presses back against me, and a smile plays on my lips. "That's it, Elli. Fuck my cock." I stop moving my hips and watch her ass rock back and forth on my cock. She's much slower, though. I let her do her thing for a minute. Then I reposition myself to lie down across her back, smashing her legs underneath her body and her arms to her back. I tangle one hand in her already messy hair while the other slides underneath her neck. I tighten my fingers around her throat until she can't move a muscle.

I'm so close that if I were to stick my tongue out, I could taste the tears running down her gorgeous face. She swallows against my hand, making me smile.

I whisper in her ear, "I'm going to fuck it now, little demon. I'm going to show you who this ass belongs to." I pull my hips back and slam forward. She screams out into the tape covering her mouth, and I tighten my hand around her throat, taking away her air. "I'm going to make you like it, Elli. You're going to come for me," I growl, unable to stop myself. I lick her tears while her body shakes, tasting their saltiness. She tastes like the ocean, and I'd gladly drown for her.

I fuck her ass, feeling powerful. Unstoppable. The sound of our bodies slapping fills her bedroom. I watch her eyes grow heavy; her body stiffens against mine. I know the moment she comes, and I let go of her neck just when her eyes roll back into her head.

I rip off the pieces of tape, and she sucks in a deep breath. Pulling out of her, I flip her onto her back once again and shove her knees to her chest. I slide back into her ass, making her scream out, but her ass takes me easily this time. No need to work up to it right now. Running my free hand over her wet cunt, I get her cum all over my fingers. I push her knees to the side just a bit so I can lean over her body, and my cum-covered hand grips her face.

"Such a good little demon," I say, looking into her heavy eyes. Her makeup's smeared across her face from earlier and even more now.

"S-in." She chokes out my nickname, trying to arch her back.

I lower my lips to hers, kissing her. My tongue enters her mouth while my cock continues to move in and out of her. She's shaking uncontrollably, and I pull my lips from hers to shove two of my fingers into her mouth. She gags, but I ignore it. "Taste that, Elli? That's you all over my fingers from my dick in your ass."

She chokes on them, spit flying from her lips. Arching her neck, she's trying to remove my fingers from her mouth, but my hand just moves with her. "I want them shoved down your throat," I tell her, making her whimper. Her throat works at the motion. "I want you to taste yourself." I slam my hips forward, my cock pounding her ass. Fresh tears run down the sides of her face when she blinks. "You're doing so fucking good, Elli. Coming for me like that. I knew you'd like it. I've got so many ways to make you come, little demon."

My balls start to tighten, and I grind my teeth. I don't want to come, not yet, but it's inevitable. She feels too fucking good. Closing my eyes, I shove forward one last time, and my cock pulses inside her ass while my body stiffens.

Removing my fingers from her mouth, I sit up. She's coughing and crying while I pull out of her ass. I smile, running my fingers over the sensitive area, watching the cum leak out of her. "That's what I wanted to see. You're going to love being my pet, little demon."

She whimpers at my words, and I smile. She has no idea just how far I'm willing to go to keep her now that I've got her. A collar, a leash, a cage. She won't be able to breathe without asking me first. And even that, I'll take away from her.

Getting up off the bed, I leave her there and enter the adjoining bathroom. I turn on the faucet and grab the towel off the countertop. I run warm water over it and then proceed to clean off my cock with some soap. Once I'm satisfied, I throw the towel to the counter and shut off the light.

I go back to her room to see her lying on her stomach, looking at me over her shoulder. Her wrists and ankles still duct-taped. "Such a sight to see," I tell her, and she whimpers, her ass lifting up in the air.

"My arms hurt," she whispers hoarsely.

Instead of acknowledging that, I walk over to the bed and grab her shoulders, forcing her to roll over on her back once again, yanking her over to me while I stand next to the bed.

"Sin ..."

"Did you think I was done with you?" I run my knuckles down her cheek, pushing the tangled hair from her wet face.

She sucks in a deep breath, her eyes looking up at me as her head lies halfway off the edge.

"Open your mouth," I order.

Her shoulders shake, and her eyes close. But I watch the way she tries to rub her tied legs together. Her cunt enjoying the way I'm about to use her mouth just like I did her ass. The pussy will come last tonight.

I take my cock in my hand, feeling the piercings. I've got six barbells along my shaft—Jacob's ladder. I can't wait to watch her choke on it. The metal through my dick will make her drool more than a dick in her mouth without them.

As soon as that thought enters my mind, that fire returns to my body, heating me up from the inside out. Like an explosion inside a tunnel that brings all the walls crashing down, crushing anything inside it. I've never known so much jealousy. My breathing accelerates at the very thought of her diary filled with the professor fucking her. I'm going to burn it. She'll start a new one. And every story in it will involve her and me.

Hell, even the fact that she has written about me in the mask making her come pisses me off because she doesn't know it's *me*.

I grab her ribs on either side, pulling her closer to me, her head now hanging completely off the side of the bed. Placing my hand underneath the back of her neck, I growl. "I told you to open your goddamn mouth."

Her eyes widen, and she swallows nervously. "Sin..."

I don't let her say whatever concern was on her mind. Instead, I push my hard dick between her parted lips, taking advantage of the situation. She'll learn I do that a lot.

Her body jerks, her tied legs kicking, trying to fight the duct tape while she chokes on my cock as I easily shove it down the back of her throat. I can feel my piercings hit her teeth, and her mumbled words vibrate my dick.

"Choke on me, Elli," I tell her, smiling. Pulling out, she gasps. I shove forward again, making her body continue its useless fight. Her head is hanging off the side of my bed, between my thighs. Her breathing is already restricted because every time my hips thrust forward, my balls smash against her nose. I've got a hand underneath her neck tilting it at an angle so I can easily slip deep down her throat.

I smile, my free hand reaching out to play with her nipple piercings. I pull on them, and her chest rises with me to try to relieve the pain. I don't even think she realizes I pierced them. I can't wait to show her the video of it.

"That's it." I pull out, and saliva flies from her mouth, covering her face while she sucks in a breath. "So beautiful." I slap her wet cheek, and she cries out. I push back into her mouth again while she takes the opportunity to breathe, and I watch her throat expand from my cock sliding down it. "That's my girl." I pant, feeling her gag. "Take it, Elli. Show me you belong to me."

If I have to tie her up and display her in the middle of town, naked with my name carved into her chest for the world to see, I will. Like I said before, she has no clue just how dark my mind can go or how violent I can be. I have no problem showing her what the devil will do to claim his little demon.

## ELLINGTON

He comes down my throat before pulling out. His piercings clanking against my upper teeth.

I immediately roll over onto my stomach, my head still hanging over the bed, but I'm no longer crushing my arms underneath me.

Saliva and cum run out of my parted lips while I gasp and cough. My blond hair that isn't stuck to my wet face falls around my head so I can't see anything other than the white carpet below me. My hands tingle as the blood rushes back to them since they're still duct-taped behind my back.

The silk fitted sheet sticks to my sweaty and hot skin.

I suck in a deep breath, my eyes blinking, trying to see through my watery lashes that are lumped together from the mascara I wore earlier in the night. I almost threw up several times. It took all I had to keep it down. Afraid I'd choke on it. I'm not an expert at deep throating, but I didn't think I was that horrible at it. Was it because of his size? Roughness? The piercings? I'm not sure, but my body enjoyed it. The way he praised me for trying even though I didn't have the choice.

I hear the sound of bathwater running, and seconds later, I see his bare feet returning to stand by the bed. His hands grip my shoulders, and he flips me over onto my back. Then he's picking me up and carrying me to the bathroom while I lie limp in his strong arms.

The big bay window positioned above the large corner Jacuzzi tub tells me it's still nighttime. He's got the bathroom lights on, though, and they burn my sensitive eyes.

He lowers me into the bathtub, the white porcelain once again crushing my arms behind my back. "Sin ..." I manage a rough whisper. "My arms ..." I sniff. "They hurt."

Kneeling next to the tub, he runs his hand down the side of my face to wipe away the tears I cried while he fucked my ass and mouth.

"I know," he says simply, shoving the wet hair off my chest and shoulders.

The warm water is still filling the large tub. It's not even to my hips yet. His hand lowers down my chest bone between my breasts, and the pad of his thumb brushes over my nipple, making me hiss in a breath.

"Why?" I lift my head and gaze at my chest to figure out why it's so tender and see a silver barbell through both of my hard nipples, making me gasp.

"You like pain."

My wide eyes shoot to his, and he's staring at the piercings he must have given me while in the house of mirrors. "They were beautiful." He takes his finger and thumb, slightly turning the bar, making me shove the back of my head into the tub and cry out. A sharp pain takes my breath away. "Now they're fucking perfect, just like you."

Letting go of them, he leans back on his knees and grabs the bodywash. I take a quick look at the water to see it's now up to my belly button. He pops the top open on the bottle and pours it into his hand, lathering them up. Then his hands are on me.

A moan escapes my sore throat as he massages my breasts. His strong hands run up and down the sides of my ribs. Then he slowly takes them up on either side of my neck.

I'm panting, arching my head back for him, knowing how vulnerable this makes me and not caring at the moment.

Opening my eyes, I direct my gaze to the countertop by the vanity and see one of my diaries sitting there. I tense. He notices and follows my line of sight before looking back at me. Mine shoots to the faucet that still runs, and I notice the water is now up to my breasts.

I arch my back, trying to pull myself up out of the water since I've seemed to slip down, but his hand wraps around my throat, keeping me in place. My heart accelerates, my thighs tightening.

He leans over the side and presses his lips against mine, and I kiss him back without hesitation. His tongue enters my mouth while his hand holds me in place. It's tender and would seem loving if I wasn't duct-taped in a bathtub while the water continues to rise.

Sin pulls away, and I try to lean into him, wanting more, but his hands prevent it. Instead, he keeps his face close to mine but right out of reach.

"Easton." His first name trembles on my lips. I know what he's doing and where this is going, and fuck, I want it. "Did you read it?" I have to know. Need to hear him answer.

"I want to know everything that goes on in that beautiful mind of yours," he responds, confirming what I already knew.

He watches a tear slip from the corner of my eye. The diaries and journals have a purpose. The journals are for class. It's to make people uncomfortable. To desensitize them for what's to come. For me, it's much more than that. I've been writing in diaries since I was a kid. It was about what I heard my mother and her clients talk about. Situations they found themselves in or wanted to be in. My fantasies have just gotten darker and darker over the years. I had to get my desires out, and I had no one that I could talk to them about. So I chose to write them.

"Do you trust me?" he asks just as soft as his kiss was.

I swallow the lump in my throat and lick my swollen lips. "Yes."

His pretty blue eyes search mine for a second before leaning forward and placing a kiss on my forehead. I whimper at the tenderness in his touch. Then he stands to his full height, leaning over the tub, and shoves my face under the water with his hand around my throat.

He holds me down, my arms and back pushed to the bottom of the tub. It's not long enough for me to lay flat, so I pull my knees up for room. Opening my eyes, I look up through the calm water to see him leaning over the edge. Pieces of hair start to float around my face, obstructing my vision.

My cheeks are full of air, and I let it out slowly, feeling the bubbles on my face. My pussy clenches, my knees moving back and forth.

I had a scene written in my diary just like this. Where I trusted someone enough to literally hold my life in their hands. Water bondage is a known kink in the BDSM community, and I've always wanted to try it. Something about risking my life while handing someone else all the power turns me on. It's a combination of bondage and breath control. Both of which I crave.

My lungs start to burn, and my chest tightens. I lift my hips and wiggle my shoulders, trying to get free of his hold. Just when I think I can't go any longer, he pulls me from the water.

# FIFTEEN

# SIN

She gasps the moment her face reaches the surface, followed by coughing. I release her neck to reach over and grab the knife I had brought in here. Leaning over the tub once again, I cut the tape that wraps around her ankles and throw it to the floor along with the knife. Then I step into the tub, lowering myself into the warm water and spreading her legs with mine. The tub is on the larger side; it's no king-sized bed, but I'll make it work.

"Sin," she breathes, her head resting back on the ledge of the tub, eyes heavy.

Fuck, she's amazing. So goddamn gorgeous.

Reaching behind me, I pull the plug but leave the faucet on. The water is so high that it's reached her neck. My added body pushes it over the sides, and it splashes onto the floor.

Grabbing my hard cock, I push into her pussy, forcing a cry from her lips. I hate fucking in water, but I've had her ass and mouth. Now it's time I come inside this cunt. I lean forward, cupping her face and forcing her to look up at me. I kiss her roughly, swallowing every sound that comes from her plump lips. My hips move, and the water splashes onto the tile and the wall.

She's sluggish, and her body is tired. I'm losing her. It won't be much longer before she closes her eyes again to sleep what's left of the night away. But I'm not going to slow down. No. I'll use her until she passes out. Well, that won't stop me either. I'd still fuck her if she were unconscious. My little demon was born to serve. She prefers to submit. Give her an order, and she'll obey.

When I pull my lips from hers, my hand goes back to her throat, and her pussy clamps down on my cock, pulling me in deeper. "That's it, Elli. Milk my cock. Make me come inside your tight cunt. Just like I did that ass and mouth."

She whimpers, her eyes closed. I scoot her away from the back of the tub, and her eyes snap open just before I shove her head back down into the water. She fights this time. Her body thrashes underneath me, and I fuck her pussy. Slamming into her while I hold her in place. Her hair floats around the surface like a cloud, shielding her pretty face from me.

I reach down with my free hand and play with her vertical hood piercing. My thumb rubs over the black barbell aggressively. "Come for me, little demon," I growl, my fingers digging into her neck so much she'll have bruises come tomorrow. I like that idea. I want everyone to know she belongs to me. No one ever tries to take on the devil because they know they have no chance of winning. He's ruthless, a savage, and has no mercy on anyone.

Her body stops fighting only to go stiff. Her cunt starts pulsing around my cock, and I smile. Waiting an extra second, I shove forward and come inside her. Grabbing the back of her neck, I lift her head from the water. For a millisecond, she doesn't seem to be breathing. I look over her soft features. Her lips are parted, and eyes closed. My free hand comes up, and I run my thumb over her lips just as her eyes snap open, and she sucks in a breath. She immediately starts crying.

I stand from the tub and pull her out, setting her on the edge. Grabbing the knife off the floor, I cut the tape around her wrists and then leave her to turn off the bath that has turned cold. Grabbing a towel off the hook on the wall, I turn to see her now kneeling in the middle of the bathroom with her face in her hands, softly sobbing.

Bending down, I wrap the towel around her and pull her into my arms, where she buries her face into my bare chest. Then I carry her into her room and lay her down on her bed. I go to pull away, but her arms wrap around my neck. "Please. Don't." She clings to me.

"I'm going—"

"Don't ... leave me," she sobs, not letting me finish, so I settle onto the bed next to her, wet and naked.

I kiss her wet hair. Within minutes, her cries subside, and her breathing evens out. When her body relaxes against mine, I know she's asleep.

Pulling away from her, I get out of bed and grab the duvet to cover her. Then I place two pillows on the bed, gently sliding one under her head. I make my way to the bathroom, grab her diary, and then go back to bed with her.

While she's sleeping, I read it as I wait for the guys to return with David and everything I need to fuck up the bastard's life.

Nothing about her fantasies in her diary surprise me. My little demon has always been curious. I was drawn to her and could never understand why. I mean, she's gorgeous, yeah, but there was always more that I couldn't explain. But we were too young. By the time she was of age, I was already into my first year of initiation to be a Lord. Orders are you have to be celibate for three years.

*Fuck my luck.*

I had never fucked a girl my age, let alone younger. I learned at a young age that if they're married, they don't want anyone to know they're fucking you. And if you pay them, well, they definitely don't want the world to know. They don't give a fuck. No questions asked, and the best part is that they don't want to know your life story and how you're hung up on your sister's best friend.

She stirs, and I look down at her face, running my knuckles over her soft skin. "Sweet dreams, little demon. Tomorrow is a new day to serve your devil."

## ELLINGTON

When I woke up this morning, I hate to admit I was disappointed. I was alone in my bed, and I wasn't tied up. The first thing I did was check my phone. Kira had texted me at some point the night before to let me know she was going to bed early and would see me at the university later on today.

That was it. Nothing from Sin. I had to spend an extra thirty minutes getting ready. I have never had to cover up so many bruises on my body before. Wrists, ankles, neck, fuck, even my thighs had them. Thankfully, it's fall time, so I could wear jeans and a long-sleeved shirt with a thin scarf.

All day, my pussy has been wet due to the way my bra rubs against my nipple piercings. I never knew they could be such a turn-on. Every time I swallow, I flinch like I spent all night vomiting alcohol. My ass is a little tender, but it's not unbearable. I think my shoulders took most of the trauma. My back and arms are really sore. Thank God this day is almost over. As soon as this last class is done, I'm going home and passing the fuck out.

I push open the door to Mr. Hamilton's class and see it's empty. It's not odd that I'm first, but the room feels colder than usual, making me shiver. He sits at his desk, his head down, watching something on his phone. Without a word, I take my seat.

The commotion makes his head snap up, and his dark eyes

glare at me. "What in the fuck are you doing?" he demands, jumping to his feet.

I look around to make sure he's talking to me. When I'm positive I'm the only student in the room, I ask, "Excuse me?"

"Get the fuck out of here, Elli," he shouts, pointing at the door.

"What is wrong with you?" I ask, my brows creasing.

"You are no longer in this class." He growls, "Get the fuck out."

"What?" I jump to my feet. "Since when?" I haven't received an email, and I sure as fuck haven't dropped this class.

He runs his hands over his dark hair. "Look, I did what he told me to do. I don't want any trouble. So get the fuck out of here and don't come back."

"What are you ...?" Easton. "Did Sin tell you to drop me from your class?" I demand.

He gives a rough laugh but doesn't answer me. I make my way over to his desk and grab his arm.

I gasp when he backhands me across the face. "Get the fuck out of here, or I'll throw you out!" he screams.

I cup my stinging face, unable to meet his stare. I can hear his heavy breathing while I hold mine. Then his hand grips my cheeks. I try to pull away, but he lifts my face so I have to look up at him. Tears burn my eyes from his hand on my face.

"You're a fucking whore." My chest tightens at his words as shame washes over me. Why am I the whore when he was fucking me? He never once acted like it was a chore to have sex with me. Now he's disgusted? He approached me, not the other way around. "Go crawl back to him on your hands and knees. Let him treat you like the worthless slut you are."

The first tear falls down my cheek, and his heated eyes watch it. Shoving me away, he causes me to stumble back. I hear the door open behind me as students finally come into class. Without another word, I turn and run out of his classroom, trying to hold in a sob.

Entering the house, I run up to my room and slam my door shut. I don't know who to be more pissed off at—my professor or Easton. He fucking got me removed from my class.

Did the professor show up last night? If he did, what happened? I passed out on the roller coaster and then woke up in my bed. But I'm not sure how much time had passed. Maybe Sin read about us in my diary that was in the bathroom. I mentioned my nights with David in there. But Sin didn't seem mad about what he had read. And when did he get the chance to even speak to David? What did he mean by he did what *he* had been asked? He had to have meant Sin, right? None of it makes sense.

Removing my cell from my back pocket, I toss it onto my bed and go to head toward my bathroom, but I pause. My feet turn, taking me back to my bed. I sit on the side and open my nightstand. Tears run down my face while my finger hovers over the app.

I open it up, and press call.

It rings once, twice, the third time, it stops, and I hold my breath waiting for him—the man in the mask—to speak, but there's only silence. Checking the screen, I watch the clock counting the seconds, so I know he answered.

I sniff, running my sweaty hand down my jeans. "I need to see you," I whisper, my throat closing up.

Professor was right. I'm a whore. I've never pretended not to be. But Sin? He's a Lord. I'll never be anything to him. I'm just something that he can control. The fact that he got me kicked out of class says so.

"Please?" I sniff again, running my hand underneath my runny nose. "I need—"

*Click.*

The phone drops to the floor after he ends the call. I numbly get up, making my way to the bathroom feeling defeated, betrayed, and abandoned. Just like I did all those years ago after my father passed away. No matter what I do, I can't escape it.

## SIXTEEN

## SIN

I enter her French double doors, not even bothering to be quiet. She had been crying. What in the fuck happened that she wanted to see me? The masked me? Not Easton Bradley Sinnett.

I'm fucking pissed. Jealous of myself that she didn't call Sin. Was I not enough yesterday and last night? Did she think I was fucking around? That she doesn't belong to me?

It's been an hour since she called. I was in the middle of something and couldn't get away right then. It fucking killed me to make her wait. But I had to wrap up what I was doing. I couldn't tell her I was coming. I can't chance her recognizing me.

I curse myself when I realize I can't fuck her. She'll know it's me. Maybe I should just tell her and get it over with. Why hide who I am now? It'll just prove my point that she's mine. Has been before she ever even knew it.

Looking over at her bathroom door, I watch her exit, wearing nothing but a towel wrapped underneath her arms. She's got her hair up in a messy bun on top of her head. Her once pretty ice-blue eyes are bloodshot, her face puffy and wet from tears. Has she been crying this entire time?

Stepping toward her, she notices me. Her legs come to a stop, and I watch her break out into tears almost immediately. She runs to me, throws her arms around my neck, and hugs me tightly. Her body shakes against mine while she sobs.

I pick her up, my gloved hands gripping her thighs, and she wraps her legs around my waist. The towel drops to the floor, and I carry her to the bed. Lying down, she curls herself into me. It's like last night all over again, but it's not the real me. It's someone I've made up—mask, gloves, hoodie, and contacts. She's come to need him more than anyone else in her life because I allowed it. Pulling her face out of my chest, she looks up at me, and my body tenses when I look closer at the perfectly placed handprint on her cheek. "Who hit you?" I don't have to hide my voice because I don't recognize myself. Rage like I've never felt before is making my skin tingle and my heart race.

"Doesn't ... matter." She hiccups.

Did she fuck David today? Maybe they got rough, and he slapped her around. The thought makes me want to rip off my mask, hold her down, and fuck her ass to remind her she's mine. If anyone is going to mark her, it should be me.

"Thank you," she whispers.

I tilt my head to the side, confused by her words.

"For saving me," she whispers, and I feel my chest tighten, the rage turning into guilt because I know exactly what she means. That's why she's attached to this version of me. The realization hits me that I might have to play two roles longer than I wanted to.

I tighten my arms around her. She closes her eyes, and I watch fresh tears run down her cheeks, more confused than I've ever been before.

This was supposed to be easy. I no longer have to hide who I am. Not with her. So why can't I remove my mask and let her see who I am?

*She won't trust you.*

Not like I want her to. Sin, she's known since we were kids—the guy she's always had a harmless crush on, and she let me use her for one night. But the mask—he's her savior. She's emotionally attached to him. And no amount of orgasms Sin can give her will break that bond.

# ELLINGTON

### *Thirteen years old*

I SIT OUTSIDE MY MOTHER'S OFFICE ON THE FOURTH FLOOR. *I'VE got a pop in one hand and a Snickers bar in the other. It's summer, so I get to spend my days sitting outside listening to her sessions.*

*Today is a man who has a fetish for role play. He likes to pretend his girlfriend is a stranger. They go to a bar separately. And then he walks over to her, buys her a drink, and ends up fucking her in the bathroom stall while his wife is at home with their children.*

*I'm taking a bite of my candy bar when I hear the elevator ding, signaling it's about to open.*

*My heart races as I jump to my feet. I'm about to run, but it's too late. The door slides open and out steps my mother's new husband.*

*His blue eyes meet mine. "Elli, what are you doing up here?" he asks, tilting his head to the side.*

*My mother's voice comes from the closed door behind me while she talks to her patient. He sighs heavily, walking over to me.*

*I hold my breath, tears already stinging my eyes. I'm going to be in so much trouble.*

*"Elli." He places his hand on his knees, leaning over to be eye*

*level with me, talking softly. "Are you listening to your mother's sessions?"*

*I can't answer. My throat closes up on me. I suddenly can't catch my breath, and I drop my candy bar.*

*"Hey, it's okay." He takes my hand and pulls me over to the waiting room area my mother designed to make her patients feel more at ease when they come to our home. "You're not in trouble, Elli."*

*"I'm not?" I manage to ask through a deep breath.*

*"No." His eyes shoot to my mother's office door and then back to mine. "How about we keep this our little secret?" He reaches up and runs his hand through my dark hair.*

*I bite my bottom lip, tasting my tears. I manage a nod.*

*He gives me a soft smile. "That's a good girl." His hand drops from my hair to my leg, and I jump. "It's okay, Elli. If you keep my secret, I'll keep yours, deal?"*

*I don't know his secret. So I just stare at him, confused by what he means but too afraid to ask.*

*"See," he scoots closer to me, his leg now touching mine. His black slacks rough against my skin. "If your mother knew that you have been listening, you'd be in big trouble."*

*Fresh tears sting my eyes.*

*"She could lose her job, Elli. And you don't want that, do you?"*

*I shake my head. My mother has already been through so much over the past year. Things are just starting to get back to what it was before my father died. "No, sir," I whisper.*

*He reaches up, rubbing the stubble on his chin. After a second, he says, "You know, Elli. I'm now married to your mother." I nod, sniffling. "She's my wife, which makes you my family too." I nod again. My mom tells me we're going to be a happy family and that everything will be okay. "So..." His hand drops back to my thigh. "Why don't you call me Daddy."*

I open my eyes, sitting up straight and gasping for air at the dream. But it's not a dream. It was a living nightmare. One I didn't understand until years later.

Even in death, he haunts me. He's been dead for two years, and he still makes my skin crawl. That was the first time he ever touched me. Years later, I'd willingly given him my virginity.

I'm used to being someone's secret. Someone's whore. That's what I'm good for. My body was made to serve men. He told me all the time how pretty I was. How sexy I was. And how much I turned him on. I hated him. That he made me want him. How good he made me feel. It was a sickness for us both.

Reaching up, I rub my swollen eyes, wishing I could erase the memory from my brain. My head is stuffy, and I have a pounding headache. My hands drop to my lap, and I look up through my lashes to see him standing at the end of my bed.

He came for me.

He's still wearing his black mask, hoodie, gloves, and matching jeans. The red contacts stare at me, and I wonder what he's thinking. I've never broken down like that. Not with him. Not with anyone.

I get up on my hands and knees, crawling to the end of the bed. He stays still as a statue as I rise up on my knees, my hands falling to my thighs. I'm naked. After he hung up on me, I took a hot bath where I cried into a bottle of wine, hoping it would help. It didn't.

"Why don't you fuck me?" I ask, my voice rough.

He says nothing. Just stands there.

I reach out, raising his hoodie just enough so I can grab his black belt and start to unfasten it. His glove-covered hands grip my wrists painfully. I whimper, my breath quickening. "Why don't you fuck me?" I demand through clenched teeth. I'm on the verge of being manic. I can feel it bubbling up inside as my mind slips further and further away from me.

The memories of James, David, and Sin... they're all too much.

He lets go, and I punch him in the chest. "Why? Be a fucking man and fuck me!" I'm screaming, tears stinging my eyes while I gasp to catch my breath. "Can you not get it up?" I try a different angle. Manipulation. Make him prove himself. No man likes to be belittled.

I've never seen his dick. He's tied me up and played with me, but it's never about him. "Come on." I give him a taunting smile. "Fuck my mouth. Come all over my face. Make me your whore." I hold my hands out wide. "That's what I am, right? Fucking use me." Tears fall from my eyes, and he just stands there watching me lose my mind.

I climb off the bed and round the bedpost, coming up beside him. He turns to now face me. "If you're not going to fuck me, then get out," I shout, pointing at the French doors. "Get the fuck out!" I shove his chest, but he doesn't budge. "You're useless," I spit at him. "Nothing but another useless cock who can't fuck."

His hand comes out so fast I don't even have a chance to react. It wraps around my throat, immediately cutting off my air. His fingers have an iron grip as he lifts me off my feet. I don't even fight him. A little piece of my heart breaks because my pussy tightens in anticipation of what's to come. How he'll use me.

He shoves me on the bed before letting go and flipping me onto my stomach. I go to crawl across it, but a hand grabs my hair, yanking me back, and a cry is ripped from my lips. My nipples rubbing on the fitted sheet makes my breath catch. They're still swollen and extremely sensitive. He holds me in place while I hear him open and close my nightstand. Then my arms are yanked behind my back. I feel the familiar roughness of a zip tie before he tightens it in place around my wrists.

Then he's yanking on my hair again, flipping me back over. I lie there looking over his skull mask. It's mainly white with black around the eyes that run down the face as if they're bleeding out. The jaw and teeth are outlined in black as well as the nose. His red eyes are glaring at mine. I can see his chest heaving through his black hoodie and hear his heavy breathing inside his mask. I've pissed him off. *Good.*

His hand lowers to his belt, and he rips it from his black jeans. Then he's wrapping it around my neck, pulling it tight, making it hard to breathe but not impossible.

I know what's coming, but it won't be enough. I need a fight. I want him to take it and make me like it. So I kick him, my foot hitting him in the stomach.

He hunches over, a grunt coming from behind his mask. He grabs my ankle, yanking me off the bed, and I fall on the floor. The impact forces the air from my lungs. I'm on my stomach, and he drops behind me. The feel of his rough jeans against my skin as his knees force mine open makes me whimper.

I hear his zipper a second before his cock slams into my cunt. I go crazy. My body thrashes against his weight. Embarrassed that I was so wet that he didn't even need to ease into me.

Fresh tears fall from my eyes, and he grips the belt, taking away my air.

His body covers mine, and his heavy breathing fills my ear while he pounds into me. I'd sob if I could breathe. The tears fall freely down my face while it rubs against the carpet. I'm going to have a rug burn when he's done with me. It'll match the handprint that I got from David perfectly.

My pussy clenches down on him, my body breaking out in a cold sweat. Suddenly, he pulls out, loosening the belt, and I choke out a sob. I hear the drawer open again behind him and then something cold slides down my ass.

My heart races. "Wait—"

He grabs the belt again, taking away my air and leaning over my back once more. "A whore gets used." His voice is a low, dark whisper, and my heart pounds at the promise it holds. "So shut the fuck up and take it."

# SEVENTEEN

## SIN

Fucking anger has me being irrational. My mind knows it, yet I can't stop. I hated to see her break. To look so fucking broken. She woke up from her nightmare, and I knew exactly what was coming. She had whispered, "Daddy," in her sleep while I was headed for the French doors. I couldn't bring myself to leave her.

I thought maybe she'd want me to hold her once again. Or at the very least just sit here with her. But she started baiting me. I tried my fucking hardest not to touch her. To let her throw her fit and turn my back on her.

But I gave in to my anger. For her. For me. I thought maybe I could make her hate the mask. Get her to realize that I'm not the good guy, after all.

She's lying on the floor facedown, ass up in the air, and I push my cock into it. If she wants to be a fucking whore, then I'll fuck her like one.

I hold the belt tightly around her neck while I watch her ass give way for my dick. I'm not easy. Her body shakes uncontrollably, and I hear her choking as she tries to breathe. My hips move back and forth, hard and fast.

I loosen my hold on the belt, not wanting her to pass out on me just yet, and she coughs before sobs follow.

I push my cock all the way inside, and she screams. Grabbing her hair, I yank her up to her knees. Her back to my front. My legs holding hers wide open.

The position allowing my cock to slide deep into her tight ass. I reach around. One glove-covered hand covers her mouth while the other falls to her pussy. I start to rub my fingers over her cunt before I shove them inside her, fucking it.

I whisper, my mouth by her ear, "Be a good whore, Elli. Come for me." I shouldn't be talking to her, but I can't help myself. If she hasn't figured it out yet, she's not going to tonight. She's got other things on her mind.

She's breathing heavily through her nose, and my cock jerks inside her ass, making her whimper.

"Is this what you wanted?" I keep my voice low. "For me to show you I'm a man? That you belong to me?" I pull my fingers out and slap her breasts, making her flinch and cry into my hand. I do it again, making sure she's got her juices on her body. If she wants me to mark her, then I will.

"You're so fucking wet." She trembles. My hand drops back to her pussy and slaps it, forcing her ass to rock back and forth on my dick. "Such a good little whore." I praise her and push my fingers back into her soaking wet cunt.

Her body struggles, and mumbled sobs fill the room while I enter a third finger. Her pussy clamps down on them, her body stiffening as she comes for me.

I remove them from her pussy and the hand over her mouth to shove my fingers that were just inside her down her throat. She sobs around them but doesn't pull away or fight me anymore.

My hand that was over her mouth drops to wrap my arm

around her waist, and I bounce her up and down on top of me, her ass fucking my cock, knowing I'm about to come. I grip her hair, shove her face down, and come buried deep inside her ass.

She lies there, legs spread wide and sobbing on the floor. With my hand on her back, I pull my cock from her ass and see they're both bloody.

*Fuck.*

I leave her there crying while I stand and walk into the bathroom. I start a bath and then go back to her bedroom. I open the top drawer of her nightstand and grab what I need before shoving it in my pocket. Then I lean over, cutting the zip tie around her wrists.

She lies there, still facedown and sobbing, then brings her hands around to cover her face from me. I grab her, forcing her to stand, and I pick her up in my arms. Carrying her to the bathroom, I place her in the tub, and she pulls her knees to her chest. Pushing herself into the far side of the tub, she's wanting as much space from me as possible.

She's about to get her wish.

I pull the cell out of my pocket that I took from her nightstand and hold it up, waiting for her to see it.

Her bloodshot eyes find mine and narrow, letting me know I succeeded. She hates the masked me. I've hurt her. I was her savior, but now I'm a sick bastard who fucked her ass until she bled while making her like it. I twist the cheaply made phone and break it in half before dropping the now useless cell into the bath water. I turn, giving her my back, and exit the French doors, knowing I will never enter them again as the masked man who saved her. It's time she depends on the real me as much as she did him.

# EIGHTEEN

# SIN

The following afternoon, I walk into Lincoln's office back at the house of Lords. He sits behind his desk, his face in his hands, but it snaps up the moment he hears me entering. "Sin—"

I drop the manila envelope on his desk, cutting him off. With a sigh, he opens it. He looks over the pictures and cell phones and decides to plug in the USB drive to his computer. He's silent for a few minutes as he goes through them. Once finished, he opens his top drawer and pulls out a picture of his own and slaps it down on his desk in front of me. "I find it odd that this woman isn't in any of those photos I just looked at."

I don't have to look down to know it's a picture of Elli tied to a hotel bed. It's the one he had shown me before when he gave me the assignment to find out just who Mr. Hamilton had been fucking.

"You were aware of her involvement. I didn't think you required any more proof," I say through gritted teeth. I don't want anyone knowing of her and David's sexual relationship. Those who know what he was doing, knows what he expected of a woman. And the possessive part of me doesn't want anyone having pictures of her being his whore. I've protected her before, and I'll continue to do so.

He sits back in his seat, crossing his arms over his chest. "I'm guessing she also has to do with you not showing up at the vow ceremony the other night?"

I don't answer.

"Your chosen—"

"Can be someone else's whore," I interrupt him. I'm still in a shitty fucking mood over the fact that Elli called and fucked the masked me last night. Me, the real me that she had spent the night before last with, hasn't heard a fucking word from her.

"That's not how this works, Sin, and you know it." His eyes harden on mine.

Leaning forward, I place my forearms on the cold surface of his mahogany desk. "As an official Lord, I can fuck whoever I want now that the vow ceremony has taken place," I remind him.

"Ellington Asher was not on the list as a chosen," he growls, frustrated with me.

A chosen must be placed on the list by her parents. A male descendant serves the Lords. A Lord who has a daughter may make her serve as well. It's his chance to show the Lords their gratitude. We all play our part in this secret society. "I don't give a fuck if she was on a list or not." I stand.

"Sin," he snaps, pointing at the chair, and I fall into it, rolling my eyes. "I don't care what you do with Ellington, but you must take your chosen."

"And if I don't?" I arch a brow, challenging him.

He picks up the picture of Elli and looks at it for a few seconds before his eyes glare at me over the top. "You either take your chosen, or I take Ellington." He tosses the pic back onto the desk. "And, Sin, you won't like what I do to her."

My hands fist, my jaw clenching. He just fucking threatened

her. You don't go against Linc. Not in here. He runs the house of Lords. The door opens behind me, and a sadistic smile spreads across his face, making his eyes light up like Christmas. "Darling." He stands, pocketing the picture and stepping out from behind his desk to greet his weekly fuck.

The woman walks right up to him, and he pulls her in for a big hug. His eyes are on mine as he lowers his hands to grab her ass in her tight pencil skirt.

I narrow mine on him. Does he really think I give a fuck where he's sticking his dick after what he just said to me about Elli? "Are we done?" I ask, standing. I've got other places to be.

He pulls away from her and gestures to me. "Darling, you know Easton."

The woman turns to face me, and her cheeks redden. My teeth clench when I realize why he was so fucking smug. *It's Elli's mother.* What the fuck is she doing here at the house of Lords, of all places, hugging Lincoln?

"Easton, I didn't see you there." She smiles at me. "I'm sorry." Her wide eyes go to Linc. "I should have called first..."

"You're fine, honey."

*Honey? Darling?*

"Sin will keep our secret, won't you, Sin?" He arches a brow.

They're fucking dating. This can't be happening. I run a hand through my hair. "Of course, Mrs. Asher." I call her by her first husband's last name to piss him off. She'll always be an Asher to me. No matter how many husbands she has.

"It's just that I know you're friends with Elli. I'd never asked you to lie..." She rambles on. "But we haven't told her yet—"

"Darling, you don't have to explain yourself to Sin," he interrupts her.

"Well, they're going to find out soon anyway. The big day will be here before we know it."

"Big—big day?" I stumble over my words, trying to figure what the fuck is going on.

"Yes." She gives me a warm smile. "We're married. We'll be announcing it soon."

My legs give out, and I fall back into my chair. She married him? A Lady is a Lord's wife. And she has rules just like her husband. When a Lord dies, his Lady is gifted to a new Lord. It's so she can't go out and date in the real world and tell all our secrets. I killed her husband two years ago. So why get married now? Some Ladies are remarried within months, others take longer. There are no rules on when they must take another Lord. It all depends on who the Lords want the widow to be with.

"Easton?" She gets my attention, and I look up at her to see her hand on my shoulder. "You okay?"

I jump up, taking a step back from them. "Fine," I lie. What the fuck is going on?

"I'm begging you, Easton, please don't tell Elli. We'll be telling her next week at dinner. We want her to have enough time to adjust to Linc moving in with us."

My heart hammers in my chest. Now his threat holds more weight. He's going to be living in the same house as my girl. It makes sense. Mrs. Asher has a mansion from her first husband—Elli's father. He was a very powerful Lord. Lincoln isn't nearly that high up on the food chain in our world. I mean, come on, he lives here with us at the house of Lords, which is just basically a frat house.

"We'll be there," I tell her, gathering myself and squaring my shoulders.

"Oh, yeah... sure—"

"We'd like to keep it to just the three of us," Linc interrupts her, still giving me that smug smile I want to cut off his fucking face and wear on mine so he has to stare at it. "You know, since we're *family* now."

I give a smug smile of my own. "I understand, but as Elli's boyfriend, I'm sure she'll want me there too. You know, for moral support." I place my hands in the front pockets of my jeans.

Mrs. Asher frowns. "What?" She looks at Linc and then back at me. "You two are dating?"

"Yes, ma'am." I nod.

Her frown deepens, looking back at Linc and then to me. "But... you're a senior at the university. And you've been initiated."

*Fuck.*

She goes on, "Elli isn't a chosen."

"Correct," Linc agrees, and I want to snap his fucking neck.

"So you're Elli's boyfriend, and you have a chosen? You're cheating on my daughter?" She speaks slowly as if her mind isn't comprehending what she's saying but trying to make sense of it.

"No—"

"Darling, you know how these things work." He chuckles, not letting me finish. "And so do they. It'll be all right."

My head tilts at his words. Why the fuck is he defending me now?

"I guess so." She nods to herself, trying to wrap her brain around why her daughter would allow her boyfriend to fuck other women as if she raised her to have more self-respect than that. She didn't, but that's beside the point.

Without another word, I turn and exit his office. I'm practically running down the staircase when I see a very fucked-up-looking Matt exiting our personal gym on the second floor. He's bleeding from the head and face. He looks to be a little lost.

I ignore him. Guys fight all the time within the house. Tell a hundred men they can't have sex for three years and well ... it never ends well. They end up taking out their frustration somehow.

I shove the front double doors open and pull out my cell. It only takes me a second to find the information that I need. Then I'm getting in my car and tearing out of the parking lot.

# ELLINGTON

WALKING ACROSS CAMPUS, I PULL MY BAG HIGHER UP ON MY shoulder. My mind goes to last night. I didn't get any sleep after my hero left. My head still hurts from crying so hard and so does my ass from him fucking it.

He proved that he was not the guy I thought he was. Maybe it's for the best. I could feel myself getting attached emotionally. Physically needing someone and mentally needing someone are two very different things.

My cell rings, and I pull it out of my pocket to see it's Kira. "Good afternoon," I answer. "Where are you?" She wasn't at the university today. Well, if she was, I missed her.

She yawns. "I'm still in bed."

I frown. "You're at home?" I bite my bottom lip, wanting to ask if Sin is there, but don't. If he can ignore me, then I can ignore him too.

"No. I'm in a bed," she says cryptically.

"Ah, I see. I need to meet this new boyfriend." I laugh, coming up to the parking lot.

"Soon," she says and then yawns again. "Want to go to the marina tonight? Just you and me?"

"Yes." I nod to myself. I could use a girls' night.

She promises to text me in a few hours, and we hang up. I'm opening my car door when I hear the screeching of tires. Looking up, I see Sin's car flying toward me. He brings it to a quick halt right behind my car, blocking mine in my spot since I'm parked up against a curb.

"Get in," he orders me through his passenger-side window.

I walk over to him and bend over to see him clenching the steering wheel. "Good afternoon to you too," I say, flipping my hair over my shoulder. I haven't heard from him. Not one word.

His eyes snap to mine, and I frown when I see them narrowed on me. "Everything okay?" I ask.

"Get in the car, Elli," he snaps.

I roll my eyes, straighten my back, and walk over to my car. "You're not going to talk to me like that," I holler over my shoulder. In bed and out in public are two very different things. Opening my door, I go to get into my car when his hand grips my upper arm. He jerks me from my car. "Hey!" I try to get away, but he drags me to his car and pushes me into my passenger side, slamming the door shut. "Sin, I can't just leave my car here," I protest, but he's already speeding away, kids jumping out of the way to keep from getting run over by him. "What the fuck is your problem?"

He remains silent but turns up the radio, and "I Hate everything About You" by Three Days Grace drowns out anything I could possibly say.

Crossing my arms over my chest, I let out a huff and watch the trees fly by as he speeds down the road. It only takes me a second to realize he's headed to my house. Now I'm really concerned. If he wanted to go to my house, then why didn't he just let me drive my car? I could have followed him. Well, okay. A quick look shows he's going almost a hundred miles an hour. I speed but, damn, not that much.

My body jerks when he slams on his brakes in my driveway. He gets out, slamming his car door. I get out much slower but start running up the stairs when I see him entering the house.

"Sin, what in the fuck are we doing?" I bark out, taking the stairs two at a time to catch up with him. He's much taller than me, so I can't get there as fast. I enter my room, and he's pulling a suitcase out from under my bed and starts opening drawers, tossing stuff into it. "Are you kidnapping me?" I ask, as somewhat of a joke, laughing it off. Because that's ridiculous, right? But my pulse accelerates at the thought. A rush of adrenaline makes my pussy clench. That's another fantasy in my diary. And I know he's read some of at least one of them.

He stops what he's doing and stalks over to me. My breath catches at the look in his eyes. He did not find that funny. Coming to a stop, he reaches out and cups my face. My lips part on their own, and he runs his thumb over them. "Is that what's about to happen, Elli? Going to make me drag you out of this house against your will?"

"No." I'd go anywhere with him. But the question is, why the urgency? Why now? Where are we going?

Leaning in, he gently gives me a soft kiss on my forehead and then pulls away. "Help me pack your bag."

AN HOUR LATER, WE'RE PULLING UP TO THE HOUSE OF LORDS. I've been here before. They have a lot of big parties. But I've never been here with an actual Lord. Just Kira. We dance, get trashed, and Uber home.

He parks his car and gets out a lot slower this time. Popping his trunk, he grabs my suitcase, then opens my door for me. "How long are we staying here?" I ask. I haven't spoken to him since he threatened to drag me out of my house. But he packed a lot of my things, enough for more than one overnight stay.

"You'll live here with me." He grabs my hand and drags me up the stone steps.

I give a rough laugh. "Live? Sin, I can't live here." With him? Since when did we become a couple just because I let him fuck me? I mean, he did read my diary, so he knows how I've felt about him for years. But that doesn't mean he feels the same, right?

"Well, you're not staying there," he argues with a clipped tone.

"Where? My home?" What the hell is he talking about?

We enter the house that I'm pretty sure was once an elaborate hotel, and it's fucking chaos. Men and women everywhere. The house smells of weed and sex. You can tell they had a party last night due to the beer cans and empty glass bottles of liquor. Trash bags sit up against the walls in the hallway that are already full but haven't been taken out yet.

He comes up to a door on the first floor and pushes it open. I step inside and look around as he closes it behind us. It's got a single bed that to my surprise is made with white sheets and a duvet. Two white pillows to match. One dresser and a door that he walks into and drops my bag. It makes me wonder when he stayed here last. Does he bring women here? Or does he stay at their place?

"That's the bathroom," he says, exiting.

I nod my head and walk in there, trying to figure out what in the fuck I'm doing here and how long I will willingly stay. Because if there's one thing I know about Sin—if I decide to leave, he'll tie me to that bed and make me stay. And honestly, that doesn't sound too bad.

# NINETEEN

# SIN

No way in hell will she stay at her house. Her mother has brought another evil man into their lives. Now, I'm not sure it's her fault. She probably doesn't know that Lincoln is using her to climb the social ladder within the Lords.

What I can't figure out is how he was able to pull it off. To get the Lords to agree for him to marry her? A Lord doesn't always need permission to marry who they want. Usually, it's set up through the families. By the time we graduate from Barrington, our weddings will already be planned. But it's different when you're a Lord's widow. The Lady very rarely gets to choose the Lord she is re-gifted to. Mrs. Asher looked to really be in love with Linc, which makes me believe that he's been winning her over for the past two years. Women are easy to manipulate. Especially a grieving woman who lost her second husband. It makes her vulnerable and needy to anyone offering her any type of attention.

But I know everything I need to know after he threatened Elli. And I won't leave her at that house for Linc to take what's mine. Willingly or by force.

Elli is very fragile and can easily be manipulated. I know

because I've done it. And I won't stand by and let Linc have his way with something that is mine. I've waited too long to get her where I want her. And no one will stand in my way. Especially not some fucking low-level Lord on a power trip.

My bedroom door opens, and I look up to see a woman enter. She's got her long dark hair up in a high ponytail. Her makeup is caked on like she's about to do a photo shoot of some kind, and she's wearing the tiniest bikini I've ever seen. Two little triangles cover her fake tits and an even smaller one covers her pussy. She's dressed in a pair of heels and clearly has not been swimming due to the fact that she's still dry.

Amelia Lane Cleary stands in my room, hands on her hips, and her injected lips smiling.

"Get the fuck out of my room." I point at the door.

Instead, she steps farther inside, closer to me. "You're lucky I'm not the jealous type. Otherwise, I'd be insecure that you didn't show for our vow ceremony." She places her hand on my chest and cocks her head. Her tongue pokes out to run across her red lips. As if she truly thinks that'll do something for me. It doesn't.

I grab her upper arm and yank her toward the door.

"Sin—"

I stop and turn to see Elli has stepped out of the bathroom. Her gorgeous eyes go from mine to the half-naked girl in my grasp.

"She was just leaving," I growl through gritted teeth, hating that I have to explain myself but also knowing I need to defuse the current situation that Amelia has put me in.

Pursing her lips, Elli goes back into the bathroom and grabs her bag. "No, I was just leaving."

I let go of the bitch on my arm and step in front of Elli. "You're not going anywhere."

Her narrowed eyes tell me she's going to run out of here, and I'm going to have to make her stay. Good, it'll give me a reason to chain her up.

"You're not supposed to be here," Amelia says from behind me. "You're not a chosen."

I close my eyes and take a deep breath. One problem at a time. I let go of Elli and turn to face Amelia. I pull her out of the room and slam the door shut behind me. Once in the hallway, I yank her to me. "Stay the fuck out of my room." She's lying. Any woman can be here at any time. She's just trying to piss off Elli, and it's working.

She huffs. "Lincoln called me. Said you wanted to see me. But here you are." She rolls her eyes so hard I hope she's having a seizure. "With her," she adds with a huff.

Of course, he put her up to this. He's fucking with my life.

"Have you told her?" she goes on.

My jaw clenches, refusing to answer that question.

"She's going to find out, Sin. Sooner or later. I don't mind if you play with her for now, but the time will come when you have to let her go."

Looking at my door, I think of my options. I have to pacify Linc for now. Running a hand through my hair, I say, "I'll call you." Then I turn, giving her my back, but she grabs hold of my arm and yanks me to a stop.

"Promise?" Her eyes drop to my jeans and slowly run up to meet my eyes, pushing her body into mine.

My fingers curl around her upper arms, digging them into her skin, and she whimpers, her knees buckling, but I keep her upright. "I said I'll fucking call you. Now go be a good little bitch and run along until I need you." Shoving her away, I turn and enter my bedroom only to find it empty. "Elli?" I bark out but get nothing. The bathroom is also clear. "Fuck." I hurry through the house, wondering how she got by me, and out the front door to see her getting in my sister's car.

"Elli?" I bark out, but she ignores me, falling into the passenger seat before Kira takes off. "Goddammit."

# ELLINGTON

## *Thirteen years old*

I HOLD MY DIARY CLOSE TO MY CHEST AS I WALK DOWN THE hallway. I see the door open, so I step inside the room.

"Elli." James looks up at me from behind his desk. "Come. Have a seat." I sit down on the black leather couch, and he gives me a soft smile. "What did you learn today?"

My stepdad found out last week that I've been listening in on my mother's sessions. He said he promised he wouldn't tell on me, but in order for him to keep my secret, I had to take notes and share them with him. "Age play," I say softly.

"Oh," he says excitedly and gets up, coming around his desk to be closer to me. He sits down on the couch. "Go on."

"Mr. Robbins likes to be his wife's daddy."

"How so?"

Swallowing, I direct my eyes back to the page. "He likes her to pretend to be his baby, and she calls him Daddy."

"Like how I have you call me Daddy?" he asks, and I nod. "See, Elli, it's okay to call me Daddy when we're alone. We're not the only ones who do it." I bite my bottom lip nervously, and he frowns. "What is it?"

"He has her wear a diaper. I don't want to wear one."

Giving me a soft smile, he chuckles. "No diaper. What about a pacifier?" He reaches up and runs his thumb gently over my lips, my breathing picking up at the touch. "You'd look so pretty with something in your mouth, Elli."

I pull back, and he drops his hand to his lap. My eyes are on my hands, and I try to calm my racing heart. "I guess..." I whisper, shrugging.

"That's my good girl," he says, gently pushing my hair behind my ear, and I raise my eyes to look at him. I like the way that sounds, and by the smile he's giving me, he does too. "What if I told you I already have one for you?" Getting up, he walks over to his desk and opens a drawer. He pulls out a black box and comes back to sit next to me. Holding it out, he says, "Go ahead, open it."

Reaching out, I push the lid open and see a black pacifier. Daddy's girl is written across it in pink letters. I've seen these before. My mom's friend has a baby, and she carries five everywhere she goes for her son. "It looks different," I speak quietly.

He sets the box down next to him on the couch and removes it. "It is." Holding it in his hands, he places it in front of me. "This is called a pacifier with a leather belt harness."

I shift in my seat, and he notices. "There's nothing wrong with being nervous, Elli. If you don't like it, I'll take it off."

I run my sweaty hands along my jeans. "What does it do?" I ask, wanting to know. Mr. Robbins said that his wife loves hers. That she sucks on it all the time. And how much it turns him on watching her.

"This"—he points at the leather belt—"goes around your head. It's like a belt you wear with your jeans. It fastens in place at the back of your head."

My eyes widen, my pulse jumping in my neck. "So I can't take it off."

He nods. "You won't be able to. But I can."

I shift again, and a funny feeling between my legs makes my breath quicken. "I don't know—"

"All you have to do is tap the pacifier with your hand, and I'll remove it," he interrupts me.

I swallow the lump in my throat, but I can't deny that my thighs have been clenched this entire time. My curiosity has me wanting to try it. To see why Mr. Robbins's wife loves it so much.

*Letting out a long breath, I nod. He said he'll take it off if I didn't like it.*

*"That's such a good girl." He smiles at me.*

*There are those words again, and the butterflies return to my stomach.*

*James gets up from the couch to stand in front of me. "Open for me," he commands, and I lick my lips before doing as he asks.*

*Putting it in my mouth, he wraps the leather around my head, and my breathing accelerates, making my pulse race.*

*"Deep breaths through your nose, baby. Breathe for me." He pulls away, and I look up at him through my lashes. "Good girl." He runs his fingers over the pacifier in my mouth.*

*I taste the rubber, my tongue exploring the weird shape. It doesn't feel as big as it looked in the box.*

*"How does that feel?" James tugs on the belt to see if it's too tight or too loose. I'm not sure.*

*I nod since that's all I can do.*

*He walks over to his desk and picks up his cell. "I'm going to set a timer for ten minutes. Think you can suck on it that long?"*

*I nod again and begin to do just that. It's like having a sucker. But when it rests in your mouth, you suck on it instead of lick it. But this doesn't have a flavor. Cherry is my favorite.*

*He sits down at his desk and begins to work on his computer, dismissing me while I sit here trying my hardest to be his good girl.*

I TOSS BACK MY VODKA, TRYING TO DROWN MY MEMORIES. It's not working. James played on the fact that I used to listen in on my mother's sessions. He would have me take notes and then discuss them with him. It was his way of trapping me. The more I knew, the more he could take it to my mother, and I'd be in trouble.

I wish I had understood that then. That I wouldn't have been so stupid. He taught me that it was okay to like what I liked. For my body to crave what it craved. I hated him for it. And I hate myself even more. That I got off on it.

I try to tell myself that I didn't know better. But I did. I knew listening in on the sessions was wrong. I knew that wanting those things I heard was wrong. I knew letting him touch me was wrong. But it felt so good. Being wanted felt good. I had felt lost and ignored for so long. I was lonely, until I wasn't.

"You okay?" Kira asks me, her hand on my shoulder making me jump.

I nod, but it's a lie. I couldn't tell you the last time I felt okay or when things were normal. Or I felt normal.

"Kira?" I hear a girl I know by the name of Sarah call out. She's dating another Lord. We saw them when we first arrived. "I'll be right back," Kira tells me.

I wave her off, not caring that she leaves me here. After I ran out of Sin's bedroom at the house of Lords, she gave me a ride to her house. I didn't ask why she was there, and thankfully, she didn't ask me. I'm not ready to tell her I've slept with her brother. She's the only stable thing I've ever had in my life, and I don't want to lose that over dick.

She took me back to the university, and I got my car and followed her to her house. We watched a movie then got ready to go out. There's a party at the marina tonight and I need to get out and drink until I pass out. Otherwise, I'd sit at home in my room all alone, staring at the broken cell phone that no longer reaches the one person I need.

I stand at the boating house, looking out of the floor-to-ceiling windows, watching kids jump from boat to boat. Some even fall into the water and their friends pull them out while they laugh at them. I wish I was at that level of drunkenness. Hell, I'd settle for some ecstasy right now. Anything to fuck me up.

I haven't been here in years. It makes me miss my old life. The one when my father was still alive. After he passed, my mother sold his yacht. Said we didn't need it. Its name was Ellington. I know it sounds stupid, but I felt like it was just another way to erase me. Another way to be forgotten. I never mattered. Not to her and not to her career. But my father? I was his girl. My father was a Lord, but my mother worked for them. Her job came before anything else. Even she and my father fought over it.

"Hey, Elli." I hear my name being called from behind me.

I turn and give Mack a smile. "Hey." I take a step closer to him. By the way his brows rise, he thinks I'm interested all of a sudden. I just want to feel something. I've lost my masked man, David, and now Sin as a friend. I'm all alone.

"Are you here with anyone?" he asks, looking around.

"No." Just as the word leaves my lips, an arm falls over my shoulders.

"There you are, baby." Sin pulls me into his side.

The use of *baby* makes me cringe. He's never called me that, and I know it's because of Mack.

"Who's your friend?" Sin goes on, and I wiggle out from under his hold and shove him away, but of course he doesn't budge. I should have known he'd show up. The place is crawling with Lords tonight.

"Mack," he answers timidly, reaching out his right hand. Sin doesn't move to shake it.

I roll my eyes, taking a drink of my vodka. I saw the way he grabbed the girl in his room. The way she looked at him like she'd do anything to please him. I know that look because I do it too.

I'm not the girl a guy falls in love with. I'm the girl he fucks until she comes around.

Mack awkwardly looks around and then turns, giving us his back before walking off into the crowd. "Go away, Sin," I tell him. "I'm not here with you."

He steps into me, his hard chest bumping mine, and I swallow nervously at the look in his eyes glaring down into mine. "Do I need to fuck that attitude out of you, little demon?"

I don't answer.

He reaches up this time to cup my cheek. "Get on your knees and open your mouth."

I snort. Yeah, right. So everyone here can record it? You can't do shit without kids pulling their cells out and posting it on the internet. "That's not happening." I give him my back.

A hand tangles in my hair, yanking my back to his front. His free hand goes around my throat, holding me in place, and whispers in my ear, "You either drop to your knees and open that mouth, or I bend you over and fuck that ass."

I whimper, and the mention of my ass has my breathing pick up. It still hurts from the masked man last night. He was so rough and made me bleed. And I liked it. I sat in the bathtub for over an hour just staring at the cell that he broke. His last *fuck you*. What did I do that pissed him off so much? That I said his dick was worthless? He proved it wasn't. Why take away my only line of communication?

"Which one will it be, Elli?" Sin interrupts my thoughts.

Sucking in a deep breath, I manage to growl, "Fuck you, Sin."

"Ass, it is." He starts pushing me forward toward a narrow set of stairs with the hand tangled in my hair, but I'm saved as Jayce walks up to him.

"Hey, man. I need to speak to you." His eyes go from Sin's to mine. "It's important."

Sin lets go of me, and I don't even look back. I down more of my vodka while I go off to find Kira. I thought coming here tonight would be fun, but now that Sin's here, I need to go.

# TWENTY

## SIN

"Make it quick, Jayce," I say through gritted teeth as I watch her walk away. I arrived just in time to see her talk to that stupid fucker Mack. He's got a thing for her. I can't blame the guy, but I watched the way his body reacted to her story when she read it in front of Mr. Hamilton's class. Over my dead body will he get a chance with my girl. He's too timid. He could never give her what she wants. Needs. Not like I can.

I tune Jayce out while I imagine where and how I'll take her tonight. I gave her the option of mouth or ass because I wanted to see just how far she'd let me go. I know her ass is sore, but she wasn't going to tell me no.

If I wasn't so jealous, I'd push her to her knees and fuck her mouth right here in front of everyone to let them see that she's mine. But even I know I can't do it. I don't want to share her. I don't even want to give anyone the image of her on her knees for me. I'd stab a man's eyes out if they saw her in such a state.

"Dude, are you even listening to me?" Jayce hits my shoulder.

"No," I answer honestly.

"Sin—"

"Call me tomorrow," I interrupt and push past him, refusing to let her out of my sight. Coming up behind her, I see the bastard is talking to her again. "There you are, little demon." I walk up to them. I noticed the way she tensed at me calling her baby. I can guess why.

Mack jumps back and then turns to run.

"I can't have friends?" she growls.

"I've known you all my life. Mack is not your friend." The only close friend she has is my sister.

"Not like I whipped out his dick and sucked it."

My jaw clenches. "Just how many men are you fucking right now? You know, besides me and David?" Here's her chance. Will she be honest with me? And what will I do if she's not?

Her fists clench. "Why? You going to take care of them like you did David?"

How does she know I took care of David? I'm assuming she's guessing. I showed up in her class with my friends and kicked him out. He had plans to come over the night that I fucked her. And then the next day, she's no longer in his class? She's smart enough to figure it out. I never did force her to tell me who slapped her or find out if he fucked her one last time. But I'll get those answers later.

Smiling, I watch her eyes narrow to slits at the fact that I just silently confirmed it was me.

"There is actually one more." She throws back a smug smile. "I was with him last night," she admits, stepping into me. "And I've never had to fake it with him." She turns, giving me her back, and walks away once again, thinking she just won.

I<small>T'S</small> <small>BEEN TWO HOURS SINCE SHE GOT IN MY FACE AND</small> practically told me that the other guy she's been fucking was better than me. *Me?* Funny, considering the other guy is me.

I can't wait to see the look in her eyes when I tell her the good news. That she's been coming for me all along.

When she walked away, I ran to my car, got what I needed, then sat back while sipping on a beer. Just waiting. I've watched her from a distance. Letting her take her time. Thinking she's actually done something by telling me someone else has been fucking her and she's been faking it with me.

It was so cute. But it'll be even sweeter when I see her reaction. I never expected her to know who I was in the mask, but it's time. Enough with this shit. She actually thinks that bastard is better than me.

I watch her walk down the dock from the boat she was on with a drink in one hand and her cell in the other. I get up from my spot and follow not far behind her. She makes her way toward the parking lot.

When she turns to walk in my direction, I duck back behind a corner. I wait for her to walk by, then I jump out behind her and throw a hood over her head. She starts screaming, but you can barely hear it over the music from the nearby boats.

I pull her arms behind her back and zip-tie them tightly. Then I pick her up and carry her over to the other side of the marina where my father keeps one of his boats. She fights, her body thrashing while she screams profanities through the hood. I smile. She needs to save her energy.

# ELLINGTON

I'm placed on my ass, and I let out a deep breath. "Sin," I growl, fighting the restraints that hold my hands behind my back. "What the fuck are you doing?" I shout.

Then I try to take a calming breath. The drinks started to hit me a while ago, and my body is swaying. No, rocking?

Am I moving, or is he moving? I'm not sure. Hot air falls on my face from the hood, making the hair inside the dark material stick to my cheeks. I'm jolted to a stop, my body swaying forward.

The hood is ripped from my head, and I shake it to try to free my hair from sticking to my wet face. "East—" His name dies on my lips when I look up to see a set of red eyes staring down at me. "What—" I can't form a sentence because my mind is running wild.

The masked man stands in front of me in a hoodie, jeans, black gloves, and his mask. His contacts seem to glow in the middle of the night while he stands before me. My heart races when my eyes drop to the chain that is in his right hand.

*Was he at the party?* Had he seen me with Sin? Mack? Is he mad? Jealous? He left me. I'm not going to play this game with him anymore. I will not rely on him. "What the fuck do you want?" I yell, jumping to my feet.

He reaches out, his hand shoving my chest and knocking me back down onto the white seat that I now realize is a boat. Taking a quick look around, I shiver at the cool air and see the speed boat rocking back and forth on the waves. No other boats are in sight, but I can see the marina to the right of us. We're far enough that if I yelled, no one would hear me. But close enough that the lights help us see out here in the middle of the lake.

I go to open my mouth to tell him to fuck off, but his hands grab at me. Gripping my hair, he holds my head down while his other hand shoves me onto my stomach. He straddles my back and wraps the chain around my neck. I hear a clicking noise, and his body weight is gone.

My arms are all of a sudden free, and I stand to face him on shaky legs. "What the fuck?" I reach up and feel the chain wrapped around my neck. It's not tight enough to cut off my air, but it's also not loose.

I slam my hands into his chest. He grabs my dress and rips it clear off my body. The fabric gives way to his strength like tearing a piece of paper, leaving me in nothing but my thong. I didn't have a bra on, and my heels are long gone. I lost them at some point when I was kicking and screaming with the hood over my head.

"What the hell is wrong with you?" I scream, my hands lifting to cover my naked breasts as if he's never seen them before.

Then he reaches up and grabs the top of the skull mask. I hold my breath as he rips it off his face. I stare wide-eyed at Sin, heart pounding, pulse racing, and blood rushing in my ears. My hands drop to my sides like deadweight, no longer able to hold them up at what I see.

"Hello, little demon." He smirks. Lifting his hand, he runs it through his hair, giving it that messy look I love so much.

"No," I breathe, shaking my head. "It can't be."

He steps into me, and I don't retreat. He cups my face, and my lips part, trying to make sense of it all. How much did I have to drink? A lot. But I didn't take any drugs. How is this possible?

"Sin?" His name trembles on my lips, and my knees threaten to buckle.

"Surprise." Then he grabs my waist and throws me over the front of the boat.

# TWENTY-ONE

## SIN

I hear her splash into the water, then a gasp follows. "EASTON!" she screams.

I place my shoe on the side of the bow, my forearm resting on my bent leg. I turn on the spotlight to see her better in the water. Her hands grabbing at the chain I wrapped around her neck that I secured with a padlock.

She manages to swim over to the boat; I didn't throw her too far out. Her hands slap at the front of it, trying to grip anything so she can crawl out of the water, but the bow sits too high for that. "Sin..." She's gasping.

"How long do you think you can swim until you get tired, Elli?" I call out.

"I...fucking... hate you." She starts crying. Her hands continue to slap against the bow.

"You didn't last night. You told me I was your savior," I remind her. "Oh, wait. That was the other man you thought you were fucking."

She bares her white teeth, gripping the chain around her neck.

I freed her hands, but the added ten pounds to her neck is going to wear her out real soon. I made sure not to secure it too tight, but enough that she can't just lift it over her head.

"Speaking of last night—I hope your ass isn't still bleeding. I'd hate for you to attract a shark," I lie, trying to scare her. There aren't any sharks in these waters.

"EASTON!" she screams, her hands slapping the water, making it splash up in her face.

She tries a new position, floating on her back to give her body a second to rest, but her head goes under. She gasps, righting herself once again. I locked the chain at the nape of her neck for that very reason. To pull her down. If the excess chain was in the front, she could hold it in her hands to loosen the weight pulling on her neck while her legs tread water. I want her to be using both her arms and legs. It'll wear her out faster.

I look over to the back of the boat where the swim deck is. She hasn't thought to swim over to it. I'm not even sure if she can see it at all. The spotlight I have on her is blinding. People in life-or-death situations don't usually stop and think rationally. They panic.

"Pl-ease," she chokes out.

"Please what, little demon?" I ask, removing my black gloves and throwing them to the side, getting comfortable.

I didn't plan on doing this tonight, but I decided she needed to know who I was. The real me. That I was the man she's come to need. I'm the guy who saves her. Even if I'm the one who puts her in these life-threatening situations.

Her head ducks under water, and she pops up a second later, sucking in breaths between sobs. It goes under again, and this time when she pops up, she's a little farther away. The distance enough to make me start worrying.

She falls under once more, and I wait, watching for her to

come back up. After a second, I stand straighter. "Elli?" I call out, but all I see are the ripples on top of the dark lake.

She's fucking with me, trying to make me think she's sinking to the bottom. She's not.

But as my eyes scan the water, my pulse accelerates. She had been drinking quite a bit.

Panic grips my chest when I see she hasn't surfaced. I reach up and yank the hoodie up and over my head while kicking off my shoes before I dive in where I saw her last. Trying to get close enough but not hit her.

I immediately come back up, spinning around. "Elli?" I shout before going back under just to double-check, and my fear doubles when she's nowhere to be seen. Diving down again, I open my eyes but can't see much. My legs kick as my hands reach out aimlessly. I feel something. It's the chain. Wrapping it around my fist, I yank on it, feeling her body hit mine. Letting go of the chain, I wrap my arm around her waist and swim to the surface, pulling her with me.

Cold air hits my face when I suck in a breath. "Elli?" I turn her around, and her head lies back, exposing her reddened neck with the chain still around it.

I grip her face with my free hand. "El—"

Before I can finish, her eyes pop open, and she rams her forehead into my face, making my vision go black and pain explode between my eyes. "Fffuucckkk!"

## ELLINGTON

I shove off his chest, my foot kicking it in the process, and start swimming toward the swim deck, gasping for air now that I'm no longer fake drowning. I'm almost there when I'm yanked back by the chain around my neck, cutting off what little air I was already getting.

"Wanna play games with the devil? Let's see what you got, little demon." He yanks me over to the back of the boat by the chain and out of the water.

I fall onto the swim deck, my head now pounding. I can feel blood running from my forehead where I made contact with his nose. I'm on my back while he sits between my shaking legs. I don't have the energy to push him away, let alone fight him at the moment.

He hovers over me, blood dripping from his busted nose and onto my chest and face. I lick my lips, and my mouth tastes like I'm sucking on pennies. I'm not sure if it's his or mine at this point.

I'm still gasping for breath when he smiles down at me. "Fuck, I love you," he whispers, his hand wrapped around my neck, crushing the chain into my already sensitive skin. "Remember that when I rip you apart."

My chest heaves, arms heavy and down to my sides. A whimper escapes my parted lips at his lie. He doesn't love me, but I can't deny the way my heart flutters at the words.

Letting go of me, he kneels on the swim deck and throws my legs over his shoulders and lowers his bloody face to my pussy.

I might as well be tied down because I can't move. My body's exhausted, my thighs are screaming, and my arms are tired. I lay on pieces of the chain, and they dig into my back, but I don't have the strength to move it. Pretty sure my hair is tangled in it too.

My back and neck arch when he shoves a finger into me, then two. A scream gets lodged in my throat when I feel a third. He pushes them in and out, fucking me while my body rocks back and forth on the roughness of the swim deck. Removing them, he licks my cunt. His tongue flicks my piercing before pulling it into his mouth.

"Sin," I cry out, arching again, the chain pulling at the angle. I'd risk my life for this. People have died for less.

My heavy eyes stare up at the stars littering the black sky, the sound of the waves rocking the boat and the feel of his mouth between my legs have the world spinning.

# TWENTY-TWO

# SIN

I sit up and look down at her spread legs. Her cum and my blood are smeared all over her smooth cunt. "Perfect," I whisper before bringing my hand down to slap it.

She jerks, crying out into the night.

Lowering my head, I suck on her nipple piercings, pulling them into my mouth. Her hands grab ahold of my hair, gently tugging at the scalp. She has no energy left. No strength. Good.

I grip her cheeks, shoving my tongue into her already parted lips. She kisses me back just as hungrily, moaning at the taste of copper mixed with her sweetness.

Pulling away, I sit up and unzip my wet jeans. I pull my hard cock out and run the head of my dick over her pussy, smearing the blood and cum. Slowly, I push inside her. Her breath catches, arching her back.

I reach up, slide my fingers between her neck and the chain, and lift her to straddle me.

Her eyes are now level with mine. My cock throbs inside her cunt while I push all the wet hair from her face. What's left of her makeup is smeared down her cheeks. The most gorgeous ice-blue eyes are so heavy she can't keep them open. Running my hand up her back, I grip the base of the chain in my hand and pull on it, cutting off her air while I bounce her up and down on my cock.

My lips find hers, and I devour them. I'm not getting much back from her, but it doesn't matter. I accomplished what I set out to do. She now understands that she's mine. And I'll do whatever I have to do to remind her who she belongs to.

# ELLINGTON

*MY SINFUL, SINFUL, LITTLE DEMON*
 *In my dreams, you will see*
 *That you are what I want you to be*
 *You're my demon*
 *I'm your devil*
 *And I will keep you chained in hell forever*

I STARE AT THE DIARY OPENED ON THE FIRST PAGE LYING ON the bed. The chain that was wrapped around my neck last night lies down the center of the pages next to the words written in Sin's handwriting.

Looking up and around the room, I see I'm in his bedroom back at his parents' house. I don't remember how we got here. Did he bring me here? If so, where is he?

I don't remember anything past us fucking on the swim deck. My heavy eyes fell closed during my second orgasm, and when I opened them, I was here and it was morning. A blank diary sits next to me. I've spent hours reading over the first page, trying to make sense of it all.

My cell beeps, signaling a text, and I pick it up to see it's Kira confirming our plans for tonight. She's either not here at her parents' or she has no idea I'm in her brother's room down the hall from hers.

Rising to my feet, I manage to make my way to his bathroom with just a little help from his wall. Turning on the lights, I see I've got bruises around my neck from the chain. Inspecting my knees, I have them there from the swim deck as well and one on my hip from when he pulled me up onto the boat.

Turning on his shower, I step inside and fall over. My shoulder hits the wall, making me groan. Why did I drink so much? I know why. To drown out the memories that were screaming in my head. But they always come back. You can't erase real life. No matter how much you try.

Falling to the shower floor, I sit under the sprayer and close my eyes as the warm water runs over me like a downpour. My mind is fucked up right now. Sin is the mystery man. I should have known, right? I should have recognized his voice. The way he walked. The hoodie. He wore one just like it at the *Freak Show*. But come on, I too have a solid black hoodie. So I can't hate myself for that one. But there had to have been other signs I just chose to miss. Or maybe I wanted the mystery man to remain just that. He didn't know the real me. Or so I thought.

How many times has he come to visit me in the past two years? More than I can count. He hardly ever spoke. And when he did, his voice was low. Barely a whisper. Hell, at times, my mind thought I heard him speak, but I was just hearing things. The mind likes to play tricks on itself.

I have listened in on enough of my mother's sessions to know that people can convince themselves things aren't real. I thought the masked man was someone I didn't know. Therefore, I never even thought to look for similarities, which brings me to another thought.

Easton Bradley Sinnett killed my stepdad.

That thought hits me like David's hand to my face. Shock and surprise make my chest tighten. Why? It wasn't for me. So what had James done to deserve to be killed? I'm not sad about it, but I am curious. From what I've heard over the years, the Lords take care of their own. Which could mean something good or bad. Depending on what you've done for them, their society can make you disappear. Make it look like you never existed.

And James's finger? Why did Sin have to take his finger and phone? What was on there that was so important? I'll never know. Sin would never tell me, and I'd never ask.

Managing to get myself up off the shower floor, I start to wash my hair with his shampoo. I learned a lot last night. Not only about Sin but also myself. I wanted to make him jealous with Mack. I wanted to push him to see how far he'd go. I got my answer. A part of me wants to know how much further he'll go before he breaks.

---

I'M WALKING DOWN THE HALL, A DIARY IN MY HAND. I FOUND my car in Sin's parents' driveway this morning. Once again, I had no clue how it got there. But I quickly ran by my house this morning on my way to the university. I catch sight of Sin walking toward me with Jayce, but he doesn't see me. He's too busy staring down at his phone, typing away. It makes me wonder who it is he's talking to.

So I'm good enough to fuck but not text or call? Not sure why I'm surprised. Or why I'm jealous. I'm more pissed off at the fact that he's the masked man who snuck into my room and got me off. I should be ashamed of what I've allowed that man to do to me. But I'm not. Instead, I want more. More from the man I thought he was and more from the man that I now know he is.

Jayce says something to him, and Sin's eyes lift from his cell to meet mine. They look cold. Unforgiving. I like that about him. He's not fake. He hates the world even though it's given him everything he's ever wanted. He pockets his phone, tucking his hands into his jeans, and starts to head for me. Ignoring whatever it is Jayce is calling out to him.

I pull my backpack farther up on my shoulder, and right before I get to him, I take a right, opening up a door into the classroom.

"Okay, now ..." Mr. Hamilton stops talking when he sees me enter. "Elli." His eyes narrow on mine.

I stand, waiting for him to kick me out, but he won't. He can't afford to make a scene—not this time—because it's not just us. Class has officially started. And if he wants me to leave, then he'll have to drag me out by my hair.

I hear the door open behind me, and by the way that David stiffens, I don't even have to turn around to see that Sin followed me in. "I've got a story to share," I state.

"Oh, I don't mind. Go ahead." Mack's currently standing at the podium and runs off to find his seat at my announcement. He hates sharing. Honestly, the guy either has a boring sex life or no imagination. You can't say pussy or cunt without his face turning red.

David crosses his arms over his chest and looks away from me. His silence tells me everything I need to know.

Making my way to the front of the classroom, I drop my backpack at my feet and place my diary on the podium. Opening it, I start reading.

# TWENTY-THREE

# SIN

I take her seat at the front of the class and place my elbow on the desk, my chin resting in my hand. She pushes her bleach-blond hair behind her ear, and I don't miss the fact that she took the time to cover up every bruise I gave her last night on my father's boat. But I guarantee the ones under her clothes are still visible if I were to strip her naked in front of everyone.

"I first met him at a bar," she starts. "He approached me and offered me a drink. One turned into more than I could remember."

I watch David shift in his seat.

"He told me I was pretty. That I was what all men wanted. I believed him. But then like the man before him, he put his hands on me."

I sit up straighter, my eyes going to David once again. He fixes his tie, his eyes on his desk.

"Told me that I was a worthless whore."

David clears his throat. "Elli, this isn't the assignment."

"Why? Why is it that the woman is always the whore?" she goes on, ignoring him. "Shouldn't he be accountable for making me wet? For turning me on."

"Elli?" he snaps, jumping to his feet.

"He had no problem fucking me, but when he found out I'd fucked another man, I was worthless. Used-up trash."

"For fuck's sake, Elli." He steps out from behind his desk and heads toward her, but I stand from her chair, causing him to stop.

"I was no longer his whore, but someone else's." Her eyes are on her paper, not caring that he's trying to stop her from spilling their secrets. "I think it's funny that because I have a pussy and he has a dick, I'm the one who should be ashamed. I'm not. He drugged me the first time he got between my legs."

*He what?* I take a step toward him, and he takes two back, almost tripping over his chair. "Ellington!"

"He had recorded it," she continues, still ignoring him. "Showed it to me when I woke up. How much my body enjoyed it. Got off on it. He promised me it'd be our little secret. But I shouldn't have to keep my mouth shut about him being a piece of shit."

"ELLINGTON!" His face turns red with anger. Silence follows and he lets out a long breath realizing she's done.

Looking over at her, I watch her close the notebook and walk out of class.


# ELLINGTON

I EXIT THE CLASS AND FEEL A HAND ON MY ARM, STOPPING me. I'm spun around and look up into a set of hard blue eyes. "He raped you?" he demands to know.

My lips thin and I look away from him.

Letting out a growl at my refusal to answer, he asks another question, "He's hit you?"

Not sure why he cares all of a sudden.

"The night you called the masked me to come coddle you. I asked who hit you, and you said it didn't matter."

Again, I say nothing. I didn't go into David's class for Sin's sympathy or jealousy. It was to cleanse my soul of anything left remaining of David. I wasn't going to let him be the one who ended it. I was. My choice, my way.

And that's exactly what I just did.

"Elli?" Sin snaps my name, causing kids in the hall to stare.

"How fucking dare you." I shove his chest with my free hand.

He's silent for a second before he lowers his voice to a deadly growl. "Be very careful how you speak to me, Elli..."

"Fuck you, Easton," I snap his first name. "You got me kicked out of Mr. Hamilton's class?" I point at the now closed door. "He was fucking pissed at me. And I didn't do shit."

He yanks my body flush with his, and I can feel how tense he is. "He has drugged you and hit you, and you're mad at me?"

"It doesn't matter." I run a hand through my hair. "Congratulations. You won." Then I rip my arm free and storm down the hall. "I'm officially no longer his whore."

He lets me go and I make it out to my car, toss the notebook into my passenger seat and speed home.

I enter my bedroom back at the house and slam the door shut, letting the first tear fall, tossing the notebook on my nightstand. I'm not upset that I'm no longer spreading my legs for David. I'm mad at myself. How do I keep doing this? Put myself in situations that I know are wrong. First James, then David, and now Sin.

"Fuck," I curse myself, needing a second to catch my breath.

My cell rings, and I look to see it's Sin. Fuck that. I press ignore and then turn it off altogether. I'm not in the mood for him right now. Or anyone, for that matter. My mom is out of town once again. Said she'd be back Monday. At least, that's what the text she sent me earlier this morning said.

I'm going to spend my evening at home. Alone. I'll take a hot shower, grab a bottle of wine, and lie in bed eating my weight in candy.

---

I LOOK TO SEE THE CLOCK ON MY NIGHTSTAND SHOWS IT'S almost midnight. My eyes are so heavy, and I can't keep them open anymore. My phone is still off. I've ignored the world. It's for the best.

Turning off the TV, I lie down under the covers and close my eyes, but they open the moment I hear something. It sounded like a door opening and closing. Sitting up, I throw off the covers and place my feet on the floor just as my bedroom door is shoved open.

Sin enters my room, and my breathing hitches when I see his blue eyes narrowed on mine. He's in front of me the very next second before I can even blink. "East—"

"Shh," he whispers, lifting his knuckles to run down my reddened cheek, making me shiver. "It's okay if you don't want to talk. In fact ..." He grabs my arm, spinning me around so my back is to his front. He wraps an arm around me from behind while the other comes up and slaps over my mouth, his fingers pinching off my nose. "I'll help you out with it."

I struggle in his iron grip. My legs kick out in front of me as my fingers dig into his forearm. I thrash around, but he holds me tightly, cutting off my air while my lungs burn and my chest heaves.

My body goes slack in his hold, and my arms fall to my sides. I expect him to let go, but he doesn't. My eyes fall closed, and the blackness pulls me under without any escape.

# TWENTY-FOUR

# ELLINGTON

I wake up, opening my heavy eyes, and I realize I'm in the passenger seat of Sin's car.

My head falls to the left, and I look over his tense body. His hand grips the steering wheel, the other holding the shifter. His defined jaw is tight, eyes narrowed on the road like it betrayed him. "Sin," I moan his name, my throat sore.

His eyes quickly look over at me and then back on the road.

I lift my ass out of the seat but can't move. My arms are tied behind my back, and he's pulled the seat belt so tight that it's locked me in place. My thighs tighten while my breath hitches. "Where are we ... where are we going?" All of a sudden, my throat is dry.

"Something I have to take care of," he answers cryptically.

"Untie me?" I ask more than demand. A part of me knows I like it, while another part tells me I shouldn't.

He chuckles but doesn't respond or make any attempt to free me. I look out the tinted windows, trying to see where we're at or where we're going. It's just woods, but I know exactly where we're going. The *Freak Show*.

My breathing accelerates as he pulls off the two-lane road and drives through an iron gate to the parking lot. He brings his car to a stop next to a white Audi that I know is Jayce's. Just as I look out of my window, I see a Black SUV pull in next to us, and it's Corbin.

Sin comes around and opens my door. He leans in, undoing my seat belt, and yanks me out of the car with his hand on my upper arm, bringing me to the back of the SUV when Corbin pops his hatch.

He spins me around to face Jayce, then pulls something over my head and down my body. Looking down, I find it resembles a black cloak of some kind. It's got a high collar on it. I can feel the material rubbing on my neck.

"Open wide," Sin orders from behind, and I do as I'm told only for him to reach around my face and shove a ball gag into my mouth. It's big, forcing my teeth open wide and I whimper around it while I feel him fasten it in place behind my head. It tastes of rubber, causing my mouth to instantly produce more saliva. My tongue explores the back of the round ball, trying to push it out of the way, but that's useless. He's secured it tight enough that the leather is digging into the corner of my lips and cheeks. The pain makes my thighs clench.

Then hands grab my shoulders, and I'm spun around. Sin lifts something in his hands and places it over my head. Thankfully, it has two eye holes so I can see. But it's hot in here. I can hear my heavy breathing echoing in my ears.

I'm guessing it's so no one can see I have a gag in my mouth. And the cloak they put over me doesn't have any arm holes, so it too hides my arms tied behind my back.

Each of the guys puts on their black hoodies and masks from last time. Corbin's is the clown, Jayce's is the skinless face, and just as I had guessed, Sin is the broken mirror. "Let's go," Sin commands, and Corbin closes the hatch.

I'm escorted by three men into what looks like a red-and-black tent. I expect some kind of circus inside but that's not even close to what I see. The tint was just painted on the front of the building. There is a guy taking tickets and two carts connected to one another. The lights are dim, making it harder to see with the small holes as eyes.

Drool runs out of the corner of my mouth, and I can't help the moan that escapes my lips when my pussy throbs. I catch sight of the kid, who's taking the tickets, frowning.

Sin grabs my upper arm, helping me into the car, and I see Corbin and Jayce get in the one attached to the back of ours. It jerks forward and Sin leans over into me, his hand gripping my throat, forcing my head back, and I whimper.

His hand tightens, taking away my air, and I struggle in his grip, although wetness fills my underwear. I try to suck in air but get nothing, and it just makes me squirm more.

"The sound of you trying to breathe makes me so fucking hard," he whispers in my ear, making my nipples harden, and it just forces another unintelligible noise from my lips due to the tenderness the piercings still cause. "If you didn't have a gag in your mouth, it'd be full of my cock."

My throat burns, my chest heaving, and tears sting my eyes.

He lets go of me, and I suck in a deep breath through my nose. A line of drool steadily runs from the corners of my mouth now. My jaw already starting to get sore.

The car jerks again, but this time to a stop, and he grabs me. I protest, but he pulls me from the car effortlessly. I get a quick glimpse at Corbin and Jayce through my small eye holes to see they also exit.

Sin pulls me through a door I didn't notice hidden in the black wall and to a stop, then he rips the mask off my head, my hair sticking to my sweaty-and-drool-covered face. I blink to see a prop tied up to a wall. His arms were raised above his head. His feet tied together at the ankles.

He's got a pair of jeans on with a black T-shirt. It's ripped, looks like a knife slashed across his skin in various places, fake blood running down the front of him. There's a mask over his head. Looks like an animal of some sort with long and thick devil horns that curl backward around to a point.

There's a red light pointed right at it.

I don't understand why we're here or what we're doing. A beeping sound makes me jump, before I hear what sounds like our cars leaving us on the other side of the wall.

Panic fills my chest, making my heart pound faster. My wide eyes go to Sin to ask what the fuck is going on, but he grips my hair in his hands, and I cry out in the gag when he yanks me forward. He brings me to a stop in front of the prop, and Jayce rips the mask away.

I scream into the gag when a set of dark brown eyes meet mine. Mr. Hamilton is the prop that's hanging on the wall. And the smell of blood hits my nose, making me gag.

"Don't do that, little demon." Sin commands in my ear, standing behind me to keep me in place. "This piece of shit doesn't deserve your pity or your forgiveness."

I shake my head, quickly trying to loosen his hold, but he just tightens it, forcing my head to look up at the dark ceiling. I start to choke on the slobber that slides to the back of my throat.

"I've been watching him." Sin goes on as if I'm not going to choke to death. "You're not the only student he's been sticking his dick in."

How did he know that I had been sleeping with my professor? I mean, he had to have known before I read off my diary today in class. But I also know that Sin is the reason he dropped me from his class in the first place. So he was aware before today.

Sin goes on. "Some even underage. He had the videos and pictures to prove it."

My body tenses at that, my breath stopping altogether.

Sin laughs roughly, the sound echoing in the room, making the hair on the back of my neck rise. "That's right, little demon. He's got a long list of girls who have been more than willing to get undressed for him."

The way he says *girls* makes my chest tighten and bile rise.

"He'll hang here for as long it takes him to die," he adds. "I made sure not to cut him too deep, or into any major organs. Bleeding to death can take hours. Sometimes days, if he's unlucky." Letting go of me, I right my head, my neck now as sore as my mouth.

Sin reaches out his hand to his friend and my diary is placed in it. I start mumbling behind my gag, trying to grab it out of his hold. I know he read my journal, but that is different than my diary. I talk about Sin in there.

"We're going to have a class." Sin states and hands grab my shoulders, pulling me down into a chair. The metal cold on my ass and thighs through the thin cloak. "You shared your fantasies, little demon. Now let me share mine." Licking the tip of his fingers, he starts turning the pages until he finds what he's looking for. "Imagine you tied to a bed down in a basement."

I stiffen, unable to take my eyes off Sin.

"Just lying there ready to be fucked. To be taken full advantage of. I softly run my hand along your thigh, and you shift on the bed, begging me to fuck your wet cunt."

My pulse starts racing. *Why is this so familiar?*

He closes the diary and tosses it to the floor, no longer interested. Leaning forward, he places each hand on an armrest, caging me in. His mask just inches from my face, and I hold my breath. "Imagine me fucking your pussy with my hands wrapped around your throat while you fight the rope that ties you to the bed."

My heart is pounding, and I'm holding my breath. Why do I feel like I've been there before? And how does he know about it? Was he watching Mr. Hamilton and me?

His hand shoots out and wraps around my throat, forcing me to lift my chin as a steady line of drool runs from my gagged mouth.

"That was the first time I fucked you, little demon. In his house."

*No.* It can't be. I try to shake my head, but his shattered mirror mask nods once. "Yes. He left you all alone in his basement. And I walked right in and had my way with you."

Tears fill my eyes. I was so mad at Hamilton that night. After my second bottle of wine, he tied me to the bed and then said he was leaving me. When I started to panic, he shoved my underwear in my mouth and taped it shut. Then there was nothing. Just silence. I knew he had left and wasn't sure when he'd return. But the longer I lay there, the wetter I got. Then I felt a touch, and I wanted... no, needed more. My body begged him to fuck me. I was practically sobbing when I came. Then I passed out. I woke up the following morning in my room, confused as to how I got home, and my car was in the driveway.

"My point is, Ellington." Sin lets go of the armrests and reaches down to grab the cloak's hem, pulling it up.

My pulse accelerates. He never calls me by my full name.

He runs his free hand between my legs, and they fall open on their own. "Is that you belong to me. I owned you before you even knew it. And I'm going to make sure you never forget that."

I go to stand, but my hair is grabbed at the crown, and my neck is yanked back. Mumbled words come from my gagged mouth, and spit flies out around the edge of the rubber ball.

Hands are on my knees, holding them wide open, and I try to fight them, but it's useless. There are three of them and one of me, and my arms are tied behind my back.

"You belong to a Lord now, Elli. And a Lord always takes what he wants."

I swallow, the feel of the cold spit that's set in my mouth making me gag.

"I vow ..." Sin's voice fills the room. "To fuck this cunt." My already soaked thong is shoved to the side and a finger enters me, causing my hips to buck involuntarily. "You vow to be mine, don't you, little demon?"

I nod the best I can, which isn't much, and moan a yes when a second enters.

"We vow to never be apart in this world or the next." He enters a third one, and my teeth sink into the rubber while I inhale sharply through my nose. "Because I will always find you, pet. No matter how far you try to run, how hard you fight me, or how long you live for me. You will never escape me."

I see a red light, almost like a flame lighting up the small room, but I can't look to see what it is because one of the guys behind me is still holding my head back by my hair, forcing me to look up at the black ceiling. Sin removes his fingers, and I sink into the chair just as hot searing pain shoots through my body.

I scream into the gag, my body thrashing in the chair, and I swear my vision fades for a second. When I come back to reality, my face is wet from tears running down my cheeks, and my body is shaking. Hands are on either side of my face and Sin's face is in front of mine, his mask long gone and so is the hand that was fisted in my hair.

He smiles. "That was such a good girl, little demon."

His hand slides behind my neck and pushes my face down. I see their crest on my inner thigh—a circle with three lines running parallel inside it. It's the size of the ring he wears. The irritated skin is red and bleeding.

He grabs my neck once again, forcing me to meet his eyes. They're wide with amusement, the corner of his lips turning up, just showing the tiniest hint of a smile. "That's a reminder of who you serve."

My thighs tighten while a mumbled whimper falls from my gagged mouth. The feel of the wetness between my legs reminds me just how fucked up I am. He was right. I like pain. My body gets off on it.

"You like that, don't you?" he asks, lifting my head to meet his eyes again. "You always wanted someone to make you feel worthy, Elli. I'll make sure you know your place. You'll be my personal little pet. I'll tie you up and play with you whenever I want. However I want."

I nod my head the best I can with his other hand around my throat. At this very moment, I realize I'd do anything for him. To be his little demon.

When I burn the world down and they ask me why, I'll tell them the devil asked me to do it. And I wanted to make him proud.

He steps back and I slump in the chair, trying to stop the tears while I shake uncontrollably. Sin lifts his hand to Corbin and a backpack appears in front of me in Sin's hand. He unzips it and dumps the contents out into a bucket that Jayce sits on the ground next to him.

My eyes widen when I see what was inside the backpack. Sin tosses the now empty bag back to his friend and reaches down, pulling a notebook with my name written on the front from the bucket, holding a lighter to it. I'm screaming unintelligible things when the pages catch, and he drops it into the bucket to light up the rest.

Sin reaches out, grabs my hair, and yanks me to my knees in front of the bucket. He comes to stand behind me, one hand in my hair, and the other wrapped around the chair as he kneels behind me. Forcing me to watch him burn my memories, my fantasies. A part of me wishes they were that easy to erase.

"You don't need those anymore, Elli" he whispers in my ear as the flames grow higher, the room hotter. I can feel the fire heating up my skin he's got me so close to it. "I'll buy you new ones. And I'll make sure you always have something to write about." promises, gently kissing my tear-streaked cheek.

# SIN

SHE'S MINE. FINALLY. IT'S TAKEN ME YEARS TO GET TO THIS point, but there has never been a doubt about what I wanted. I always knew I would go to great lengths to get her.

I let go of her, taking a step back and she slumps, kneeling on the floor watching the fire, her mumbled cries filling the room.

Corbin pulls his cell out of his pocket and types away a message. Jayce turns to look at David. I was going to let him live. I didn't think he was that big of a threat. But after I heard what she had to say in his class today, I knew I had to take care of him. For her.

She sniffs, getting my attention, and I look down at her. The cloak is still shoved up to rest around her waist, so she's looking down at her inner thigh, where I branded her with my ring.

I pull the cloak back into place, and her pretty eyes meet mine. Fresh tears spill over the bottom lashes and run down her cheeks. Along with drool.

*Fuck, she's gorgeous.*

If I could, I'd keep her like this forever.

She is officially mine. Technically, she can't be my chosen, but I can have more than one. The vow ceremony wasn't a tradition in the Lords' eyes, but I still made it happen. You're supposed to dunk your chosen in water to cleanse them from past fucks. And it's done in front of a congregation to show ownership. Two fellow Lords who happened to be my best friends were enough. She wears our brand. She'll belong to me until the day she dies.

"Let's go," I say, reaching out and grabbing her upper arm. I pull her to her feet, and she sways a little.

She starts mumbling behind her gag, her eyes widening. I ignore her obvious struggle to remind me that she's still gagged and restrained. She's not getting loose anytime soon. Her shoulders shake, and I slip the mask back over her face to cover it up.

Corbin puts out the fire before we exit through the back, and I lead her to my car and place her in the passenger seat. I close the door and turn to my friends. "I'll come get him in the morning," I inform them.

Jayce adds, "I can meet you here. Just let me know what time."

Corbin is still typing away on his phone, but he gives a nod.

We say our goodbyes, and I get into the driver's seat. Reaching over, I rip off her mask, and her heavy eyes look over at mine. She's getting tired. Her adrenaline is starting to wear off.

I run my thumb over the ball covered in her drool, and she moans, her hips lifting off the seat. Reaching across her, I grab her seat belt and fasten it, locking her in.

---

I CARRY HER UNCONSCIOUS BODY INTO HER HOUSE. I overheard that Linc is out of town until this weekend. Since her mother is also MIA, I'm guessing they're together. So I'd rather take her here than my parents'.

I kick her bedroom door open and lay her on the bed. Her heavy eyes open, and she looks up at me, trying to roll onto her stomach to release the pressure on her arms tied behind her back.

"Stay," I order, pressing her shoulders into the mattress. "I'm going to clean your thigh."

She nods, and I walk into her adjoining bathroom. I grab what I need and then go back to the bedroom. I sit on the side of the bed, yanking the cloak up her legs, high on her waist. Then I grab the cotton shorts and underwear, pulling them off to where she's naked from the waist down.

I take the washcloth that I already have soap and water on and gently run it over the raised red skin.

She screams into the gag, her body turning away from me.

I get up, push her back onto her back, and straddle her legs, right below her knees. "I've got to clean it," I tell her.

She nods, her eyes held tightly shut while tears run down the sides of her face. I clean it up as quickly as possible and then bandage it.

Reaching into my pocket, I pull out my pocketknife and pop it open. She looks up at me, breathing heavily through her nose, and I cut down the middle of the cloak and her shirt. When I had entered her room earlier, she was already in bed for the night, so she wasn't wearing a bra. When I push it off her shoulder, she's now naked underneath me.

I get up off her legs and spread them wide, centering myself between them. My fingers run over her soaked cunt. "I love how wet you get," I mumble when I push one finger into her. "I'm going to enjoy pushing you, little demon."

Arching her back, she moans. I unzip my jeans, releasing my hard dick and rub it over her entrance before pushing my cock into her tight cunt.

I lay down on top of her, my arms behind her knees, spreading her open wide for me, and I start to fuck her, loving the way her mumbled cries sound as I make her mine.

# TWENTY-FIVE

## SIN

I've spent all weekend inside Elli. I've dreamed of having unlimited time with her, and I've taken advantage of every second. I've woken her up, and I've fucked her while she was still asleep. She has let me have my way with her. But then again, it's hard to stop me when her hands are tied. Or tell me no when she's gagged.

I enter the house of Lords and make my way to the only elevator that has access to the basement. We were called in. We can have an assignment at any given time once we're initiated. So the fact that I was balls deep inside her mouth when I got the text still has me hard.

The house was given to the Lords years ago, along with many other properties all over the world. It was once a hotel. A bunker was added in after the Lords took it over. We train down here to shoot, to hunt. We spent a lot of our first two years down here learning how to take what we want.

"Hey, did you see what's going on?" Jayce asks me as I sit down at the large table. Looking around, it occurs to me that only the seniors were called in.

"No. Been busy." My cell went off, saying I had to be here. Otherwise, I'd still be with my little demon.

"It's Judge Mallory," Corbin whispers, leaning forward and placing his forearms on the table.

"What about him?" Jayce asks Corbin.

"It was on the news. Break-in at his house, shots fired. Body found." He shrugs. "That's all that was said before his security broke the camera of the reporter standing on the front lawn."

Pulling my cell out of my pocket, I put in my code and look over the camera I have of Elli in her room. I placed it there the second time I visited her a couple of years back. There were times I wasn't able to make it to see her, but I was able to watch her. I wanted to know if any other man was ever in that room. And if so, I'd take care of him. Thankfully, there never has been.

She lies there on her stomach, her arms spread wide, and each wrist tied to a bedpost. She's naked, her ass up in the air. I told her if she moved, I'd know it and she'd be punished. A part of me hopes she does. I love making her cry.

The elevator dings, signaling its arrival before opening. I close my cell and look up to see Ryat, Prickett, and Gunner enter.

They take their seats, and I don't miss the tension between Ryat and Matt. I still have no clue what's going on there.

My eyes catch sight of Lincoln walking off the elevator, and I stiffen. He was out of town, but he must have returned early. I saw that Elli's mother texted her yesterday that they were having guests over for dinner tomorrow night after she returns from her weekend away. I haven't told Elli I know about it, but my ass will be there. He'll have to throw me out and then explain to her mother and Elli why.

He claps his hands and gets right to the reason we're here. "I'm guessing everyone has seen the news by now and is aware of what's happened."

We all say yes. If Corbin told us what he saw, then I'd say I'm caught up enough.

He plops down at the head of the table. "I need two volunteers for an assignment. I can't give you any other details other than the job might take a day, might take three weeks. That all depends on how long it takes you to get it done."

"Ryat and I will handle it," Matt speaks before anyone else can say a word.

A silence blankets the room as all eyes shoot to Ryat. He sits there looking unaffected. If he's pissed or worried, he's not showing it.

"Ryat?" Lincoln asks him for confirmation.

"Sounds good, sir," he answers.

"Perfect. You all are dismissed." Linc gets up and exits like he's the one with a woman tied to a bed waiting to be fucked. Which he probably does. There are fifteen seniors in this room right now, and I guarantee at least three of us has a girl tied up and waiting for us to get back to them.

I stand and make my way to the elevator, pulling up the footage again to see she's relaxed on the bed. Her body now flat, her head to the side. She looks like she's sleeping with her eyes closed. Smiling, I pocket my cell. *Punishment it is.*


# ELLINGTON


MONDAY EVENING, I LOOK AT MYSELF IN MY FLOOR-LENGTH mirror, my hands running down my white halter dress, red heels, and matching lipstick. Kira and I are meeting up after I'm done with dinner. My makeup is done heavy, and my hair fixed in a high pony. We're going to go out. I'm going to pop some pills, get hammered, and then go home with her and crawl into bed with

Sin. If he's home. He spent all weekend here with me. Now that my mother has returned, I don't want to be here.

Gripping the hem of my dress, I lift it to look at the brand on my inner thigh. It's had a bandage over it the last couple of days. Sin cleans it and changes it out for me. I hate that I love it. That he's claimed me in a way no one ever has before. In a way, it makes me feel accepted. Even I know that's fucked up. That my childhood has me accept something that most of society would find wrong.

Putting my dress back in place, I respond to Kira as I make my way downstairs and into the formal dining room. I sit down at the table.

"Ellington?"

I look up to see my mom enter with a few members of her staff. "Are you okay, honey? You look a little sick." Before waiting for me to answer, she turns to them, barking out orders, then faces me once again, crossing her arms over her chest.

"I'm fine, Mom. Just tired."

"Well, if you wouldn't stay out all night with random men like a raccoon digging through trash, you wouldn't be so exhausted."

I nod, picking up the bottle of champagne from the middle of the table. "You're right, Mom." I toss it back, sucking it from the bottle.

She frowns but then orders her little bitches to bring a new bottle since I've claimed this one. She walks out and I pull it away from my lips, sucking in a deep breath.

"A glass, Miss Ellington." A member of her hired staff sets a champagne flute in front of me. His way of telling me my mother won't appreciate my unruly manners in front of our guests.

I reach out, pick up the crystal flute and then slam it down on the marble floor next to my chair. It was from my mom's second wedding. A gift from my *daddy*.

His eyes narrow on mine as I stare up at him. "I'm sorry, it slipped."

"Quite all right, miss. I'll get you another one," he says tightly, turning toward the hallway. I hear him snap his fingers, ordering someone to the formal dining room because picking up my messes are beneath him.

Reaching down, I pick up a piece and hold it in my hand. My pointer finger runs over the sharp corner. I hiss in a breath when I see it's cut me. The slightest drop of blood pops out before running down my finger. I pull it into my mouth and suck. The taste reminds me of what Sin and I did on the back of the boat. Fuck, I want him even more now than I ever have.

Why? Because I know he's as fucked up as I am? Because he has known it was me this entire time? He showed up for me when I needed him. He held me in my bed. That has to mean something, right? That it's more than just sex?

And the mystery man. He's done so many dirty ... no, filthy things to me. Some I begged for. Other times, he didn't allow me that option.

I hear laughter coming from down the hall and I curl my hand around the glass to hide it. She enters, and my eyes meet a set of brown ones. My breathing picks up. I've only ever seen him twice in my life.

*I SIT IN THE GRAND HALL ON THE COUCH, EYES ON THE FLOOR.*

*"Who would do this?" my mother cries. "Who would kill James?"*

*"I don't know, Laura. But I'll find him. I'll take care of it. There will be retribution."*

*I lift my eyes to look at the bastard who sits across from me. He's got his arms around my mom while she sobs into his side, but his eyes are on me. They drop to my dress, and his brows crease when he* looks at my wrists. The marks still visible from the zip tie the mystery man used to tie me up after he killed my stepdad.

The front door opens, and my mom jumps to her feet. "Anything?" she begs.

"No, ma'am." The officer shakes his head. "No proof of forced entry."

"He must have been at the party," Lincoln growls. "Check the list."

"We have ..."

"Then double, triple-check it, for fuck's sake," he snaps, and my mom's body shakes. "I want to know how he had access to this fucking house."

My bedroom. I watched him leave out of my French doors to my balcony. He must have entered the same way. I never lock them. I prefer to leave them open at night and listen to the wind howl in the trees. It's soothing.

"Are you okay, miss?" A man comes up to stand in front of me.

I look up at him through my lashes. They're clumped together. His eyes drop to my dress and heels. I know I look like shit. They think it's because my stepdad is dead, but it's because I allowed his killer to fuck me with his gun. My pussy burns. I'm pretty sure I'm getting an infection. But I don't give a fuck. It was worth it. To be fucked by the very thing that killed the man I hate? I'll take an infection any day for the price of freedom.

"She's fine." Lincoln scoffs.

"She's in shock." My mother cries, "She hasn't spoken since ... since Linc found the body."

I didn't even know Lincoln was attending tonight. I wouldn't have stayed home if I had. But that doesn't mean anything. It was packed full of guests. And I stayed to myself. Always do.

"Let us call EMS to check her out." The officer doesn't wait for anyone to answer. He speaks into the radio on his shoulder and orders an ambulance.

"Why?" my mother screams, making me flinch. "Why did this happen? Again?" She's now sobbing on her knees by the couch.

Lincoln walks up behind her and places his hands on her shoulders. "Laura ..."

"He was so good to us. He loved us." I whimper at her words, and the officer notices.

"Are you going to get sick, miss?" he asks me.

"She's fine," Lincoln snaps at him, but the officer doesn't look away from me.

Am I? No. I wish I could expel every touch, every kiss, every motherfucking memory of him, but I can't. Only death will offer me such mercy.

A new officer comes walking down the stairs and hands a pill bottle to the one who hovers over me. "Found this in the bathroom by his body."

"What are they?"

The man lowers his voice. "Viagra."

My body shudders. I've been lucky enough the past year that he's needed help getting it up. It wasn't as fun for him to fuck me when it had to be scheduled. A part of me—the sick part—was ashamed of myself that I no longer did it for him. The other part told her to shut the fuck up.

"Someone removed his finger," another man states, coming down the stairs.

My mother's shrill scream that follows the officer's statement makes my ears ring. I had watched the mystery man cut it off. He didn't know I was there, but I was. Stunned to silence at first. He thought I was going to talk. He has no idea how well I can keep a secret. One of those secrets is sitting across from me, holding my sobbing mother.

The front double doors fly open, and three men enter the family room in solid black three-piece suits. "That's enough, gentlemen. We'll take it from here."

*They're Lords. Powerful men at the top of their food chain.*

"With all due respect ..."

"Get the fuck out of Mr. Roland's house," one commands. His voice booming over my mother's cries

*I want to correct him. This isn't James's house. It was my father's, who left it to my mother in his death. But I can't make my lips move.*

"We've got medics on the way," the officer who called me an ambulance argues.

*Another man enters the house and the Lords gesture to him.*

"We brought our own." He crosses his arms over his chest. "Last time I'm going to say it."

*Understanding the officers are outnumbered and outpowered, they exit the house as the Lords follow Lincoln upstairs to where the body remains.*

*The doctor walks over to me while my mother falls onto the couch, the sobs that come out of her mouth irritating me. Did she really not know what kind of man he was? I thought she put on a show. Pretended to love him because she had to. I guess I was wrong.*

THAT WAS TWO YEARS AGO, THE LAST TIME I HAD TO SEE Lincoln. But that's not why my hand tightens on the piece of glass I'm holding. My breath quickens at the pain as the jagged edges cut into my skin.

"Why is he here?" I demand.

"Elli," my mother scolds me. "Don't speak that way. I'm sorry, Linc."

"It's quite all right. This will be an adjustment for all of us."

"Adjustment?" I repeat the word, and my eyes drop to the diamond on her left hand. A sharpness in my chest takes away my breath. "Mom—"

"Laura, we've got a problem in the kitchen," her head chef says, interrupting me.

"I'll be right back." She pats Lincoln's chest and follows the man out.

He places his hands on the table across from me, wasting no time. "Hello, Elli. It's been too long."

"Not long enough." I swallow, my tongue all of a sudden heavy. "Get out of this house," I add, ignoring the way my body trembles in the chair. James may have fucked me, but he took his time getting under my skin. Making me believe that I needed him. Lincoln is not that kind of man.

He smirks. "Didn't you see the ring, baby?" I jerk at the nickname. "Daddy's home. And by the way you've been acting, I see you've forgotten your lessons."

A cry escapes my lips, my body sinking further into the chair, trying to escape him.

His eyes drop to my hand, and his smirk grows. "Already bleeding for me, I see."

Tears blur my vision, and my throat is closing, making it hard to breathe.

"When I get my hands on you, those six years with James will feel like heaven."

I don't walk out of the formal dining room, I run, down the hallway and through the foyer, needing to get out of this hell. I yank both front doors open and rush outside, only to run into a hard body. A yelp escapes my lips in surprise.

"Whoa." Hands grip my upper arms, and my legs buckle, but he wraps his arms around me, making me whimper. "What the fuck happened, Elli?" I hear Sin's voice, and I bury my face into his shirt. The familiar scent envelops me, and I begin to cry.

# TWENTY-SIX

# SIN

She clings to me, and I look up over the top of her head to see Linc standing in the hallway just outside the formal dining room. He smirks at me, and my teeth grind. My arms automatically hold her tighter.

"Linc?"

"I'm coming," he calls out to her mother, but his eyes are on Elli before disappearing.

The double meaning isn't lost on me. "Hey?" I pull her away from me, and tears run down her face. I rub them away with my thumbs while cupping her cheek. "What happened?" I demand.

Her big eyes meet mine, and I watch fresh tears spill over her bottom lashes. A trail of black runs down her cheeks, smearing her makeup. "I can't stay here. Not right now." She sniffs.

I nod, grabbing her hand and walking her down the steps and over to my car. I open the passenger door, and she falls into it, fixing her dress that had ridden up.

Getting in, I start the car and pull out of the driveway and through the open gate. I feel something on my back. Wetness? Reaching around, I run my hand over my shirt. Looking at my hand, I see it's bloody. "The fuck?" I look over at her and see her sitting ramrod straight, her hands in her lap and they're covered in blood. "Elli? What in the fuck?" I bark. "Why are you bleeding?" Did he hurt her?

Her head drops to her lap, and she uncurls her shaking fist.

"Christ," I hiss when I see a small piece of black glass embedded into her palm.

With her free hand, she yanks it out, and blood starts running down onto her bare legs. The hem of her white dress soaking it up.

I slam on the brakes, bringing the car to a stop on the side of the road, and reach around to the back seat. I grab my duffel bag and unzip it to find a T-shirt of mine. I rip a piece off the sleeve and grab the duct tape. I take her hand, ball up the now ripped sleeve and hold it over the wound on her palm and then rip the end of the tape off with my teeth before wrapping it around four times, taping it with pressure to stop the bleeding. I then throw everything into the back seat again.

Gently grabbing her face, I pull it to look at me. Her eyes have never looked so hollow. They are the prettiest color of blue I've ever seen but right now they look dull—lifeless. "What happened?" I ask, worried for her sanity. I've seen her break down before, but she looks like she's about to lose it.

Swallowing, she whispers, "She married him."

It wasn't a question. "Elli—"

"She's doing it ... again," she chokes out. "Why him?"

My chest constricts at her words. I knew Lincoln's threat was one I should take seriously. But I didn't realize until now that he had hurt her before. "What did he do to you, Elli?"

She swallows nervously but doesn't answer me.

"He's raped you." I take a guess. He and James were close. I can only assume that if James used her, he let others as well.

Her bottom lip trembles, and she whispers, "I didn't say no."

My teeth clench, and I wish I had killed him when I got rid of

James. "How old were you?" I can't fix the situation unless I know what has happened. And I promise, I'll fix every problem she's ever had.


# ELLINGTON

## *Eighteen years old*

I'M LICKING MY LIPS WHEN KIRA COMES TO STAND NEXT TO ME. *She watches herself in my bathroom mirror while she runs her hands through her curled hair.*

"Did you ever answer Michael back?"

"No," I say, *popping the top of my lipstick and start applying it.*

"Girl, he's hot. Go for it."

"Not interested." *There's only one guy I want, and it's not Michael.*

"Speaking of guys you're not interested in... so yesterday I was in the kitchen with my mom, and Sin walked in. My mother told him he should take you out."

*I drop the lipstick in the sink I'm leaning over, red streaks now covering the marble.* "What? Why would she say that?"

"She loves you. Duh. Plus, I think she's tired of him fucking her friends. Gross." *She shudders at the thought, then makes a gagging noise.* "Well, he was. He's in initiation now." *Laughing, she adds,* "He can't fuck anything at the moment, and it's made him an even bigger dick to be around."

"What did he say?" *I shrug as if I don't care. But I do. He's the one I want.*

"He laughed, like it was a joke, grabbed his water, and then walked out."

*My heart sinks. The words hurt more than they should. I know we have no future. He wouldn't want me. Not after what I've been* through. Plus, he'll be a Lord. He's probably got an arranged marriage in place to a pretty virgin who has been saving herself for only him. That's what they care about. Innocence. No man wants a whore.

"She really does love you, though." She throws me a bright smile.

"I love her too," I say, opening the top drawer next to the sink. Reaching up underneath it, I feel around for the little baggie I taped in place. I pull it down and wiggle it in front of her. "Want one?"

"Yes." She claps her hands before taking the ecstasy I offer her.

We both pop one in and then grab the bottle of vodka, each taking a gulp. "Let's go get the night going."

Turning off the light, we exit my bathroom and bedroom. We make our way downstairs and are headed toward the front doors when we pass his office.

"Elli," I hear him call out, and I release a sigh. I thought he was gone for the night. My mother left this morning for a girls' trip with Kira's mom. We've had a night out planned for three weeks now. Our first week as freshmen at Barrington University starts next week. We wanted to get out to celebrate our last week of freedom.

We enter his study to see him at his desk. Another man sits on the black leather couch. I've never seen him before. A younger guy, around our age, sits across from him in a chair. All eyes are on us. Mine go to my stepdad. He's looking at Kira with disgust,. his fatherly instincts ashamed of her for wearing a tight miniskirt, heels, and a black bralette.

Then his eyes are on mine, and they darken even more. I learned at a young age that lust makes men primal. They're fucking animals when they see something they want.

"Where are you two going?" he asks.

"Blackout," Kira answers, and I fist my hands.

I was going to lie. He doesn't like me going there. Bad things always happen at Blackout. But what do you expect when a Lord owns a nightclub? Tyson Crawford is what they consider an outcast in their society. He doesn't give a fuck about anything or anyone. I like that about him. He's also hot as fuck. I'd let him fuck me. Too bad I'm not allowed to fuck anyone else other than the man looking at me right now.

"Well," he stands and buttons his suit jacket. "Go along, Kira. She'll meet you there."

Her blue eyes meet mine, and I can see her wanting to argue, but I give her a soft smile. "I'll be right behind you." Lie. I already know I won't be leaving this house tonight. Not since my mother is gone. He'll have all night to do whatever the fuck he wants with me.

"Okay. See you later, Mr. Roland."

She turns from me, and he walks out from behind his desk. The only reason I let her go is because I know Sin will be at Blackout tonight. Otherwise, I wouldn't let her go there alone. But she's safer anywhere else in the world other than this room. That, I do know.

"Come here," he commands. No longer putting on a show for my friend that is now gone.

Like a dog trained to obey its owner's command, I walk toward him. My feet are heavy. I stop, and he grips my cheeks painfully, making me whimper. His eyes search mine and then fall to my lips. "Did you take anything?"

I close my eyes, my heart racing. "Yes," I whisper honestly, unable to lie about the drugs. I learned my lesson that he always finds out when I do.

"Pills or powder?" he demands.

"Pills."

He pushes me away, and I rub my face. "It was only o—"

He slaps me across the face before I can finish. Then I feel his fingers in my mouth. Shoving them down my throat, and I begin to gag. Instinct has me fighting, and I slap at his chest, pushing him away while I step back.

He yanks me behind the desk and pulls my skirt down my legs

*along with my underwear. Then he shoves me facedown onto the surface, making it rattle. Seconds later, I hear him removing his belt. "Hands behind your back."*

My heavy breathing fills the room, and I avoid looking at the other two men who are present. We've never had an audience before. But he knows I fantasize about multiple men. He makes me tell him everything. I bring them behind me and cross my wrists before I feel the leather wrap around them.

"You've trained her well." The one on the leather couch finally speaks.

I glance over at him to see he's got his hands steepled in front of him and one leg crossed over the other. His head tilted to the side while his dark eyes are on mine. "Take notes, kid." He speaks to the younger guy that sits across from him.

"We've been doing this for quite some time." James grunts. "Haven't we, baby?" His hand runs over my pussy. His fingers slowly enter me, just enough that I push against it. "It's all about the long game." He goes on, pushing them in a little deeper, making me whimper.

My eyes are growing heavy. The pill starting to kick in. My face rests on the cold surface of his desk, and my ass wiggles.

"It hasn't always been easy, but I've found that she responds the best to beatings than anything else. She likes it rough." His fingers spread me wide, and I moan, my eyes falling shut. "You've got to train their minds before you touch their bodies."

"Sounds like you've done all the hard work for me," the kid says, and laughter follows.

I ignore them and focus on the fingers teasing my pussy. They feel too good. My legs spread wider for him, and he removes his fingers, making me groan in frustration.

"What did you take, Elli?" I hear him ask. His voice sounds far off.

"Hmm?" I mumble, my tongue heavy. I'm in a tunnel, far from anyone else.

A hand comes down on my ass, and I wiggle it, wanting more. My skin is starting to tingle, the room growing hot. Why didn't he remove my shirt too?

"I said, what did you take?" he barks, that sting on my ass following, but I don't feel it as much as the last time.

"Dude, she's fucked." The kid laughs once again.

I don't know what they're talking about. All I know is that I need something. Seconds later, the head of his dick is at my entrance, and my lips part on a shaky breath when he enters me.

He hates when I do drugs because he can't reach me when I'm in bliss. My mind is free of anything or anyone. The drugs make it feel ten times better, though.

"Fuck her mouth, Lincoln. Until she's throwing up whatever she swallowed," James commands, and my pussy grips his dick, making him moan.

"My pleasure." My heavy eyes watch the guy stand from the couch. His hands go to his belt.

"After she pukes, fuck it some more until nothing is left other than the cum you force her to swallow." James pulls his cock out and then slams it forward. I'm aware of the wetness running down my thighs.

"What if she tries to bite my dick off?" he asks, laughing, now standing directly in front of the desk. His zipper is undone and his cock is in his hand.

I lick my numbing lips.

James pulls out of my pussy, slapping my ass once again. "She won't. The whore loves to choke on cock."

"You do know that if she took Molly, puking will only make her roll harder, right?" the kid speaks.

James stills, his cock buried deep into me. He leans over my *back, gripping my hair, and yanks my face off the desk. Growling in my ear, he demands, "Is that what you took?"*

*I can't even keep my eyes open, let alone answer. The side of my face stings, and my eyes open just enough to see the man standing in front of me slap me again. My vision goes blurry, and I can't tell if it's the drugs or unshed tears. I couldn't care less either way. "He asked you a question, bitch."*

*"Fuck it anyway," James snaps, his hips starting to move once again, shoving mine into the side of his desk. "I want it rough and messy."*

I YANK OFF MY SEAT BELT, OPEN THE PASSENGER DOOR, AND fall to my knees. Thankful that the car was already on the side of the road.

"Elli?" I hear Sin call out, but I'm already on my knees and vomiting on the gravel at that memory. Just like I was made to do that night. The drugs may have affected my ability to function, but the memories are seared into my brain like the brand Sin gave me on my thigh.

My stomach tightens, and my shoulders begin to shake. I manage to puke again, then I start to dry heave since I haven't eaten much today.

"Elli ..." I see him come up in my peripheral. I hold out my hand for him to stay back and start dry heaving again.

When I have nothing else to give, my head bows, my knees tucked underneath me with my hands on my thighs. I start coughing and fist my hands. I'm a fucking wreck. Why? I've lived with this for years. Why can't I control it now?

"Here, let me help you up." Hands grab my arms, pulling me to my shaky legs, and I shove him away before pulling the hem of my dress down to cover my pussy where it had ridden up.

"Stop, Easton." His jaw tightens at his name. "Why?" I ask, the back of my hand running along my mouth.

"Why what?"

"Why now? After all these years? Why are you everywhere all the time?" I ask, unable to escape him. How did he know to be at my house tonight? Was it just a coincidence? No, I don't believe in those. Especially when it comes to Sin.

He steps toward me, and I take one back. He pauses, shoving his hands in the front pockets of his jeans.

"You've been sneaking into my room for two years, but we never had sex. Then I start sleeping with David, and you decide to fuck me?"

"Elli—"

"You tricked me." I interrupt him, not really caring what his answer to that is. Sin doesn't need a reason. He just does shit whenever he decides he wants to. Plus, I know about their vow of celibacy. It took me a few days to figure out why he waited so long. "Made me think you were someone else."

He's silent.

"How long would you have let that go on?" That, I do want to know.

"How long would you have continued to fuck me, the masked me, and David?" he snaps, avoiding answering my question and asking his own. "For fuck's sake, Elli. You'd think one dick would be enough."

I slap him across the face with my good hand. I do it again, but he grabs my wrists before I make contact. I yank it free, but the momentum and heels on the uneven road have me falling, my side skidding across the gravel. He doesn't laugh at me. Instead, he stares at me with pity. My chest squeezes, making it hard to breathe.

"Come on." He steps forward to help me up again, and I turn around and jump to my feet, dusting off my hands and fixing my dress again. Fuck, I should have worn jeans tonight and tennis shoes.

"I'll walk."

"No," he growls. "Get your ass in the car."

I take another step back.

"Elli!" he snaps. "Get your ass in my fucking car. Now. I'm not leaving you here on the side of the road. It's not safe."

I give a rough laugh. The part of me that wants a fight rears her fucking head, and I say, "I'm sure I can suck someone's dick for a ride."

He reaches out, grabs my arm, and drags me back to the car. Shoving me inside, he slams it shut, and I grab the bottle of champagne I had brought with me when I ran out of my mom's house. Trying to erase the vomit taste, I take a big swig. I wait until he's in the driver's seat with the door shut before I shove mine open and run. Needing the head start.

"Fuck," he hisses, followed by the sound of his door slamming shut.

I hear his feet pounding the gravel behind me as I run off into the woods. Ducking under branches and jumping over large limbs.

I'm panting, my heart racing, but I don't look back. I just need to keep going. I'd rather be alone than coddled. He fucked me ruthlessly that night after the Freak Show and then as the masked man. Why is he going soft now? Because he found out I'm a whore? He's always known that. I've heard the whispers about me throughout high school and then Barrington. I just never gave a shit. No one really knew me and what I've been through, and those who think they have can go to hell.

I'm hit in the back, causing me to fall to the ground. I knew I wouldn't get far with my heels on. A cry is ripped from my lips as pain shoots up my shoulder and hip.

My arms are grabbed, and I'm shoved onto my back. I look up to see an angry Sin hovering over me. He straddles my stomach, and I slap at his face. "Get the fuck off me." But he grabs my arms, shoving them above my head and pinning them to the uneven ground.

Sticks and rocks dig into my back, and I scream as loud as I can with frustration into the woods, trying to buck him off, but it's no use.

"I love it when you scream for me." He smiles down at me.

Tears sting my eyes, and I close them tightly, refusing to look at him and show any vulnerability. He's already seen me weak. I can't take it anymore.

# TWENTY-SEVEN

# SIN

I release her wrists and shove her back onto her stomach.

"Get off me," she growls, her hands now digging into the ground, trying to crawl out from underneath me.

"Why do you do this?" I laugh at her attempt to get away. She's not going anywhere. I unzip my jeans, pull out my hard dick, and then shove her legs open wide, making her whimper.

Then I reach up, grab her arms and pull them behind her, holding them captive parallel to her back. With my free hand, I slide my cock into her soaked pussy. "Fuck, he did a number on you, didn't he?"

"Fuck... you," she chokes out.

I saw the way she looked at me when I showed her pity. So I'll see how she reacts to the opposite. Letting go of my dick, I reach out and grab her hair. I rip her face up off the ground as my cock starts fucking her cunt. No foreplay. "Tell me, Elli. Did you beg James to fuck you, like you beg me?"

"St-op." She begins to sob.

I release her forearms and she pulls them from her back to reach out in front of her. I lie down on her back, my weight pinning her down, both of my hands now tangling into her hair, and place my lips by her ear. "Want me to be your *daddy*?"

She goes wild. Her body thrashing against mine, her legs kicking. Mine spread hers wider to try to control them. Her fingers digging into the ground, while yelling out profanities into the night.

"Be a good girl, *baby*, and come on my cock. Like you did him for all of those years." I pull out of her pussy and slam my hips forward.

She's sobbing uncontrollably now.

"Did he share you?" I growl, doing it again.

The force making us move across the ground. She's going to have scratch marks on her face from the loose limbs. I know I can feel them scraping through my jeans on my knees. She's wearing a thin dress. "Did he watch Linc fuck you?" I shouldn't be jealous. I know that no matter the situation, it wasn't like she chose to fuck him. But I've read her journal for Hamilton's class, she fantasizes about multiple men fucking her. I would give her the world, but that's where I draw the line. "Did you come for him too?"

Her pussy pulses around my cock and my teeth clench.

"Is that what gets you off, little demon?" I go on, my hips more forceful with each thrust. I want to pull out and fuck her ass, but even I know I wouldn't be able to control myself right now. "Want me to force my friends to fuck you while I watch? Hmm?" I slam my hips forward. "Want me to tie you to my bed at the house of Lords and let them come in one by one and take their turn?" My breathing is erratic, the words giving me a sour taste in my mouth.

"I...hate...you." She continues to sob.

"No, you don't." My teeth clench at her refusal to answer my question. "You can't hate anyone that shows you any kind of affection." I reach around and grab her face, my hand going over her mouth while my fingers pinch off her nose.

She's going to come for me, and I know what she needs to do it.

Her fingers claw at my hand, tearing the skin, but I don't let go. My cock fucks her pussy while I take away any chance of breathing.

Our bodies rock back and forth on the ground in the middle of the Pennsylvania woods until I feel her coming on my cock. Just like I thought, it doesn't take long.

I let go of her face and sit up on my knees. She lies below me, no longer moving. My heavy breathing fills the open space and blood rushes in my ears. Flipping her over, her head falls to the side before her body starts convulsing with a coughing fit.

Her heavy eyes open and she looks around aimlessly. "There you are." I smile. My hand pushing the hair that's covered in twigs and leaves away from her tear-streaked face. It's red and irritated in places from the ground. Leaning down, I place my face in front of hers. "I will always win, Elli. No matter how low I have to go, you will not beat me at this game."

She whimpers, her eyes still unfocused.

"Run from me, I'll chase you. Challenge me, I'll break you."

Fresh tears fill her eyes and I'm not sure if they're in surrender or fear. It doesn't matter.

"I'll never set you free, little demon. It's best you understand that now." She licks her wet lips. "Because I'd hate to have to kill us both." If I can't have her, no one will. But I also would never want to survive in a world where she doesn't exist. Death would be heaven compared to a life without her being mine.

Letting go of her, I sit up on my knees, grip the hem of her now ruined dress, and shove it up to her neck, exposing her breasts to me. My hands run up her prominent ribs and grip her tits. I watch her head fall from side to side, she's still trying to catch her breath.

"You came on my dick, Elli." My eyes drop down to watch it slowly pull out before pushing back inside her. "Now it's my turn."

Her breathing is shallow, her eyes still unfocused. I'm aware that I might have gone too far, but I can't help myself. She gets me so worked up.

I push into her one last time, filling her cunt, and then pull out. I squeeze the head, watching the last little drop fall onto her swollen pussy. Then I push inside her again, making her whimper. "Goddamn." I groan. I can't get enough of her. I watch the way my cock fucks her while she lies there gasping. My eyes fall to the brand on her inner thigh, and I want to wrap my mouth around it and sink my teeth into the delicate skin to hear her scream. But I won't. Not right now. I'll get my chance. I have the rest of my life to do whatever I want to her.

"S-in," she manages to choke out my name.

I smile down at her. "Yeah, beautiful? Tell me that I'm the only one who is going to fuck you now."

"Only...you."

"Only me, Elli." I thrust my hips forward. "I want your cunt to take all my cum, little demon. Like your mouth does when I force you to swallow."

Her neck arches while she lets out a moan.

"That's it," I say, entering her again. "That's my good girl. Take it all, Elli." Once satisfied, I pull out and watch her cry while curling into herself. I zip my pants, stand, and pick her limp body up into my arms, carrying her to my car.

# TWENTY-EIGHT

# SIN

I take her to my parents'. Not wanting to go back to the house of Lords with her because Amelia is probably hanging out there since I have yet to call her since the day she barged into my room there. And I'm not taking Elli home. I place her in my bed and shut the door, heading to my sister's room.

Her door is cracked open, so I walk right in. She's sitting on her bed, her back facing me. "Hey, I—"

"Fuck, Sin." She jumps to her feet, spinning around to face me. "Fucking knock." She wears a towel wrapped around her body underneath her underarms. Her hair is down and wet. Her eyes quickly shoot to the bathroom door and then quickly return to mine.

I step farther into her room. "What's going on?" I ask.

"Nothing," she growls. "But you can't just barge into my room like that."

"It was open," I say defensively. "What were you doing?" My suspicion rises. She's up to something and she doesn't want me to know. Which isn't like her. My sister isn't the kind to hide things.

"That's none of your business. Get the hell out of here." Her hands grip the towel tighter while her eyes narrow on mine.

"I—"

Her bathroom door opens, and her eyes go wide and her head snaps over to watch the man exit. "Hey, babe ..." His eyes meet mine and he curses under his breath. "Shit."

"Are you fucking kidding me?" I shout at Corbin. "What the fuck is this shit?" I bark. "Get the fuck out of her room."

"Man, I'm so—"

"Don't apologize." She stops him. "We didn't do anything wrong."

"Are you serious?" Didn't do anything wrong? It looks like my best friend is fucking my sister. And that is definitely wrong. "Get the fuck out." I point at the door I stand in front of then look at her. "When Dad finds out—"

"Dad knows." She squares her shoulders. "I'm Corbin's chosen."

My eyes go from hers to his. She glares at me while my best friend's eyes soften with... regret? Maybe that's wishful thinking. How could he not tell me this? He knows how I feel about her being involved with a Lord. It's unacceptable. My parents have spent their lives hiding her from our world. Why would he agree to this? "No." I shake my head and spin around.

"Sin?" my sister calls out, but I ignore her, running down the stairs.

I shove my father's study door open so hard it knocks a hole in the interior wall. His eyes snap up to meet mine and he jumps to his feet. "I'll call you back." He hangs up the phone without waiting for a response.

My sister runs in behind me still clinging to her damn towel. "Daddy—"

"You let her be Corbin's chosen?" I shout. "Have you lost your goddamn mind?"

Corbin enters behind her but thankfully he took a second to pull on some jeans. I ignore him completely. "Sir—"

"Oh!" she interrupts him again. "So we're just going to pretend that you're not fucking my best friend? But I can't fuck yours?" she yells from behind me.

I whirl around on her, and I want to strangle her. He won't love her. My sister isn't like other chosens. She was a fucking virgin. Saving herself for marriage. She hasn't had the life that Elli had. My parents have sheltered her. "He's just using you for pussy."

"Sin—"

"Maybe I'm just using him for dick." She crosses her arms over her chest, interrupting Corbin once more.

"Enough!" my father roars. "Kira, leave us."

"But, Dad—"

"Now," he snaps at her.

She turns, her hair whipping her in the face, and I'm surprised that Corbin follows her too even though my father didn't dismiss him. She slams the door shut behind them.

I turn on him. "A fucking chosen?"

He runs his hands through his hair, taking in a deep breath. "Corbin came to me requesting to be her Lord. He wanted her."

I snort. "I'm going to fucking kill him," I growl under my breath.

"We asked your sister. She wanted to be his chosen."

"You can't be serious."

"As Corbin's chosen, he can protect her."

"Tell that to Tyson Crawford," I bark, remembering what he went through his senior year.

He sighs. "What happened to Whitney Minson was unfortunate, but I trust Corbin with your sister. I believe him when he says he'll do what needs to be done to protect her."

My ass falls into the chair across from his desk. Jayce has been going on and on about what I missed during the vow ceremony. But Corbin? Not one word. Now I know why he didn't care to push me to go. He knew all along he'd be fucking my sister in front of the Lords. And that makes sense now as to why I watched Elli get into my sister's car outside the house of Lords. I thought she had called her to come pick her up, but I kept wondering how my sister got there so fast. Well, Kira was already there with Corbin.

I lift my head to glare at my father. "Do what you have to do to make Elli my chosen." There has to be something even though the ceremony has happened. I've made her mine, but I want everyone to fucking know it. I want the Lords to acknowledge it.

His eyes soften. "Easton. Nicholas was adamant that he never wanted her to be a chosen. He did not want her connected to the Lords in any way."

"He's dead," I growl, making him stiffen. "Has been since she was twelve. I think things have changed."

He rubs his temples.

I stand to my feet. "Did you know that she's been raped? For years?" His jaw clenches. "James was grooming her. She was a child, for fuck's sake," I snap.

He walks over to his safe and punches in the code before opening it up and grabbing a box. Then he comes over and places it in my lap. "Dad," I growl. "Are you fucking listening to me?"

"Open it."

I rip off the lid and look down, my breath catching at the box full of pictures. I pick one up. It's of Elli lying facedown on a wooden table. She's got to be around eighteen. Maybe seventeen. Her arms tied behind her back, her ankles also tied, and her legs brought up and secured to her arms—hog-tied. She's crying, tape over her mouth. I throw it to the floor and pick up another. She's naked in a room kneeling. The picture taken from behind showing marks across her back and neck. I toss it and grab another. She wears a collar with a leash, nothing more. Strapped to a black X with a blindfold over her eyes. "Where did you get these?" I ask barely over a whisper.

"Who do you think put the hit on James?"

My head snaps up to look at him wide-eyed. "I ... I don't understand. You knew what he was doing to her? All those years?" I'm not sure at what age he started raping her. But I do know that he lived in the same house as her for over five years. A lot can happen during that time.

He shakes his head. "No. I had my suspicions. But could never prove it. And the Lords, well, they don't care about how women are treated." He sighs. It's why he and my mom have tried so hard to shelter my sister. "But I got these in the mail one day. Anonymously. I made copies and sent those to a founding family member with the request to have him terminated." He fists his hands. "Nicholas would have burned the world down if he had been alive. He wouldn't allow anyone to hurt her. And I promised I'd take care of her. I failed him." He hangs his head.

I look at another. She can't be more than sixteen. She's face-down, ass up in the air and there's blood running down her bruised legs. The picture of her innocence taken tells me everything I need to know about how long it had been going on.

I look at my father. "Did you request me to have the assignment?"

"No. It was either someone wanting you to fail and get killed in the process. Or a joke that you were to kill him since I requested it."

"And his phone?" I ask.

He cocks his head.

"The assignment had me remove a finger and deliver his cell. There was something on it that the Lords wanted."

"No." He sits down.

I run a hand down my face. "I went through it. He had pictures of her. They started from when she was as young as thirteen." When he married her mother. They weren't all sexual. There were some of her in bed sleeping. In others, she was wearing a bathing suit and swimming in their pool. The older she got, the more X-rated they became. In some, she was looking at the camera, and in others, she had no clue.

"Maybe they knew he had evidence on his phone," my father offers as an explanation.

"I deleted them," I announce.

"You what?" he barks. "Easton, you can't tamper with what they want."

"I wasn't going to hand a phone over with inappropriate pictures of her on it. She was underage in some of them." I shake my head. No way in hell would I allow the world to have those. Who knows what the Lords would have done with them.

He stays silent but I can tell he's angry with me now. I grab another picture out of the box, unable to stop myself, and my chest tightens. She's crying, blood running from her busted lip and a handprint on her cheek.

How did he do this to her, and I not see it? I mean, it wasn't like I saw her on a day-to-day basis. Once I started at Barrington, my life revolved around the Lords. I lived at the house of Lords. Was always serving them. You don't get much freedom and downtime until you're a senior and are officially initiated in. But still, how did people not notice marks on her? Her mother? My sister? Did he keep her caged in a private location somewhere that no one could see what he was doing to her? I close the box and stand.

"Have you tampered with her birth control?"

I come to a stop and turn to face him but don't answer.

His jaw clenches. "Whatever you've done, reverse it. If you've replaced her pills, put the correct ones back. If you've given her something to counteract the shot, stop it."

I look away, my hands running through my hair. When I look back at him, I see disappointment in his eyes. "So you don't care if

Corbin knocks up Kira, but you care if I get the woman I love pregnant. Got it." I know my friend, and he's not wearing a condom when he fucks my sister. And who knows if she's being smart.

His face softens a second before he masks it. "Why do you think Linc married Laura?"

My brows pull together. "You know about that?"

"Have a seat, son." He gestures to the chair I stood from. I fall back into it. "I was best friends with her dad before he even got with Laura. They fell in love immediately. She was his chosen. They got married before they even graduated from Barrington. They wanted to start a family as soon as possible. Laura had a rough pregnancy. Bedridden, very sick. She went into labor six weeks early. Me and your mother were there when they wheeled her back for an emergency C-section. Elli wasn't breathing. Laura was bleeding. She ended up having a hysterectomy."

"What does this have to do with Lincoln?" I demand, wanting him to get to the point.

"Linc wants an heir. An Asher heir."

I frown. "But you just said Laura can't have more kids. Even if she could, she's not an Asher..." I trail off, finally understanding. "No." I shake my head. "Elli wouldn't..."

"Do you think he'd ask her to have his child?" he snaps. "He's inserting himself into that house to get close to Elli. He saw what James did. He'll do the same. You can't watch her twenty-four seven, son."

He's right, and I don't like the pit I feel in my stomach that I can't keep her from harm. That she'll end up like Whitney Minson all over again, and the Lords will cover it up like she never existed. I'd lose my mind, just like Tyson did. After she died, nothing and no one mattered to him. Hell, he gave up his future, knowing that one day he'll get his chance at revenge.

My father shakes his head. "Lincoln will wait for his opportunity, and he'll fuck her. Every chance he gets. Against her will or by manipulation. Whatever it takes. Elli is a good girl and I hate what she's been through, but she's been groomed for too long. You can't reverse that type of psychological damage. You know that firsthand."

My eyes narrow at that. "So you're saying I'm using her." Haven't I? I've pretended to be someone else to get her off. I used her body. That night at the Freak Show, afterward at her house. Fuck, she liked it. So did I. Which one of us is more fucked up? Even now, I don't want to be soft with her. I want her crawling on her hands and knees to me. Begging me to fuck her. To make her my whore. She's so pretty when she cries. When she begs. The way her body leans into mine. The way her lips part when she's begging to breathe.

"I'm saying when he gets the chance, he'll take it. And if you've tampered with her birth control, she'll be having his child. Not yours."

My hands fist at that thought. Elli will be my wife and she will have my kids. No one else's. "He warned me. Told me to take my chosen, and if I didn't, he'd do things to Elli. He already knew he had plans in place." How will I keep her from that house? That's her home. Elli may be willing not to go back but her mother will ask questions.

"There is one more thing." He sighs. "Amelia..."

"I don't want to talk about her." I shake my head.

He flexes his jaw. "Son, it's not going to go away. Plans have been made..."

"Without my approval," I argue.

"It's the way it is. You will do what's best for your children just like I'm doing what's best for you and your sister." I'm well aware he left my mother out of that statement. I know where she stands.

Getting up, I turn and leave his study, ending the conversation. I enter my room to find it empty. Rushing into the adjoining bathroom, I shove the door open, making her yelp in surprise.

"It's just me," I say, closing it behind me.

She stands in front of the sink in her dirty, ripped dress. Her knees are scraped along with her arms. She's covered in dried blood from her hand and due to the roughness of how I fucked her in the woods off the side of the road.

"Let me help you." I take a step toward her, and she crosses her arms over her chest. I stop and her eyes drop to the floor.

I don't like this Elli. The timid girl who acts afraid. I want my little demon who slaps me across the face, fights me knowing she can't beat me. Moving closer slowly, I gently grab the hem of her dress. "Lift your arms," I whisper.

Lifting her arms above her head, I pull the material off and let it fall to the floor. She stands before me in nothing but her underwear, her heels long forgotten over in the corner. I walk over to the shower and turn it on.

When I turn back to face her, she's standing there shaking, head down. Her bleach-blond hair matted around her face. There are twigs and leaves in it.

I reach out, grab her hand, and pull her into the shower. Placing her back against the sprayer, I face her and unwrap the duct tape and remove the shirt from her hand. I look at the wound. It's stopped bleeding. Honestly, it could probably use some stitches.

"I need to clean it," I tell her, and she nods.

I gently wash it and she stands silently still while I clean the rest of her, along with the brand on her leg and piercings. They're both healing so nicely. Leaning her head back, she closes her eyes and I wash her hair with my shampoo.

When it's rinsed clean, she lowers her head, and her bloodshot eyes meet mine. "I'm sorry," she whispers.

I grip her face in both of my hands. "Don't fucking apologize to me, Elli. You have nothing to be sorry for."

She sniffs, her chest rising. "I ... I don't know what's wrong with me." Fresh tears fill her eyes.

I tighten my hands on her face, making her whimper. "Listen to me, Ellington." I wait for the tears to spill free so she can see me clearly before I continue. "Nothing is fucking wrong with you. Not a goddamn thing."

"But—"

"But nothing," I snap, interrupting whatever bullshit she was about to say. "You're perfect."

She begins to cry harder at my words. I understand how fucked up they are. She's who she is because of the childhood she had. And I'm the way I am because of the Lords. They fucked us both up in different ways.

"It's you," she whispers, her plump lips trembling.

"What is?" I ask, my eyes searching hers.

She licks her lips, dropping her eyes in shame before whispering. "What I've always wanted."

I've known how she's felt about me for a couple of weeks now. Ever since I read her diary that night after I brought her home from the *Freak Show*. But to hear her say it out loud, I'm unable to put into words how it feels for her to acknowledge that.

I release her face and run my knuckles down her neck to feel her racing pulse. I press my body into hers, my free hand wrapping around her thin waist, holding her to me. "I'm not going anywhere, little demon," I say, and she sniffs, biting her bottom lip nervously. "I will be whoever you need, whenever you need me." I can be the guy who holds her when she needs to break, and I can be the guy who chases her into the woods and fucks her ruthlessly.

I'm willing to be her devil as much as she's willing to be my little demon. I never want her to second-guess my intentions. For some, pain is where they find comfort. Elli is that someone.

With my hand on her neck, I force her eyes to meet mine. I give her a soft kiss on the lips and her hands wrap around my neck, her left leg lifting to hook around my hip. My hand falls to it, gripping her soft skin.

I'm going to show this woman that one man can be everything she needs.

## ELLINGTON

MY HANDS REST ON THE EDGE OF THE COUNTER, HEAD DOWN as I stare at the two pills.

I started using drugs when I was sixteen. The day after I lost my virginity to James. I hated that he made me feel so good. I knew it was wrong. But my body had been starving for three years. Craving something I couldn't have. I cried when he left my room, and I stayed up all night, unable to close my eyes, afraid he'd come back and make me want more.

I tried to convince myself that I wasn't the problem. That I had sat and listened to so many couples over the years talking to my mother in her sessions that I wasn't as screwed up as I thought. I mean, some things I couldn't understand why someone would take pleasure in—like being pissed on. Why? I couldn't find the appeal of a golden shower, not even after watching videos. But then I realized that what I had experienced with James had felt good, no matter how wrong it was. So maybe what they had done also felt good.

To each their own, ya know. That's when I told myself I'd try anything at least once.

Grabbing the neck of the wine bottle, I pick up the pills with my other hand and toss them in my mouth. Closing my eyes, I toss back the bottle and swallow them with a big gulp. If I have to get through this day, I'll be fucked up.

Hanging my head, I suck in a deep breath and open my eyes. I stiffen when they land on a set of blue ones standing behind me.

Sin leans up against the doorframe dressed in an all-black three-piece suit with his arms crossed over his chest. Eyes on mine.

I've been staying here at his parents' house for five days now. I thought it would be odd staying here, but it's felt more like home than my actual home ever did. I get up, he takes me to Barrington. Then when I'm done, we come back here. It's felt normal. And there's a pit in my stomach that keeps telling me not to get attached. It won't last forever. It's like a dream you don't want to wake up from.

Wiping my wine-covered lips with the back of my hand, I turn to face him. I know he saw me take them. He's known I do drugs. He caught me at a party once in high school passed out on a bathroom floor. I woke up the next morning with a text telling me to watch who I get fucked up around. I never did thank him for that.

"Getting the party started early." The corners of his lips turn up into a smirk.

"Something like that." I push off the counter and walk over to him and he pushes off the doorframe. His hands going to the waist of my floor-length dress. I chose black silk. I thought it'd be fitting. I'm not celebrating shit. I'm in mourning. "Why don't you help me out."

"Anything." He wraps his arms around me, pulling my body flush with his.

"Fuck me." I gently kiss the corner of his lip. "I want your cum dripping out of my pussy when I give my toast."

He pushes me away, spins me around, and slaps my ass. "Bend over and pull up your dress," he orders, not needing to be told twice.

# TWENTY-NINE

# SIN

She's been quiet since we left my parents' house. A quick glance shows her in my passenger seat, head resting back, and eyes closed. The drugs starting to hit, if they haven't already. I've never been one to do drugs. I'm not even much of a drinker, to be honest. Part of being a Lord is always being at the top of your game. You don't want to be called out on an assignment and be too fucked up to complete it. Or worse, be too fucked up and get yourself killed.

I've never thought much about why she does them. I should have asked after the first time my sister called me crying in a bathroom at a party while Elli lay unconscious on the floor.

**Seventeen years old**

*I push my way through the kids at the house, Corbin right on my ass. We were hanging out with a couple of girls when my sister called me, frantic and hiding while at a party. Coming up to the bathroom door, I try to open it but find it locked. "Open the* damn door," I yell over the music, pounding my fist on it. "Kira." I hit it again.

It swings open the next second and I meet my sister's wide eyes. "Oh, thank God, Sin. I can't wake her up."

I push my way in, and Corbin enters, shutting it behind him. I see her best friend on the bathroom floor rolled up into the fetal position. Her skirt has ridden up on her thighs, showing off part of her ass. Her hair fanned out and covering parts of her face. "Elli?" I ask, shaking her shoulder.

Nothing.

"Ellington?" I push her hair away and open her eyes to see they're dilated. "What did she take?" I ask.

"I don't know." My sister sniffs. "I didn't see anything. Elli doesn't do drugs."

"She took something," I bark.

"Maybe she was drugged," Corbin offers. "How do you feel?" He turns to Kira, his hands on her shoulders, checking her eyes as well.

"Fine," she answers.

"Did anyone give you two drinks?" he snaps, making her jump.

"Yeah, but they poured them from the same bottle, and I feel okay," she cries, wrapping her arms around herself.

I roll her on to her back. "Ellington?" Still nothing. I place my fingers on her pulse and feel it racing. Yanking the hoodie up and over my head, I order to Corbin, "Hold her up."

He kneels behind her, lifting her to sit up by her underarms and I place my hoodie over her head. It's longer than the skirt she's wearing. And the last thing I need is a bunch of guys taking pictures or recording her pussy on display while I carry her out.

Once it's on, I place my arms underneath her legs and back, picking up her unconscious body. Corbin helps pull the hoodie down into place to cover whatever it can. "Get the door. And clear me a path," I bark out.

*"Come on." Corbin grabs my sister's hand and yanks her out of the bathroom as I carry Elli out of the party with all eyes on us.*

I took her home and placed her in her bed. I had every intention of going back to that party and demanding who the fuck drugged her, until I went to leave her room that night and found a bottle of pills on her nightstand. It pissed me off. My sister was right, Elli had never done drugs before. Not that I knew of anyway. Before her father passed, our families spent a lot of time together. I knew her.

I never thought to ask her why she started doing them. I should have. Maybe then I would have paid more attention to her life changing right before my eyes. It had to have been James. I saw the signs but pretended not to care. That I didn't have the time to get involved. She was sixteen, for Christ's sake. I knew not to fuck her. Because I'd be going into initiations soon. I knew touching her once and then not being able to for three years would be the worst kind of torture. Plus, I knew that she would one day be mine. I'd have the rest of my life with her.

That night was also the night that rumors started flying about her at our high school. They said she hooked up with several guys that night. She never denied it. I knew the truth, and she didn't seem to care what others thought. All she had to do was ask me, and I would have ripped their fucking heads off. I would've done anything for her then, just like I will now. The only difference is, now she doesn't have to ask for my help. I'll do whatever I think is necessary.

"You okay?" I ask, reaching out my hand to her leg. I gently grip her thigh and squeeze.

Her head falls to the side, her heavy eyes meeting mine, and she gives me a small smile. "I will be soon."

Fifteen minutes later, I'm pulling into the driveway of her

mother's house and the valet opens my door. I walk around, thanking the man who opens hers, but I grab it. "Elli, we're here." I reach in and grab her hand.

She manages to open her eyes and turns in the seat to place her heels on the ground. I pull up her dress, so she doesn't step on it and rip it. Once she's out, I don't let go.

Even though she's been mine since the last time I attended a party here two years ago, this is our first official public night together. By the time we leave this house, everyone will know that she belongs to me.

# ELLINGTON

### *Twelve years old*

"DAD? DAD?" I SCREAM. THE WORDS SO LOUD IT HURTS MY *own ears.*

*I run over and wrap my arms around his thighs, trying to lift him. "Dad, please," I beg, trying to lift them again. But he's too heavy.*

*I rush into the adjoining ballroom and grab a chair. I drag it across the floor until it's right beside him. I stand on it, grab his waist and try to lift once again. But my feet slip off the side of the cushion and I fall off the edge. The chair tips over with my arms still wrapped around him. The extra weight making the rope break, and we both go falling to the marble floor.*

*I can't breathe. My chest hurts and I grit my teeth trying to lift his weight off me. "Help me!" I manage to shout out. "Someone ... help me...Dad."*

*I'm able to roll him off and I straddle his stomach. "Daddy!" I shout, yanking on his shirt. Sobbing, my fists start hitting his chest, trying to bring him back but I know he's gone.*

. . .

I BLINK, MY HEAVY EYES ADJUSTING TO THE SECOND-STORY banister where I found my father's body hanging when I was twelve. I never visit the west wing. Not since that day.

The coroner had said there was nothing that I could have done. Or anyone for that matter. When I found him, he had been dead for several hours. I had just arrived home from school. My mother was out of town for the week.

I lay there with him on the floor for over an hour before someone found me. They had to pry me away from him. Mrs. Sinnett arrived and took me home with her to their house until my mother returned early from her trip the next day.

Sin stands silently next to me. He's been hovering more than before. I can't breathe without him watching ever since I had my breakdown on the side of the road and then again in his shower. Thankfully, he doesn't speak. He too stares up at the banister that once had a rope wrapped around it. Today, the grand staircase that leads up to it is decorated with white roses and twinkling lights. Makes me want to vomit. It's like she's celebrating my father's death. This house is over fifteen thousand square feet, and she couldn't do this in another wing? Or outside? Any other place on earth?

"Miss Asher. Mr. Sinnett." My mother's head of the house—Francis—nods to both of us. The way his eyes linger on mine tells me he knows I'm on ecstasy. He'll probably run to my mother and tell her. I hope he does.

He picks up one of the three candles that sits on the round table in the center. It's a got picture of my mother and Lincoln. They're hugging, both smiling on a beach. You can see their wedding rings. It's obviously very recent. Since they married. Why she chose to elope with him and then come back here and have a reception is beyond me. I can assure her that no one here gives a fuck that the Lords have passed her onto to another piece of shit. It's an endless cycle. I've already fucked four Lords. I can only hope that I'll never fuck another, let alone marry one.

Francis takes a box of matches and pulls one out, lighting the candle. Then the other two. Waving the match afterward blowing it out.

I shake my hand free of Sin's and numbly pick one up. Holding it to my face, I feel the heat from the flame. I've never been suicidal. But then again, is it something that takes time? Or do you just think *I want to die and end it all?* My father never seemed to be unhappy or gave the impression that he hated his life. Not that I could see. I think that was one of the biggest questions I had—why?

Why that day? Why this banister? Why no note to say good-bye? Had he decided he was going to end his life when he kissed me goodbye that morning before his driver took me to school? Did he have it planned the night before when he tucked me into bed and read me a bedtime story?

None of those things were out of character for him. He was always in a great mood. Made time for me and my mom. Of course, there were times the Lords called him to serve. And his work was very demanding. But he made sure to include us. To make sure we were aware that we were loved and valued.

The flame between my fingers blows around from my heavy breathing. It's crazy what one little match could do. What a flame so small could destroy. I want to see it light up the sky. I walk over to the stairs and hold it out, letting the tip of the flame kiss the flowers where they start to wrap around the banister, lighting them up.

"Ellington!" Francis yells at me and runs over, throwing water from the flower vase that sat on the round table to put it out.

I watch the smoke rise before disappearing with disappointment and jealousy. I wish I could do that. Just float away, fade into nothing.

He continues to curse under his breath and barks out orders to have the flowers replaced. Just like my mother did my father. I know she wasn't the same after he died. But it didn't take her long to fall in love with James. She thought he could do no wrong. He came in and swept her off her feet and made me fall to my knees.

When is it my turn? When do I get to destroy shit and get rewarded? Maybe I'll try my hand at that tonight. See how far I can get. Giving Francis my back, I walk off. I'm in the mood to fuck some shit up.

# THIRTY

# SIN

I look at the man who is glaring at my girl as she sashays away.
"You need to control—"

"If she wants to watch this house burn, I'll hand her the fucking matches." I yank them from his hand and pocket them in my dress slacks. Then I follow her.

She stumbles in her heels, and I come up beside her, wrapping my arm around her waist to stabilize her.

I watched the way she stared at the staircase. I remember my mother bringing her home to stay the night with us. She was a wreck. Cried for hours in my sister's room. The sounds she made broke my heart. It took everything in me not to run in and hold her in my arms. To tell her everything would be okay. But I knew that would be a lie. I knew that there were more storms to come before things calmed down. And I'm not only talking about the fact that she had lost her father.

He had been a well-respected Lord, making her mother a Lady. She would be given to another Lord. Elli's life was about to change in more ways than one. And honestly, my little demon hasn't been the same since.

We enter the ballroom to see all the round tables covered with white tablecloths, expensive crystal vases full of flowers. White leather chairs sit at each one. Silver and white balloons float over our head, covering the ceiling.

"Elli. Sin." A man nods at us dressed in a suit. "Let me show you to your table."

We follow him to the front of the room, and he sits us at one of the round tables that is directly next to a long table that faces the room.

I pull out her chair and she falls into it. I sit next to her.

"What can I get you?" he asks.

"A bottle of champagne," she answers.

"A water, please," I say, gripping a hold of her chair and pulling her closer to me. Then I slide my hand into the slit of her dress and grab her thigh.

She looks over at me and you can't mistake she's on something. Her eyes are heavy and dilated but she still looks every bit of the gorgeous woman I'm addicted to.

Ellington Asher is my drug. I'd never tell her she can't do something, but she won't do it without me by her side. She can't protect herself. Not like I can.

The server brings her bottle of champagne and a Markham crystal decanter filled with water. He places a champagne flute in front of her seat and a glass in front of mine. He fills hers with the champagne and she stops him. "I don't need that." She grabs the bottle from his hands and drinks from it.

I hide my smile while he fills my glass full of water with the decanter. "Thank you," I nod to him, and he walks away, frowning at her.

My eyes scan the room and I see my parents enter. They make their way to our table. I stand, hugging my mother and greeting my father. My sister and Corbin enter next. They too come over to sit with us.

I haven't spoken to Corbin since I found out he's fucking my sister. I get it. She's old enough to do what she wants, but he kept it from me. Would I have freaked out had he come to me and told me what was happening? Honestly, I'm not sure, but we'll never know now.

"Hey, guys. I was told that this is my table."

I look up to see Chance Beckham pulling out a seat and sitting down. He's a Lord. Attends Barrington and is a senior with us this year. He grew up with me, Jayce, and Corbin. We've never been close friends, though.

Not very many Lords know who he really is. But I do.

My hand is still on Elli's thigh, and I feel her stiffen. I look over at her, and her face has paled. Leaning into her ear, I whisper, "Are you going to get sick?" I watched her take two Mollies and now she's drinking. I can only imagine what her body is feeling right now.

Pulling away, I look over her face and she makes no move to acknowledge I spoke to her. "Elli?" I shake her leg a little. "You okay?"

She blinks, her eyes dropping to the table, and she nods, but I know she's lying.

Letting go of her leg, I grip her hand in mine. "Come on—"

I'm in the process of pulling her to stand, when the room bursts out into cheers and applauds. Everyone is on their feet, and I know her mother and Lincoln have entered the room from the other side. Making their grand entrance to walk down the aisle and sit at the head of the room.

Falling back into my seat, I turn to face her. I grip her face, forcing her to look at me. "Talk to me. What's wrong?"

"I'm fine." She swallows.

"You're lying," I growl. "What the fuck is it?"

She reaches up, shoving my hands off her face, and straightens her shoulders. Picking up the bottle of champagne, she takes a big gulp. "Drop it, Sin. I told you I'm fine." She wipes her painted red lips with the back of her hand.

# ELLINGTON

### *Eighteen years old*

I'M ON THE FLOOR, FACEDOWN, AND I CAN'T OPEN MY EYES. *They're too heavy, but I can hear them talking. Laughing at me. I wish I cared enough to get up and leave. But I can't. The drugs have kicked in, and I'm long gone. Lincoln did just what James told him to do while he fucked me. I'm exhausted. They tossed me to the side once they were done. Like the trash he tells me I am.*

*Instead of feeling embarrassed, I feel good.*

*Hair is pushed from my face and knuckles gently run down my cheek.*

*"Take her to her room," I hear James order from behind me, sitting at his desk.*

*Hands flip me over onto my back and I'm lifted into a set of arms. One of mine hangs off to my side while the other lies across my stomach. I manage to open my eyes and look up to see the kid carrying me out of James's office.*

*The one that was sitting on the couch that looked around my age. His green eyes drop to look over my face and run down my body. I'm still naked from the waist down.*

*If I could fight him, I would, but I can't even feel my own lips let alone get him to let me go.*

*He pushes my bedroom door open and places me on my bed. Gripping the hem of my shirt, he yanks it up and over my head and then unfastens my bra.*

*"N-no—" I manage to say, my tongue heavy.*

*He smiles down at me. It's not soft or inviting. Reaching out, he runs his knuckles over my face once again. His thumb then making its way over my parted lips. "Don't worry, Ellington. I'm not allowed to touch you. Not yet anyway." Leaning down, he places his face in front of mine, his hand dropping to curl around my neck, holding me in place as if I had the strength to fight him. "But one day, you will belong to me. And when that day comes, you'll beg for drugs to numb the pain I will cause."*

I throw back another drink of the champagne, my eyes on the man who sits across from me. It's him. The kid from James's office that night. I haven't seen him since then. I never knew what he meant, and I never asked anyone.

James would have lied, and I had only ever seen Lincoln one more time at the party that night James was killed. I thought maybe I had dreamed it, made it up in my head. I was rolling my ass off. Thought my imagination got the best of me.

But here he is, at my mother's reception. *Why?* Who the fuck is he? And why is he at this table? I know why I'm here. I'm the bride's daughter. Sin is my date. Mr. and Mrs. Sinnett have been friends of my mother's since before I was born. Kira brought Corbin. This kid doesn't fit. I know he's a Lord, but so what? Almost every male in this room is.

I ignore Sin's eyes on me. I'm not ready to go there with him. How much can he find out about me before he just throws his hands up and says *fuck it, you're not worth all the trouble?* I don't want to find out.

I'd take Sin any day over what others would do to me if given the chance. Easton Sinnett may want to break me, but he's the only one that could put me back together after he's done.

I trust Sin with my life. Anyone else, not so much.

My mother and Lincoln make it to the front of the room and

take their place at the table next to us. It faces the ballroom. Giving everyone a look at the happy couple. I want to puke.

When Sin asked me if I was going to be sick, I wanted to laugh, but now I can taste the bile rising. I swallow it down with another drink of champagne. Out of the corner of my eye, I see Mrs. Sinnett frown at me. I hate how weak I look to her right now. She has always been a second mom to me. Sometimes more than my own.

When I found my father dead, she held me while I cried in Kira's room. She rocked me to sleep like I was an infant needing to be coddled. The next day, my mother showed up to get me and she was so distraught she never even looked at me. She never asked me if I was okay. She never once thought to offer me support. I was the one who found him, for fuck's sake.

I know she was his wife, but I was his daughter. It didn't matter. I never did. Why would I then? Why would I now?

The kid leans over to Sin and Corbin, saying something I don't hear, making them both laugh. Of course, Sin knows him. They're the same age. Both Lords. Have lived at the house of Lords since freshman year. Thankfully, Barrington is large enough that you can easily avoid someone who you don't want to run into. And I've never had any classes with them because they are seniors.

I throw back another drink and close my eyes. I take in a deep breath, feeling the room spin. I want it to swallow me up. A hand on my thigh makes me open my eyes and I come face-to-face with a set of pretty blue ones. They search mine before dropping to my chest that the black, silk dress shows off. He doesn't say anything, but I can see the question all over his face.

*Am I okay?*

No. I'm losing my goddamn mind. But it won't be the first time. And honestly, I'm tired of fighting to stay sane. Going crazy would be a vacation.

"We want to thank you all for joining us today," I hear Lincoln call out to the room that quiets down for his speech. "Laura and I couldn't be more thrilled to welcome you all to our home..."

That bile returns and my chest heaves as I force it down. *Their home?* I wish I had that candle to set it on fire.

"To celebrate the beginning of the rest of our lives," he finishes, and everyone cheers, clapping like he's the president addressing the United States of America.

He's not important. I know that much. He's not as powerful as my father or James was. So why does he think he is?

"Like my husband just said," my mother starts, and I watch her smile to their guests. I hate to admit that she looks lovely in her white dress. It's off the shoulders, tight fitting, showing off all of her curves. She wears a set of pearls around her neck that my father got her for their wedding anniversary just two months before he passed away. I want to rip them off her neck. She doesn't deserve them. "We are very lucky to have so many friends and loved ones to share this special day with us." She raises her glass. "Thank you again, for all the love and support..."

I'm unable to hold in the laughter that comes from my numbing lips. The room falls silent, and I feel eyes on me. "To the happy couple." I lift the champagne bottle and then down a big gulp. Time to fuck shit up. I can't take it anymore. I want to watch it all go up in flames like the flowers.

"Elli," Kira whispers, leaning into the table.

I push my chair back and stand, turning to face the table at the front of the room and smile. "Really, Mom, do you expect us to believe you actually love him?"

People gasp at my question and my mother's injected lips thin. Lincoln stretches his neck, fixing his tie. Good, I want to make the bastard as uncomfortable as I can.

"I mean, he's a Lord." I laugh at that. "Did you pick him, or did the Lords tell you he was the one you had to marry?"

"Ellington," she snaps, walking out from behind her table.

"Because between Dad and James ... you married down." My laughter grows. "Am I right?" I turn to face the crowded room full of guests.

A hand grabs my upper arm, and I'm being dragged backward. I almost trip over my heels but I manage to stay upright as I'm shoved through a door.

# THIRTY-ONE

## SIN

"I 'm sorry about that, ladies and gentlemen." Linc stands from his chair. "Elli's ... not well." He goes on, walking away from the table. "Just give us a few minutes." He rushes out of the room.

I push my chair back and jump up from my seat. "Easton," I hear my mother call out, but I ignore her as I follow them.

Shoving open the door to the adjoining room I saw Laura drag Elli into, I see we're back in the west wing where she stood and stared at the banister that her father hung himself from.

Elli now stands in front of her mother who has her finger in her face.

"You're not needed here. This is a family matter," Lincoln states, stepping in front of me. I punch him in his face.

He doubles over, covering it with his hands. "Je-sus," he mumbles.

"What the fuck?" Laura snaps, looking over at me. Then her eyes go back to her daughter. "What the hell is wrong with you?" she demands. "You're fucking on something, aren't you? Drugged up, as usual."

Elli starts laughing. "Don't act like you care now, Mom. You've never cared before."

"Elli—"

"You've never cared about me at all." Her voice rises.

"Stop being so damn dramatic." Her mother rolls her eyes.

I hear the door open behind me and I look over my shoulder to see Chance has followed us to get a view of the show. Giving him my back, I dismiss him.

Laura notices and then looks back to her daughter as well. "I don't want to see you again until you're sober." Her heels clap on the marble as she walks over to her husband. She grabs his arm and starts to drag him back to the party when Elli speaks.

"Why him?" she demands, hands fisted down by her sides. "Why out of all the Lords did you pick him?" Her eyes fill with tears. "He's nothing like Dad was."

Laura turns and walks back over to Elli. Hands on her hips. "Your father was a self-absorbed son of a bitch. Just like you," Laura growls.

Elli's eyes narrow on her mother. "Father was too good for you," she states.

I step closer, expecting her mother to slap her, put her hands on Elli in some way. If she does, I'll break her nose too. I'm not above hitting a woman. Her face will match her husband's.

Instead, Laura has the audacity to look wounded by Elli's words. "You're just like your father. And that's exactly why you'll die like him." A tear runs down Elli's cheek, her chest heaving as her breathing picks up. "Do us all a favor and get it over with. Take a few extra drugs next time. Just don't die in this house." Laura snorts. She storms off but only to turn back after a few steps, deciding she's not done. "I have given you everything. And this is how you treat me, you ungrateful little bitch?"

Elli throws her head back laughing, the motion making her stumble in her heels, throwing her off balance. I step forward to catch her, but she rights herself. "Seriously? You think I asked to be raped?"

"Raped?" Her mother's mouth drops. "You think I didn't know that you sat outside my office listening to my sessions? You think I didn't know that you tricked James into fucking you?"

Elli's watery eyes go wide, and she gasps. "Tricked him? I did no such thing—"

"You really think that I wasn't aware that you were a whore who spread her legs for *my* husband?" She's yelling in Elli's face.

Ellington doesn't say anything, instead she stares at her mother with tears in her eyes. The only parent she had just admitted that she knew what was happening but chose not to protect her. Not to stop it.

"I saw everything. And you should thank your lucky stars for James. Because when I wanted to ship you off, he was the one who talked me into letting you stay under my roof." With that, Laura spins around, and her narrowed eyes meet mine before they go to her husband. "Get her the fuck out of my house," she orders him and then she storms off into the other room, not giving a shit about her daughter.

I watch Elli silently cry, her pretty eyes dropping to the floor, her small body shaking.

"Chance, you heard my wife," Lincoln growls, wiping blood off his face. "Take her home." Then he too exits, following after Laura.

Chance moves toward Elli and I step in front of him, blocking his way. "Touch her, and I'll break your fucking arm," I warn.

He halts, his eyes going to my girl then back to me. Raising his hands, he nods to me once and starts backing up until he turns and walks back into the ballroom.

I PLACE HER IN MY BED AND GO TO STEP AWAY BUT SHE reaches out, gently tugging on my arm. "I'm just getting undressed," I assure her, and she lets go. I remove my button-up and slacks. Then I shove my boxer briefs and socks off until I'm naked and crawling into bed next to her. On my side, I prop myself up on my right arm and run my free hand over her tear-streaked face.

She hasn't spoken since her mother turned her back on her and left her standing broken all over again. I walked over, took her hand, and escorted her out of the house. The night was over.

Her heavy dilated eyes open to meet mine. "Lie to me again."

I frown. "I've never lied to you."

"When ..." She licks her lips. "When we were on the boat, and you told me you loved me." Her eyes seem to soften. "I want to hear that again."

She thinks I lied? Why would I lie? To get between her legs? I've been there for years. Elli has never been the kind of girl who needs to be told what she wants to hear to get in her pants.

My hand slides down her stomach to her pussy. Arching her back, her eyes fall closed as I play with her piercing. Gently pulling and rubbing before I slide a finger into her. She's wet enough. The fact that I came in her just two hours ago helps.

Plus, she's still on the drugs. Her body is going to react to the simplest touch, lightest kiss.

I lie flat on my back, grabbing her arm and pulling her on top of me.

Her eyes spring open and I look up at her now straddling me. "Fuck me," I order. "Sit that tight cunt down over my cock and fuck it. Get yourself off, Elli. I want to watch you come."

She's abandoned her previous request for my own, just like I knew she would, and adjusts herself to slide onto my hard dick.

My neck arches and I hiss in a breath. I've never had a woman on top before. Her hips start to move back and forth, her hands on my chest. She's gentle. Slow and steady, but it feels amazing.

I open my eyes and lift my hands to wrap around her neck and squeeze. Her delicate hands grip my forearms, but her hips don't stop. She fucks me as if her life depends on it.

*It does.*

"That's it, Elli. I feel your pussy getting wetter. Come on, little demon. Be my good whore and come for me."

She swallows against my hands and her cunt clamps down on my dick while her fingers loosen their grip on my forearms, arms falling to her sides. She comes as her head falls back.

I roll to my left, pushing her onto her back and letting go of her neck.

Her body convulses and she coughs while breathing heavily. Her face wet with tears and my cock covered in her cum.

I lean down, my tongue licking at her parted lips to taste the lingering champagne and tears. It's a delicious combination.

"That's what it feels like to love you, Ellington Jade Asher. It's goddamn fucking consuming. Suffocating." I slide my hand underneath her head to grab her hair and yank it back, giving me access to her neck.

I run my tongue over her racing pulse to her jaw. And over to her ear. "I'll never lie to you, little demon. I will beat that ass black and blue. I'll fuck that pretty mouth and I'll take this cunt whenever I want. But always remember, Elli, that I love you. And no man on this earth will ever come close to feeling what I feel for you. And if he thinks he does, I'll rip his fucking heart out." Just the thought of another man loving her makes me see red. No one can be who she needs like I can. "Do you understand me, little demon?"

"Y-yes," she answers breathlessly.

"That's my good girl."

# THIRTY-TWO

# SIN

I walk into the house of Lords and enter the kitchen. I left Elli passed out in my bed back at my parents' house because I had a meeting an hour ago. Thought I'd run by here to grab a few things from my room on my way back to her.

"Sin, where the fuck have you been, man?" Gunner asks, slapping my back.

"Busy." I avoid his question.

A few guys sit around the large kitchen table. One of them is Matt. He's got his head down while he texts away on his cell, but you can't miss the bruises and swollen eye that he has. They look new.

"Matt, you look like shit." Chase notices him and laughs. "Get in a fight?"

"Shut the fuck up," he growls, getting to his feet and walking out.

Jimmy plops down beside Prickett and smiles. "Heard Ryat fucked him up while they were on their assignment."

Prickett ignores him. I'm not sure what's going on between all the guys in the house. I haven't been here much ever since they had their vow ceremony. But I've seen it every year for the past three. Once the guys get their chosens, there's chaos between the Lords. Men fighting over pussy they want and can't get.

Every Lord that is attending Barrington has a room here until they graduate, but it's not like we are required to check in every night. We're allowed to come and go as we please. Especially the seniors. Once the Lords take chosens, they're hardly ever here. Too busy out fucking anything they can.

"I don't know why you guys fight over chosens." Chance shakes his head. "They're nothing special."

"They're like anything else. Some are better than others," Gunner agrees, taking a bite of his sandwich. "Mine's worth it." He gives a sly smile with his mouthful.

I'd kill a man if it meant I could take Elli as my chosen. No questions asked.

"Yeah, well..." Chance leans back in his chair. "Mine sucks."

"In a good way, right?" Chase wiggles his eyebrows.

"No. She fucking sucks. All she does is cry. All the fucking time. I mean, I like using women, but I want one that actually enjoys the sex."

Prickett gets up from his seat. "You shouldn't have picked a virgin, dude."

Chance snorts. "It wasn't my choice. Her family owes mine. She's payment." He rolls his eyes. "I've got to chase down whores just to get off."

"Wait." Chase lifts his hands. "You've got a chosen that cries, and that's keeping you from getting off?" He snorts. "Just gag her so you don't have to hear her cry if it bothers you that much."

Chance has his face in his hands. He drops them and looks up at Chase who comes to stand next to me. "I've tried that. Nothing works. She sobs. Like, just looking at me upsets her. She's terrified." He shakes his head. "Some men might be into that, but I sure as fuck am not. And I'm afraid every time I gag her that she's going to make herself vomit. I don't want to kill the poor thing."

Chase slaps my back, walking over to me but looking at Chance. "Take some notes from Sin here. He found his own whore and won't even touch his chosen."

Chance sits back in his seat, his eyes on mine. He wants Elli. I don't blame him, but how things went down last night at the reception proves my suspicion. I almost feel sorry for the bastard, that he'll never know what it's like to be with my little demon.

Turning, I walk out of the kitchen and to my room. I've just slammed the door shut when someone knocks on it. I yank it open. "What?" I bark. My eyes hardening when I see who stands before me. "What the fuck do you want?" I look out into the hall to see we're alone.

He steps into my room, pushing me out of the way in the process. Grabbing my door, he closes it shut behind him. "I think we can help one another out."

I snort. "I don't need help." *What the fuck is he talking about?*

He pulls his cell out of his pocket and I stand silently, wondering what the fuck he's doing while he scrolls through messages. When he finds what he wants, he holds his phone up into my face. My wide eyes go to his.

Nodding, he adds, "Like I said, I think we can help each other out." Locking his screen, he drops his phone to his side and steps into me. "Unless you want to lose everything." He shrugs carelessly. "Up to you." He turns and grabs the doorknob, ready to leave my room, but I reach out and slam my hand on it, keeping it shut.

He turns and walks farther into my room, and I turn to face him. I've got two options. One—let him live. Two—kill him right here, right now. "You've got five minutes," I say. Depending on what he has to say will depend on which option I choose.

## ELLINGTON

I wake and roll over onto my stomach, moaning as I bury my face into the soft pillow. A warm hand runs up and down my back softly before grabbing my shoulder and pulling me to face a wide-awake Sin. I also don't miss the fact that he's already dressed in jeans and a T-shirt. I'm still naked.

"What time is it?" I mumble. God, it feels like I've been sucking on sandpaper all night and my head is throbbing. I should know better than to drink while rolling.

"Almost noon," he answers.

I cover my face with my hands. "Why didn't you wake me?"

"Well, I figured after the night you had, you needed as much rest as you could get."

Sitting up, I push the rat's nest I call hair from my face.

He gets out of bed, and I watch him walk into his adjoining bathroom, remembering last night. My mother admitting that she knew I slept with James. But obviously not the truth about it. She wanted to ship me off. He talked her into letting me stay in my own home? What had James said to her?

Exiting the bathroom, Sin hands me two Advil and a glass of water. "Take these."

I toss them in my mouth and swallow.

"Get dressed."

I fall onto the bed, stretching my arms above my head. He watches me, his head tilted to the side. I wonder what he's thinking. Is he visualizing tying me to his bed? To use me for the day? I'd gladly let him. Or fight him. Either way, I'd enjoy it. I just want him to take my ability to think away. "Why?" I finally ask when he just stares at me.

"I've got somewhere I want to take you," he answers vaguely and turns to go enter his closet. A second later, he returns, and my heart picks up at seeing the black silk blindfold hanging from his hand.

"Right now?" I pout.

"Right now." He grabs the duvet and yanks it back to expose my naked body to him. He slides a hand down my inner thigh, and I spread them for him. Cupping my pussy, he lowers his lips to mine and whispers, "Trust me, you want to see it." Then he pulls away and tosses the blindfold on my chest.

I take in a deep breath and pray that the medicine kicks in soon.

---

I'M DRESSED AND IN HIS CAR IN LESS THAN THIRTY MINUTES. He orders me to put the blindfold on before he'll go anywhere, so I slide it on, blanketing me in darkness. I like it.

But nervousness takes over and I start bouncing my knees. What the hell are we doing? Is he not taking me home? Although, that is the last place I want to go. I'm sure my mother has packed all of my shit and kicked me out. If I were younger, she'd probably ship me off to boarding school like she tried to do back then. Or Lincoln would.

Either way, I can't live there anymore. Not after what Linc said to me when I was supposed to have dinner with them. I was too young to know any different with James. He trapped me. I won't allow Linc to do the same.

A hand touches my thigh and I jump.

"You're okay," comes Sin's calming voice, and I take in a deep breath.

I haven't mentioned what he said last night to me when I asked him to lie. I remember every word he spoke. Even though I almost passed out. He told me he loved me. It had been real, so he says. But was it?

I don't know what love is. I've never experienced it. I think there's different types of love out there for all types of people. Do I love Sin?

Absolutely. In the *I'll kill for you* kind of way. He could make a saint unholy with only his voice. He could make an angel fall from heaven with just a single look.

And me? Well, I'm no saint or angel. I'm a slave for him. I couldn't deny him anything if I tried.

The fact that he'd rip someone else apart for just thinking they could love me turns me on. It's the fucked-up toxic side of me that wants to test it.

He softly rubs his warm hand up and down my thigh and I feel my body relaxing into the seat, hoping I don't fall asleep. I'm still exhausted. My body sore and tired.

The radio plays, drowning out my heavy breathing and quieting any conversation we could potentially have. I don't mind it. I'd rather not discuss what I did last night.

My body jerks and I realize I had fallen asleep. It's still dark and I can feel the blindfold over my eyes and his hand still on my thigh. If he notices, he doesn't mention it.

The car rolls to a stop and his hand disappears for a second before I hear car doors opening and closing. He grabs my hand, pulling me out, and places his hands on my shudders to get me to stand where he wants me.

Then the blindfold is removed from my face, and I blink a few times to adjust to the bright sunlight.

A house sits before me. Three stories tall, nothing but glass and black brick. "What ... what is this?" I turn to ask him.

He doesn't say anything. Instead, he takes my hand and pulls me up the seven stairs and pushes open the two large stained-glass doors. We enter the house and I look around at the white marble flooring and black accent inlays. The walls are a dark gray and there's a grand staircase to the right.

"Did you rent this out?" I ask him.

"Have a look around," he says, gesturing for me to step farther into the house.

I take a right and see it's a formal dining room. A large table that can seat a party of twenty is facing several floor-to-ceiling windows overlooking the woods. Black curtains are open to show the perfectly manicured lawn. I take a left, entering the kitchen. It's like the rest, black-and-white floor with black countertops but the backsplash is red to give it a pop of color.

There's a piece of paper on the island. I pick it up and my heart races as I read the words.

*Welcome home, little demon.*

I look up to see him leaning up against the island. Arms crossed over his chest, eyes on mine. "Sin," I whisper, my throat closing up. My eyes quickly scan the room, waiting for the punch line. This has to be a joke, right?

Walking over to me, he cups my face. His free hand wraps around my waist and pulls me into his hard body.

"I don't understand." I bite my bottom lip nervously.

"I bought us this house, Elli."

"But why?"

Letting go of my face, he reaches down and grips my thighs, lifting my ass to sit on the island. He steps between my parted legs. "Because I wanted you to have a place to come home to. Our home." A soft smile tugs at his lips while the blood rushes in my ears. "A place for you to feel safe."

I just stare at him, trying to slow my racing heart.

"Say yes, Elli. Tell me you'll move in with me."

Where else would I go? This man I'd do anything for is giving me the best gift I've ever received. He wants to live with me. Here in our house. Just the two of us. I'm not one of those girls that need to be married. I actually never want to get married. But to live with him? To be his every second of every day? That sounds like heaven to me. "Yes." I nod, sniffing. "Of course."

He picks me up off the island and I giggle. Actually giggle like a lovestruck teenager. He carries me back to the formal dining room table and sets me on my feet. Then he's ripping off my shirt, shorts, and underwear.

"What are you doing?" I ask, still laughing. I've never felt happiness like this before. It's like bubbling inside me wanting to escape.

"I'm going to have my first meal in our home." He lifts me up, placing my ass on the table. Pushing on my chest, he forces me to lie down. I put my heels on the table and spread my legs for him like the good girl he wants me to be. I'm so fucking needy for him. "Touch yourself for me," he urges me.

Sitting back in the chair at the head of the table, he watches me play with myself, my fingers dipping in and out of my pussy. I hear him shift in the seat and then hear him removing his belt from his jeans.

"Come on, little demon," he coaxes, encouraging me. "Make yourself come all over this table."

My fingers pick up speed, going deeper, and my hips lift off the surface. My heavy breathing and moaning fill the room. I'm close. My body rocks back and forth, my heels dig into the table, and I whimper.

"Sin—" I'm so close. I can feel it. Almost there...

He rips my hands away from my pussy, and I cry out.

"Sin?" I sit up, panting. "What—"

He wraps his hand around my throat, cutting off my words. He leans in, his lips tenderly kissing mine. "Lie back down, Elli."

I do as I'm told, and he grabs my hands. Wrapping his belt around my wrists, sliding the end through the silver buckle, he then presses my arms to my upper chest. He takes the remainder of the belt around my neck before tying it off, securing my wrists to my neck.

He pulls my ass to the end of the table and kneels, throwing my shaking legs over his shoulders. He licks my cunt and I arch my back. "You're going to come all over my face, Elli. The first meal I have, will be your pussy."

# THIRTY-THREE

# SIN

I get out of bed when I hear the doorbell ring. A look at my phone on the nightstand shows it's five in the evening. *Right on time.*

Leaning over the bed, I push her blond hair from her face. "Elli, wake up." I kiss her warm cheek, making her stir.

"Hmm?" she mumbles.

"Wake up and get dressed."

Her eyes flutter open, and she looks around aimlessly before they land on mine. The doorbell rings again and she sits straight up, eyes now wide.

"Get dressed and meet me in the dining room," I say, pulling on my T-shirt from earlier and getting my jeans on. I exit the room without further explanation.

Opening the front door, the man smiles at me as he enters. "Good evening, Easton."

He follows me into the formal dining room, and he sits down at the table that I fucked Elli on just hours ago. His briefcase right where she lay wide open for me. Opening it up, he pulls out the papers that are needed and hands them to me.

I quickly scan them over, making sure everything is there that I requested. Nodding, I lay them on the table, and he pulls out a pen for me. I'm signing the last page when she enters.

"What's going on?" She yawns, pushing her tangled hair from her sleepy eyes.

"We've got to make it official." I pull out the chair and she sits down on it. "This is Mr. Tate. He has brought everything we need to sign in order to close on the house."

She frowns at first but then nods.

"Everywhere you see a yellow tab is where you need to sign," I inform her, pointing at the one on the first page.

"Okay." She licks her lips before looking up at me. She looks like she wants to question it. As if I'd have any doubts that I want to spend the rest of my life with her in this house. I don't. In fact, she has no clue what I have planned. For her, for us. Nothing short of death will take her from me.

Her eyes drop to the papers, and she signs the first one. Then I reach down and grab the corner of the paper, pulling it back just enough for her to see the tab at the bottom of the next page. After she signs, I do the next.

When I pass the fifth page, I look up at the man who sits across from her, and he gives me the slightest nod. I smile to myself, turning the page to the next.

My cell vibrates in my pocket, and I pull it out with my free hand to see it's a text.

See you tomorrow.

I ignore it, pocketing it once again, and giving Elli all my attention as she continues to go through the paperwork, signing her name. She has no clue what I'm doing, but she will eventually. And then it'll be too late.

256

## ELLINGTON

LAST NIGHT WAS OUR FIRST NIGHT IN OUR HOME. AFTER THE guy left with all the paperwork signed, Sin carried me to our bed. We never left. Not even for dinner.

It was weird but nice knowing that we were going to wake up together. Knowing this is going to happen every day makes me smile.

I've never slept so peacefully in my life. The way his arms wrap around me makes me feel safe. And the way he fucked me... God, even the sex feels different, and it's amazing. I'm on a high that I've never reached with drugs before.

I roll over and reach out for him but feel nothing but the cool sheets. My eyes open when I hear the bathroom door opening.

"Good morning, little demon." He walks over to me and kisses my forehead.

My eyes fall shut. "Where are you going?" It's a Saturday. We said we were going to stay home all day and do nothing but each other.

"I have to go to the house of Lords. Take care of some business." He kisses my forehead again. "I'll be back before you get up."

"Okay," I whisper. I hear the faint sound of the doors opening and closing as he makes his way out of the house. I pull the covers up to my neck when my cell rings.

Opening my eyes, I reach out and pick it up off the nightstand to see it's Kira. "Hello?"

"Hey," comes her soft voice.

I sit up, pushing my back into the white padded headboard, bringing the covers with me. "Hey, everything okay?" I haven't spoken to her since the wedding reception two nights ago.

"Are *you* okay?" she asks.

"I'm fine, Kira." I sigh, dropping my eyes to the comforter.

"I ... I feel like so much is going on right now. With you and with me. We haven't really had a chance to stop and talk. Just hang out."

"We've been busy." I love my friend, but I also understand that she's seeing someone. I've never been one of those friends that is needy. I can go days, weeks even, without talking to you and then call you out of the blue and pick up where we left off, like we never went a day without seeing one another.

"Let's get together tonight?" she suggests. "You, me, and the guys."

"I'd love that." She still hasn't come out and told me she's seeing Corbin but the fact that she was with him at the reception was all I needed to know. I also saw how Sin didn't speak to him once. So I'm guessing that's not going well. I haven't told her we moved into this house. Well, technically neither one of us have moved our things in. Thankfully, the house came fully furnished, so all we have to do is get our clothes and a few other important things.

"Great, I'll have Corbin message Sin."

We say our goodbyes and I close my eyes, lying back down to get some more rest. My body is exhausted.

MY EYES OPEN WHEN I HEAR THE SOUND OF THE FRONT DOOR opening. Looking at my cell, I see he's been gone for almost two hours. I stretch, feeling good that I went back to bed after talking to Kira.

A smile tugs at me lips when I hear the sound of his shoes walking to the bedroom. Our bedroom.

Fuck, it's crazy to know that he just came home to me. The bedroom door opens, and he enters. I instantly sit up. "Everything okay?" I ask when I notice the way his jaw is set in a hard line. His pretty blue eyes narrowed in anger.

"Fine," comes his clipped answer as he walks over to my side of the bed.

"Sin—"

He grabs a hold of my hair and yanks me down to the bed, cutting me off. My breathing accelerates when he leans over and places his face in front of mine. "You know the best part about coming home to you?"

I whimper at his words, but I manage to whisper, "What?"

With his free hand, he runs his knuckles over my nipple piercing. "That you're already naked in our bed waiting for me to use you."

I lift my hips off the mattress, my pussy clenching. "Yes," I agree. Sin can use me any way he wants, whenever he wants. I'm his.

# THIRTY-FOUR

# SIN

I enter our bedroom to find her lying in bed, her phone in her hand watching a music video on YouTube. "We're leaving in thirty," I inform her.

She sits up straighter, her cell falling to the bed. She's been in here all day. I'm not sure if it's the drugs wearing off that make her tired or if she's just trying to catch up on her rest, but I like it. Her naked in our bed, all day long. I've used her for most of it. But we have plans.

"Corbin called. He and Kira want to go out."

"Oh." Her voice gives her away. She already knew. I know Kira called her earlier this morning after I left the house. They set it up. Like making me hang out with Corbin will help our already tense friendship. It won't. But we're going to a club, so it's not like we'll actually be doing much talking.

"Sin, I'm going to need more than thirty minutes." She looks at the clock on her cell.

I grip a hold of her neck, forcing her back to the bed, and she sucks in a sexy breath as I run my tongue over her lips. Fuck, I'll never get enough of her smell, her taste. "If you're not willingly walking out of this house in thirty minutes, then I'll throw you over my shoulder and carry you out."

I don't want to go but I said we would, and I'm a man of my word.

Her lips smile against mine. "Promise?"

"Always." I push my lips to hers softly, giving her a kiss, and her hips rise up off the bed, wanting more. She's not getting it. Not right now. Pulling away, she lifts her hands and runs them through my hair. I groan, my eyes falling closed.

I love tying her up and playing with her, but I also love when she touches me.

"We could stay in," she offers. "I'm sure our bed is more fun than wherever we're going." She continues to play along as if she has no clue. I'll let her.

"Don't worry, little demon. I'll be bringing you back home and tying you to this bed."

"Sin," she whimpers, her hips lifting again.

"You'll lie here next to me the rest of the night, helpless, until morning when I finally decide to let you come."

Her hands yank on my hair, pulling my head to the side, and she sinks her teeth into my neck, making my cock rock fucking hard before she sucks on it. I don't stop her. I love that she wants to mark me. I want the world to know I belong to her just as much as I want them to know she belongs to me. "You're going to run out of time," I remind her.

"Maybe I just want you to drag me out of this house."

Pulling back, I slide my arms under her legs and lift her out of bed as she fights me while laughing.

## ELLINGTON

I CHOSE A BLACK PLEATED MINI SKIRT AND A WHITE CROP TOP with a pair of Vans. Comfortable but still stylish. Kira messaged me earlier and informed me that Corbin and Sin agreed on Blackout tonight. I wasn't surprised they picked a club instead of going to a dinner. Somewhere that required actual conversation.

My hair is up in a high pony, and I didn't put much makeup on. Just some powder, blush, and lip gloss, and topped the look off with mascara. It's enough to cover my face but definitely not full glam.

We're in his car while he drives us down the curvy two-lane roads before he pulls into the back of a parking lot. It's packed but I'm not surprised. Everyone comes to Blackout to get fucked up. I see a familiar car pull up and park a few spots from us and I jump out to see Kira exit Corbin's passenger side.

She runs to me and throws her arms around me. God, I've missed her so much. "You have so much to catch me up on," I whisper as I watch Sin eye his best friend up and down. Obviously still not happy about this, but if I know my best friend, he sure as hell can't stop it.

"Let's go get fucked up." She gives me a big smile.

Corbin takes her hand and Sin grabs mine, slowing me down to let them walk a little ahead of us. I look up at him and he glares at me. "No drugs."

His words catch me off guard and I come to a complete stop. He does as well and turns to face me. "Excuse me?" I demand. I know I've got a problem, but he's never seemed to care before. Why would he now?

"You can drink all you want, but do not take any drugs," he commands, eyes boring into mine.

I want to be mad. Tell him to fuck off. I wasn't planning on doing any, but now I want to. Who the fuck does he think he is? We move in together and he's going to tell me what I can and can't do now?

"Elli." He snaps my name, making me jump.

"Yeah." I shake my head, swallowing nervously. Confused by his tone. "No," I correct myself. "I won't. I don't have any on me."

He snorts like that's going to stop me, but he drops it and pulls me across the parking lot and into the back door that Corbin holds open for us.

---

TWO HOURS LATER, I'M PRETTY DRUNK. HAD A COUPLE OF shots and am on my third drink. Me and Kira are making our way to the bathroom, leaving the guys sitting at the table. Her hand in mine and she's practically skipping. "I'm so happy to see you happy."

She throws me a drunken smile, her eyes practically closed. "I'm in love."

"That—" I'm cut off by running into a hard object. It knocks us back a few steps.

"Hey, ladies." The guy smiles at us, but I don't miss how his eyes drop to my chest before going to hers as well. I know him. His name is Marcus, and he goes to Barrington University. He is the *it guy* if you want drugs. I've even bought from him before. It was a couple of years ago, though, at a Halloween party.

Another guy stands next to him; I know him from the university as well.

"Sorry," I say and sidestep Marcus, pulling Kira behind me as we try to squeeze between him and the wall.

His hand shoots out, stopping us again. "It looks like you two could use a little help." He reaches for me, and I take a step back, bumping into Kira.

"We're good." I push his hand away. Sin is still not in a good mood. Kira and I don't give a fuck about the guys, but you can tell they're not happy about being here with us tonight. And Sin's been watching me closely. I keep thinking about what he said to me in the parking lot, and I wonder if tonight is a test somehow.

"You could be better," the other guy says, making Kira gasp. She thinks he means our looks; I know he means drugs.

Marcus reaches up and rubs his chin, looking at me. "Need a party favor tonight?" he asks.

Kira answers before I can. "No."

I'm sure that's for Sin and Corbin's sake. She doesn't want Corbin or her brother to know that she's tried them with me before. If Sin knew she did, he'd lose his shit.

The Lords would never. Getting high or taking any kind of substance to inhibit their behavior goes against their oath. They are always on their A game.

"How about you, Elli? Want a little something?"

I bite my bottom lip. The need to be good for Sin battles with the need to rebel just to see what he'll do if I go against what he said. Reluctantly, I shake my head. "Not tonight."

"Come find me when you change your mind," Marcus adds, winking. "If there's anything I can give you." And then they continue down the hall.

I roll my eyes, entering the bathroom with Kira. She starts fixing her hair in the mirror. "God, I'm so glad I'm no longer part of the dating scene."

"Yeah," I mumble, walking into a stall and pulling up my skirt. "So, you and Corbin. Fill me in. All the details." I've been a shit friend.

"Yep. He's so great, Elli." She sighs.

Exiting the stall, I walk over to her and start washing my hands. "I hope he's good to you."

"Amazing." She bats her eyes.

Man, the girl has it bad. I'm happy for her. "Sin didn't look so happy."

She snorts. "I don't care what he thinks. And neither does

Corbin." Unlocking the door, she pulls it open and in walks the last person I want to see tonight. Sin's chosen.

Amelia's eyes look over me before pulling her lip back with a snort. I hate that I turn to watch her go to the sink. She opens up her Hermes clutch and reapplies her lipstick. Eyes meeting mine in the mirror. Thoughts of her fucking my boyfriend run through my mind and jealousy courses through me like electricity.

Popping her lips, she turns to face us. Placing her hands on her hips, a smile spreads across her face. "How's it feel to be two for two, Elli?"

My brows pull together, confused by her question, but it's Kira who actually asks. "What are you talking about?"

She looks from me to Kira, then back to me. Taking a step closer, the smile just grows. "You mean your best friend doesn't know about *Daddy* and his friend?"

I stiffen at her words. The blood rushing in my ears. How would she know? She wouldn't. She's digging. Staying silent, she snorts and looks to Kira. "She's fucked both of her stepdads." Leaning forward, she whispers in my ear, "What do you think your mother would do if she found out?"

My hands fist down by my sides. My mother knows about James, just not the truth. The story he told her. I'm sure it was that I came onto him. Threw myself at him. But my mother has no clue about Lincoln. Or she would have mentioned him too.

Pulling back, Amelia shrugs. "I mean, if my daughter slept with my husbands, I know what I'd do to the fucking whore."

"Who told you that?" Kira demands, pushing me to the side. She thinks it's a lie. A horrible rumor being spread about me. I've never told her.

Pushing her hip out, Amelia looks down at her nails. "Your brother."

"He's fucking lying," Kira shouts.

"Was he, though?" She tilts her head to the side. "Let's ask

Ellington. Elli, tell us that James and Lincoln didn't both fuck you in James's office."

I'm trying to catch my breath. Unable to answer even if I wanted to. The betrayal I feel from Sin all too consuming. Why would he tell her? When did he tell her?

"Elli?" A hand touches my shoulder and I jump back from Kira. Her eyes full of pity watching mine fill with tears. I knew it was too good to be true. Sin isn't the kind of guy you fall in love with and marry. He's the kind that uses you until he gets bored and moves on.

"You know you're a pity fuck, right?" Amelia continues at my silence.

"Shut up!" Kira snaps at her.

But she doesn't. Instead, she steps back into me. "You're an easy fucking lay that he feels sorry for. He might be fucking us both, but you're the one he'll dump once he's decided you're no longer worth it."

Kira begins to laugh, making Amelia's face tighten. "Seriously? Now we know you're lying. Because my brother is not fucking you."

Amelia opens up her clutch and removes her phone. She then holds it up in front of us and a video starts to play. It's Sin's room at the house of Lords. There's no sound but the video is as clear as day. He's sitting on the bed, fully dressed, his back up against the headboard staring down at his phone in his hands. Sin looks up and then you see Amelia enter his room. He gets to his feet, setting his cell on the nightstand. She walks right up to him, and they waste no time. She removes her sundress. He removes his shirt. She kicks off her heels and then pushes her underwear down her bony legs. She's not wearing a bra, her fake breasts on full display for him.

He gestures to the bed, and she crawls onto it, rolling onto her back. Standing beside it, he pulls rope out from the headboard and ties both of her wrists above her head.

She closes her eyes, arching her back, and spreads her legs wide for him. He lowers his hands to his jeans and undoes his belt. Pulling it from the loops, he then wraps it around her neck, letting the excess lay down the center of her chest. When he turns to open his nightstand. I slap her phone out of her hands.

"Bitch," she snaps, bending down to pick it up.

My heart is racing, my stomach in my throat. I want to deny it, but it was right there in front of my face. He was wearing the same clothes that he left our house in just this morning. He lied to me. Told me it was Lord related. But was that a lie? She's his chosen because he's a Lord. I just never questioned what it was.

He fucked me when he got home. In our bed. In the house that he said he got for *us*. I let him touch me and he had just been with her.

"You taped it?" Kira barks. "Sin is going to kill you when he finds out." She stabs her finger into Amelia's chest. "And I will tell him. I promise you that. Right fucking now." She spins around to rush out.

Amelia bursts out laughing, making my friend pause. "Oh my God, this is better than I imagined." Her laughter grows, the high-pitched sound hurting my ears. "He never told you..." She slaps her stomach, doubling over.

"Who never told me what?" Kira yells at her.

She rights herself and pushes her hair from her face. She's almost in tears she was laughing so hard. "Every Lord has cameras in their rooms at the house of Lords."

Kira's face pales, her eyes now wide. Swallowing, she whispers, "No—"

"Yes." Amelia steps into her. "Corbin has been recording you every time you let him fuck you in his room. And then he shows it to all of his friends, laughing while they all watch how shitty of a lay you are." With that, she flings her hair over her shoulder and saunters out of the bathroom.

Silence fills the bathroom and I place my hands on the countertop, my head dropping. I'm trying to breathe once again.

"Did you know?" she whispers.

"No." I had no clue my boyfriend was fucking Amelia. I mean, she's his chosen. I just never thought about it. But of course, he is. And as far as the cameras in their rooms? I've only been in his once and we didn't do anything. I stormed out, saw Kira in the hallway, and begged her to get me the hell out of there.

"He would not sleep with her." Kira denies it. "She is—"

"His chosen," I shout, pushing away from the counter to stare at her. "I'm nobody. Nothing. She is his chosen. She's important." Even the Lords don't want me. For some girls, being a chosen means something to them. Their chance to serve. I had always thought it was disgusting. But now? Now I realize I'm nothing to Sin other than a pity fuck. That's worse. "Did you not see the video?"

"That could have been weeks ago." She runs a hand through her hair. She's focusing on my situation to avoid her own. I saw the hurt in her eyes that Corbin hadn't informed her he's been recording them.

I don't even bother telling her that video was from this morning. She's got her own shit to deal with now and it just makes me look like an even bigger stupid bitch. "Don't tell Sin about the video. Or that we spoke to Amelia."

She bites her red-painted lip. "Give him a chance—"

"If you can keep a secret about fucking Corbin then I think you can keep my secret of what just happened," I snap. Sin doesn't deserve a second to explain why he's cheating on me. It'll just be another situation where I look like a stupid slut.

She sucks in a deep breath, squaring her shoulders, and I run a hand through my hair, trying to slow my racing pulse.

"Your secret is safe with me." Then she turns and exits the bathroom.

"Fuck."

Staying a few extra seconds, I make sure to clean up my face and get my breathing under control. Just when I think I've finally gotten myself together, I exit the bathroom and make it back to the bar. I can see our table from here, across the room. Corbin and Kira are gone. Not surprised. She probably told him they were leaving. Not like he'd care; Sin isn't speaking to him anyway.

I catch sight of Sin sitting there, sipping on a beer, the same one since we got here. It's got to be warm by now. And I'm also not surprised to see the queen bitch herself standing right there. Her hands on the table as she's leaning over, her tits in his face. Again. Just like in the video.

What I am surprised about is the way he looks up at her. It's with hatred. How he used to look at me. Back before he found out what I whore I really am.

Any normal person would know that this thought process isn't healthy or rational. But it's how I think. I love the Sin that doesn't give a fuck. That he holds you down and wants to mark you. I don't want a man who is afraid to break me. And I thought that was him. I was wrong.

I spin around to rush out the exit and hit a hard body. "Sorry." Looking up, I sigh. *Not again.*

"I feel like you're doing that on purpose." Marcus laughs. His eyes drop to my hands and then frowns. "Where's your drink?"

"Don't have one," I shout over the music.

"Well, that won't do." I let him grab my arm and pull me over to the bar, knowing I'm going to piss Sin off and not giving a fuck.

# THIRTY-FIVE

# SIN

"You never called me back today." Amelia arches a brow.

"Been busy."

She plops down beside me, and I scoot over to put some space between us. Honestly, if Elli sees this, I expect a beer bottle to go flying toward my head. The thought makes me smile. I like it when she's in a mood. It'll just make what I have planned on doing to her later when we get home even better. I love when she makes me take it.

"You're wasting your time with her."

Her words get my attention and I turn my head to face her but say nothing.

My silence just aggravates her even more. "She's not good for you." Her hand falls on my inner thigh and she leans over to place her lips by my ear. The new position giving me a direct line of sight to the bar.

I see the back of Elli standing there with a drink in her hand. My teeth clench when I see the guy next to her, his hand on her lower back, at the top of her ass. They're laughing. He pulls away, reaches into his pocket, and pulls out something. She opens her fist, and he drops it in. Then she turns around and takes the shot that the bartender sets down in front of her.

"Let's get out of here. Go to my place. I want you to tie me to my bed this time and fuck me." I hear words being spoken in my ear, but I can't acknowledge Amelia. Or look away from my little demon letting another man put his hands all over her.

*What in the fuck does she think she's doing?*

A hand gets my attention and I realize that Amelia's practically sitting on top of me. Her hands rubbing my cock. I'm not even hard. And she's licking my ear.

Reaching down, I grab her wrists. She whimpers, trying to pull back, but my free hand grips her chin, holding it in place. "Touch me again and I'll break your fucking hand. Do you understand?"

"Sin." She gasps. "You're hurting me."

To further my point, I tighten my grip and she screams. But we're in a fucking club, no one is even looking back over at us.

"Sin..." She sniffs, adjusting in her seat. "I'm serious." Tears fill her eyes.

"I'm fucking serious," I growl through gritted teeth. "When I want you again, I'll call you." Then I shove her out of the booth and onto her ass.

A few girls try to help her up, but she pushes them away and runs off crying.

I get out of the booth and make my way to the bar, wondering what in the fuck Elli thinks she's doing.

Coming up to the bar, I look around and don't see her, but I do see the guy she was talking to. I recognize him. His brother plays football at Barrington. "What's up, Marcus?" I get his attention.

"Sin, what's up, man?" He gives me the handshake half hug and slaps my back a few times. "What's going on?"

"Not much." I gesture to the bartender for a shot, because that's what any guy would do at the club, and look around for her again. Still nothing. Where the fuck did she go? "Here with anyone tonight?" I dig, not wasting any time.

He throws his head back laughing. "Never come with pussy, Sin. You know that. Gotta keep your options open so you can choose which one you want."

I nod in agreement like I fucking understand that. It's not like I've been clubbing for years taking home random pussy. "Any prospects?" I go on.

"Yeah. We're about to leave." He throws back his shot.

My heart picks up. Is she really going to leave with him? This has to be a joke, right? We fucking live together. "Do I know her?"

He slams the now empty shot glass down. "Doubtful." His eyes drop to the skull ring on my hand that signifies I'm a Lord. We all wear them while attending Barrington. Well, those that know we exist. There have been rumors going around for years about who we are and what we do. "She's a nobody."

My teeth clench at his words. *She's fucking mine.*

He looks down at his phone and sighs, putting it away.

"What's up?" I nod to it. Maybe she skipped out and texted him that she couldn't meet up tonight.

"Had a friend who was going to join us. Guess he found someone else."

"So you *and* a friend were going to take this woman home?"

His eyes meet mine and he smirks. "We wanted to surprise her, if you know what I mean."

Yeah, I do. He's going to leave with my little demon and share her with his friend. I want to slit his throat right fucking here in front of everyone. But where would that get me? "That's a gamble," I add. "The last thing you need is a rape charge come Monday morning." He knows she's drunk and on drugs. Drugs that he gave her. Her going to the cops won't do her any good after they're done with her. Sure, she might have bruises on her, but they could say she liked it rough. There's always a way around it.

273

Throwing his head back, he laughs, his Adam's apple bobbing. "You have to know the right one to pick, man. This girl..." He slaps my arm excitedly. "She's so fucking easy. Been fucking her professor."

It takes everything in me to keep my face blank. How the fuck does he know that?

"She won't say shit to anyone. And if she did ... no one will believe her." His eyes drop to my skull ring again as I twirl it around my finger, trying to keep my composure when I want to fucking explode. "How about you? Want a piece?"

He wants me because of my Lord status. The cops can't touch us. We've got Lords on the inside in uniform. Any time one of us does something illegally, it's not swept under the rug. It's completely shredded. "Yeah. I'm free." I'll teach them both a lesson they won't forget.

# ELLINGTON

I EXIT THE BATHROOM ONCE AGAIN TO FIND MARCUS standing ready and waiting. I let him grab my hand and as he walks me through the club, I glance over at where we were all sitting and it's full now with people I don't know.

Sin took her home with him. It makes this decision even easier. Fuck him and his fucking lies. It's over. Whatever it was, I'm done. He can have his chosen. And I'll have whoever I want.

Walking outside, I get into Marcus's car. Thankfully, he turns the radio up, so we don't have to talk. There's nothing to say.

I need to calm my nerves. My entire body is vibrating with betrayal that I feel from Sin. It's not just the sex but that he also told Amelia about James and Lincoln. She's got a big mouth. She'll go and tell everyone.

Good thing I don't give a shit what people think. Not like

anyone would believe the truth anyway. If my mom didn't, no one will.

He brings the car to a stop, and I see we're at a log cabin. "Your house?" I ask. Marcus isn't from here. His family lives in California. Kids come from all around the world to go to Barrington. It's for the elite. Doesn't matter about your grades, all your parents have to do is pay a significant fee each year and you're in.

"Yeah." He unlocks the front door and holds it open for me.

I follow him into the open kitchen, and he grabs a bottle of vodka. "Drink?"

"Please." *Fuck, yes.* Give me the entire fucking bottle and I'll just drown myself in it.

He pulls out two shot glasses and fills them to the brim.

I take it from him and toss it back, hissing in a breath. He comes to stand behind me. His hands on my thighs. I feel him push up my skirt.

I reach out and grab the empty shot glass I set down and fill it again. By the time I toss it back, his hand is between my legs. I throw the glass to the floor and hear it break. Lifting the bottle, I take a swig when he pulls my underwear to the side.

Tears sting my eyes but I refuse to let them fall. I will not let Sin hurt me. I will not give him that kind of power. He made his choice, and it wasn't me.

Taking another drink, his finger slips inside my pussy and I whimper. Guilt tightening my chest. *Why?* He was cheating on me. Fucking someone else. Then came home to the house he said he bought for us.

After he was finished making me come on the formal dining room table that day, we signed papers. He had everything there and ready for us to make it our home. It took hours to go through, to finalize, but it's ours.

So why do I feel guilty? He's the one living two lives.

"You're so wet." Marcus pulls his finger out and pushes it back in.

"I ... I don't think—"

"Shut the fuck up." He slaps my ass, and a cry leaves my numbing lips.

My hands grip the vodka bottle tighter, and I close my eyes. I hate that I want Sin right now. That my body can feel the difference. He's been getting me off for two years. He knows it better than I know myself.

Thoughts of him and Amelia enter my mind and I bite my tongue to keep a sob in. I imagine him and her in our bed. Her tied there while he gives her what I want.

Marcus pulls his finger out and then his hands run up my back, he grips my hair at the scalp. Pulling me to stand, he spins me around. His free hand grips my chin painfully, his face in front of mine.

I stare into his green eyes, and he smiles at the tears in mine. "Crying already, baby?"

I flinch at the pet name.

"I haven't even started yet." Then he presses his lips to mine.

I don't kiss him back and his tongue shoves its way between my lips. He tastes like cheap beer. My arms stay at my sides while he holds me in place by my face and hair. I'm numb, my heart shattered. I've never known pain like this. It's as if someone has stabbed me and I'm bleeding to death. I can feel my life slipping away. I pray the alcohol takes it all away soon.

When he pulls back, I'm sucking in a deep breath. He spins me around, shoves me over the counter, and kicks my legs open with his shoes.

"I hope you like it rough." Letting go of my hair, he brings my hands behind my back, and before I realize what he's doing, I feel handcuffs tighten on my wrists.

I kick my legs out and go to scream but he lays his body on top of mine, pinning me down onto the counter, his body weight taking my air away. "Because we're going to fucking use this body as it was intended for."

*We're?* "We?" I manage to rush out as fear grips my chest.

His weight is lifted from my back and he grips my hair, yanking me to stand. "What do you think?"

I frown, confused by the question, but he spins me around and my legs threaten to buckle at what I see.

Sin leans against the entrance to the kitchen. Arms crossed over his chest and eyes on mine. My heart is in my throat. The blood rushing in my ears is all I hear.

He pushes off and takes a step toward us. I go to run but Marcus wraps an arm around my neck, tight enough that I can't breathe.

Sin comes to stand before me. His hand runs down my breasts over my shirt, and I fight the hold Marcus has on me.

Reaching into his pocket, Sin pulls out his pocketknife. He pops it open and slices down my shirt. My chest heaves when his fingers lightly run over my ribs and pull down my skirt. It falls to the floor.

When his cold eyes meet mine, he finally answers, "She'll do."

# THIRTY-SIX

# SIN

Marcus laughs at my answer while she stares at me wide-eyed. She is going to hate me when I'm done with her, but I don't give a fuck.

My skin is on fire, my pulse racing. She let him touch her. Finger her. Put her in handcuffs, for fuck's sake. Forget the fact that she belongs to me. The things Marcus and his friend could have done to her are endless.

Has she learned nothing about men? Fuck, growing up in a world knowing that Lords even exist should be enough to terrify her.

"Hear that?" he asks her, his mouth by her ear while she struggles in his grip. "You're good enough to be our whore."

She whimpers, tears fall over her bottom lashes.

"Put her on her knees," I order.

He lets go of her neck and shoves her to the kitchen floor. She cries out when they hit the tile.

I grip her ponytail and yank her head back. She goes to speak but I press the tip of the knife to her cheek.

I stare at her unblinking. Her wide eyes go from mine to

Marcus. "Don't kill her before I get my turn." He laughs, a smile spreading across his face at the thought of what he's going to get to do to her. "We're going to fuck you up, you little whore. You'll be begging for death before we grant it." He stands and leans his back against the wall, crossing his arms over his chest, getting comfortable to enjoy the show.

I'm going to give him one. "Drugs?" I question him.

"Gave her a little something," he answers.

"What was it?" I snap, glaring at him.

"Something to put her in the mood." His eyes are on hers kneeling in front of me. "She'll enjoy being used. Well, until she loses consciousness anyway."

I look at her, and sure enough her eyes are dilated, eyelids growing heavy. "Did she ask for it?" I need to know if she went to him for something, or if he just offered and she took it. Not sure why, it's not going to change how I treat her.

He snorts. "She didn't have to. The slut's a druggie. Sold to her in the past. Saw her at the club and took the opportunity."

She whimpers and my eyes drop to her pierced nipples, and they're hard. I tilt my head, watching the way her chest rises and falls as she breathes.

I kneel before her, my knuckles run over her breasts and stomach. They drop to her thighs, and I gently run the back of my knuckles over them. She shifts on her knees that rest on the cold floor. Her throat moving when she swallows. I get to her underwear. "Spread your legs," I demand.

She sucks in a deep breath but doesn't argue. She opens them the best she can. I drop the knife to her underwear, cutting them away. I want her nude. I want her vulnerable. I want her to understand that her life is in my hands.

I run my fingers over her pussy, and she closes her eyes in shame. The movement of her chest picks up while her heavy breathing fills the room.

"I told you she's a fucking whore." He laughs, making her sob. "She gets off on this shit. Just loves being used and abused."

I stand. "Open your mouth. Stick out your tongue."

Her eyes go to Marcus who leans against the wall to my right, and I slap her across the face, making her cry out. "Open your fucking mouth, bitch, and stick out your tongue," I command.

Sniffing, she licks her lips then parts them, doing as she's told. "That's a good girl," I praise her and her shoulders shake. I run the tip of the knife along her lips, barely touching them. Then drop it to her tongue. I watch the soft pressure making an indention down the center. When I'm almost to the tip, I apply a little bit more pressure, and cut the skin.

She pulls back, crying as blood flows from the cut, falling onto her bare chest. "Gorgeous."

My free hand drops to unzip my jeans and I pull my cock out. I'm so fucking hard for my little demon right now. I want to beat her ass black and blue, but I want my cock covered in her cum when I do it.

Blood drips from the tip of her tongue that sticks out of her open mouth onto her chest and the floor at my feet. Any other time, I'd be happy. But right now, I want to hurt her. Make her cry and beg me to forgive her. Tell me she's sorry that she's put us both in this situation.

Taking my hard cock in my hand, I run it over her bloody lips and push it into her mouth. She gags, her body pulling back, but I don't let her go anywhere.

I watch saliva and blood fall from the corners of her luscious lips as I fuck her mouth. She's crying, tears freely flowing down her pretty face.

"Fuck," I moan, loving the way she looks like this. I'll have to do it again sometime.

I'm balls deep in her mouth when my free hand pinches her nose. Her eyes go wide, and she thrashes under me on her knees, but I don't let up. I fuck her until her eyes roll into the back of her head and her body goes slack.

I pull out and come all over her drool and blood covered chest. Stepping back, I let go of her and her head falls forward while she begins to cough and sob.

Lifting her face to look up at me, her eyes are heavy. She looks dazed. Could be the alcohol, or the drugs. Either way, she's about to pass out. Drool and blood slowly run out of her mouth. "Such a good little demon."

She whimpers, her eyes falling shut, and I allow her to fall to the floor onto her side in the middle of the kitchen.

I hear the faint sound of the front door opening and closing, making me smile.

"Hey, I'm next." Marcus whines like a fucking child, pushing off the wall.

"You're right." I stand and turn to face him. "You are next." Then I throw the knife, enjoying the shrill scream that follows.


# ELLINGTON


I OPEN MY HEAVY EYES AND GROAN. I'VE GOT A POUNDING headache. Sitting up, I rub my eyes with the palm of my hands. I press a little too hard, causing stars to dance across my vision.

Opening them, I blink rapidly before they focus. My breath hitches when I see Sin sitting across from me on a couch. He's got his right ankle propped up on his knee. His arms fanned along the back cushions. His blue eyes on me.

Unblinking. He doesn't look mad or satisfied. Just blank.

That's not what has my heart racing. It's the fact that I'm not restrained. No duct tape, no rope, no handcuffs.

He looks too calm for what he did to me earlier.

I swallow nervously and look away from him. My eyes scanning the living room for Marcus but it's just me and Sin. I know we're still at the same house. Why are we here?

My eyes drop to my chest, and I see I've got dried blood on it. I'm still naked. Reaching out, I grab the blanket that was draped over me and hide myself.

"You do not want to play this game with me, little demon." He finally speaks. His voice sounding as calm as he looks. "I will win every single time. No one can beat the devil."

My eyes lift to look at him through my lashes, and he cocks his head to the side. My tongue is throbbing where he cut it, but I no longer taste blood.

He stands and walks over to me. His movements force me to sit up straighter and lift my head in order to watch him. Coming to a stop in front of me, he reaches out his hand.

I take it.

He lifts me to my shaking knees and removes the blanket. He opens it up and wraps it around my shoulders. Lifting his hand, he runs his finger over my trembling lips. His eyes stay on mine, anchoring me in place. I've always known Sin would have power over me. We just never got close enough to see how much.

Now that I do, I'm terrified. Not of him. But what I'd do for him.

He slips his thumb into my mouth, and I stick my tongue out. He gently runs it over the cut, and I whimper. "Say you're sorry."

I blink at his command. *Sorry?* Am I sorry that I made him jealous last night? Am I sorry that I left with a man I intended to let fuck me? Am I sorry that I put myself in a position that could have potentially gotten me raped by multiple men and left in a ditch to rot? No.

I might have been drunk and fucked up, but my mind was clear and made up. Fuck Sin, his lies, and his cheating ass. Lifting my chin, I narrow my eyes on him. "I won't."

I expect him to be mad at my refusal, but instead he gives me a breathtaking smile. One that shows off his dazzling white teeth. Then he leans in and whispers in my ear, "We'll see."

He grabs my arm and pulls me into the kitchen. I gasp, yanking to a stop when I see Marcus sitting in a chair. His wrists tied to the armrest. Each ankle tied to a front leg. Jayce and Corbin stand behind him. There's a vertical cut in his white T-shirt and a blood stain around it.

"What the fuck, Sin?" Marcus snaps when he sees us.

"Go ahead, tell him." Sin gestures toward Marcus.

I step back but Sin grabs my arm, yanks me forward, and stands behind me where I'm right in front of Marcus's chair, staring down at him.

"Tell him, little demon," Sin says, pulling my tangled hair, that at some point fell out of my ponytail, off my chest to rest down my back.

"Let me out of this chair," Marcus yells up at me. "Right now, Elli. Get me the fuck out of—"

"Enough," Sin barks at him. "Let the woman speak." He wraps a hand around my throat from behind, forcing me to look up. "Who do you belong to?"

"You," I whisper, unable to deny it.

"Who fucks you?" Sin goes on.

I swallow the knot in my throat. "You do."

Sin yanks the blanket free of my shoulders and I stand naked in front of them. His free hand drops to my inner thigh, and my breath catches when his fingers run over the brand he gave me. "And who owns you?"

"You..." My breath hitches. "You do."

"You guys set me up," Marcus screams, making me jump. "You sick fucks." The chair rattles as he yanks on the rope that ties him down. "Let me go."

"Not until my girl tells me she's sorry."

There's that damn word again. "I already told you," I say through gritted teeth. "I'm not."

He whispers in my ear, "You will be." He shoves me into Jayce who I hadn't seen move to stand on my right. I try to push him away, but he spins me around, pinning my hips into the edge of the large island. He manages to slide his arm between the crook of both of mine, pinning them in place behind my back. While his free hand goes over my mouth.

"Corbin." Sin nods to his friend. He takes a chain and holds it out to Sin. He picks up a small handheld blue tank off the counter and I start thrashing against the island and Jayce, knowing what it is. Sin turns on the blowtorch and starts heating up a small area of the chain that Corbin holds between his fists.

"What the fuck, man?" Marcus shouts.

Once Sin is happy with it, he nods to Corbin again. He returns to his spot behind Marcus who is trying to watch him by looking over his shoulder. "Open wide," Sin orders, and Corbin lowers the heated chain over Marcus's head from behind and pries his mouth open with it, successfully placing it between his teeth.

I begin to cry, yelling *I'm sorry* but no one can hear. Not between Marcus's screams and Jayce's hand over my mouth.

Sin walks over to the table and grabs another chair. He picks it up and sets it down in front of Marcus, backward. He straddles the seat and places his arms over the top of the chair. "You touched my girl and that's unacceptable."

Marcus still thrashes around in the chair, drool already leaking out of the corner of his mouth.

Sin places the blowtorch to Marcus's right hand that hangs off the armrest of the chair.

I'm yelling into Jayce's hand that *I'm sorry*, but no one can hear me since it's still over my mouth. Marcus is spitting through the chain. The smell of burning flesh makes me start to gag.

Sin pulls it away and Marcus slumps in his chair, his jeans turn darker as he pisses himself. Sin inspects his mouth. "Broke a few teeth biting down on that metal, huh? That's a bitch." I see blood mixed with the drool now running onto his already blood-stained shirt.

"Look at her." Sin points over to me. When Marcus makes no attempt to do so, Sin jumps up from the chair, grips Marcus's face and shoves it to the right to get a look at me. "See her. She's not a nobody."

Sin watches the tears fall from my eyes with a proud smile on his face, and a sob racks my body. "She's mine. And that makes her the most important person in the world. Understand?"

Marcus sniffs, and nods his head the best he can, which isn't much with Corbin pulling on the chain and Sin's hand on his face. He lets go of him.

He kneels in front of Marcus, holding out the blowtorch in front of his last good hand. Marcus throws his head back, sobbing. His bloody covered chest heaving. "I watched this one slide under her skirt where you proceeded to finger her cunt. My cunt. It has to go."

Marcus sobs and Sin presses it to his flesh. Marcus's entire body stiffens, his veins protruding in his neck. His skin red like he's burning from the inside out.

I'm screaming at the top of my lungs. Tears and snot run down my face over Jayce's hand as he keeps me pinned in place.

Sin stops and Marcus's body sags in the chair. He looks over at us. "Let her go."

Jayce steps back, letting me go. I pry my hips and lower stomach from the island and take a step toward Sin but fall to my knees. They're numb. Blood cut off from how hard Jayce had me pinned.

"I'm ... sorry," I say through a sob. "I'm so sorry."

He turns the blowtorch off and sets it on the counter. Then he walks over to me. Kneeling, he places his forearm on his thigh.

"That's my girl." Leaning forward, he gently presses his lips to my forehead. "Such a good little demon."

I cover my face with my hands, and I feel him lift me up. "Clean up this mess," he barks before carrying me out of the house.

# THIRTY-SEVEN

## SIN

I stand at the end of our bed. She's passed out. I brought her home, gave her a bath, and she was out before her head hit the pillow.

Her and I are a lot alike, if you think about it. Lords are trained, groomed, and manipulated. You can put fifty average men in a room with a hundred Lords and they'll be able to pick each one of us out. Even if they weren't aware our secret society existed. Why? Because we're raised the same. We're conditioned to think a certain way. We're meant to be possessive, dominating, and fucking vile. Death means nothing to us.

James took the training he got from the Lords and used it on Ellington. Where I spent three years of celibacy for initiation. He put her through three years of initiation too. She listened to grown adults talk about their fucked-up fetishes and kinks. Her body craved it but was never allowed a release.

Am I mad that she willingly left Blackout with Marcus? Absolutely. Can I blame her for it? No.

I'm the fourth man she's ever been with. But what if she wouldn't have caught me that night at the party killing James?

What if she hadn't seen the masked me save her? I wouldn't have been getting her off those two years. She would have worked her way through the college. Man after man. Dick after dick. I had to keep her at arm's length but satisfied at the same time.

No one knows how fucking hard that was. It was like dangling a piece of meat in front of a starving man.

Elli needs constant reminding that she's owned. That she belongs to someone. Otherwise, she feels lost. Like a child roaming the streets looking for their parents who don't give a shit about them.

My cell begins to vibrate in my pocket, and I pull it out. My brows crease when I see who it is. Exiting the bedroom, I answer. "Hello?"

"My office. Twenty minutes," he snaps before hanging up.

Pocketing my cell, I walk back into the bedroom and kiss her forehead, pulling the covers up to her neck. "Sweet dreams, little demon. I'll be back."

---

I STEP INTO THE BACK ENTRANCE AND TAKE THE ELEVATOR UP to the third floor. Exiting, I knock on the door.

"It's open," he calls out.

I step inside to see Tyson Crawford leaning his ass against his desk at Blackout. It's seven a.m. and he's dressed in black slacks and a matching button-up with the sleeves rolled up. Like me, I highly doubt the man has been to sleep. "You wanted to see me?"

"Sit." He points at the couch to his right. Tyson never has been a man of many words if you're not a close friend of his. He gets to the point and doesn't give a fuck if you like what he has to say or not.

I fall into the leather and lean back, getting comfortable.

He hands me a card. I take it, frowning as I read over it.

"Detective Haynes. Don't know him. Or her." I go to hand it back, but he walks behind his desk and sits down. Picking up a remote, he turns on the TV that hangs on the opposite wall.

Over twelve different angles show multiple cameras displaying the surveillance of Blackout. He clicks on one that is focused on the parking lot. It shows me and Corbin walking in with the girls through the back entrance. He goes to another camera and fast-forwards a little, showing the girls going to the restroom. They bump into Marcus and another guy I know of. They then enter the bathroom, no longer in view. He fast-forwards some more and you see my sister rush out. A new angle shows her walking up to our table, slapping Corbin, and then storming off. He follows after her. I smile at the memory. Then another angle shows Elli exit the bathroom looking pissed. Why did they both come out so mad?

She stops and looks in the direction that we sit. Another angle at the bottom shows Amelia sitting beside me. But she looked mad before she spotted the booth. She turns and runs into Marcus again. This time she lets him pull her over to the bar. He places his hand on her back and Tyson pauses it.

"Want to tell me why the girl you arrived with left with him?"

I turn to face him but stay quiet.

"Sin," he growls. "Detective Haynes left Blackout five minutes before I called you. They've recovered a body. And it belongs to this guy who has his hand on your date."

I smile.

"Goddammit, Easton," he snaps my real name.

I've always liked Tyson. He was a senior when my class was a freshman. He stayed to himself a bit more from what I saw. But he was always ruthless. Then he lost his chosen, and well, he gave up everything for Blackout. I hope whatever he asked for in return was worth it.

"Did you show them the surveillance?" I finally speak.

"No." He shakes his head. "Blackout doesn't cooperate with the police."

"Well, then that's that." I slap my thighs and get to my feet.

"You're not stupid, Sin. So don't act like it."

I tilt my head. "What is that supposed to mean?" I wanted them to find his body. He's got a friend who was going to fuck my girl with him. I want Marcus's death to be taken as the threat that it was intended to be.

"It means if you don't want the girl you love to find out you're fucking someone else, don't bring them both to the same place."

I snort.

He picks up the remote and rewinds one of the many angles to the women's bathroom again. It shows Kira and Elli entering and a minute later I watch Amelia enter as well. I step closer to the TV as time goes by slowly. He had fast-forwarded over this earlier. Finally, the door opens and out walks Amelia with a smile on her face. Not much later, Kira runs out, then I see Elli. She pauses, wipes her wet cheeks, takes a deep breath, and walks down the hall into the open club. She sees me and stiffens. Then her eyes find Marcus and it's over. I can tell. Whatever was said snapped something inside her and she was done with me.

Well, sucks to be her because I'm not letting her go.

He shuts it off and speaks, "Next time you plan on doing something over pussy in my club, I expect to be informed."

"Thanks," I growl, headed for the door.

"Sin?"

"Yeah?" I turn to face him.

"Marcus?" He leans back in his seat.

"Taken care of," I say. They won't get anything off what the guys left for the cops to find.

He nods. "Next time, give me a heads-up."

"Yes, sir," I say and go to open the door but stop when I see someone was about to enter.

"Sorry I'm late," Ryat Archer announces, entering the room. Last time I saw him, we were at the house of Lords sitting in the basement when Matt volunteered himself and Ryat for an assignment.

"Just in time," Tyson informs him. Then he looks at me. "You'll want to sit back down, Sin."

Shutting the door, I walk over to the couch across from the one Ryat sits down in. He looks like shit. Busted lip, black eye, and some bruises on his upper neck. He's wearing a hoodie, making it hard to see anything else, with a set of dark jeans. You can tell they're older. I wonder if Matt got a hold of him like he did Matt.

"What the hell happened to you?" I can't help but ask.

He grunts but doesn't answer. Me and Ryat aren't close, but he is with Tyson. The Lords are like anything else. There are cliques within us. Ryat didn't grow up here in Pennsylvania like me, Jayce, and Corbin. He's from New York. Moved here after high school graduation to attend Barrington.

"I was on an assignment," Ryat states and I nod.

"I'm aware. What's that have to do with me?" I wonder.

He bows his head, running his hand through his dark hair. "Normally, I wouldn't do this, but if I were you, I'd want to know." He lifts his head, and his eyes meet mine.

A cold chill runs up my spine when he speaks. I watch his lips move, hear his words, but with the blood rushing in my ears, I'm unable to process what he's saying to me. One thing is for sure, everything is about to change. And I'm going to owe Ryat big time.

# THIRTY-EIGHT

## SIN

I t's a little after nine in the morning when I pull into the driveway. Pulling my cell out of my pocket, I call my father's number. He answers on the second ring.

"Son."

"Make the call," I say, looking over the house that sits in front of me.

He sighs. "It's for the best, East—"

"I didn't ask for your opinion," I interrupt him.

He lets out a deep breath, getting irritated with my attitude but I don't care. After what Ryat told me, I need to make some changes. And they need to be made as soon as possible.

"I'll make the call. But, son..."

*Click.*

I hang up, get out of the car, and enter the house. I find her in the kitchen standing at the island. The first thing I notice is the bag packed at her feet. It can't have more than a few items of clothes and her toothbrush. It's all we've brought over so far. I place my hands in the pockets of my jeans and stare at her.

"I'm leaving," Elli announces, lifting her chin.

295

I sidestep to make sure I'm not blocking the exit.

Her shoulders fall but she quickly recovers. My little demon wants to be chased. Held captive. She just thought she belonged to me before, but things are getting ready to change. And not in her favor.

Huffing, she reaches down and grabs her bag, and I wait until she passes me before I turn and speak. "You won't get far."

She comes to a stop, slowly turning back to face me, her ice-blue eyes narrowing at my statement. "Excuse me?"

I step into her and reach up, pushing some loose strands of bleach-blond hair behind her ear. "Go ahead, run away if that makes you feel better about yourself. But you won't get far."

"Sin." She sighs, getting annoyed. "What you did last night was unacceptable. You almost killed—"

I laugh, cutting her off. *Almost?* She shoves my chest.

"You didn't care last time I killed a man for you. Or the time before that." I'm up to three dead men for her. And I'll kill many more if need be.

Her eyes drop to the floor, and I reach out, cupping her face while running my thumb over her bottom lip. "Let that be a lesson, Elli. If a man touches you, it'll be the last thing he does." I push my thumb between her lips. The action forcing her head back to meet my stare.

Wrapping her plump lips around it, she creates suction as I slowly pull it out. "Was that my punishment?" she whispers, remembering what I did to her last night.

"What?" I frown.

"Cutting my tongue," she explains.

I smile at her. "No, little demon. That was for fun."

She whimpers, and I love the way her breathing picks up at the thought that making her bleed was meant to be fun. She can try to tell me she didn't enjoy it, but we both know that would be a lie.

"I have something much more enjoyable in mind for your punishment."

Nibbling on her bottom lip, she asks, "Enjoyable for you or for me?"

"That's for you to find out."

## ELLINGTON

My heart is hammering in my chest. A shiver running down my spine. I had every intention of walking out that door. Telling him to fuck off.

*Did I, though?* If so, then why did I wait for him to return home to make the threat of leaving? I wanted him to stop me. Grab my hair, drag me back to bed, and force me to stay. I know what I did was wrong. I need to be punished. He needs to remind me that he still wants me. Needs me. It's the fucked-up part of me that wants to be owned. I don't know who I am without him.

"Hand me your bag," he orders.

Reaching down, I pick it up and hand it to him. He places it on the island and unzips it. Looking inside, he must be satisfied because he zips it up and grabs my hand. He pulls me out of the kitchen, down a hallway, and into what I'm going to make the library. I can't wait to fill it full of books. One full wall is nothing but floor-to-ceiling windows overlooking the woods out back.

He pushes on the far wall and a door opens that I didn't even realize was there. Flipping on a light, we walk down a set of stairs and into an open room.

A coldness runs over me, making me shiver at what I see. It's a basement. I've been in one before. David had one at his house. He tied me up and left me there one night. But that was the first night that Sin fucked me. Made me his.

Letting go of my hand, he commands, "Strip down." Then he throws the bag on a countertop over in the corner.

Slowly, I pull the T-shirt I was wearing—it's his—up and over my head. Then push the shorts down my legs, along with my underwear. I feel shy all of a sudden. Embarrassed as my wide eyes look over the ropes, chains, and belts hanging on the far wall. Each one different than the other. There are various colors and sizes.

He turns around and I see my white Dior heels in his hand that were in my bag. Coming up to me, he kneels. "Place your hands on my back to steady yourself."

I do as he says and lift my right foot off the cold concrete floor. He slides it on, followed by the other. He stands to his full height, and I smile nervously up at him. "My Prince Charming."

His face is blank, his eyes void of any emotion. It makes my pulse race. He grabs my hand once again and pulls me to the center of the room.

There's a black leather-wrapped post that stands in the middle. One vertical post with a horizontal one that sits right at my hips with my six-inch heels on.

I run my fingers along the soft leather, watching him out of the corner of my eye walk over to the far wall. He grabs some chains, a couple of belts, and then turns, opening a drawer. I can't see what he gets out of it.

When he turns to walk back to me, my eyes snap to stare at the silver ring that hangs from the top of the vertical post that is right in front of me. My breathing picks up.

He crouches down again, behind me this time. The chain wraps around my right ankle, the coldness of it making me shiver. He picks up a short double-ended metal hook. One is connected to the floor, the free end is latched through two links that are in the chain around my ankle, securing it in place.

Standing, he goes to my other ankle. He grabs it, and pulls it farther apart, almost knocking me off my heels. I grab the post in order to keep myself from falling over as he does the same thing to the left ankle.

Standing behind me, he leans into me, and I feel his jeans rub against my ass and thighs. "Look up," he commands.

Swallowing, I look up at the black-painted ceiling. He slides something around my throat. I feel the leather wrap around and hear him fasten it at the nape of my neck.

I try to lower my head but can't. My hands shoot to whatever it is he put around my neck, my heart hammering in my chest. "Sin—"

"It's a posture collar," he interrupts me before I can ask what it is.

My hands begin to sweat, and I try to shift on my heels, but they're tied too far apart, secured too tightly. My breathing accelerates and my pussy clenches. He's going to make me pay. I hate that I'm excited. That I want him to mark me. As if the brand on my inner thigh will fade away.

He walks around in front of me, and I look at him over the vertical post. My heels putting my chin level with the top. He's still got four, maybe five inches over me. Pulling another one of those double-sided metal hooks out of his pocket, I lower my eyes to watch him connect one side to the ring that hangs from the top of the post. Then he grabs my neck, pushing my head back painfully and I hear it click again.

Letting go of me, I try to pull away, but he secured the collar to the post. "Easton?" My voice shakes. My hands come up and grab at the metal hook. I try to unhook it, but he slaps my hands away.

He takes a longer chain and holds my hands in one hand while the other lays the chain across my wrists, then he brings both ends back over the center and pulls on them, securing my wrists together with one chain. He yanks on it, fastening it down to the horizontal bar that runs across my hips but on the inside of it. I'm immobile. Totally at his mercy. My pussy is wet, but my body is shaking, and I want to cry happy tears that he didn't let me leave. That he's going to fight for me. Force me to stay.

He stands back, his eyes running over me, and smiles.

"Please," I whimper, trying to yank myself free, knowing I'm not going anywhere.

Stepping back into me, he tilts his head to the side. He reaches out and runs his knuckles down the side of my face. "Do you have any idea what it felt like to watch him touch you? Know that he kissed you ...was going to fuck you."

"Sin," I lick my lips, needing to explain. "I was mad..."

"Mad?" he repeats the word, slowly nodding his head. His eyes boring into mine. "So every time you get *mad*, I have to expect you to throw yourself at any random guy."

My teeth clench and my tied hands fist. "You're cheating on me. I was just doing what I saw you do."

"I've never cheated on you," he argues.

I give a rough laugh. "Quit fucking lying to me. I saw you."

He gives me a smile and leans in, pressing his lips to my forehead. I try to pull away from his touch but there's nowhere for me to go. "I hate you," I growl, yanking on my restraints, knowing it's a lie. I don't hate him. I love him. Even knowing that he fucked Amelia, I still want to be with him. "I fucking hate you." I begin to cry, the bitter words hard to swallow.

"No, you don't. Not yet anyway," he says calmly.

"Sin," I growl, hating that he knows me so well.

He reaches out, gripping my face, squeezing my cheeks tightly. "Just remember, little demon, that I love you. Because what I'm about to do to you has nothing to do with love."

His hand drops from my face and I spit on him. It's the only thing I can do at this point. It lands on his cheek and chin. I expect him to slap me, or to grab my face again, but he doesn't. Instead, he turns his back to me.

# THIRTY-NINE

# SIN

I wipe my hand down my face while I hear her scream out followed by the chains rattling. She's not going anywhere. This is her punishment. Last night in the kitchen on her knees was nothing.

I'll just keep reminding her who branded her thigh. I open a drawer and grab what I want. Walking back over to her, I stand behind her this time. Loving the way her back is arched due to how I tied her to the posts. I had it made just for her. I've had years to imagine how I'd fuck her. The ideas are endless.

My eyes drop to her lean legs and watch them curve up to her bubble butt. It's pushed out, giving me full access to her ass and cunt. Her chin is pulled forward, the collar connected to the post and her hands down in front of her chained to the horizontal one that pushes her hips out.

She tries to turn her head to watch me, but she can't due the collar chained in place. I grip her hair and yank her head back. She screams out into the room at the motion, and I shove the metal ring gag into her mouth. "Open wide," I order, making sure it's behind her bottom teeth. "Wider, Elli. I know how big that mouth can

301

get." She whimpers, her body jerking and trying to pull away, but I manage to get the top behind her teeth as well. "That's a good girl," I say, bringing the leather straps around her head and fastening the buckle in place. Making it tight enough that it pinches her cheeks, and she can't push it out with her tongue.

I walk around the front of her and see tears already in her pretty ice-blue eyes. I grip her cheeks, lowering my face to hers. "Since you like to spit..." I place my lips in the center of the gag and spit into her mouth.

She gags, her tongue sticking out as she tries to spit it back out. But it's useless. She closes her eyes tightly and I watch tears run down her cheeks. "I love when you cry for me," I say, making her whimper. "Look at me, Elli," I command and her eyes slowly open. Her lashes wet and eyes red. "When I'm done with you, you won't be able to crawl, let alone run away from me."

Leaving her in place, I go over to the counter again and open a drawer, grabbing a couple of more things that I need to get started.

I first take the belt and wrap it around her upper thigh and the horizontal bar, securing it, making sure she can't move her ass. Then take another belt, doing the same to the other thigh.

I pop open the lube and run it over her ass, watching it run between her cheeks and drip to the floor. She's screaming, her body thrashing, thinking she knows what's coming. She has no clue.

I then pour the lube over the butt plug. I take my soaked fingers and reach between her spread legs from behind and rub her pussy. She was already wet, but I make sure to push my fingers into her, getting the lube everywhere I can.

Once I'm satisfied, I pull them out and rub the tip of the plug along her ass, down to her pussy. I push it into her cunt a few times before running it back up her ass and push the tip inside. She whimpers and I press my hand on her lower back, feeling her tense up. "It's going in whether you relax or not."

She cries, her shoulders shaking, and I push. Her ass opening up like I knew it would. "That's it, little demon. Almost there." I push it farther into her ass, the muscle widening to allow the head in. It disappears totally inside her, and I push my thumb on the wide base to make sure it's all the way in there.

I lean over her back and place my hand over her sweaty forehead, kissing her wet cheek, tasting her tears. "Good girl," I whisper. "You're such a good whore. Taking what I give you."

Sobs rack her body and I give her another kiss. Letting go of her, I step back and admire my girl.

*Fuck, she's incredible.*

I grab the dildo and lube it up as well. Then I lower it between her tied legs and run it over her pussy, smearing more of the lube to make sure it's ready before I slowly push it into her from behind. "You will learn, Ellington, that my cock is the only one you're ever going to need. And I'm more than willing to remind you anytime you need that."

Unintelligible noises come from her gagged mouth while I push the dildo in and out of her. "Look at the way your body begs for it, little demon. To be fucked." Her hips try to move back and forth on it, but I've got them tied with the belts, so they don't go very far. "Let me help you." I unfasten one belt at a time. It gives her hips two inches of movement. Enough for her cries to turn to moans.

Gripping the base of the dildo, I pick up the pace, fucking her cunt with it as if it's my cock. Which it is. She just doesn't know it yet. The chains rattle and her breathing picks up while I fuck her pussy roughly. I want her to get off. The punishment isn't not coming.

Her body stiffens, gargled moans come from her mouth, and when her body sags, I remove the dildo. It's covered in her cum.

I unfasten my jeans with one hand, and then unzip them. Pushing them down my legs, I let the material gather at my ankles, not caring to remove them completely. I grip my hard cock and slide it into her soaked cunt, groaning at the feel of it pulling me in.

I reach around to her drool-covered chin, pulling it back, knowing that the chain won't allow her to go far. But also, not caring. This is supposed to hurt. She gets off on that. "This is the reason for the gag." I hold up the dildo that is a replica of my cock, piercings and all, for her to see. "I had it made just for you, Elli. I told you my cock would be the only one to ever fuck you again and I meant that."

I push the tip of the life-like dildo into her mouth, her watery eyes blinking rapidly. She shifts, her throat working as I push it down into her open mouth. She gags, her body fighting the restraints. "Almost, Elli. I know you can take it all." It's not going to taste very good with the lube on it, but I don't give a fuck.

She blinks again and fresh tears spill over her bottom lashes while I look down at her. "You're doing so good, come on, Elli. Swallow it." It disappears into her mouth, and I hold it there, her chest heaving, body jerking. I pull out of her cunt and slam forward, making her fight me harder. "This is what you wanted, little demon. Every hole filled. To be used like the whore you are."

Pulling my hips back, I let my cock slip out and enter slower this time, feeling her pussy clenching around me. "Remember I told you, I'd fuck your mouth with a dildo covered in your cum." I pull it out of her mouth, and she coughs, spit flying from the gag. "So pretty. I love when you look like this. Take it again for me. Show me how good you are at swallowing my dick, Elli."

I push it back into her mouth, feeling her work her tongue to allow it to slide in easily. "I'm so proud of you." I kiss her cheek. Unable to stop myself, my tongue licks at her tears and I moan, pushing my cock into her soaked pussy at the same time. "You're doing so good."

She blinks, fresh tears running down her face, and I reach around with my free hand, pinching her nose. She bucks her hips, the sound of the posts rattling fill the room. "You'll learn that I can take whatever I want from you, Elli," I inform her, my cock just teasing her cunt while I hold her nose with the dildo still down her throat. "Your sight, your hearing, your very breath." I pull it out and let go of her nose. The dildo is soaked from her saliva and lube, but she's cleaned the cum off it. "Don't forget that you serve the devil. You will beg me on your knees for a mercy that will never come."

I pull my cock out of her pussy and step back, she slumps against the posts. I reach down and turn the butt plug, making her body jerk, tensing up.

I lower the dildo to her cunt and push it in and out a few times, getting her juices all over it again. Then I step back into her, shoving my cock roughly inside her pussy. "Again," I tell her, reaching around, and she sobs. I smile, pushing the dildo into her mouth. When it hits the back of her throat this time, she gags again. "Don't vomit, Elli. Breathe through your nose."

She blinks rapidly, tears pouring down her face. She relaxes her body, and I hear her breathing heavily through her nose.

"That's it." I kiss the side of her face. "Keep it down."

The end of the dildo has a big base. I had it made to where I can connect a leather belt to it and secure it around her head if I ever feel like leaving it in her mouth while I use the rest of her. But she's not ready for that. She'll get there, though. I'll train her to take it like her ass accepts my cock.

Just takes practice. Consistency is key.

An hour a day down here with me and she'll be able to do anything I want. Take anything I want.

I shove my cock in and out of her cunt, slamming into her. Her body tenses and I feel her come once again. "That's my girl," I say. "I just want to make you come over and over."

She makes a gagged moan.

I push forward, coming inside her cunt, and then pull out. I remove the dildo and toss it across the room. Kneeling behind her, I pick up my jeans and pull them to my hips, fastening them in place.

Then I pull up a black leather stool and set it right behind her ass before I place the belts on either upper thigh, holding them in place. "Can't have you moving around for this," I tell her and slap her ass.

She moans and I grab what I need before going back to sit on the stool. I take the peroxide and pour it onto the cotton ball. Then I wipe it across her lower back, right above her ass, centered between her two dimples. I have to clean all the sweat and bodily fluids off. I'm not trying to give her an infection.

Once it dries, I pull on my gloves and turn on the wireless machine. She starts screaming into the room, not knowing what I'm doing, but I ignore her.

Dipping the end of the needle into the black ink, I flatten my left hand across her now flawless skin, while using my right to tattoo her lower back.

I've pierced her nipples, and I've branded her with the Lords' crest. But that's not enough. Anyone can have something pierced, and any Lord can brand a woman. I've seen it done countless times over the years during my time at the house of Lords. But a tattoo that I do just for her? One that no other bitch will ever have?

That's ownership. It's another way for me to mark her. Another reminder of who she belongs to. It might not be plastered across her chest, but I'll know it's there and so will she. And if any man ever gets the chance to get her naked enough to see it, then it'll be the last thing he'll see before I rip his fucking head off.

I come to a stopping point and wipe the blood off that runs down her back to her ass. "You're doing so good, Elli," I say, and she shakes with a mumbled sob. "Almost done."

## ELLINGTON

ONCE AGAIN, I WAKE UP WITH A POUNDING HEADACHE. I can't move. I've never been this sore in my entire life. I'm pretty sure my throat is swollen. Is that possible? It's hard to swallow and breathe.

I get up, throw on some clothes, and make my way to the kitchen to look for something to eat because I'm starving, when I stop dead in my tracks. My mother sits at the island. Lincoln in front of the open fridge.

"Honey." She frowns seeing me. Walking over, she reaches out and tries to run her hand through my tangled hair. "What happened to you?"

"I can guess." Linc snorts.

I take a step back, her hand dropping to her side. "What ... what is going on?" My voice is rough, throat scratchy. "How did you know...?" I start to cough and clear my throat. "How did you get in?" How did they even know this is where I was?

My mother smiles at me like she didn't tell me to kill myself just days ago. "How did I get in?" She pulls a key from her pocket and sets it down. "My key."

"Where did you get that?" My voice shakes while trying to catch my breath. Why would Sin give her a key to our house?

"I bought this house for you."

My heart races at her words. "No," I say, shaking my head. "You didn't."

She frowns. "Who do you think owns this place?"

"Me. And Sin."

"Oh, honey." She starts laughing and looks over at Lincoln who gives me a pity look. "Why, why would you think that?"

"Because he bought it..." I trail off as they both start to laugh. "We signed paperwork. He added me to it." I've never bought a house before. I don't know what it requires but he had everything ready. Said it was done and ours.

"I did not raise you to be this naïve, Elli." My mother shakes her head. "Me and Lincoln bought you this house while we were away getting married. It was Lincoln's idea." She points at him and my stomach drops. Why would he want to buy me a house? He wanted me at home where they are. He even told me, said he'd make those six years with James feel like heaven.

I'm still asleep. This is a nightmare. It has to be.

"He wanted to give you a gift. Since we eloped and knew the wedding announcement would be ... hard on you. It's a gift. From us." She opens her arms out wide, gesturing to the house.

I shake my head, taking another step back. "No."

She sighs heavily, looking at Linc, but he shrugs. Obviously not knowing what to do or say to make me believe their lies.

"Yes, Elli. This is from us. Here..." She opens her large Louis and pulls out a set of papers. "These are your copies. I brought them for you to have." Handing me a manila envelope, my shaking hands take it.

Opening it up, I pull out the deed to the house. It's got multiple signatures. It looks the same as what me and Sin signed. But my name is nowhere on it. Just my mom's signature and Linc's.

"You'll need these too." She hands me another set of papers. "This is the trust. It's all yours. Free and clear."

"This has to be a joke," I whisper more to myself. They printed off the fake papers online to fuck with me.

"Seriously." She huffs and digs out her phone this time. A few seconds later, she's showing me emails. It's between her and a real estate agent. The woman sent her pictures of this house. It's fully furnished, just like it was the day me and Sin arrived. It talks about a cash sale. Closing date. How she wants it ready before she gets back.

My heart is hammering. *He lied.* He lied about Amelia. About this house. About how he loves me. What else hasn't been the truth? I fall into the chair at the island and try to keep the tears back.

"Honey." She places her hand on mine and I look up at her. "The house isn't the reason we're here."

"What is?" What else could it fucking be? And where the hell is Sin? After he was done with me last night in the basement, he gave me a shower and laid me in bed. Did he lie down with me? I can't remember. What time is it even right now? How long have I been out?

"Me and Lincoln have decided on your future."

"My future?" The headache I already have intensifies.

She nods. "We've found you a husband."

"No." I jump to my feet. "I'm not getting married, Mom." We've talked about this. She knows how I feel.

"We—"

"Darling, have a seat," Linc interrupts her, and she nods, doing as she's told. "See, Elli, after the incident at the reception. We've decided that it's time you settle down. Become a Lady."

"I don't want—"

"This isn't up for discussion, dear," my mother states, her tone harder than before. "You will settle down with a respected Lord. And you'll be initiated into a Lady." She reaches out and grabs her purse. *End of conversation.* "The wedding will be in two weeks," she states and Linc walks over to grab her hand.

Wedding? *Two weeks? Initiated?* "Wait," I shout desperately as they go to exit the house. "Can I choose? Who I marry?"

"No. It's been decided. Lincoln met with him this morning. And he's agreed." She lets go of his hand and walks over to me. She cups my face. "You're lucky anyone will marry you, Elli. With your ... past and current situation." Her eyes roam my tangled hair and swollen face with disgust. "You'll see this is for the best."

My chest is so tight it hurts to breathe. I always feared this would happen. She'd dictate what I do, who I can date. The older I got, the less I thought about it. This has to be Lincoln. He's making an example of me. Getting her to throw me away for good. "What about Sin?" I whisper.

She frowns. "He's already promised to marry, Elli. Jesus, did he not tell you anything? You know how this works. Honestly, I don't even know why you dated him in the first place knowing it couldn't go anywhere."

*Couldn't go anywhere?* I never thought about marriage, but I also never thought about him marrying either. "No." I shake my head. How long had I been asleep, for Christ's sake? "He's not..."

"The families announced their engagement this morning, Elli." Her eyes soften and she sighs.

My shoulders shake. *This morning?* After he fucked me in this house. "Who?" I lick my cracked lips. The gag from our time in the basement yesterday was rough on them. "Who is it?"

"Amelia Cleary." She smiles. "She's lovely. The whole family. Her mother is a friend of mine." She reaches up and pats the side of my cheek. "She's the one who sold us this house."

*He's marrying his chosen?* My legs give out, and I fall into my seat once again. She kisses my cheek. "I'll see you Thursday. We'll do lunch." Then she takes Lincoln's hand and leaves my house. Their house?

It's supposed to belong to me and Sin. How ... What happened? He told me yesterday that I was his. He's branded my inner thigh. He tattooed me ...

*"Look at that," he whispers in my ear. His arms have to hold me up, my legs too tired.*

*Opening my eyes, I look over my shoulder to the mirror in the bathroom to see SIN across my lower back, right above my ass. It's red and a little bloody. I whimper and he brings my face to look up* at him while he stands in front of me. "You ... tattooed me." My voice is rough. I had an idea what he was doing. I could hear the buzzing and feel the needle in my skin. I got off on it. The pain, the fact that I knew he was claiming me again in his own way turned me on.

Cupping my cheek, his blue eyes search mine before he lowers his face, so close our lips almost touch. "You're goddamn right I did." I whimper. "It's a reminder that you belong to me. Always have and always will." Then his lips capture mine in a breathtaking kiss.

I REFUSE TO BELIEVE HE TATTOOED HIS NAME ON ME yesterday and then announced an engagement this morning. That's not something you do on a whim. He would have known they were going to announce it.

"Sin?" I call out, my voice cracking in the now silent house.

Getting to my feet, I run to our bedroom. I open the closet door and my breath catches, all of his stuff is gone. No. This can't be happening.

I run back to the bed and pick up my cell. I call his. "You've reached Sin—" Straight to voicemail.

I do it again. Same. I decide to call Kira. She answers on the second ring. "Where are you?" I rush out, not even waiting for her greeting. Entering the kitchen once again, I grab my car keys.

She yawns. "House of Lords."

"Is Sin there?" I'm sliding a pair of shoes on that lay by the front doors. Bending over makes the skin across my back pull tight, reminding me of the tattoo that is now there for the rest of my life.

"I haven't seen him."

"Is his car there?" I demand.

"Elli—"

"Kira, please. Check for me." I'm running down the steps and to my car parked in the driveway.

"Let me look." She sighs. A moment later she answers, "Yes, it's here..."

I hang up and smash on the gas, tossing my phone to the passenger seat. Making it to the house in ten minutes when on any given day it would take over thirty. I rush inside, ignoring the stares that the guys give me. I'm running down the hallway and shove his bedroom door open. It's empty but his bathroom door is open. I enter to find him fresh out of the shower, jeans low on his hips. A towel in his hand drying off his hair.

"Is it true?" I ask, swallowing the knot in my throat, afraid of his answer. My mind telling me to shut the fuck up, turn around, and leave. To save myself the heartache that I already know is coming.

He lifts his head, those blue eyes harder than ever. The Sin I fell in love with. Would do anything for. Would let him do anything to me. The fact that I've got his name on my back proves just how far I'm willing to go to be his.

Ignoring me, he moves to stand in front of the mirror, giving me a side view. "I don't have time for games," is his monotone response.

*Games?* I grip his arm, yanking him to face me once again. "This isn't a fucking game, Easton," I snap. "Is it true?"

His jaw clenches and he looks away from me.

My breath catches. My hands lift to cover my mouth and I take a stumbling step back into the door, closing us in. "All of it?" I can't help but ask. I need him to say it. He's never been afraid to tell me the truth before, even if it hurt, so why is he avoiding answering me now? And why does it feel worse than if I knew he lied about it?

He turns to face me again, moving to stand in front of me. His eyes on mine. "Did you really think I loved you?"

Tears sting my eyes, and I feel like I just jumped off a high-rise, my stomach now in my throat.

"What did you think was going to happen, Ellington?" He uses my full name, making me whimper. Lifting his right hand, he takes a piece of hair between his fingers and twirls it around. "That I'd make you an honest woman? Have kids with you?" He snorts at that ridiculous idea.

The first tear falls down my cheek. He lets go of my hair to run his knuckles through it. "You've always been a whore, Elli. I'm a Lord. Will be a powerful one. And I'm going to make a woman a very respected Lady." My stomach tightens. "You're the kind of woman we fuck on the side. Not the one we come home to."

I can't breathe. Can't move. My vision is fading in and out, and I think I'm about to lose consciousness. I never wanted to be a Lady, but for Sin? I'd be anything he wants me to be. And if I had to marry a Lord, I want it to be him. "I don't believe you," I say, shaking my head, refusing to process his words.

His blue eyes search mine and I take in a shaky breath. "You said you loved me," I manage to get out.

He smiles, a sinister one that makes his eyes light up. "Those were just words, Elli. You're the stupid girl who believed them."

"You..." I take a second to swallow the knot in my throat. "You said that I belonged to you."

His perfect lips that made me weak in the knees yesterday make the hairs on the back of my neck stand when they curve into a smile. "You're right. I did say you belong to me, but I never said I belonged to you."

"Sin?"

I stiffen as a female calls his name from inside his room as if God himself is laughing in my face for believing every word Sin ever said to me.

"One minute," he answers, his voice louder to carry through the closed door we're leaning up against, making me jump.

"We're going to be late, babe. The caterer was able to work us in. I don't want them to cancel on us," she goes on.

Caterer? For what? Their wedding? He's really marrying her? The girl he said he wasn't cheating on me with? Was it cheating? Were we ever really together? My mother was right, I know the rules the Lords have but I stupidly believed that I was special. That he would pick me over her. Why? Because I was a fool for him?

She's supposed to be his chosen. A chosen and a Lady are two very different things. And a Lord doesn't always marry his chosen. So why her?

It's soul-crushing to think I would ever get what I want. I never have before. Sin is no different.

I can't help the sob that bubbles up and he slaps his hand over my mouth, pushing the back of my head to the door. Leaning in, he presses his hard body into mine, his face dropping to whisper in my ear, "You were always meant to be to someone's secret, Elli. You're a good fuck, I can't deny that. But no one will ever love you. Not the real you."

He shoves me to the side, grabs his shirt off the counter, and rips the door open, slamming it shut behind him, hiding me in his bathroom. "Let's go," I hear him say.

"What were you doing in there?" she asks him, obviously thinking something is up.

"Nothing," he answers. Then I hear his bedroom door open and close as he leaves with his future bride.

---

"In here," Kira states. "Put her in bed," she tells Corbin who carries me.

After Sin left me in his bathroom, I fell to my knees. Crying so hard that I crawled to the toilet and got sick. Kira found me and had Corbin drive my car home while she drove me.

I curl up into a ball, no longer crying. My mind has gone numb, I wish my body would too. The tattoo burns more than the brand ever did. I can feel it throbbing, a reminder that I was so fucking dumb to let him tie me up and have his way with me. He's right, no man could ever love me.

"Hey." She kneels beside the bed to get eye level with me.

"Did you know?" I whisper, finally speaking to her. There's been nothing to say since she found me. She knew I would show up when she informed me Sin was there. And then I overheard Corbin tell her when they entered the bathroom that he had seen Sin and Amelia arguing while he rushed her out of the house. My car was parked right out front. A part of me hopes that Amelia saw it and put two and two together. But if she's as dumb as me, she won't even care. She'll take him any way she can get him.

She sighs. "I found out this morning."

I sniff. Why didn't she tell me? Warn me? Did she not stop to think how I'd find out? She's known that I'm sleeping with her brother. Not that I'm in love with him, but it was obvious that we were together and that I was distraught when I found out he was sleeping with Amelia when she found us in the bathroom. "How long have they known?"

"I don't know."

"Three weeks," Corbin answers, leaning up against the doorframe.

"Babe," she snaps at him.

"Three weeks?" I whisper, my throat closing up on me all over again.

"They were going to wait until next year after she graduates from Barrington," he goes on. "But her mother decided to move it up."

Her mother? Did she do it because of my mom? She told me

315

this morning in my kitchen that they are friends. Did they plan this? "I tried calling him..."

"He's blocked your number," he adds matter-of-factly.

"Corbin," she snaps at him.

"She deserves to know." His cold eyes meet mine. "It's over, Elli. It'll be best for you to come to terms with that sooner rather than later."

Kira jumps up and goes over, slamming the door in his face.

# FORTY

## SIN

"What do you think about this, baby?" Amelia calls out and I grind my teeth at the nickname. Elli hated it and so do I. It's too sweet. Too generic.

Walking over to her, I look at the sample of plates they have out before us to taste. They all look like overpriced shit, if you ask me. But what do I know? "Doesn't matter," I say, pulling out my cell from my jeans pocket and walking away to get some privacy.

I pull up the camera footage just in time to see Corbin's eyes look at me through the screen as if he knows I'm watching, then Kira slams the bedroom door in his face. My sister walks over to the bed and I watch Elli bury her face into the pillow. Kira rubs her back, but Elli pushes her away.

"Babe?" Amelia barks out. "What are you doing?" She's in front of me the next second, trying to get a look at my phone.

I lock it, narrowing my eyes on her. Opening my mouth to speak, it rings in my hands. **Tyson** lights up the screen. "Hello?" I answer, stepping away once again to put some distance between us.

"It's done. You have a meeting. Friday morning. Ten a.m.," he answers in greeting, getting to the point. "Meet me at Blackout. I'll drive."

"You're coming too?" I can't help but ask. Surprised by that.

"That's the only way they'll see you," he growls, obviously not pleased with the situation but understanding how important it is to me.

I nod to myself. "Thanks, man." Knowing that I'm not only going to owe Ryat but I'm also going to owe Tyson as well.

He hangs up without another word and I turn to see Amelia glaring at me. Arms crossed over her paid-for chest. "Why is Tyson Crawford calling you?" she demands, pushing a hip out.

"It's nothing." I give her my back, going to look at the camera again.

She grabs my arm, her nails digging into my skin, making me grind my teeth. "Easton—"

"None of your goddamn business," I snap, spinning back around to face her. Silence falls over the room. All eyes are now on me.

The woman who is helping us plan our wedding gasps. Her eyes wide, hand now over her injected lips.

*Fuck this day.*

I reach into my back pocket and remove my wallet. Handing my card to Amelia, I say, "Get whatever you want. Just don't expect me to care." Then I walk out the front door and go to my car. I fall into the driver's seat and pull up the camera footage.

Elli is lying in the bed, eyes closed. She looks to be asleep. Pulling up the rest of the house where I've installed cameras, I see Corbin and my sister in the living room. I turn on the volume to the max setting to listen in.

"Why did you tell her all that?" she growls at him. "Elli is fragile."

"Like I said, she deserved to know." He shrugs. "Sin's marrying Amelia. The poor girl needs to get over it and move on."

"Oh, because that's so easy." Kira laughs but it holds no humor. "Would I be that easy to get over?"

"Kira," he snaps. "Don't start..."

"What would you do if I dumped you to marry someone else? Hmm? You'd just let me walk away?"

"That's different." Corbin runs a hand through his hair.

"That's a cop-out if I've ever heard one." She rolls her eyes and steps away from him.

He reaches out, grabbing her upper arm, and spins her around. She goes to push him away, but he pulls her in, kissing her.

I go back to the camera in the bedroom, not wanting to watch that shit, and see the bed now empty. I sit up straighter. *Where the fuck did she go?*

Pulling up another camera, I look at the bathroom. It shows her walking up to one of the double sinks. Her hand over her face. She turns on the faucet and cups the water, rinsing out her mouth.

I turn on the volume as my sister enters. "Knock, knock."

Elli looks up at her, tears silently falling down her puffy face.

"You okay?" she asks softly.

"Fine," Elli answers and starts to walk back toward the bedroom.

"Did you get sick again?" my sister asks her.

"I'm fine, Kira." Elli ignores her question.

"Are you pregnant?" Kira asks, and Elli comes to a stop.

She slowly turns around to face my sister. "No." Shaking her head, she runs a hand through her tangled hair.

"Are you sure? Maybe you should take a test," my sister offers, her voice so low that she sounds afraid to even put the thought into Elli's head but also concerned for her friend's health.

"I'm not pregnant, Kira. I'm on birth control," Elli argues, getting irritated. Turning, she goes to walk off again when my sister speaks.

"But what if you are?"

Elli's shoulders fall and she sighs heavily, but she doesn't respond. Instead, she goes into the master suite and crawls back into bed, pulling the covers up and over her head to block out the world and her best friend.

# ELLINGTON

I SIT AT THE RESTAURANT, STARING AT MY WATER. KIRA'S words keep echoing in my head that I might be pregnant.

It's not possible. But that would be my luck, right? Having Sin's baby. The universe fucking me one last time. I highly doubt my future husband wants to raise another man's child. Hell, I've already got his name tattooed on me. At least that can be covered up with another one. And my mom said it yesterday that I was lucky a Lord even wants me. Add a child and fuck that shit.

A part of me hopes I am. It'll give me an out. I'll tell the Lord that I'm supposed to marry I'm pregnant and maybe he'll throw me to the side, and I'll get to go on with my life. Alone. Far away from here where nobody knows me. Sin will be busy with his wife and starting a family with her, he'll never even think about me, let alone look for me. The thought makes my breath catch and chest tighten.

"Ellington?"

I look up to my mother who sits across from me. "Yeah?"

She sighs, her eyes falling to her phone Checking the time, I'm sure. Counting down the minutes until she gets to leave. I don't even know why she wanted to go to lunch with me anyway. And I don't know why I crawled out of bed in the first place today. I didn't even brush my hair or take a shower. Just threw on a pair of shorts and T-shirt along with some tennis shoes and walked out the door.

Standing, she gets my attention once again and I see her smile. "Darling."

Lincoln comes up to the table and I roll my eyes. Of course, he's here. I'm not surprised that she didn't tell me we were having a guest. Why would she want to eat with me alone?

He kisses her cheek and then looks at me. "Elli, it's good to see you out of the house."

I say nothing.

"I hope you ladies don't mind but I brought company." He gestures to my right, and I look over, my heart pounding in my chest.

"Of course not," my mother says excitedly.

The kid leans over and shakes my mother's hand, and she blushes. His green eyes meet mine and I feel like I'm going to puke again. *It's him.* The kid from James's office, then their reception.

"Ellington." He nods to me and takes the seat to my right.

I stare at him wide-eyed, unable to speak, trying to hold down the piece of toast I managed to eat for dinner last night.

"Elli, don't be rude, honey," my mother scolds me. "I'm sorry, she's not feeling well."

She's right. I was, but not now.

"That's quite all right." He gives her a dazzling smile. "We can do this another time." Pushing up from the chair, he goes to leave but my mother stops him.

"No, please. Sit down. She'll be okay. She just needs some food in her system."

"I'll get the server," Lincoln says, standing and leaving us alone with the surprise guest he brought.

"Who are you?" I ask, unable to stop myself. Why is he here? With Lincoln, of all people?

He looks at me, his green eyes drop to my chest for a quick glance before meeting mine. "I'm Chance Beckham. But everyone calls me Becks." His shoulders are back, chest bowed like he's proud of that name. Like I should know who the fuck he is.

I don't.

"Elli," my mother calls my name and I look over at her. She's smiling, her teeth on full display. She looks so happy it makes my stomach knot. "Chance here is Lincoln's nephew."

My breath hitches.

"And he's going to be your husband."

# FORTY-ONE

# SIN

I was at Blackout a quarter to nine this morning. Tyson was already ready like I knew he would be. I sit in the passenger seat while he takes the sharp curves of the Pennsylvania roads. We're climbing, making our way up into the mountains on a cloudy, cold day.

I've got my cell in my lap, an earbud in my ear watching Elli on the screen. She's sleeping. She's been doing it a lot this week. She came home from lunch with her mother yesterday, and they got into another huge fight. Her mother stormed into the house yelling; Elli told her to go to hell. It got dirty like the reception argument.

Chance Beckham is who they are forcing her to marry. I'm not surprised. I figured that's who Lincoln would pick. It's a way to throw it in my face that he won. He's thinks he'll get unlimited access to her if his nephew is her husband.

He's not as smart as he thinks he is.

I look over at her nightstand. She's got a pregnancy test and an empty bottle of wine next to it. I watched her take it last night and she actually looked disappointed that it was negative. However,

323

she then celebrated with a bottle while watching a horror film before she passed out.

"Why are you torturing yourself?" Tyson finally speaks to me since I arrived at Blackout almost an hour ago.

I close the phone and remove the earbud, not really sure what to say so I keep my mouth shut, watching the woods pass by.

My cell rings through the silence and it's Amelia. I hit ignore and run a hand down my face.

Sitting up straighter, I see a sign coming up that says *Carnage*: 10 miles.

"Be direct," Tyson speaks, obviously noticing the sign as well. "To the point. Don't fuck around. The Spade brothers don't like having their time wasted."

"Got it." I nod. "How long have you known them?"

"Long enough," he answers cryptically.

Not even sure why I asked. My phone rings again and this time I answer. If I don't, she'll just keep calling. "Hello?"

"Don't forget we've got dinner with my parents tonight," she says in greeting.

I groan. Seriously? This could have been a text. "I won't."

"My mother and I have an appointment with the florist. So I'll just ride with her and meet you at dinner." She pauses. "Unless you want to go to the florist too? Then we can ride together..."

"I'll meet you at dinner." She knows I want no part of planning the wedding. I couldn't care less about it.

"Okay, love you..."

I hang up and immediately pull up the cameras inside Elli's house again. She's still in bed sleeping. Locking my phone, I close my eyes, sighing. Tyson was right, I've got to stop torturing myself.

Tyson pulls up to old wrought-iron gates. Rolling down his window, he presses in a code and both open, allowing us access. I look over the tall trees that line both sides of the two-lane road.

It's curvy along with a few hills. Once the trees clear, a medieval-looking building comes into view. "I didn't even know this place existed."

"Most don't." Tyson goes on, "Just because you're a Lord doesn't mean they tell you everything."

Pulling into the circle drive, we both get out and make our way up the fifteen steps and into the double doors. It looks as rough and old as the outside.

A man dressed in a black-and-white butler uniform nods to us. "Please follow me, gentlemen."

He takes us to an elevator that we ride to the sixth floor. Opening up, we step off and into a room. "The Spade brothers will be right with you," he states and then exits, closing the doors behind him.

Tyson falls into a chair, checking his cell. I walk over to the floor-to-ceiling windows overlooking the woods. Listening to the doors open behind me, I turn around to see three men enter.

I'm not sure what I expected but it's not what I see. One has dark hair that is shaved close to the sides but longer on the top. He's wearing a black long-sleeved shirt with a pair of holey jeans and black combat boots. Ink covers his knuckles and his neck. A cluster of snakes wrap around his throat all the way up to his jawline.

The second guy has a white T-shirt on, showing off both of his sleeves. One catches my eye. It's of a woman. She's dressed in a nun costume that covers her entire body; all you can see is her face. She's got a ball gag in her mouth with a line of drool running down her chin, her makeup smeared, and she has an upside down cross on her cheek. My eyes lift to his blue eyes, and he smirks, catching me staring.

The third guy wears a backward baseball hat with a hoop nose ring. He's dressed in a black T-shirt and jeans. He's covered in ink as well, but I can't make them out due to the blood splattered on him. He removes a rag hanging out of his back pocket and wipes off his hands before reaching out and turning to Tyson. "It's been a while."

"You know how it is." Tyson shakes it, not even bothered.

"What can we do for you?" the first one who entered asks, picking up a pack of cigarettes off the desk and pulling one out. Like Tyson said, no bullshitting.

"I want to see your roster," I state.

Silence falls over the room while the guy lights his cigarette and takes in a long drag. Blowing it out, he chuckles. "This is a joke, right?"

"No. I'm looking for someone and I want to know if they're here or not."

Taking his time, he takes another drag, his cheeks caving in on the inhale, the end burning red while his green eyes glare at me. Letting it out, he says, "If someone is here, then it won't matter if we confirm it or not." Shaking his head, he adds, "They won't be leaving. To the world, they no longer exist."

## ELLINGTON

I'M HOLDING THE BOTTLE OF WINE BY THE NECK, DOWN AT MY side, as my bare feet pad against the cold floor. My life is over. My plan of a career gone. I might as well drop out of Barrington at this point. Chance told me I won't be working. Ever. My job is here. In this house. One day raising his children. Well, those weren't his exact words. He was on his best behavior in front of my mother at lunch yesterday when he told her he'd take care of me. She looked more than thrilled to be handing me off like an infant that requires round-the-clock care, and she no longer had the time for me.

At this point, I give up. I'll die a slow and agonizing death.

Is this why my father committed suicide? Because he just saw no end in sight? How long will I be able to take the life that Chance will make me live? Forget what I want or need. He'll use my body however he wants, and I'll pop out some kids while he fucks other women and I pretend not to know. It's like Sin said in his bathroom, the Lords have women on the side. When you're told you can have anything you want, women included, why would they be satisfied with one?

Lifting the wine, I take a gulp. Tipping it back too far, some runs down my chin and covers my T-shirt. It's Sin's. I found it in the back of the closet underneath a stack of my jeans. It still smells like him. I had the urge to burn it like he did my journals and diaries, but I couldn't bring myself to do it.

Entering the dark living room, I walk over to the floor-to-ceiling windows and open the black curtains. I look over at the dark woods that line the back of the property.

Lunch went about how I thought it would. Fucking terrible. Then Linc and Chance showed up and it just blew up from there. I ordered a few drinks after that, and my mother had to bring me home. We fought. Once again, she called me a used-up whore and told me that I should kiss Chance's shoes for thinking he can make me any kind of Lady. I had a few more drinks after she left.

Then I remembered that Kira thought I was pregnant. I had her bring a test over and when it was also negative, we celebrated by having a few shots of the Everclear she brought with her.

*It's for the best.*

Hell, maybe all the drugs and shit I've consumed will prevent me from having Chance's children and he'll throw me away. Like every other man who's come into my life. A Lord needs to reproduce. It's part of their commitment to the society. If you don't have anything to offer to it, then they don't need you. And the Lords want their army.

Deny a man sex for three years, then give him a chosen as a reward, marry him off and he's more than willing to knock up his wife. Boom! Next generation of Lords and Ladies are growing up. Rinse and repeat.

A cold chill runs up my back and I stiffen. My heart picking up at the shadow I see in the window standing behind me.

My skin begins to tingle, the fear and adrenaline making my breath hitch. "What do you want?" I ask, knowing exactly who it is.

"Little demon." Sin's voice comes from behind me.

I close my eyes, my hand curling around the neck of the wine bottle tighter. The hair is pulled off my shoulders to lay down my back and goose bumps break out across my skin. "Why are you here, Sin?"

"Isn't it obvious?" he rasps against my neck. His lips tenderly kissing right behind my ear.

"I'm getting married," I say, hoping it pisses him off as much as the news about him marrying Amelia did me. I want him to fucking break. It's my turn to destroy something.

"You were serving me long before he came along, little demon," he says, and I whimper. Of course, he doesn't care that I'm being forced against my will to marry another Lord.

"Leave," I whisper. "Please."

"I can't do that, Elli." His arm comes around my waist and slides up my shirt. His gentleness makes my breath hitch. Sin is never gentle, but I don't stop him. I've missed him too much. Just the fact that he showed up has my heart hammering in my chest with excitement. "You still think of me." He chuckles darkly when his fingers run over my nipple piercings. I haven't brought myself to remove them.

No matter how hard I try, I can't seem to erase him.

His hand slides through the collar of his shirt I have on, and he wraps his fingers around my neck, making me arch it.

His free hand grabs the bottle that hangs to my side. Bringing it up to my lips, he says, "Open."

He pours the wine down my throat, and I choke on it. Making it cover my face, neck, and clothes. It splatters across the window I stand in front of. "Sin," I snap, pushing him away and turning to face him, his hand now slipping free of the shirt.

The open curtains now behind me give the room a little light from the outside porch lights streaming in. He's dressed in his black jeans and black hoodie. All he's missing is his mask, contacts, and gloves to be my hero. I hate that the guy who saved me is the same guy who no longer wants me. "Get the fuck out of *my* house," I growl, walking past him. My shoulder bumping into his.

"Get on your knees," he orders.

A laugh bubbles up my chest and spills out of my lips. I turn around to face him. The look on his face tells me he was not joking. "You get what you give, Sin, and I don't give a fuck anymore." With that, I turn, giving him my back and heading to my bedroom.

His hand grips my hair, and he yanks my back into his front.

"Sin," I growl, my hands grabbing at his forearms. Digging my nails into his skin, I hope I make him bleed. "Let go of me." My legs kick out as he lifts me off my feet, carrying me over to the back of the couch. My pussy clenching with excitement. He's here for me. And if he's here for me that means he's not there for *her*.

"Is this how we're going to play, Elli?"

I whimper and wetness pools in my underwear. *No. No. No.* "Just leave. Ple-ease," I beg him. My heart hammering.

He chuckles, pinning my front into the back of the couch while standing behind me. "Going to fight me?" He grabs my hands and yanks them behind my back, pinning them in place while gripping my forearms together in one hand. His free hand grabs my hair, yanking my head up, forcing me to stare up at the ceiling, panting. "Make me take what already belongs to me?"

I try to wiggle free but there's nowhere to go and my thighs clench. Hating myself more than I could ever hate him. James was right, I respond better to beatings. Bruises and scars are what I get off on. Why am I like this? Would I have been this way had my father never died and my mother had not married James? We'll never know. "Fuck you, Sin," I manage to grind out.

Another dark chuckle. "Go ahead, little demon. If fighting me makes you feel better about yourself, I'm okay with that."

Another whimper escapes my lips, and he yanks me from the couch. Turning me around, he lets go of me and I slap him across the face.

He reaches out, painfully gripping my neck with both of his hands, taking away my air. Placing his face in mine, he smiles when he speaks. "We both know that I have no problem taking what I want."

# FORTY-TWO

## SIN

Her body fights me but she's weak and drunk. I've been watching her all day on the cameras. It just wasn't enough. This is much better. Pretty ice-blue eyes wide with terror, her small body pressed up against mine. Fuck, I've missed her, and it's only been five days.

Her hands slap at my arms, her body jerking in my grasp. Lips parted, and I watch her long, dark lashes flutter when her arms drop to her sides. "That's it, Elli. Such a good girl." Leaning forward, I press my lips to hers gently, feeling the softness of them against mine.

I don't give a fuck what either of our future's hold. She will always be mine. I'm here to remind her of that.

Pulling back, I see her eyes roll back into her head and I let go of her neck, her legs give out and I catch her. She lies across my arms, dazed and coughing. I lay her on the couch and leave her there, knowing she won't be going anywhere anytime soon. I've got to get some things together because I'm going to be staying the night. Maybe a couple.

I SIT ON THE COUCH, MY ARMS FANNED ACROSS THE BACK, MY eyes on the TV. It's on but muted. I'm not one to really watch much television, but I've got to do something to pass the time until she wakes up.

My eyes go to the chair that sits facing me. When I returned from the basement, she was passed out on the couch like I knew she would be. I picked her up, undressed her and brought a chair in from the kitchen. She's sitting up, her legs spread wide open, ankles tied to each front leg. I also tied her knees open to it. Her arms are behind her back, draped over the top of the chair and tied down to the back, and I stuffed a pillow between her and the back of the chair to push out her hips.

I want her open. Vulnerable. Able to see everything. She's got the posture collar on to keep her chin up and three pieces of tape over her mouth. Two in an X, then the extra across both.

She stirs and a smile tugs at my lips. It takes her a few minutes for the fog to lift and reality to sink in. Wide eyes meet mine and she begins to mumble behind the tape. She jerks, her body fighting in the chair.

I watch her nipples harden and her hips lift off the seat as much as possible. I lean forward, grip the chair, and yank her to where it touches the end of the couch, my legs spread wide for her to sit between them. I run my hands up and down her thighs and she whimpers.

"About time you wake up for me." My hand slides between her legs and my fingers spread her pussy wide open for my thumb to run over her clit, making her jump. The way I've got her seated, her hips are pushed out farther than her chest. So I've got enough access to her cunt to play with. Most of her weight is back on her underarms that are draped over the back.

This isn't about being comfortable. It's about being mine.

Pulling away, I shove the chair back a little and to my left so I can reach the coffee table in front of the couch. I pick up the little pink egg and the lube. I pop it open and cover the silicone with it. Then I turn to her, my hand going back between her legs. She mumbles unintelligible words behind the tape as I fuck her with my fingers a few times before slipping it inside her.

I hold up the remote and her watery eyes go from mine to it. "Remember when I tied you up and got you off with the wand?" I ask, smiling at the memory. It was back in the beginning when I snuck into her room as her savior. "You got off, what, five or six times?"

She blinks, her chest heaving.

"We're going to do that again." I turn on the remote and her back bows, body stiffening for a brief second before she starts thrashing in the chair.

I sit back, my eyes falling to her body, watching her hips ride the chair as if it's my cock inside her. She's sucking in breaths through her nose, her taped cheeks caving in, and nipples hard. "Gorgeous," I say, and she whimpers.

She screams into the tape and her body goes stiff as I watch her come. I shut it off and she slumps in the chair. Watery eyes meet mine.

Lifting my hips up off the couch, I remove what I want out of my jeans pocket. Her eyes widen when she sees me remove the lid. "That's one." I lean forward, running the tip of the black Sharpie down her chest about three inches long. Putting it back on, I smile at her. "I don't want to lose track. And I don't expect you to either. When forced to orgasm over and over, your mind tends to turn to mush."

She whimpers again, trying to turn her head away from me but the collar keeps it in place. So she closes her eyes instead. I allow it.

My cell rings. I answer, placing the call on speaker, and set it down next to me on the couch. "Hello?"

"Hey, babe." Amelia's voice fills the room.

I stare at Elli and her eyes widen when she realizes who's on the other end. I turn on the remote again and watch her body fight in the restraints.

"Where are you?" Amelia goes on. "We have dinner with my parents. We're waiting on you."

Elli blinks, fresh tears running down her cheeks.

"I'm not going to make it." I turn up the vibrator to the highest setting, loving the way Elli's body tenses.

"What?" Amelia whines. "But, babe..."

"I won't be home tonight."

Elli sobs, understanding that she's going to be my plaything all night long. I'm going to put her body through heaven, but it's going to feel like hell. I'm going to make it brutal.

Amelia sighs heavily but then adds, "Well, you can make it up to me tomorrow then." And by the way her voice drops, you can tell she means me and her in bed.

"Whatever you want," I say and watch Elli's hips lift off the chair again, getting ready for number two. Her body unable to control itself. Elli sucks in a deep breath through her nose, her body bowing.

"Love you," Amelia speaks.

I end the call just as Elli comes again. I turn off the vibrator and watch her come down from her high, sinking back into the chair. She opens her heavy eyes, and they land on mine. They narrow, she's angry with me. Not enough, though. She's nowhere near where I need her to be. "If it makes you feel any better, I don't love her either."

She sobs, her body shaking.

"Where were we?" I pick up the Sharpie and write another

tally on her chest next to the last. "I hope these come off before your wedding night," I say, and she closes her eyes tightly.

Her mother has officially announced her daughter's engagement to Chance. When you plan on having a wedding in two weeks, you've got a lot of time to make up for. And her mother wants it big, flashy.

I'm going to make sure it's a day my little demon never forgets.

"I'd hate for Becks to question your loyalty to him."

She shakes her head the best she can and screams into the tape.

"Do you know what they do to Ladies who cheat on their Lords?" I go on as if she cares. "Doesn't matter if it's rape or she willingly spreads her legs. Cheating is cheating. I'm not saying I agree, but those are the rules." I shrug, watching her hatred for me grow every passing second.

I raise my hips again to retrieve my pocketknife. I open it up and run it along her shaking thigh, careful not to cut her. "Her Lord drags her to the cathedral kicking and screaming. He strips her naked, ties her down at the altar in front of the congregation. Then an offering basket is passed around to his fellow Lords who fill the pews. But instead of collecting money, they pass out razor blades. Then, one by one, the Lords stand, go to the altar, and cut his Lady. Blood is a price we all must pay."

I run the tip of the blade up between her legs and her body goes stiff. Slowly, I drag it upward and over her stomach. "Of course, there are rules. Her Lord gives orders. Don't cut too deep. No more than two inches long. Stay away from her cunt ... It can be as few or as many rules as he wants. She's his wife. His offering."

I bring the knife to her breasts and flick the piercing with it, making her flinch. "I've heard stories but only seen it once. My sophomore year. He returned home early from an assignment to find her on her knees for his brother. He shot his brother, killed him right then and there. Decided she needed a more painful fate. He only had one rule, make sure she was dead by the time they were done. God, I'll never forget the screams. How they echoed. It went on for hours. So much blood. That's how I learned not to kill David so soon."

Her heavy eyes meet mine when I bring the knife back down between her legs. "The point is to make the Lady as ugly as possible. It doesn't matter if he loves her or not. It's the fact that she stepped out on him. We are all about loyalty, devotion. That's what I love about you, Elli."

She whimpers at the use of the L-word.

Pulling the chair back between my open legs, I place the knife to her taped lips, and she shakes uncontrollably. Her eyes are on mine, and I watch them swim in tears, wondering how long it will take to break her. She's too strong for her own good. Blinking, they spill over her bottom lashes and down over the tape.

"He trained you well, Elli," I say, and a sob racks her body. "But it's time you learn who you really are." My eyes go to the red dot in the corner of the room up in the ceiling. If you didn't know it was there, you'd never see it. I hid it well. I look back at her. "You may become Chance's wife, but you will always be my whore." Then I turn on the vibrator with the remote, tossing it across the room, and sit back, enjoying the sound of her muffled cries and moans with the Sharpie in my hand, ready to keep score.


# ELLINGTON


I'M LYING ON THE SHOWER FLOOR, BODY SHAKING. I DON'T know how long I've been in here but I'm sure the water is cold by now. I don't feel it. I'm numb. Too tired to move, to even open my eyes.

I don't know how long Sin was here. Time didn't exist. At one point, he untied me from the chair and carried me to my bedroom. He continued on my torture there. Vibrator, belt, tape, and rope. Any position he could think of, he fucked me.

I would pass out and then wake up again. It was an endless cycle of pleasure that my body begged for.

I keep having flashbacks, though. Bits and pieces coming back to me.

"GOOD GIRL, ELLI," SIN WHISPERS IN MY EAR. "FUCK," HE groans, and his hand slides into my already tangled hair. "You're doing so good."

Pushing the side of my head down into the mattress, I don't even fight him. There's no point. I've got nothing left. He's on a mission to kill me—death by orgasms. Is there a better way to go? No.

The sound of the headboard hitting the wall fills the room along with his heavy breathing. He's close to coming. Again. "That's it." His hips push forward, moving to push my face down into what was once our bed. "Goddamn, Elli. Your cunt feels so good."

I can't breathe, but that's nothing new. At this point, I'm not even sure how I'm still alive. I've lost count of time and days since I found him standing in my living room. I've been his toy to play with. To use however he wants, and my body has loved every second of it.

His hand in my hair raises my face and I suck in a breath through my nose since I've still got tape over my mouth. He only takes it off to fuck my mouth then applies new pieces once he's done using it.

My legs are spread wide, my back arched painfully high, and my restrained arms are pinned between us behind my back. They rub against the fresh tattoo and the pain turns me on even more.

I can't decide if I'm in hell or heaven.

My pussy pulses around his pierced dick as he fucks me ruthlessly. At this point, I can't tell you how many times I've come but the tallies on my skin keep track for me. "That's it, little demon. Show me how much you love being my whore by coming on my dick."

I whimper, unable to make any other noise, my body stiffening as I do exactly what he wants. Dots flash across my vision, my breathing halting altogether. My eyes roll back into my head as my muscles start to spasm. He controls every part of me, mind and body. I can't stop it.

Shoving his hips forward, he stills as his cock pulses inside me. Pulling out, he lets go of me and I fall onto the bed, trying to catch my breath.

I feel him get off the bed but I'm too tired to open my eyes as tremors rack my body. He grabs my ankles, pulling me farther down the bed to the footboard. He spreads them wide and wraps something rough around each one. Rope. I'm spread wide open for him.

His hand grips my hair, and he moves my head to the other side. "Look at me," he commands.

My heavy eyes open and he's leaning over the side of the bed, his face in front of mine. His free hand grips my taped cheeks while his eyes search my tear-streaked face. I haven't been able to stop them. On top of pain, my entire body is overstimulated. It's vibrating from the inside out.

Letting go of my cheeks, his hand brushes the matted hair off my face and onto my sweaty back. "You're so fucking perfect." His knuckles run down the side of my face. "But I'm going to ruin you, Elli."

I swallow at his promise.

"Chance will never be able to satisfy you. You will look forward to my visits. You will beg for me to use you. To make you my little whore."

He steps away and I close my eyes, thinking I'm going to get a *nap, but they open when something cold slides between my ass cheeks. He's not done with me.*

*Seconds later, I feel pressure from his fingers. My legs try to close but I realize that's why he tied them open. His finger easily slips inside my ass, in and out, spreading me, preparing me to take whatever he wants to give me. I don't even flinch when the butt plug slides into place. Instead, a moan comes from my taped lips.*

*Then I'm bathed in darkness. I blink, trying to figure out if I passed out or not, but nope. He turned the light off. Then I hear the bedroom door open and close as he leaves me hear waiting for him to use me again.*

"ELLI?" I HEAR KIRA CALL OUT FROM MY ADJOINING bedroom, pulling me out of the memory. "Ellington, where the fuck ...?" She barges into my bathroom and rushes over to the shower. Yanking the glass door open, she steps inside fully dressed. "What the fuck, Elli? I've been banging on your front door for fifteen minutes. I finally broke a window." She reaches out to touch me but hisses in a breath when her hand feels the water. "How long have you been in here? The water is freezing." She stands, turning it off, and bends back down. "Come on. Get up." She grabs my arm and pulls me to sit. "How long...?" Her voice trails off, her eyes dropping to my exposed chest and stomach. "What the fuck?" she whispers. "What are those?"

I don't answer.

"Are they tallies?" she goes on.

I nod, unable to speak. My jaw is so sore from gritting my teeth. I had never come so hard in my life. And that doesn't include the way he used my throat. I hate that I wanted to please him. That my mind thought if he saw how good I could be, then maybe he'd choose me over Amelia. Like I ever had a chance at being his.

"One, two, three, four, five, six, seven ... Jesus, Elli." She stops counting.

I know there are so many more. When he took me to the bedroom and flipped me over, he started keeping track on my back. My pussy is swollen, it aches. "I can't get them off," I whisper.

I've scrubbed for I don't know how long. I tried a scrub with a loofah. All it did was rub my skin raw. My chest is red, and it made me bleed a little.

"What?" Her eyes go over to the jug that sits next to me and she picks it up. "You're bathing in bleach?" she barks.

It wasn't the best idea I've ever had but the thought of Chance kicking me to the curb made me desperate. If he tosses me to the side, my mother will no doubt send me away. "I was going to try." I need them off.

Sighing heavily, she stands. "Come on." She grabs my hand and helps me to stand on my wobbly legs. "I know what will help."

# FORTY-THREE

## SIN

I'm standing in my bedroom back at my parents' house with two other Lords when Corbin's phone rings.

He looks down at it and sighs. "It's Gunner. He's called me three times in the last hour. Ryat is losing his shit over Blakely..." It rings again, cutting him off. "Hey, man." He walks over to my bathroom. "I don't know anything. I didn't attend the party..." He closes himself inside, giving the two of us privacy.

"You did good," the other Lord states.

I snort. "We'll see."

My bedroom door opens so hard it bangs against the interior wall, leaving a massive hole from the knob hitting the drywall. "You sorry son of a bitch..." My sister's words trail off when her eyes meet mine and then go to the guy standing next to me. She takes a step back as if one of us pushed her. "No." Her wide eyes go back to mine. "Easton, please tell me this isn't what I think it is."

I run a hand through my hair. I knew this would happen, I just thought I'd have more time.

"Please," she begs. "Tell me that my best friend is not an assignment."

I look over at Chance and he crosses his arms over his chest, glaring at her. I know he isn't going to say shit. We both have too much to lose.

"How could you do this to her?" she asks me.

I remain silent.

"You can't just let her go?" My teeth clench. "Huh? Just let her be." She runs over to me, slapping my face. "You piece of shit." She slaps me again.

"Stop!" Chance orders, placing a hand on her chest, holding her back.

"Don't fucking touch her," Corbin barks, stepping out of my bathroom, hearing the commotion while pocketing his cell.

"Then handle your bitch," Chance says.

She looks at her boyfriend, tears now in her eyes. "You knew? Everything you said to her ... you were lying?" Her voice shakes, showing how hurt she is that he didn't fill her in on our plan.

Like a mask sliding over Corbin's face, it goes blank. We've been trained to shut down, to keep secrets from others no matter who they are.

"Why didn't you tell me?" she asks Corbin.

But it's Chance who answers. "Because it's none of your goddamn business."

She looks at Corbin, expecting him to stick up for her, but still, he says nothing. She sucks in a deep breath, and I know she's about to go off on me. "I just left Elli's. She was in the shower scrubbing herself raw. She was going to use bleach," she shouts, getting angry with me again. "Fucking bleach, Easton." She slaps me again.

This time, Corbin comes up behind her, wrapping his arms around her, pinning hers to her sides. Picking her up off the floor, she tries to kick me but she's too far away now. "You fucking bastard," she spits out. "She loves you."

My chest tightens.

"She loves you and you've ruined her."

"What do you think I'm doing?" I snap, unable to stay quiet. "Huh? I'm trying to keep her alive."

He sets her down on her feet again. "By killing her?" she snaps. "God, Sin, just let her go." She begins to cry. "Let her be with Chance." *Over my dead body.* "Let her have a life without you. All you do is hurt her. Lie to her. Cheat on her."

"I've never cheated on her," I growl, not listening to that bullshit again.

"We saw you!" She's screaming so loud it's hurting my ears. I've never seen my sister this distraught before. Since I left Elli passed out in *our* bed, I've been worried about the state of mind I put her in. I'm doing what has to be done, doesn't matter if I agree with it or not. I've got to prove myself. "Amelia showed us the video in the bathroom," she goes on.

I look over at Chance and he shakes his head, not understanding either. "You don't know what you're talking about," I argue.

"Quit fucking lying to me! I'm not going to believe your bullshit anymore. We saw you and Amelia in your room at the house of Lords. We watched her get undressed, crawl into your bed and then you tied her down ..." She pauses to catch her breath.

"And what?" I demand, my heart picking up at what she's describing.

"Elli knocked the phone out of Amelia's hand, obviously done watching her boyfriend cheat on her." She huffs. "But it was clear, Easton. You're a lying, cheating piece of shit." She rushes me again, but Corbin reaches out and grabs a hold of her hair, yanking her back.

"Babe, calm down," he growls, holding her in place while she fights his hold.

"And you told her about James and Lincoln," she goes on. "Why? To make yourself feel better? You're no better than them. Taking advantage of her."

My jaw clenches. "This conversation is over," I growl, hearing enough.

Corbin picks her feet up off the floor and spins around, dragging her out of my room kicking and screaming. Normally, I'd be concerned where he's taking her, but right now, I don't care.

"How the fuck does she know all of that?" I ask myself.

"Amelia," Chance answers.

"How the fuck did she know?" I narrow my eyes on him.

He raises his hands. "I haven't told that bitch shit."

"That only leaves one other person."

---

It's been two days since my sister barged into my room and I still have no clue what's going on. I can't ask Amelia because then she'll know that I know. I'd rather keep her in the dark as much as possible. She's obviously talking and the less she's aware that I know, the better.

Entering my father's home study, I see him sitting at his desk. "Got a second?" I ask.

"Have a seat." He gestures to the chair across from his desk.

I fall into it. "If this is about your wedding—"

"It's not," I interrupt him.

He nods, sitting back and getting comfortable. "What do you need?"

"What do you know about Carnage?" I ask.

His body stiffens, eyes narrowing for a brief second before he masks it. But he avoids my question. "I know that you need to stay away from there."

"Why? Because of the Spade brothers?" I go on and he sighs. They refused to give me any information the other day. But I'm not going to give up so easily. My future with Elli is on the line. And I'll do anything to save it.

"They're not blood related," he states. "They're called brothers because like you and me, they took an oath to one another. They share everything."

"What's their secret?" I wonder.

He arches a brow. "Secret?"

"Why them? They're Lords, right?" I can't figure out how they ended up there. Of course, Lords are like anything else in the world. Some are richer than others. Some are smarter, more ruthless. How did they get control of a fucking city? Carnage covers hundreds of thousands of acres in the middle of nowhere tucked back in the mountains. All surrounded by barbed wire fence taller than any man could get over. Only has one entrance and exit that I've seen so far.

My father's jaw sharpens as he turns his head to look away for a second. I know more than he wants me to. Is it supposed to be a secret that they are one of us?

"How did they end up there?" I continue to dig at his silence.

"End up there?" He gives a rough laugh, eyes now back on mine. "Son, they are Carnage. They run that place like it's hell itself. They may be Lords, but they don't think like us. They don't handle things like us. They can't function out in the world like you and me. They're trained differently. Their initiations were different. Everything about them is different."

"You make them sound like machines." I snort. "Everyone has a weakness." *Elli is mine.* The fact that I'm digging around proves it, but I can't let anyone know. The Lords will use it against me. They will take what you love and ruin it just because they can.

He tilts his head to the side, confused by my question.

"You saying they've never been in love?" Impossible.

He cracks a smile. "There's always a woman. I can't say love was involved, though."

"One woman?" I verify, sitting up straighter. He had said they share *everything*.

He nods. "There are several stories that involve Carnage. One is she was killed. The other is she escaped."

I frown. "So she was a prisoner there, or a patient?"

He shakes his head, getting irritated with all my questions. "Why do you care?" His eyes narrow on me.

I sit back, crossing my arms over my chest and shutting my mouth. I sound too desperate. "Just curious. Heard some rumors and wanted to know if they were true. I find it odd that they're kept a secret."

He goes to open his mouth, but his cell rings and he digs it out of his pocket. "It's Malcom," he announces, and I roll my eyes. My future father-in-law. "Give me a second." Placing the phone to his ear, he smiles. "Hello, Malcom..." Opening up the door to the right, he steps out of his office, knowing I'm not fucking leaving, and he wants privacy.

I pull up my phone and click on the app to see Elli. She lies in bed sleeping. She's been doing it a lot lately. She's not eating enough. Between how much she's been drinking and what I've done to her body, she's exhausted.

Locking my cell, I pocket it and catch sight of the box that my father had shown me the other day. Full of pictures of Elli. I get up, walking over to it. Pulling the lid off, I pick one up.

She's young. Underage for sure. She's blindfolded, tied to a dingy mattress in a basement. It's dark but the flash lights her up. She's clothed in a yellow sundress. The thought of her in this kind of situation so young makes my pulse race. That I should have seen signs. That I should have paid more attention to her.

Scanning the photo, I see a mirror on the wall above her head. I squint, trying to focus on what I see. It's a man, standing there staring down at her. *It's James.* You can't miss him. He's dressed in a button-up and slacks. His arms crossed over his chest, eyes on her.

*Who the fuck is taking the picture?*

346

I hear the knob on the door open and I shove the picture into my pocket and put the lid back on. I'm falling into the seat when he steps back in, cell now in his hand. "We're having drinks tomorrow night with Malcom."

"*We* are not," I state.

He sighs. "Son..."

"I've got somewhere to be." I stand, needing to get the fuck out of here.

"Easton?" he calls out, and I stop and turn to face him. "Whatever you want with Carnage, let it go. There's a reason you didn't know they existed. They are unbeatable. One of them is lethal, but all three of them ... you don't know suffering until they decide to drag you into their world. Nothing survives there."

I flinch at his words, praying that he's wrong. I look away from him, not wanting to reveal what Ryat told me. He didn't have to come to me like he did. I'm thankful for that, but I won't betray his trust or loyalty. So I say, "The girl—"

"She's gone, Easton. If she escaped, her time on the run will run out. If she's dead, she got lucky."

She has to be alive. My future is in her hands. But if I go by what my father just told me about the Spade brothers, they could already have her chained to a blood-covered cot in a padded room. For all I know, they killed her years ago and then came up with the rumors to cover their tracks.

"I'll drop it." It's not the first lie I've told my dad and it won't be the last either.

He clears his throat, letting me know this conversation isn't over just yet. Picking something up off his desk, he walks over to me. Holding out a white envelope, he says, "This arrived for you today."

"What is it?" I ask, taking it from him. My blood runs cold when I read over the black writing.

*Please join us for an engagement party...*

It's Chance and Elli's party invite. I wad it up and let it fall to the floor where it belongs. Then, without another word, I turn and leave his office.

# ELLINGTON

I STAND IN MY ROOM BACK AT MY PARENTS' HOUSE IN FRONT of the floor-length mirror tucked into the corner. My makeup and hair are done. I've just got to get dressed.

But I can't seem to force myself to do it. This is it. My mother is throwing me and Chance a party. We'll officially be announcing our engagement tonight in front of all of her and Linc's friends. Just another sea of Lords and Ladies that they want to drown me in.

I hate that Sin is on my mind. Kira was able to get all the tallies removed from my skin. I'm pretty sure she took a layer off with it, but all reminders of that night have been erased as if it never happened. And I haven't seen him since. It's like when the masked man broke our only way of contact and left me crying.

I feel inadequate. Like he's too busy with Amelia. She's fulfilling all of his needs, so I'm long forgotten. Left to rot in the bottom of the tub like that useless cell phone.

I hear the click of the doorknob and I turn around to see my door open. I stiffen when Linc enters. "Get out of my room," I say, trying to straighten my shoulders, but my voice cracks, giving away that after all these years just being around him affects me.

The smile on his face tells me he noticed it. Shutting the door, my heart begins to beat wildly in my chest when he locks it. "This will only take a few minutes."

I rush over to the adjoining bathroom door, thinking I can get in there and lock him out, but he beats me. I whimper and take a step back when he steps into the doorframe, arms out wide, blocking it.

Reaching out, he grips my chin, forcing my head back. I take in a deep breath, glaring at him down my nose.

"Get on your knees and thank me," he orders, getting straight to why he's in my room.

My legs begin to shake. My breathing becoming labored. "Fuck you," I spit in his face.

Letting go of my chin, he slaps me across the face so hard it knocks me to my hands and knees. Opening my watery eyes, I see it's where I first willingly lay down for the masked man. I dig my nails into the carpet, refusing to cry at the sting lingering on my cheek. I'm so tired of looking so weak.

"You know, Elli..." he starts as his shoes walk away from me and over to my bed. "James took his time with you at first due to how young you were. Legal age of consent in the state of Pennsylvania is sixteen." He makes it sound okay. That James was somehow a gentleman for waiting until the state says I was old enough to give consent to be fucked. "I'm honestly impressed he was able to wait that long. I would have fucked you the moment I took over this house."

"I never asked him—"

His laughter fills the room, interrupting me and sending a chill up my spine. "You're right. You never asked. You begged him long before then."

My throat closes up because I can't argue that.

He opens my top nightstand drawer before shutting it. He turns back to face me, and I try to get up on my shaking legs and run to my door, but he grabs my hair. I cry out as he yanks me back and bends me over the side of the bed, pinning my legs to it with him standing behind me.

I scream as he brings my arms behind my back and zip-ties my wrists. My stomach sinks and I can't hold back the tears that fill my eyes.

"They can't hear you down there, Elli. Everyone is in the west wing getting ready for your party."

Yanking me off the bed, he shoves me to my knees. My head falls forward and sobs rack my body, so hard I can't catch my breath.

"You will open that mouth and you will thank me for everything I've done for you."

I raise my eyes, trying to catch my breath and slow my racing heart. Now is not the time to freak out. I glare up at him.

"See, Elli..." He unzips his black slacks. "Your mother wanted you to marry Sin." My eyes widen at that. "She confided in me after your meltdown at our reception that she felt he would at least keep you busy. That she knew about your father and his father having some sort of agreement that after you graduated Barrington, you were to marry him."

*My father wanted me to marry Sin?*

"But of course, your father is dead, so whatever agreement he and Mr. Sinnett had is void now. So I convinced her that you should marry Chance. He's a better Lord for you. He'll control you like a Lady should be. Sin would go soft on you. He loves you too much."

He's wrong. He has no clue what he's talking about. Sin hates me. His actions have proven that.

"And David, you owe me for David. I sent him to you. Told him that you were such a good whore and needed to be fucked. You make Sin weak. He'd let you run all over him. But Chance? He doesn't give a fuck about you." Reaching down, he runs his knuckles over my cheek that he just slapped. "You may marry him, but you will serve whoever he tells you to."

"You mean you?" I grind out. "That's why you're forcing me to marry your nephew, because you think he'll let you fuck me." If my father and mother really wanted me to marry Sin, I do know one thing—he may not be faithful, but he'd never let another man touch me. And that just wouldn't work for Lincoln.

He chuckles lightly. "You're so smart, Ellington. James used to tell me how dumb you were. Just a cunt to fuck. But I knew you were smarter than he gave you credit for." Reaching inside his unzipped slacks, he pulls out his dick and I lean away. He tangles his hand in my hair roughly, making me cry out.

"Enough talk. It's time for you to be a good fucking whore and thank me for all I've done for you."

My teeth clamp shut, and I shake my head the best I can with his fist in my hair. This isn't like last time in James's office. I'm not fucked up on drugs. Or begging for it.

He sighs, disappointed, and all but rolls his eyes. "How about Sin?"

My heart stops and I look up at him through watery eyes.

"If you don't open your mouth, I'm going to report him to the Lords."

I freeze. What does he mean report him?

"See, Sin was given an assignment, off the books. Of course, he didn't know that. It was more of an experiment on my end. I wanted to see just how far he'd go for his little demon. And poof, the guy ended up dead. Photos of you naked and being used— gone. All for you, Elli. Imagine my surprise when I realized just how much he cares for you, a used-up whore."

Tears fall down my cheeks. David. Linc set Sin up by hooking me up with David. But why? What made him think Sin was even interested in me?

"So, this is the last time I'll make this offer, Ellington. Open your mouth and thank me for not getting the man you love stripped of his title."

I hate that I care what happens to Sin. He saved me. Although he then used me until he got bored. But that's my fault, right? I believed his lies. I fell in love with someone he really wasn't. I can't let them strip him of his title. Not because of me. I'm tired of being the reason people get hurt. This is my future. Being passed around and used.

They're all right. I'm the whore. I'm nothing. Sin has a future, and I'm not going to let him lose it because of me. I'm not like them. Licking my lips, I close my eyes and part my lips.

"That's a good slut," he praises, and my shoulders shake as his cock slides into my open mouth.

---

I KNEEL ON THE FLOOR, THE BLOOD RUSHING IN MY EARS. I watch him zip his pants. He grips my face and I stare up at him in a daze. Everything is blurry. He says something then lets go of me. The zip tie is cut and my arms fall to my sides. I hear him exit, the door shutting.

My chest heaves and I scramble to my feet. Running into my adjoining bathroom, I fall in front of the toilet just in time to vomit.

"Oh my God, Elli." I hear Kira now standing next to me.

I do it again. My stomach muscles tightening, thighs clenching and chest burning. I expel what Linc forced me to swallow. It's like déjà vu.

I just wish I was as fucked up as last time. I've got some in my dresser that I can take once I know I'm done throwing up.

She grabs my hair, holding it since Linc fucked up my updo with his fist in it. Once I'm done, I flush the toilet and sit back on my legs.

"Have you eaten today?" she asks, going over to the sink. Turning on the faucet, she runs a washcloth underneath it to get it wet, then hands it to me.

"Y-es." My voice rough, throat burning.

I abandon the washcloth on the floor and stand on shaking legs. I go over to the faucet, cup the water and wash my face while rinsing my mouth out.

"Elli," she speaks softly. "I think you should take another pregnancy test."

"Not this again," I mumble under my breath.

"I'm serious. It could have been a false negative. Or maybe you're not far enough along yet..."

"I'm not pregnant."

"Did you and Sin use a condom?" she asks.

"Are you and Corbin using protection?" I glare at her.

"I'm not the one vomiting," she snaps defensively.

"I'm fine, Kira," I sigh. "I promise."

I exit the bathroom, entering my bedroom once again, and she follows. "Are you trying to hide this pregnancy because Sin is marrying Amelia?"

I spin around to face her. "What?"

"Is this some sort of revenge?" She places her hands on her hips. "Because he won't marry you?"

I'm so close to the fucking edge I'm about to jump. I don't know how much more of this bullshit I can take. "Your brother doesn't give a fuck about me, Kira. And I get it. I do. I was just a fuck. Take some notes. Your day is coming." I give her my back.

"What does that mean?" She grabs my upper arm, spinning me around.

"It means Corbin is the same."

"No—"

"They're all fucking Lords, Kira," I snap at her for being as stupid as I was. If I can save her this heartache, I will. "They took an oath. Women don't mean shit to them."

Her eyes drop to the floor. The same spot I was just kneeling and gagged for Linc. "My brother loves you."

I throw my head back laughing. It's manic sounding, my entire body shaking from it. "Well, I don't love him." The bile returns but I swallow it down. I never told him I loved him and now I'm glad. Imagine if he knew he had that much power over me.

"You have to tell him you're pregnant," she urges.

"I'm not fucking pregnant!" I scream "Jesus Christ, Kira. I'm not fucking pregnant. Let it go. Worry about yourself. Huh? Who the fuck knows if Corbin is being faithful to you."

She slaps me across the face, and I don't even feel it. I'm too numb at this point. Losing my goddamn mind over a game that I can't win.

She storms out of my room, and I find myself walking over to my dresser. I open it up and pop two pills into my mouth. Then without thought, I enter my closet and numbly pull the dress that my mother got me to wear tonight for this party off the hanger, slipping it on over my head. If life has taught me anything, it's that it doesn't stop when you need rest. You swallow your cries and you lift your chin. Because life doesn't give a fuck about you. You either take it, or you let it kill you.

*Never trust a man unless you know what he'd do to survive.*

I get it. Because for once, I understand what my father did, and it doesn't sound so bad.

# FORTY-FOUR

## SIN

I stand next to Corbin and Chase in the ballroom when I see my sister entering. I can tell from across the room she's crying.

"What's wrong?" I ask the moment she rushes over to us.

"We're leaving," she barks at Corbin.

"What's wrong?" he asks her, and she ignores him too.

"I'm fucking leaving. Come with me or don't." Spinning around, she goes to storm off, but I grab her arm and yank her back. "Sin—"

"Answer our fucking question right now," I growl in her face, my fingers tightening on her skin. She looks to Corbin but all he does is cross his arms over his chest, also waiting for an explanation.

I love my sister to death and would do anything for her, but she chose this life with the Lords. She had every chance to run the other way, and she didn't. Corbin isn't the guy she thinks he is. He's a Lord and that will always come first. No matter how much he loves her. The Lords always like to test us with things that we love.

"I found Elli upstairs vomiting," she finally admits, letting out a long breath.

My brows crease. "She's sick?"

"She's been sick," she snaps, trying to yank her arm free, but I don't let go. "I think..." She nibbles on her lip. "I think she's pregnant, but she doesn't want anyone to know."

I let go of her arm, dropping mine to my side. She steps into me instead of running off. "If she's pregnant, then you can choose to marry her, right?" Her blue eyes are big and full of hope. She wants me with Elli as much as Elli does. She wants me to be the better guy and pick her best friend.

"It doesn't work that way." Corbin is the one who speaks when I refuse to answer.

Her eyes go to him. "Why not?" she snaps, irritated once again.

"Sin would get to decide if he wants it or not," Corbin goes on.

Her wide eyes go back to me and she takes a step back. "No. You wouldn't do that to her," she says, understanding what her boyfriend means.

"It's complicated," Corbin goes on.

I don't hide anything from him. He may have gone behind my back, but I've accepted what he did. He's still my best friend. I won't let his love for my sister get in the way.

"Easton," she speaks softly. "You can't do that to her."

"I'm a Lord," I say. "I can do whatever I want."

With tears building in her eyes, she looks to Corbin, and when he says nothing, she spins around and rushes out of the ballroom.

"Fuck," Corbin hisses.

Placing my hands in the pockets of my slacks, I make my way out of the ballroom and upstairs, not even bothering to try to talk to him about what just went down. He can choose to follow Kira or not. Not my relationship, not my problem.

I enter Elli's room like I own it and see the French doors open to her balcony. She's standing on it, back to me, forearms on the railing.

Stepping outside, I watch her body stiffen, feeling my presence. "Why are you here?" comes her soft voice. It doesn't sound mad or curious. Just tired.

"Your mother invited me."

"Of course, she did." She sighs, pushing off the railing and turning to face me.

My eyes scan over her puffy cheeks, bloodshot eyes and ... they're dilated. I grind my teeth. "You're fucked up." It's not a question.

She blinks slowly, her pretty eyes heavy.

My eyes roam over the rest of her face and make it to her cheek. *Is that a handprint?* I step closer, pinning her back into the railing, and reach up to touch her cheek, but she drops her face. "Who the fuck hit you?" I demand.

"Your sister," she answers, lifting her chin to meet my eyes.

I can't tell if that's a lie or not, but my sister wouldn't hit hard enough to leave that red of a mark. "Elli—"

"Please leave," she begs.

My eyes search hers and they start to fill with tears. "I'm tired of seeing you." Her bottom lip begins to tremble. "I'm tired of hating myself because of you. I'm just so tired..." She closes her eyes tightly and fresh tears come pouring down her face. They open and land on mine, pinning me where I stand. "I'm tired of being the whore that no one can love."

"Elli—"

"My father taught me that life isn't fair." She places her hand on my chest, pushing me back, and I allow it. "I'm marrying Chance and I'm going to be a devoted Lady, Sin. Because I'm tired of being your whore. It isn't worth it." With that, she walks around me and out of her bedroom.

With shaky hands, I pull my cell out. Something happened.

357

That's not the same Elli I left unconscious in our bed just a week ago after I spent all weekend with her. No. She was right where I needed her to be. On the edge. She's jumped off headfirst and I won't be able to get her back.

I pull up the cameras I have set up in her room. I see her getting ready, standing in front of the mirror. Her door opens and my blood runs cold as Linc enters. I turn up the volume. I watch, my eyes glued to the screen and my hands tightening on my phone to the point I might break it while he threatens her...

With me.

She opens her mouth for him because of me.

He fucking uses her because of me.

I'm shaking when he leaves her and she runs to the bathroom getting sick. I see my sister enter and I don't even bother watching. She lied like I knew she had. I watched him hit her twice. One when she refused to give him what he wanted and the second time when she was on her knees sucking his cock. My sister might have done it as well, but she never mentioned Lincoln in her room, and I know why.

Pocketing my cell, I run down the stairs. "Elli?" I shout her name. The ballroom is now full of guests mingling around. She didn't even take the time to redo her makeup. She just washed it off completely and left her hair down. "Elli, I need to talk to you." I step forward.

"That's not happening." Linc steps into me.

I fist my hands; I want to rip his fucking head off, but I can't. Too many eyes on us, watching. This was a test. I know that now and I can't fail. I'll lose her for good. Forever. My entire body is fucking vibrating I'm so furious. Hot fire touching my skin, and I'm practically panting.

"I'll handle this." Chance places his hands on Lincoln's chest and he steps back.

"Take it outside," Linc orders Chance. I get one last look of

Elli standing in a sea full of people and I realize just how unsafe she is. No one here will protect her. Not like I will.

"Come on," Chance growls and I let him drag me out of the room, through the house, and out the double doors onto the front porch before I get myself killed. If that happens, there's no telling what they will do to her. "What the fuck, man?" he demands softly, his eyes scanning the property. "You trying to fuck shit up?"

I pull out my cell and go to the footage, turning up the volume and hold it out to him. My heart is hammering in my chest. I start to pace, my hands gripping my hair. I should have known the moment I realized she had taken drugs. It's her escape. Her way of coping with performing actions that she knows are wrong.

"Fuck." He runs a hand through his hair, watching wide-eyed. His jaw sharpening when he hears what Linc tells her. After he's done and it gets to the end, he hands it back to me. I pocket the phone with shaking hands. Chance's arms fall to his sides. "I'm sorry, man—"

I punch him in the face, knocking him back.

"Jesus, Sin—"

I grab his tuxedo and yank him to me, his chest bumping into mine. "Anyone, and I mean any-fucking-one touches her again and I don't give a fuck where we are or who's watching, they're dead."

"I didn't know he was going to do that," he snaps in my face, a steady flow of blood running from his busted nose.

"And after I kill him, you'll be next," I promise, shoving Chance away from me. "Now get your ass back in there, and don't leave her fucking side." I point at the house.

"Calm down, man." He raises his hands, quickly looking around, but everyone is inside. The party has already started. "I'm as pissed off as you are, but we can't do anything yet."

I know that but it doesn't mean I like it. "Keep your eyes on *my* wife. If anything happens to her, I'll dig them out of your fucking head with a butter knife," I threaten.

I walk across the circle drive, over to where they have valet set up, and he pulls my keys to go get my car. I yank them from his hand and stomp my way to where it's parked. Dropping into my car, my phone rings.

"Easton." My father's voice fills my car before I hear a door open and close as he hides away from the crowd inside of the house. "What the fuck just happened? Chance just returned with a bloody nose."

"It's nothing," I say through gritted teeth.

"That was not nothing. Where the fuck are you? Amelia and her parents are looking for you."

"I had to leave."

He sighs. "Son—"

I hang up and drop my phone in my lap. My blood is boiling, I can't stop shaking. He threatened my status with the Lords, and she did whatever he wanted. I hate that. She shouldn't be protecting me. It should be the other way around. But the Lords have my arms tied. She'd hate herself more than she already does if she knew the very people she saved me from, are the same ones keeping me from her.

I knew Lincoln would try something, but I figured he'd at least wait until after their wedding. To use me against her makes my chest tighten. No wonder she hates me. She let him have some-thing that wasn't his. She protected me like I have her all these years. But what did it cost her? Her sanity. She's no longer the same. James toyed with her. Made her beg to be fucked. Linc will make her beg him to stop, which he won't do. He lied to her, my father and hers never had an agreement for us to marry. It's just another way to hurt her. Make her feel like she was close to getting what she wanted, but he had the power to take it away.

My phone rings again but I press decline when I see it's my father. I have nothing to say to him right now. I squeal out of the driveway. I make my way down the dirt road parallel to the house where I used to hide on my bike when I would sneak in to see her, and pull my cell out. I'm watching her stand next to Chance in the ballroom. No smile on her face. She doesn't even look fucked up, just blank. She's no longer my little demon. She's Ellington Asher, the girl they wanted to break. The girl who has no idea just how powerful she can be.

I'm her only hope.

I PULL UP AT BLACKOUT AND RUSH INTO THE CLUB AND UP TO Tyson's office.

"Call them back." I barge through the door, not even bothering to knock.

He looks up at me from behind his desk.

"Tell them I want another meeting," I demand.

"Sin, the Spade brothers don't work like that. They may be Lords but it's not the same as you and me."

"You don't answer to the Lords," I remind him. I'm not going to pretend to understand what the fuck the Spade brothers actually do for the Lords, and I couldn't care less.

He fists his hands. "You're born a Lord; you die a Lord." Growling, he adds, "No one is untouchable when it comes to taking their oath." Running a hand through his hair, he sighs. "You'll just be wasting our time. They told you no..."

"There's a woman," I interrupt him.

Leaning back in his chair, he glares at me. His eyes give him away. I didn't tell him her name, or any-fucking-thing about this bitch, but he knows exactly who she is and that she's important to them.

"Maybe we can find her? Trade her or something."

He gives a rough laugh. "Trade her? You understand that *if* you could locate her, and hand her over, you'd be no better than Linc."

I snort as I turn from his desk and begin to pace. That burning sensation still crawling all over my skin. I could kill a hundred men right now with my bare hands. I wish I wouldn't have killed David. He'd be a good candidate to torture right now.

"I'm serious, Sin. You'd be throwing this girl to a pack of wolves. They would rip her apart piece by piece. She is the reason they are the way they are."

He talks as if I know what he means. I don't and, again, I don't care. Walking back over to his desk, I slam my hands down on it, making his eyes narrow on mine. I've never known Tyson to be soft. He's ruthless, a fucking legend to all of us. "Afraid I'll never forgive myself?"

He chuckles at that as if it was a stupid thought. "Forgiveness doesn't exist in our world."

Maybe he feels sorry for the girl because he thinks she's an innocent. His chosen changed him. Tyson's path as a Lord was going to make him a billionaire. A respected and powerful CEO with the perfect family that would have included kids and a dog. He gave it all up when his chosen was killed. She was slaughtered for something she didn't do. He loved her. As much as a Lord can love a woman anyway. It put her in harm's way, and she paid the ultimate price.

I won't allow that to happen to Elli. I'll burn this mother-fucking world down before I let a man take her from me. I'll love her no matter how I get her back, broken or not.

"I don't give a fuck about her." I finally answer his previous question regarding the woman. Let the wolves have her. If it means I can have my little demon back, then so be it. I'm willing to spill blood, even if it's not mine. No one ever cared about Elli, so why should I care about some bitch that I don't even know?

"It doesn't matter."

"Ty—"

"She's long gone, Sin. You won't find her."

*Fuck!* I fall onto the couch and lean back, my hands covering my face. I'm running out of options. Out of time. I know Elli. She's going to stay fucked up twenty-four seven. She'll die of an overdose eventually. By accident or on purpose, won't matter.

"Go home, Sin," he dismisses me. "Get some rest and think twice before you get irrational over pussy."

His cell rings and I stand, about to walk out, when he gets my attention by lifting his finger his to lips to signal for me to be quiet. I frown but nod.

Answering his phone, he places the call on speaker. "Hello?"

"Tyson," the guy speaks. "Something has been brought to our attention." I recognize the voice. It's one of the Spade brothers, but I'm not sure which one. My one and only meeting with them was very short.

"And you're calling me why?" Tyson asks, crossing his arms over his chest.

"The kid you came in with the other day."

"What about him?" he goes on.

"Bring him over tomorrow. We'd like to see him." The guy hangs up.

Tyson locks his cell before looking up at me. "Looks like you've got one more chance."

# ELLINGTON

I stand in the ballroom, my eyes on a man who stands at the opposite end. I know him. I've seen him before. He came over to my house. He brought us papers to sign when Sin said he bought the house for us. I should go over there and ask him why he did that when it was a lie. Why go through that much trouble? But my feet are planted where I stand. His blue eyes are on mine, staring at me. He doesn't care that I've caught him. Lifting a champagne flute to his lips, he takes a sip.

A hand grabs my arm and I'm pulled out of the ballroom. My feet are unable to keep up and I trip but thankfully don't fall on my face. "Christ, you're on drugs. Again." It's Lincoln. "Goddamn it, Elli. Can't you stay clean for a day?"

I groan as he brings me to a stop, spinning me to face him. "What the fuck did you say?" he demands in my face.

I'm not even here. The Molly has kicked in and I'm drinking. I no longer taste him in my mouth. I could be drooling for all I know.

"Hmm? What did you say to Sin?"

I blink, my eyelids heavy, making everything kinda blurry.

He raises his hand to slap me, but it stops in midair. "Just what do you think you're doing?" Chance growls.

I blink again, realizing that Chance's hand is wrapped around Lincoln's wrist, stopping him from hitting me. I didn't even flinch, the thought of pain makes my nipples harden. I want to feel something. I wish Sin were here to hurt me. To make me beg him to push me further than my body wants to go.

Linc yanks it free and steps back. "I'm having a conversation with my stepdaughter."

Bile rises at those words. While wallowing in my own self-pity, I forgot that he's married to my mother. I've officially fucked two of my mother's husbands—while they were married to her. I'm a horrible person.

"Why is she fucked up?" Chance asks Linc.

He snorts. "Because she's a fucking druggie. You knew this. It's what she does."

Chance turns to face me and cups my cheeks. I lean into his cool hands. They feel so good. "Are you okay?" he asks.

A laugh bubbles up and I can't help but let it out, making my body shake.

"Elli?" Chance frowns, shaking me a little.

"She's fine," Linc snaps.

Chance lets go of my face and walks me over to a chair, pushing me down into it, then he turns to his uncle. "What the fuck do you think you're doing? Your wife is here, for fuck's sake." I tilt my head, their conversation confusing me. She is? I haven't even seen my mother tonight. This party may be for me and Chance, but she threw it for herself. It's a way for her to show off that I'm not a complete waste of space in her life. Becoming a Lady is a big thing in our world. Not sure when becoming a slave was something to be proud of.

Linc straightens his shoulders. "We had a deal—"

"Yes, I know what he agreed on," Chance snaps, interrupting him. "But she's not my wife *yet*. So keep your hands to yourself until then."

Lincoln's eyes narrow on me and I smile at him. At least I think I am. My lips are numb.

"Sin knew something—"

"Sin is watching her every fucking move," Chance goes on, taking a step back and running a hand through his dark hair. Not sure if he's aggravated at me or his uncle. "Jesus, you're a grown-ass man. You once went three years without pussy. Keep it in your pants for another week before you ruin this for us both."

Lincoln fixes his collar and glares at me while he speaks to Chance. "I want her on the wedding night."

Chance lets out a huff.

"I'm serious, Becks. It's not like she's a fucking virgin and you'll be the first one there. I want her after the wedding. Hell, you can be there and watch, but I want to fuck her before you do. I've earned that."

Chance nods. "Yeah, you're right. Fine. She's yours first, the night of the wedding."

Linc pushes past him and walks toward me. Bending over, he grips my chin, forcing me to look at him from where I sit. "Did you hear that, Elli? I told you I'd get my fair share of you."

"You'll never be as good as Sin." I'm not sure why I said it, but I couldn't stop the words if I wanted to. I'm going to marry Chance, and he's going to let my stepfather fuck me along with who knows who, but they'll never be Sin. And I'll remind them of that any chance I get. He may have never loved me, but he knew exactly what I wanted when I needed it.

I expect Lincoln to get mad but instead he just smiles and shoves my face away, pushing me back into the chair. "You may not be a virgin, but you will bleed for me on your wedding night when I cut his fucking name off your back. I'll mail it to him in a baggie. It'll be my wedding gift to him after he makes Amelia his wife."

Not sure why Linc would do that, Sin won't give a fuck about it. But I'm not going to tell him that. Lincoln can figure it out on his own.

# FORTY-FIVE

## SIN

I stand in the formal dining room, my hands stuffed into the front pockets of my slacks. I'm looking out the floor-to-ceiling windows when I see the headlights coming down the driveway. I walk into the grand foyer and yank both doors open, stepping out onto the porch in the cool night. The car comes to a stop, and I make my way to the passenger side door. Ripping it open, I see Chance step out of the driver side.

"She's out," he says in greeting.

My eyes drop to Elli who is slumped in the passenger seat, still wearing her evening gown from their engagement party.

Leaning over, I unfasten her seat belt and pull her into my arms, I carry her inside the house and to the master suite. Lying her in bed, I turn to see Becks standing in the doorway. "Get the fuck out of this house," I growl, going to throw him out if he refuses to leave.

He places his hands on my chest. "Sin." He sighs. "I'm sorry."

I grab his button-up and drag him to the front doors where I shove him outside. He almost trips on the porch. "What the fuck, man?" he barks.

"Stay the fuck away from her until the wedding." I slam the doors in his face.

Making my way back to the room, she's where I left her. Lying on her back, arms out and head tilted to the side. The hem of her dress has ridden up to expose her thigh.

I walk over, grab the material, and rip it down the center, exposing her chest to me. Then I remove my shirt, shove my pants down my legs, and kick off my shoes before removing my socks. I crawl on the bed to sit between her legs.

My hand drops to her cunt and I run two fingers over it. She's not wet. Spitting on my fingers, I run them over her a couple of times before I push them inside her, getting her pussy ready for my cock.

I take myself in my hand and push inside her, my arms behind her knees spreading her wide and slamming my hips into hers. "I want you to be sore tomorrow," I tell her, watching her breasts bounce from the force. "You won't remember that I fucked you, but you'll feel it."

# ELLINGTON

I BLINK, MY EYES HEAVY AND DRY. MY HANDS COME UP TO MY face and I groan. Where am I? Sitting up, I look around the bright room and squint, the light too bright. I'm back at my house.

How did I get here?

My body aches. My pussy is sore, and it takes everything I have to get to my feet. I manage to wobble to the bathroom, and it hurts when I wipe after I use the restroom. What did I do last night? I don't remember much after Linc came and visited me.

I slip on a T-shirt and a pair of underwear since I'm naked and then make my way to the kitchen. My mouth is dry, I'm dying of thirst.

Walking through the living room, I push my tangled hair from my face and enter the kitchen. I stop dead in my tracks when I see Sin leaning up against the island and Corbin next to him.

"There she is." Corbin notices me first.

My eyes are on Sin. Blood rushes in my ears as his eyes drop to my bare legs and slowly run up over the T-shirt that barely covers my pussy.

I take a step back and turn around, only to find Jayce walking toward me. Stepping to the side, he walks right past and enters the kitchen, tossing his backpack on the counter. "It's all there."

Sin pushes off the island and nods to me. "Grab her."

I go to run but Corbin grabs me and drags me into the kitchen, picking me up off my feet as I kick them out, trying to get myself free. It's useless. He places me on my bare feet and grabs a hold of my hair, holding me in place.

"You should be more careful what you choose to swallow," Sin finally speaks to me and my stomach drops.

Did Linc tell him what I did? That I willingly opened my mouth and let him fuck me to save Sin from the Lords? Fuck, I hope not. I'd rather him think I begged Linc to fuck my mouth than let him know I did it for him.

Sin turns and grabs a glass out of the cabinet and then the bottle of Everclear off the counter that Kira brought over last week. Unscrewing the lid, he pours the alcohol into the glass until it's half full. His eyes meet mine when he lifts it and takes a small sip. Sin never drinks any hard liquor. What the hell is he doing?

Setting the glass down, he opens the backpack and pulls a baggie out. I gasp when I see what's inside. My drugs that I had stashed in my bedroom at my parents' house. "What the hell are you doing?" I demand.

Unzipping the baggie, he then dumps the contents into the glass of Everclear. "Sin—"

"Like I said, you should be more careful what you choose to

swallow." He pulls a box of matches out of his jeans pocket and lights one before dropping it in the glass. His eyes meet mine when he speaks again, "I told you no drugs."

The only time he's mentioned drugs was when we were walking into Blackout. My eyes narrow on him. "You can't tell me what to do. You don't own me, Easton!"

I watch the Mollies start to break down as they sit at the bottom, underneath the flames, the small amount of cocaine disintegrates. There wasn't much there, but it was all I had left.

"I'll just go buy more." I shrug, as if I don't care. "They're easy to get."

His eyes narrow on me. Coming around the island, he grabs a hold of my shirt and yanks me forward, forcing Corbin to let go of his hold on my hair.

My body slams into the front of Sin's hard one. With his free hand, he reaches into his pocket and pulls out a familiar pink sleeve. "Remember how I told you I fucked you that first night at David's? When I found you tied up in his basement?"

My wide eyes meet his and I suck in a deep breath, feeling the hairs on the back of my neck rise.

"What I didn't mention is that I replaced your birth control that night when I took you home afterward."

I can't breathe. My chest tightening and legs wanting to buckle.

"Why do you think I fuck you every chance I get, Elli?" He goes on at my silence, "Because I'm attracted to you?" He shakes his head. "It's because whether you want to or not, you'll have my child." Letting go of my shirt, he reaches up and cups my face. "If you're not already pregnant, you will be soon. And, well, let's just say that no woman who is pregnant with my child will be doing drugs." His eyes drop to my legs. "How does your pussy feel this morning? Hmm?"

I still can't catch my breath, let alone speak. Is that why I'm sore? Because me and Sin had sex? Why can't I remember? Well, I know I was fucked up, but I've never been that far gone before.

He smiles proudly at the fact that I'm in shock, my lips unable to work. "I fucked your cunt last night in *our* bed and you didn't move. Imagine if I had been a stranger, Elli. Someone taking advantage of you in such a vulnerable state." He makes a tsking noise with his tongue against his teeth. The smile drops off his face and he reaches up, wrapping his hand around my throat but not cutting my air off. "If I even think you're on drugs, I will shove my fingers down your throat until you vomit all over yourself. And if that doesn't work, I'll have your stomach pumped. Do you understand me?"

My eyes search his while blood rushes in my ears. How had I been so stupid? I take my birth control religiously. But for him to switch them out. How did I not notice? "W-why?" Is all I can manage to get out.

"Because I own you," he says simply. "He may marry you, but you will always belong to me."

# FORTY-SIX

# SIN

I sit in Tyson's passenger seat, watching my phone just like last time. Elli sits on the bed, rocking back and forth, silently crying. I left her in the kitchen earlier today after I made her watch me set her drugs on fire.

Pretty sure she's still in shock. The anger will hit her soon and she'll try to get back at me. I'm ready. I needed to get her pissed. I was tired of seeing her depressed. All I keep thinking about is how I'm going to walk into the house and find her dead because she thought it was her only way out. Just like her father.

Now I didn't lie. I did replace her birth control weeks ago and I expect her to be pregnant soon, if not already. I'm not as concerned as Kira, though. I've read up on it and it can take time. She's stressed, doing drugs, drinking. Her body may not be capable of getting pregnant right now, she hasn't been eating regularly, but it will happen. If I have to drag her down to the basement, tie her up and fuck her nonstop until she pees on a stick and it says she's pregnant, Ellington Asher will have my children.

Tyson brings his car to a stop and rolls down his window. I

lock my cell as he punches in the code, and the gate opens, allowing us access to Carnage.

He brings the car to a stop once we hit the circle drive and we get out, making our way up to the double doors. The same man from before greets us. "This way, gentlemen."

We follow him up a set of stairs and down a long hallway. We're not going to the office again, that's clear when he pushes a door open, and we begin to descend a new set of stairs.

He walks us down a darkly lit hallway, and we come to a metal door at the end. He knocks twice before pushing it open, making it squeak loudly.

"Gentlemen." He nods, holding it open for us.

I enter first, giving him a nod of my head while Tyson follows me. The door closes, shutting us inside.

"Tyson. Sin." The man with the tattoo of the gagged nun on his arm greets us, leaning up against the far concrete wall. "So glad you guys could make it." His lips turn into a sinister smile that instantly puts me on alert. But I push down the urge to start throwing punches. I'm not even going to pretend that I don't need them. We all know that I do.

"Why are we here?" Tyson asks, getting to the point, crossing his arms over his chest.

No one answers him. Instead, our eyes fall on the guy who kneels in the middle of the concrete room. Patches of his dark hair is missing. He's in a straitjacket and on his knees. Naked from the waist down with his head bowed forward.

One of the brothers steps up to him. "Are you hungry, Oscar?" he asks.

The man's head snaps up, his sunken blue eyes wide and wild. His lips cracked and dry. He looks feral. Like a rabid dog that's kept chained up.

The Spade brother holds a plate in his hand. Small pieces of steak cut up on it. The other brother removes a pocketknife from his pocket and holds it out to him.

The one kneeling stabs a piece of steak with the tip of the knife and holds in out to the guy in the straitjacket. Oscar leans forward, not wasting a second and closes his lips around it, knife and all. When he pulls back, he smiles and blood covers his crooked teeth, now slopping on the piece of steak. He stabbed himself in the process of grabbing the steak.

"That's a good boy, Oscar," the Spade brother praises the guy. "Want another?"

"Yes, yes, yes," he rushes out, nodding.

The Spade brother stabs two pieces this time, making them cover more of the blade. Holding it out, the guy once again wraps his lips around the knife, sliding his mouth along the edge of the blade, removing the steak. Blood drips from his smacking lips.

"You left some of the juice." The Spade brother holds it up in front of his face and the guy hungrily licks the blade. Cutting himself over and over to get every little drop. "Good, isn't it?"

"So good." The guy closes his eyes and moans. You can't miss the fact that he's now hard.

"You earned this, Oscar." The Spade brother shoves the last few pieces of steak onto the floor and the guy leans over like a dog and eats it up off the dirty concrete.

All three brothers turn to face me and Tyson. My body stiffens, wondering what the fuck we're doing here and why they wanted us to see that. I mean, the Lord in me tells me it's a warning. To show just how fucked up they are.

*They are Carnage. They run it like their own personal hell.*

My father's words echo in my mind.

"What if I told you we'll give you what you want," one states, and my pulse picks up with anticipation. "But you have to give us something in return."

"I'd say name your price and it's yours," I say without hesitation.

The three of them smile but I hear Tyson curse behind me, knowing that I might have just signed my life away.

# ELLINGTON

I sit in my car parked outside the house. My knees bounce, and my hands are sweaty. After Sin left me crying in the kitchen, I crawled into bed and spent all day trying to figure a way out of the life I've been given.

There's no escape. I could run, but where would that get me? A life of always looking over my shoulder? There's probably a tracking device on my car. After what Sin said about my birth control, I've learned I know nothing. He's been one step ahead for months. Years, actually.

I look at my clutch that sits in the passenger seat. I made sure to check, double-check, triple-check ... I'm not pregnant, and I hate how fucking sad that makes me.

Why do I want to have his child? Why do I want to put that kind of burden on him or her? Knowing that Chance—my husband—wouldn't be its biological father?

Fuck, what would happen to me if Chance ever found out? The child would be shunned. What would the Lords do to them? Sin is supposed to be powerful. But his future has been kept a secret. I overheard James talking about Sin and his dad. How high ranked he was, and how high Sin would be.

What if I died while our child is young? Would Sin take him or her in? What if the kid needs medical treatment and blood work reveals that it's not Chance's?

My mind hasn't stopped going through every scenario that ends badly for my imaginary child. I had to try to ignore the possibility that will never be. I'm in no shape to be a mother. I wish Sin's and my past was different. And that we could be happily married and making a family, but that's not the cards I get to play.

Instead, I'm marrying a man who plans on loaning me to whoever wants me. Who knows if he'll make me have his children.

To help keep my mind off my useless life, I was scrolling social media and saw where Kira's friend Sarah was at a party. I wanted to come. I need to get fucked up. Numb. Sin burned everything I had. Well, technically it didn't burn, but it's ruined nonetheless.

So I got up, showered, and got ready like my life isn't exploding into a million pieces.

Getting out of the car, I leave my clutch but grab my phone.

I enter the house and squeeze my way through the crowd. Barrington had a football game tonight and they won so the entire school is here celebrating. Barrington isn't known for their athletics so whenever they win at any type of sport, everyone celebrates.

When parents pay millions a year for kids to attend, they don't need to have a good athletic program.

Walking into the kitchen, I see Sarah standing at the large island, a drink in one hand and her other holding the hand of a Lord by the name of Gunner. I've seen him around. The ring on his finger is hard to miss when you know what to look for.

She looks over and smiles at me. "Elli." Pulling away from Gunner, she wraps her arms around me.

I look over her shoulder to see Gunner searching behind me. His eyes scanning the room before they drop to mine. He sees I'm alone.

*He'll tell Sin.*

Good. Let that motherfucker know I'm not at home crying over him.

"Want a drink?" she asks, pulling away.

I'm not as close with Sarah as Kira is, but I've spoken to her before. Her and her friend Blakely. I haven't seen her around much lately, though. I feel like everyone's lives have changed since the Lords had their vow ceremony. "I'd love one," I answer, pushing a piece of hair behind my ear and avoiding Gunner's stare.

She looks over to the guy making drinks and orders me one before looking back at me. "Did Kira come with you? I messaged her earlier and she never read it."

"I haven't spoken to her." I need to apologize to her. Just because Sin didn't turn out to be the guy I wanted him to be doesn't mean that Corbin can't be who she wants. Not everyone has my bad luck.

"Here you go." The guy hands Sarah the drink and she gives it to me.

"Thank you," I say and lift it to take a sip, but an arm falls over my shoulders, pulling me into a body. I look up into a familiar set of green eyes.

"Hey, Elli."

I let out a nervous breath, thankful it's not Sin. "Hey, Holland." It's Marcus's friend that I ran into at Blackout.

He lifts his eyes to Gunner and nods, but Gunner doesn't acknowledge him in any way. His eyes are still on me, making me nervous. Just to further my point, he finally speaks, "Where's Sin, Ellington?"

The way he uses my full name makes my heart race. The Lords have a way of making the simplest word a threat. "I don't know, Gunner." I give him a tight smile. "Why would I know that?" Lifting the drink, I take a gulp, hissing in a breath at the burn.

"Gunner—" Sarah says softly, placing her hand on his chest.

He ignores her. "Does he know you're here?"

My eyes narrow on him. "Why don't you call and ask him?" I don't know why I'm engaging in a fight I can't win.

*Lie.*

I know why. I want to bait him. I want Gunner to call Sin and tell him I'm here. I want to see him show up and drag me out of here, kicking and screaming. I want everyone to see that I belong to him. That I'm not a secret anymore. I want the world to see that he's cheating on the woman he's going to marry. Fuck my consequences with Chance. It'll be worth it. Just to know that someone would tell Amelia that Sin cares about me.

"Sin?" Holland questions, finally joining in on the conversation. "Since when would he care about you?"

My shoulders drop at his words. The truth hitting me like a slap to the face. The only reason Gunner knows anything is because he's a Lord. Amelia was probably right that they all sit around and laugh about the women they fuck. I'm just another girl on his long list of hookups.

Even if Sin came barging into the party and dragged me out, no one would think twice as to why. He did it once and the only rumors that started spreading the next day was that I fucked three guys. None of which named Sin as one of them.

I take a big gulp of the drink while Gunner glares at me once again. Sarah looks uncomfortable, biting her bottom lip nervously.

"Want a little something stronger than that?" Holland asks, breaking the tension and taking the drink from my hand, setting it on the counter. "Come on." He doesn't even wait for an answer.

I allow him to pull me out of the kitchen and down a hall. He brings me to a set of stairs and into a new room. It's darkly lit with neon signs hanging on the back wall. Guys and girls sit in chairs and lounge on the couch, a pool table is to the right and a small bar in the corner.

"Hey, man." Holland commands as we enter, "She needs something."

I frown, looking at the guy he's talking to. "Mack?" He sits back reclined in a chair.

"Elli." He jumps to his feet, pulling me in for a hug that lifts me off mine. Setting me down, he frowns, looking over my face. "What?"

"Nothing," I answer, shaking my head. I didn't think he was the type to party but then the thought of him at the marina comes to mind. But still, even then he was so shy. Acted innocent. So why is Holland asking him for drugs?

Holland slaps his shoulder. "Give her your best."

Mack frowns. "You sure?"

Holland nods. "Positive."

Mack starts digging into his pocket and removes a tiny plastic baggie. He opens it up and pulls out a white pill. Handing it over, he says, "You only need one."

"What is it?" I ask.

"The best Molly you'll ever have," Holland answers, winking at me, and I toss it into my mouth, not bothering to even think about it.

Mack hands me a cup and I take a gulp of the mixed drink, swallowing the pill.

"Thanks, man," Holland tells him.

"Give it fifteen minutes and you'll be good," Mack adds.

I go to hand him his drink back and he shakes his head, pocketing his hands. "You keep it."

Holland grabs my free hand and pulls me out of the room. We're walking back down the hallway when my cell vibrates in my pocket. I wore jeans tonight because I knew I wouldn't be sober. I'd rather not flash anyone. Pulling my hand from his, I look to see it's Kira. "Hello?" I shout over "Lilith" by Ellise.

I can hear her voice but can't make out what she's saying. "One sec."

I step into a room and turn on the light. It's a half bath. "Hello?" I repeat.

"Where are you?" she shouts, thinking I still can't hear, and it makes me flinch.

"At a party." No need to lie. I'm not sure if Sarah finally got a hold of her or not. Kira and I have been friends for too long to lie to one another. We may not agree on some things, but I'll always tell her the truth.

"Elli," she sighs. "Are you fucked up?"

"Not yet," I answer honestly.

I hear her whispering, and I guess she's telling Corbin what I'm up to. "Who are you there with?" she goes on.

"What's with the twenty questions?" I look up to see the door open and Holland enters, closing it behind him, obviously tired of waiting for me in the hall.

"Elli, please leave," Kira goes on as Holland comes to stand behind me. He places his hand on my hips and I shove them off.

He holds them up and chuckles like it's funny. *I'm not there.* I didn't come here to get laid. The only guy I want is Sin. And I hate myself for that.

"Elli?" she snaps when I ignore her.

"I'm fine, Kira. I'll call you tomorrow." I hang up and turn off my cell, knowing I'll try to call Sin the moment everything goes numb. Even if he has me blocked, I don't want to know that kind of heartache when I hear him on his voicemail.

"How about we have a little fun?" Holland offers, pulling a bag of his own out of his wallet.

Taking a sip of the drink that Mack gave me, I pray it helps the pill kick in soon. He said give it fifteen minutes. "I don't know..."

"You're here to get fucked up, right? Let's get fucked up." Without another word, he pours the white powder onto the counter and then removes a credit card. He hands me a hundred-dollar bill and I start rolling it up while he gets to separating the cocaine into two lines. I guess one can't hurt.

# FORTY-SEVEN

## SIN

We're driving back from Carnage in silence. I can feel the tension in the car. The Spade brothers are going to give me what I want, but they didn't tell me what it'll cost me.

It doesn't even matter. I know it won't be money. *A soul for a soul* comes to mind. And I'd hand mine over without thought. Loving someone is being selfless and Elli is worth that. She deserves nothing less. After everything she's been through, what I've put her through. A part of me hates that she still loves me because I know she deserves better. The other part of me is glad she does because I wouldn't be able to walk away from her even if she hated me. We've gone too far to turn back now.

Reaching into the back pocket of my jeans, I pull out the picture that I still have. I can't stop thinking about it. The thought of knowing someone else was there unsettles me more and more. The fact that she was in that situation at all makes me want to kill James over and over, but add the fact that now I know more were involved...

It has to be Linc, right? He knew about her and James. But

what if it's not? Who else is alive and knows what James did to her? Did this other guy do it too? She hadn't told me about Linc until her mother married him, so who else could she be keeping secrets for?

"What's that?" Tyson finally breaks the silence. His tone tells me he's still angry with me but curious enough to ask.

"I found this older picture of Elli. James is in it." Tyson knows her past. I've filled him in. He wasn't going to help me out without knowing everything. I figured it couldn't hurt to have him on my side. Even if he doesn't agree with what I'm going to do to end it.

He frowns. "Meaning?"

"Meaning someone else took it."

He nods to himself. "You think it's Linc?"

"It has to be."

He goes to speak but my cell rings and I see **Gunner** written across the screen. "Hey, man…"

"Where the fuck are you?" he demands.

I frown, hearing the faint sound of music in the background. "With Tyson on our way to Blackout. What's up?"

"I don't know what's going on with you and Amelia—congratulations on the engagement, by the way." I roll my eyes at that. "But I figured you'd like to know that your plaything is at Harrison's house party."

"What?" I snap, pulling the phone from my ear and placing it on speakerphone so I can look at the cameras in our house. She's nowhere on them.

"Yeah," he goes on. "I was standing in the kitchen, and she walked in. Sarah got her a drink, but Holland came up and took her for something *more*."

"Motherfucker!"

"Tell me what to do, Sin," he says while I track her location, but her cell it off. Good thing I know where Harrison lives. "Want me to let her go? Or remove her from the party?"

"We're twenty minutes away," I growl, knowing a lot can happen in that amount of time. No telling how long she's already been there. "Drag her out of there by any means necessary," I say through gritted teeth.

"Thought so," he mutters to himself.

"Gunner?" I speak before he can end the call.

"Yeah?"

Tyson slams on the brakes to make a U-turn as I hold up the address to show him. "Are you there alone?"

"No, Prickett is here somewhere."

"I want Holland." If he came and got Elli, it's because he has plans for her. I killed his best friend, left his body to rot as a warning. Elli doesn't know that but I'm sure Holland does.

"Got it." He hangs up and I throw my phone down.

"Fuck!"

"We can be there in fifteen." Tyson slams on the gas, now going the opposite direction.

"What the fuck is she thinking?" I growl to myself. I ruined her drugs, so she went out to get more. I haven't checked on the cameras in over two hours because we were at Carnage. I didn't have any reception in there.

My cell rings again and I bend down to pick it up off the floor where I threw it. "Let me talk to her," I demand when I see it's Gunner again and immediately put him on speakerphone.

"Where the fuck are you?" he rushes out.

"On our way. Why?"

"I've got her, but, Sin ..."

"What?" I sit up straighter when he trails off.

"She's in trouble."

"What kind of trouble?" I ask, my heart racing.

"I found her unconscious. Her breathing is rapid, she's burning up. I can't get her to wake up."

"What—"

"She's overdosing," Tyson speaks.

"Fuck. Hold her head," Gunner barks at someone.

Overdosing? No. She may do drugs, but she knows her limits. There's no way she would take too much. She's smarter than that. "What's going on?" I snap. "Gunner?"

"She's vomiting," he states. "Hold her head, Sarah."

"I'm trying," I hear her cry.

"Can you get her to Blackout?" Tyson demands, doing another U-turn.

"Blackout? She needs a hospital," Gunner argues.

"I'll take care of it," Tyson assures him. "Gavin can meet us at Blackout."

I look at the address again. "They're closer to our house. So are we." Blackout is on the other side of the city. I understand why Tyson suggested it, but she could be dead by then.

Tyson nods. "Send him the address and we'll meet them there."

Gunner hangs up and I go to call him back, wanting to stay on the phone with him, but my cell vibrates, alerting me of a text.

UNKNOWN: We know where your loyalty lies. Let's see about hers.

"FUCK!"

"She'll be okay," Tyson says.

"Fuck. Fuck." I fist my hands before running them through my hair. "It's the Lords. They want to test her. Fuck!"

Tyson doesn't seem surprised. Why would he? This is what they do. They see someone in a vulnerable position and use it against you. Only the strongest get to wear the crest. Only the ones they deem worthy get rewarded.

"One thing at a time," Tyson speaks. "Send Gunner the address to the house." Then he picks up his cell to make the call we need.

I'm pacing the living room of the house with Gavin. He works for the Lords. Tyson called him to meet us here. Thankfully he was closer than we were and was already waiting for us when we arrived. Tyson stands over in front of the floor-to-ceiling windows looking out into the dark woods.

The front double doors open and I rush to them, thinking it's Gunner with Elli but it's Chance. I go back to pacing.

"I got the text," he states at our silence.

I don't have time to think about that right now. Her loyalty won't matter if she's already dead when Gunner arrives.

"Where do you want her?" Gunner calls out, rushing into the house with an unconscious Elli draped across his arms. A crying Sarah enters behind them.

"In the bedroom," Gavin commands, pointing to the hallway. I hurry in front of him to lead the way for Gunner where Gavin is already set up for her.

Gunner places her on the bed and her head rolls to the side. I don't miss the fact that she's still dressed in her jeans and a T-shirt. Which makes me think that whatever Holland planned on doing with her wasn't sexual. He didn't want to fuck my little demon, he wanted to kill her.

"Elli?" I demand, grabbing her face. It's clammy and cold, her skin is pale, lips blue. "Elli?" I shout her name, shaking her, but nothing. No response at all. It makes my chest tighten.

"What did she take?" Gavin asks, running his knuckles up and down her chest bone, but still nothing. She moves like a rag doll with his harsh movements—lifeless.

Gunner holds on to a sobbing Sarah who stares down at Elli. "I don't know. I found her that way."

Gavin looks at me and then to Chance who has followed as well. "What does she normally take?"

Running a hand through my hair, I say, "Uh, ecstasy, cocaine..." I try and think of everything I burned and have seen her have in the past. "She had some benzos." Chance doesn't know. He's not around her enough so he stays silent.

"Fentanyl?" Gavin questions. "Opioids?" He lifts her eyelids and I get a look at her beautiful ice-blue eyes; the pupils are constricted.

"No." I shake my head. "She wouldn't—"

"Tyson, hand me the Narcan that's in my bag," he interrupts me, not believing my answer.

Tyson rips open the package and hands the nose spray to Gavin. I hold her clammy hand while he tilts her head back. Placing it into her left nostril, he pushes the plunger into her nose.

"Help me turn her over," he orders, stepping back from the bed.

I grab her shoulder, rolling her toward me.

"Place her hands under her head." I do as I'm told. "Tyson, bend her left knee, making it to where she can't roll onto her stomach."

We get her into position, and I kneel down next to the bed, staring into her eyes. They're somewhat open, seeing nothing. The makeup she went out wearing tonight is smeared across her gorgeous face. Had she been crying? Did she try and call me? She needed me and I wasn't there for her.

"Now what?" I ask Gavin, licking my lips nervously.

"We give it a couple of minutes. If it doesn't seem to work, I've got another one."

"You need to leave," Tyson grabs my arm, pulling me to stand.

"What? No." My eyes are on Elli and I see she blinks, starting to come to, and I let out a sigh of relief. "Elli—"

"Yes, Sin," Tyson growls at me. "Chance is here. That's who she needs."

"No!" I snap, watching her eyes look around aimlessly. Gavin starts to talk to her, and I watch her begin to cry. *Is he fucking serious?*

Tyson shoves me through the bedroom door. Gunner exits with a sobbing Sarah, and he closes it behind them, shutting her in there with Gavin and Chance. "You've come this far. Don't ruin it. Chance is who she needs to be with right now. Not you." Then he turns and enters the bedroom, closing me out once more.

## ELLINGTON

I WAKE ONCE AGAIN, FLINCHING AT THE BRIGHT LIGHT ABOVE me. I've had a hard time staying awake. My eyes so heavy, my mind too foggy. Rolling onto my side, I start to shake, my body cold.

"Here." I hear a man's voice before a blanket is draped over me.

Lifting my heavy eyes, I see Tyson stepping back, which gives me a view of the guy standing over by a wall. I groan when I see his green eyes already on mine.

"Where am I?" I ask, ignoring him and scanning the room.

"Home." Tyson is the one who answers.

How did I get here? Pushing myself up to a sitting position, the room spins and I bow my head, my hand applying pressure to my temple. "What..." My tongue is heavy, my throat raw. "Happened?" I feel high, but off. Everything aches.

"You went to a party and got fucked up. Like usual," Chance growls, clearly aggravated.

"Don't act like you care," I mumble, not remembering much. The last thing that comes to mind is me standing in the bathroom with Holland. We did a couple lines and I started to feel different ... wrong. Then everything went black.

389

He sighs. "If you think being a druggie will make me call off the wedding, you're wrong."

Of course, he won't. That would mean luck is in my favor.

"Here's her purse," I hear Tyson say and I look up just as he hands my clutch over to Chance. How did he get that? It was in my car. How did I get here? Did Tyson find me? Did he bring me home?

I look over to the other man that stands in the room. He's older. I recognize him from when the Lords brought him to our house after James was killed. He checked on me then. I remember him telling me his name is Gavin when I woke up for the first time earlier. I couldn't keep my eyes open and fell back asleep. He promised me that I was okay. That everything would be oaky. I just needed to rest.

Chance gets my attention when he rips open my clutch and tenses while staring into it. Reaching inside, he pulls out all five pregnancy tests I took earlier and holds them up. "Celebrating?"

No. More like drowning my sorrows. I don't answer.

He throws them across the room, hitting the wall so hard that two of their caps fall off. He walks over to me, and I straighten my spine.

"Who the fuck are you sleeping with?" he demands.

I clench my teeth, refusing to answer. I will not give up Sin. It'll make me look stupid. Desperate. He does not deserve my loyalty, but this isn't about him. It's about me. He didn't come to save me from the party. I will not spend the rest of my life with Chance paying for what Sin did to me. Some things a woman has to take to her grave. This is one of those that I will die for.

"I asked you a question," he shouts in my face, making my headache intensify. "Huh? Who the fuck are you fucking?"

Swallowing, I flinch at the soreness but remain silent.

He grabs my hair and yanks me off the bed. I'm unable to hold myself up and fall to my knees on the carpeted floor.

Sucking in a deep breath, I say, "You didn't ... care when I sucked Linc's dick." Taking a deep breath, my chest feels like it's on fire. "Not sure why you'd care if I fuck one." Fuck Chance and the fact that he's going to decide who I can and can't sleep with. At least Sin makes sure I'm satisfied. At least he won't pass me around.

Chance reaches down, gripping my face, and shoves my head back so I have to look up at him. Thankfully, other parts of my body are in so much pain that I don't really feel it.

"You think this is funny?" he demands. "Think you can fuck whoever you want, whenever you want?" He doesn't even give me the chance to answer, not like I will anyway.

He lets go of my cheeks and slaps me across the face, the force making me fall onto my hands. I feel the bile start to rise but I swallow it down. My cheek is now throbbing and drool runs from my parted lips. The room spins and I wonder if I'm going to pass out again. I pray that I do.

"You know, Elli. I thought we could make this work. That although you'd be somewhat of a nuisance, you'd be a submissive wife who had learned her lesson many years ago. After all, James taught you how to behave."

I whimper at the sound of his name. Sometime over the last couple of weeks I had forgotten that Chance saw firsthand how I was with James. How my body would betray me. Make me beg for something that no one should want.

"If sex is what you want, then sex is what I'll give you." He grabs a hold of my hair and yanks me from my knees. He shoves my back into a wall, moving his hand to wrap around my sore throat, cutting off my air. I don't even fight him. Let him knock me out. I don't have to stare at him if I'm unconscious. Placing his face in front of mine, he bares his white teeth. "I will offer you to all the Lords at the cathedral."

Tears sting my eyes at his words. It's what Sin told me about.

How a Lord treats his wife who cheats. Sin had said *rape or willingly,* she will be punished for her affairs.

"I'll tie you down to the altar, spread wide open. I'll let three at a time come up and use you until every Lord has fucked you. It'll take days."

The first tear spills over my bottom lashes and he smiles.

"You will be known as nothing other than our whore. And I'll make sure you earn that title." He lets go of my neck and I fall to my knees once more, sucking in a breath.

"So-unds fun," I manage to get out through the coughs. I no longer care. I'd rather him just kill me. That would be the best outcome at this point. Chance has no use for me. He won't play with me for long. Not like Sin. Chance will realize I'm not worth it and just get rid of me. For good.

I hear Tyson laugh. Chance slaps me, the force making me fall face-first to the floor where my body starts to have uncontrollable jerking movements. I feel like I'm having a seizure of some sort. Thankfully, it stops, and I just lie there, eyes heavy while extra saliva fills my mouth.

"Believe me, Elli. You won't enjoy it." He kneels down next to me. "Last chance, baby." I whimper, knowing he called me that on purpose. "Who are you fucking?"

I'm having trouble catching my breath. I'm not sure if it's from the drugs or his hands on me, but I sit up, pushing my back into the wall, and glare at him. "You're going to let your uncle fuck me after our wedding." I pause to take in another shaky breath. "Not sure why it matters who I fuck now."

# FORTY-EIGHT

# SIN

I'm pacing the living room when I hear the bedroom door open and close shut. Next, I see Chance coming down the hallway that leads to the master suite.

"Move up the wedding," I demand, walking toward him.

He drops his head, running his hand though his hair and looking conflicted "I don't know—"

"Move up the fucking wedding," I bark.

"Sin, man." He raises his eyes to meet mine. "She's in bad shape. Tried to commit suicide."

I shake my head. "No, she didn't."

"She needs to be admitted." He ignores me. "For observation. A seventy-two-hour hold—"

I land a fist to the middle of his nose, knocking him to his knees on the floor.

"Goddammit," comes his muffled growl. "I think you broke my nose this time." He looks up at me, blood dripping down his face onto the carpet.

"Say that again, and it'll be your jaw," I warn.

He gets to his feet, and I take a step back so I don't snap his fucking neck. I need him right now. Just a little longer.

"Listen." He raises his hands, watery eyes softening. "She's not well."

"She's fine."

He shakes his head. "Jesus, Sin, listen to yourself. She's in the bedroom, puking her guts up because she went out to a party and took drugs. She can barely stay conscious. Whatever you said or did was too much for her."

He's right. I did this to her. I've pushed her too far. But I can fix it. "She didn't do this." She may have went there planning on doing something, but Holland saw an opportunity and took advantage of her. He wanted to hurt her, to hurt me. She was his revenge for Marcus. My little demon wouldn't do this to herself. She's stronger than that.

"Maybe you should give up." He sighs. "Everyone has a breaking point. Her father got the job done, one day she will too."

I step into him, my chest hitting his so hard it pushes him a step back. "Are you going back on our deal?" I'm tired of listening to what he thinks I should do. Or who he thinks she is. He has no idea.

He looks away from me, and after a long second, he shakes his head. "I'll make the call. Make sure she shows up and that she's sober." With that, he turns and walks out of the front doors, slamming them both shut.

A soft sob hits my ears and I ignore Sarah. She sits with Gunner over on the couch. They haven't left. Sarah wanted to wait and see how Elli is doing and Gunner didn't argue with her. Plus, he had a text about fifteen minutes ago that Prickett is on his way here.

Tyson and Gavin enter the living room. "How is she?" I demand.

"The Narcan worked."

"But she'll be okay?" I urge.

"Yes. I've given her something to make her comfortable." He looks around the room. "Where is her husband...?"

"I'm her husband," I snap, interrupting him.

He looks at Tyson, who nods, and then looks back at me. "She needs to rest, but she'll be okay. You can call me if you have any questions or concerns."

I walk into the kitchen and grab a bottle of water, needing to try and calm my nerves. Tyson follows me. I fall down into one of the barstools at the island and run a hand down my face. "How bad was it?" I ask through the knot in my throat. I have cameras in the bedroom but couldn't bring myself to watch them. Afraid it'd have me barging in there to protect her. As much as I wanted to, I couldn't intervene. It would have made it worse for her.

Tyson shoves his hands into the pockets of his jeans. "She passed, if that's what you're asking. Congratulations. She's all yours."

Dropping my head, I interlock my fingers behind my neck, letting out a long breath. "Yeah, but at what cost?" Will she forgive me? No. Do I care? Also no. She's mine now. No one can ever take her from me. I'll spend the rest of my life—no matter how short that will be—fighting to protect her.

Dropping my hands onto the island, I look up at him.

"We all pay a price, Sin. Some more than others. What it ends up costing us depends on how bad we want it."

Looking over to the entrance of the kitchen, I see Gunner walk up. "Prickett's here."

I jump up from the barstool and run back into the living room. "What the fuck happened?" I demand. Gunner had said that Prickett had some information for me. He had seen her as well at the party.

Prickett sighs, coming to stand in front of me and Tyson. "I was in the game room when Elli entered with Holland. He went to

Mack and said she needed something special. Mack questioned it but Holland had assured him it would be fine. Elli questioned what it was. Holland told her it was the best Molly. She, of course, believed him and took it. After Holland removed her from the room, another girl who had seen the exchange went over to Mack and said she wanted some ecstasy. Mack said he didn't have any."

"What the fuck are you saying?" I demand, trying to figure it out.

"I'm saying what Mack gave her and what Holland told her it was, were two very different things. After Gunner found her in a bedroom and carried her from the party, Holland was overheard bragging about giving Elli a pill laced with fentanyl. And then I guess she also snorted some that she thought was cocaine."

"Fuck, she's lucky Gunner found her when he did," Tyson speaks.

"Were you able to get Holland?" I demand, looking at Gunner. I haven't asked because of the situation he found her in. My plans to fuck him up were put on hold.

"No. I found her in the bedroom. I needed Prickett's help to get her out of the party without anyone seeing what was going on and to the car. I came straight here, and I had Sarah follow us in Ellington's car. That way it wasn't left behind for anyone to see. I figured Holland would go back to check on her in the bedroom, and I wanted him to shit himself wondering where the fuck she went."

I run a hand through my hair, frustrated. *I'll get him.*

"I went back in with every intention to get him for you, but he was surrounded by people. I figured I'd let him run his mouth. When you're ready, let me know and I'll help you," Prickett adds.

I nod.

"It doesn't make sense." Gunner frowns. "I asked her where you were. Then asked her if you knew she was there. Holland asked why you'd care what she is doing." He shrugs. "I thought they were friends, but after the way he ran his mouth about what he did to her, that's obviously not the case. He just left her there. In the room alone. To what? Die? Thinking others would see it as an overdose? Possible suicide? Everyone knows her dad succeeded years ago."

That's what I'm thinking Holland's plan was, but I tell them the truth as to why he did what he did to her. "I killed his best friend."

---

I WALK INTO THE MASTER BEDROOM TO FIND HER LYING IN the fetal position on the bed, eyes closed. Crawling in bed next to her, I push her hair from her face. She's shivering. I pull the comforter up and tuck it under her neck.

"I'm sorry, little demon," I whisper, kissing her forehead. "It's going to be okay. You're going to be okay."

Her dark lashes flutter open, unfocused ice-blue eyes look around until they meet mine. "S-in?"

"I'm here, Elli." Fuck what Tyson said. I'm not leaving her. There's no one else here to make sure she's okay. I don't want her mother or Linc to know what happened. She'll throw her in an institute. Toss her into a rehab center and leave her there, never checking on her. Linc will just fuck her, possibly feed her addiction with more drugs.

I'm all she has. I'm all she's ever had, and I'm not going to let her down anymore.

My phone starts vibrating in my pocket, and I pull it out to see it's Amelia. I reject the call. Placing my cell back in my pocket, it goes off again and I see she's texted me this time. I open it up to see it's an announcement.

Chance has moved up his wedding to Elli. Just like I told him to. I grind my teeth. Of course, she would send me that. She wants to rub it in my face that the woman I love is marrying someone else.

If she only knew.

Elli gets my attention, rolling away from me. She struggles to get comfortable and shoves off the covers. "What can I do?" I ask her, placing my hand on her back.

She's still dressed, and she's covered in sweat. Her body trembling. "Elli?" I say, giving her a shake but she doesn't answer. I get up and lean over her, feeling her head, she's burning up. I lower my hand to her neck, to feel her pulse. It's racing.

Her body jerks and she sits straight up.

"Elli?" I ask, watching her place her hands out in front of her face and she starts to dry heave.

I pick her up in my arms and rush her to the en suite bathroom. I barely get her in front of the toilet in time before she gets sick. She's so weak she can barely hold her head up, so I do it for her while also holding her hair out of the way.

Once she's done, I strip her down to her underwear and carry her back to bed. I get her a cool wet rag and place it on her head and put a trash can next to her. I pull out my cell and call Tyson. Everyone left about twenty minutes ago. It's just me and her here.

"Hello?"

"Something is wrong," I tell him in greeting. "She's getting worse. Not better."

"Hang on, I'll add Gavin to the call."

I wait impatiently as I grab her a water from the fridge and rush back to the bedroom. I know Gavin had said she needs to stay hydrated. She needs to sip on some water, especially if she's going to be getting sick again.

Gavin connects to the call. "Tyson—"

"What the fuck is wrong with her?" I snap, interrupting him. "She's vomiting. Shaking, her pulse is racing, and she's sweating, like drenched in it."

"Everyone is different, but she can be experiencing side effects."

My teeth grind. "So you gave her something to fix her but it made her worse," I growl.

"Narcan only works on opioids. If she swallowed or snorted anything else, it will not have an effect on those drugs. Plus, Narcan in most cases is only in your system for thirty to ninety minutes. But it can trigger the onset of withdrawal symptoms in the body." He pauses. "It could also be that many opioids remain in the body longer than it takes the Narcan to wear off. Meaning, she could be experiencing the effects of the overdose now that the Narcan is out of her system."

I sigh, running a hand through my hair, watching her lying in bed, her eyes closed once again. The doorbell rings and my eyes snap up.

"I can—"

I hang up on them and pocket my cell, pulling the top sheet only up to her neck. Knowing she's burning up but also not wanting her naked if someone is here. Walking over to the tall dresser, I yank open the top drawer and grab my gun, tucking it into the back of my jeans, making sure my T-shirt covers it. I turn on the fan on my way out of the room and shut the door behind me.

Making my way to the front doors, I come to a stop when they open, and three men enter the house like they fucking own it. Three men that I didn't give this address to, but somehow know exactly where I am. Which means they know where Elli is. "Brothers." I nod to them as they all stand in the grand foyer, dressed in black, covered in ink, looking like they want to cut my head off.

"We've come to deliver a package," one says, stepping to the side. Another grabs the man who was hidden behind him and shoves the guy forward. "You've got one week to deliver, Easton."

He calls me by my first name, and I step closer to them, wanting to protect Elli who is down the hallway behind me. I don't want them anywhere near her. "Or we come and collect." His blue eyes look around, taking everything in before they meet mine again. "And we'd hate to have to destroy everything to get what is owed to us."

## ELLINGTON

I ROLL ONTO MY SIDE. MY HANDS GRAB AT MY STOMACH, AND I groan. I feel nauseated. My body is shivering. Everything hurts. It's hard to breathe.

"You're okay, Elli." I hear Sin's voice, but I don't see him. My eyes are tightly shut. I'm probably imagining it.

"What's wrong with her?" I hear a voice ask off in the distance.

"She's fine." Sin's voice is much louder, he's closer to me. I feel his hands grab at my shoulders, avoiding answering the question. "Go wait for me in the other room."

I reach out and grab a hold of a pillow. I pull it over my face, the light too bright it's hurting my eyes even though they are closed. I feel like I'm spinning, my body jerking involuntary.

"I will not—"

I sit up, abandoning the pillow as saliva fills my mouth. "I'm ... going to be sick," I manage to mumble to no one in particular.

My hair is grabbed, and something is placed on my lap. I throw up, my stomach muscles tightening, the acid burning my throat. So much to the point I'm dry heaving. Tears sting my eyes, making what little vision I have blurry.

"You're okay." Sin rubs my back. "You're going to be okay."

I fall down onto my back and roll over into a ball, shivering.

"What the fuck is wrong with her?" that far off voice demands.

I hear Sin sigh. "She's having withdrawals."

"She's an addict?"

"No ... yes. She was drugged. Needed Narcan. I think it's thrown her into withdrawals."

"Christ."

I feel the bile rising again, and I can't hold it down. Hands grab me and lift me up into the air, I bury my face into the hard chest and wrap my shaking arms around his neck.

"Make yourself useful and remove the sheets. There's a clean pair folded on the dryer," Sin calls out before I hear a door slam shut and then he's placing me on a cold floor just as I get sick again.

---

I OPEN MY EYES AND DON'T FEEL LIKE I'M DYING, SO THAT'S A plus. Not my normal self, but better than I remember.

Rolling over, the curtains allow a soft glow into the dark room, and I see Sin is lying next to me, eyes closed and lips slightly parted. He's sleeping. I'm so confused where he came from. How I got home. And why he's still here. Shouldn't he be with Amelia? And where did Chance go? Did I imagine him being here in this room with Tyson and the doctor? No, it was real. Chance reminded me exactly what my life will be like once he marries me —hell.

Sitting up, I look over at the nightstand to see an empty bottle of water. My mouth is so dry, I need something to drink. Getting to my feet, I wobble a little before getting my balance under control. I open the bedroom door and make my way down the hallway, using my hand on the wall. There's a throbbing sensation right behind my eyes and I feel nauseous.

Entering the kitchen, I open the fridge and grab a water. When I shut it, I see a figure standing over in the corner and I scream, my heart racing and causing me to sway on my feet.

"Elli?" I hear Sin call out before rushing into the kitchen. He flips on the light, and I turn to face him to see he's wearing nothing but a pair of black boxer briefs and holding a gun in his right hand. "What's wrong?" he asks, his hard chest heaving at his heavy breathing. His eyes dropping to my bare legs, making sure I'm physically okay as they quickly run up over the T-shirt of his I'm dressed in.

"I saw someone." I turn around to point them out, but my breath gets lodged in my throat. He moves out of the corner, stepping toward us and I take one back, matching it. I bump into Sin, and it makes me yelp in surprise.

"Elli—"

I turn to face Sin once again. "I'm hallucinating," I rush out.

He places his gun on the counter and cups my face in both of his warm hands. I'm trembling, trying to catch my breath. Heart still pounding and that throbbing sensation behind my eyes now intensifies. "What's wrong with me?" I whisper.

His blue eyes soften as they roam my face. "You're fine, Elli."

I lick my lips. "No. I went to a party ... did drugs."

He sighs heavily. "I know and we'll talk about that later, okay?" One hand releases my cheek to push hair from my face.

My legs are shaking. To the point my knees are knocking into one another. "Sin, I'm seeing ... things." My throat closes up on me. What did I take? How long have I been out? Is Sin even here? Am I dreaming?

"Take in a deep breath," Sin says, doing so himself, hoping I'll follow.

I don't. Instead, my shaking hands come up to wrap around his wrists and I close my eyes tightly, hoping that when they open, I'll be lying in bed by myself. And this will be a nightmare. Maybe it's a bad trip.

"Elli?" Sin barks my name, and my eyes spring open to see him still holding on to me. "Take a breath. You're okay."

I shake my head the best I can as tears start to sting my eyes.

"It's true, princess," the man speaks behind me, and a whimper escapes my parted lips.

Sin nods his head at me as if to give me encouragement and then lets go of my face, placing them on my shoulders and turning me around. I stare wide-eyed at a set of blue eyes I haven't seen in years. He doesn't look the same, but I'd recognize him anywhere. "D-dad?"

# FORTY-NINE

## SIN

Nicholas Asher takes a step closer to us and she takes another back, stepping out of the kitchen. His eyes go to mine and then back to her.

"No," she whispers. "I saw you ... you were dead."

"Ellington," he says her name and another whimper comes out of her trembling lips.

She wraps her arms around her waist. "I found you." He runs a hand through his hair at her words. "I held your body." She takes another step back, eyes on the floor, unable to look at him. "You're dead. Have been for years."

His jaw sharpens and he looks to me. I glare at him. I don't know the story as to how he's alive and standing here in the kitchen either. I just know what Ryat had overheard while he was on his assignment and that if the rumor was true, Tyson knew where he was—Carnage.

The Spade brothers dropped him off two days ago, but I've spent all of my time with Elli. She finally stopped vomiting around midnight last night and was able to get some rest. I woke alone in bed to her screaming.

"Let's sit down, okay?" I turn to look at her. "There's a lot we need to talk about." I'm not just meaning her father coming back from the grave.

A tear runs down her cheek, but she nods. I take her hand and grab my gun off the counter with my free one. Making our way to the living room, she and I sit down on the couch. Her father takes the seat across from us.

I don't miss the way she pushes herself closer to me. Her bare leg touching mine. I grab the blanket off the back and place it over us since she's in a T-shirt of mine and I'm only wearing boxers.

"Elli—"

"Nicholas." The way she says his name is so cold, detached. She's putting up all her walls, confused and hurt. She feels she's been lied to all these years. I get it. I didn't expect this to be easy. Not after everything she's been through.

His jaw sharpens at the use of his name. "It's weird you not calling me Daddy. Guess you're not twelve anymore."

A sob escapes her lips, and she places her hand over her mouth, eyes dropping to her lap.

He looks at me, brow arched.

"One thing at a time," I growl. "How the fuck are you alive?" I demand, wrapping my arm round her shoulders and pulling her into my side. My free hand holds my gun resting on top of the blanket. I understand he's her father, but I'm also aware he's been MIA for nine years. I don't know if that's by choice or something he planned.

He runs a hand through his hair. "You don't die at Carnage unless the Spade brothers are done with you," he states.

"How did you survive hanging yourself?" Elli asks, her voice soft and eyes still downcast, looking at her shaking hands on her lap. "You were ... cold," she adds softly.

"Jesus, Elli. Do you really think I tried to kill myself?" he barks out.

She lifts her eyes to look at him through her lashes. "I was the one who found you. I lay there on the floor with your dead body for over an hour. You. Were. Dead."

He shakes his head. "I was set up."

"How were you set up for suicide?" I wonder. I mean, it's not impossible. Look what Holland tried to do to Elli, but the Nicholas situation is a little different. No drugs were involved. Not that I know of anyway.

He leans forward, placing his elbows on his knees. "Someone did die that day, but it wasn't me. It was Nathaniel."

I frown, Elli remains silent.

"Nathaniel was my twin brother."

I sit up straighter. "You don't have a twin brother." I would know that. Our families grew up together and I would have remembered that.

"I did." He nods. "My father had an affair on his Lady and got my mother pregnant. My father took me, let our mother keep my brother. When I was of age, I went into initiation. Wanting to be a Lord. I had found my brother and reached out, but he didn't want anything to do with it." He shrugs. "My father wanted nothing to do with him. He was shunned by my father and my mother who raised me. But he was in my life. A lot, actually. He was always needing money, bailed out of situations that he couldn't afford to do himself. Of course, not many knew he existed. But he was killed to make it look like I committed suicide. And I was handed over to Carnage."

Silence falls over the room and I feel Elli's body shaking as she leans into my side.

"What about you?" His eyes go to his daughter. "Why and how long have you been doing drugs?"

She stiffens, but her head stays down. She's not going to answer him. Admitting what has happened to her is too much for her to explain to her father.

"Why don't you go start a bath." I lean in and kiss her temple. Nick's up for sharing but I know she sure as fuck is not. He may be her father but right now he's a stranger to her. "I'll be there to join you in a minute."

She slowly gets to her feet and starts to walk toward the hallway. Her father stands and she runs out of the living room. I hear the bedroom door slam shut seconds later.

"What the fuck is going on with her?" he barks at me.

I expected it to go this way, honestly. I figured she'd be more confused than excited. But in the long run, she'll come around. "Your death ruined her life," I say simply.

He groans. "Mine hasn't been sunshine since I *died*."

I stare at him as he looks over at the hallway she ran down, the gun heavy in my hand. He needs to know what's going on because once again, things are going to change. I'm going to give him one chance. He'll either help me or get in my way. Might as well find out right now which one it's going to be.

"Your wife remarried," I begin with and he snorts. "To James, a year after you died. He spent the first three years of his marriage grooming your daughter." His body stiffens. "He then took her virginity at sixteen. And continued to rape her until I killed him two years ago. He made her call him *Daddy*, so forgive her for not calling you that."

He turns, giving me his back, running his hands through his hair. He curses under his breath. Turning back to face me, I add, "We recently found out—at your wife's third wedding reception— that she was aware James was fucking Elli. But when Elli said she was being raped, your wife said she was willingly throwing herself at her husband."

"Motherfucker!" He grabs a glass off of the coffee table and throws it across the room. It hits the far wall and shatters to a million pieces.

I can only imagine how he feels. I'm sure you don't get to let out your frustration at Carnage. He'll be a walking time bomb now. Nine years of pent-up aggression. That's what I need. Someone who won't think twice about making others bleed. I need help if I'm going to take down who I think is involved. And of course, she needs her father. She may not feel that way right this second, but she will.

I head toward the hallway, knowing that Elli is waiting on me, but he stops me.

"What did you offer the Spade brothers in exchange for me?" he asks.

I look at him over my shoulder. "Whatever they wanted."

"Easton..." he growls.

"Get some rest, Nick. We'll try again later. We've only got a week for her to come around."

# ELLINGTON

I SIT IN THE TUB, HOT WATER UP TO MY CHEST, MY EYES staring straight ahead, but I don't see anything.

My father is alive. Has been for all these years. No. I don't believe it. How did no one not know? He was dead. In my arms.

*"Daddy?" I cry, my arms wrapped around his neck as we lie side by side on the cold floor. The rope still wrapped around it.*

*"Elli, he's dead." Hands tug at my arm.*

*"Noooo." I sob, hanging on to him tighter.*

*"Elli, sweetheart, you've got to let go of him." I hear Mrs. Sinnett say softly.*

*Hands grab at me again and this time I'm yanked from him. I scream, my hands reaching out, trying to grab a hold of him, but I'm too far away. "DADDY!" I sob as warm arms wrap around me, pulling me into a soft body. I turn and bury my face into her. She picks me up and I let her carry me out of the house as if I'm an infant who can't walk on her own.*

I blink and see Sin sitting in front of me in the tub, the water now turned off. His legs on either side of mine. His hands on my bent knees. His eyes follow the tear that runs down my face and I realize I'm crying. "How did you know?"

"Another Lord overheard something. He came to me, and I had Tyson make a call."

He doesn't want me to know who told him. Maybe it's for the best. I sniff. "What did you do?" If my father has been gone for almost nine years, it cost Sin something in order to get him back. I know how the Lords work.

"Don't worry about that," he says, his hands running up and down my thighs. "He's here now."

My eyes drop to the water, and I feel fresh tears stinging my eyes. Lifting them back to meet his, I ask, "Why are you here, Sin?"

He sighs, his chest rising and falling, and my eyes drop to the Lords' crest branded onto it. It makes me think of the one he gave me on my thigh. Has he given one to Amelia yet? If not, will he once she becomes his wife? "Because there's nowhere else I want to be."

My eyes meet his again and he reaches out, rubbing his thumb through the tears on my cheeks. "Amelia—"

"Don't worry about her," he interrupts me, once again avoiding my question.

I pull back and move my legs to the side, knocking his hands off of them.

"Elli," he sighs.

I stand, making the water splash around, and get out of the tub, hearing him get out as well. I dry off and make my way to the bedroom, yanking the covers back and crawling into bed. "Go home, Sin," I say, watching him exit the bathroom. Rolling over, I turn away from him.

He yanks the covers back and lies down next to me. "I am home, Elli." He wraps his arm around me from behind.

I turn in his arms and shove my hand into his bare chest. "This isn't *our* home, Sin. Leave."

He shoves me onto my back and straddles my hips. I reach up and slap his face, but it's weak. I'm not one hundred percent myself yet after the party. The room has stopped spinning and I no longer have a bad taste in my mouth since I brushed my teeth, but my head isn't one hundred percent. Like a throbbing sensation right behind my eyes. Not bad enough to hurt, but enough to irritate me.

Grabbing both of my wrists, he pins them down on either side of my head. I try to lift my hips but he's sitting on them. I growl.

"Get angry, little demon. It'll just make this that much sweeter."

"S-in," I cry out, frustrated, and turned on. I need him to take me to that place where my mind doesn't work. Where I don't have to wonder why my father is alive and in my house or why I got fucked up at a party. Or why Sin's here with me and not with Amelia. "Please leave."

Letting go of my wrists, he grips my throat, forcing me to arch my neck. He lowers his lips to mine, whispering, "Beg me to leave while I fuck your cunt, Elli."

I whimper before he takes my breath away completely. My pussy clenches while my hands claw at his back and my nails dig into his skin, making him hiss in a breath. My heels dig into the sheets, pushing up, but he's still on top of me. I can't get any traction or leverage to get him off of me. The worst part? I don't want him to. This is what I wanted. For him to drag me out of the party and fuck me. To want me. To need me like I need him.

It's that toxic trait that I need to be owned. Put in my place.

Hurt me, fuck me, make me come. I'll never learn but I want him to think I can. That I'm somewhat able to be saved. Even though we both know, deep down, I'm too broken to change now. Sin may be the devil, but I'm the sinner. Doing the same thing over and over, knowing that I can't be saved.

He runs his tongue along my parted lips before murmuring, "I don't know what you were trying to accomplish by going to that party, but I'm going to punish you for it."

I arch my neck more, trying to breathe, and it just gives him better access to it. He repositions his hand, still restricting my air, and I see dots dance across my vision. My hands that are digging into his back drop to my sides and my eyes start to fall closed.

# FIFTY

## SIN

I watch her eyes roll back into her head while her body softens underneath mine. Her lips are turning a pretty blue color and her face is going pale. I shouldn't be this rough with her, not after what she's been through the last two days, but I can't help myself.

Now that I know she's okay—not going to die on me—I want to tie her to this bed and fuck her ass, making her bleed while she cries, begging me to stop. She deserves that.

Letting go of her neck, her eyes open and she looks around aimlessly, trying to get them to focus while she starts coughing. I get up off her hips, flip her over onto her stomach, and reposition myself between her legs, spreading them open wide.

Taking my hard dick in my hand, I rub her pussy with my other, feeling how wet she is. I push into her, my cock spreading her cunt wide to allow me in, making her gasp. Leaning over her back, I wrap my hand around her mouth from behind and lower my lips to her ear. "What you did was stupid and reckless, little demon—exactly what I told you not to do."

She mumbles against my hand, but I don't care what she has to say. Pulling my hips back, I shove them forward, stretching her cunt and loving the way her body fights mine.

"You're still so weak, Elli. That's what happens when you get fucked up."

Her pussy pulses around my dick and I kiss the side of her face. Her hands dig into the fitted sheet, and I feel her body try to lift mine, but I spread her legs wider, pressing my body into her to keep her in place. "Fight me, little demon. Show me how bad you want me to take it from you."

She tries to move her head so she can try to dislodge my hand, but I dig my fingers into the sides of her cheeks, making her whimper and eyes close.

"I love when you fight me. When you pretend that you don't want it, but your pussy is soaking wet, Elli. Tells me just how much you love being used."

Her hands slap against the headboard as it hits the wall, not caring if her father can hear us or not.

"There's a reason my name is the one tattooed on your back." I pull my hips back and shove them forward, making her cry into my hand. "Because I own you, little demon. I think you forgot that."

As her pussy clenches around my dick, I smile. I'm going to use her as often as I can in the next week because the clock has officially started ticking.

---

I STAND IN THE KITCHEN, FIXING BREAKFAST, WHEN I LOOK AT the clock on the stove. It's almost noon and Elli is still asleep in our bed. She was practically unconscious by the time I finished with her. She needed a distraction. A chance to get out of her head. She loves to get fucked up, but sex is her drug of choice. She loves the power exchange it gives her, leaving her helpless and at my mercy.

My cell starts to ring, and I answer it. "Hello?" I say to Chance.

"I moved up the wedding," he says in greeting.

"I know." Amelia sent it to me again when I didn't respond to her the first time. I've ignored every call and text from her since. "Now call it off."

A silence lingers on the line before I hear him whisper-growl, "What the fuck?"

"Call off the wedding, Chance. It's no longer needed." My eyes look up when I hear commotion, thinking Elli has woken up and I just got caught, but it's Nicholas.

"Are you fucking serious?" he roars. "This wedding was your idea. You told me—"

"Exactly. It was my idea, so why the fuck are you refusing to cancel it now?" I demand.

He lets out a growl. "It makes me look stupid, Sin."

"It makes you look like you don't want to marry a druggie. I don't see where that makes you look stupid." I sit down at the table across from Nicholas and slide a plate over to him. "Eat," I command. "You look like shit."

To my surprise, he smirks at me and begins to dig in.

"Easton—"

"Make the announcement, Chance. You've got twenty-four hours." I hang up and set my cell down. Placing my elbows on the table, I bow my head, running my hands through my hair and pushing it off my forehead.

There no longer needs to be a wedding. My ticket is sitting right in front of me. I made the deal with Chance before I even knew Nicholas was alive. And even when I found out, there was no guarantee the Spade brothers were just going to hand him over to me. I needed several eggs in my basket. Now I've got the golden goose.

He wipes his mouth with the back of his hand and leans back

into the seat, slouching into it. His eyes drop to my ring that has the Lords' crest on it. He looks at it longingly, as if he wishes to have one himself. "So I've got a week," he speaks, starting where our last conversation left off.

I imagine freedom isn't as good as it sounds. Carnage is all he's known for so long. It's like a prisoner who is getting out on parole after serving thirty years but knows they won't be able to function in the real world. Cage a person long enough and they believe they can no longer fly.

"You're not going back to Carnage." I stand, picking up his plate and placing it in the sink.

"What?" He jumps to his feet. "They said a week until they collect."

"You're free. Don't fuck it up." I go to return to the bedroom, but he grabs my upper arm, spinning me around to face him. His face inches from mine, eyes narrowed. "What did you do?" he demands.

"What needed to be done," I say simply.

"Easton—"

# ELLINGTON

My father's eyes meet mine over Sin's shoulder and he stops whatever he was about to say and lets go of him, stepping back. Sin turns to look at me and sighs heavily.

I heard enough to be confused even more. I don't know what Carnage is or why my father was there, but I didn't like that Sin said he did what needed to be done. If it involves the Lords, it'll require flesh and blood.

My dad runs his hand through his hair, pushing it back off his forehead as if he's trying to fix it. To look more presentable in my presence. It's weird to see him. It's him but he doesn't look the

same. He was always in shape, took care of himself. But he's skin-
nier than I remember him ever being. His hair is graying, and his
eyes look dull. They were always a pretty blue. Not as blue as
mine and my mother's but just as beautiful. He's got a scar across
his right cheek that wasn't there before. Another on his forearm.
They both look like they've been there for years.

"Sit down, Elli. You need some breakfast," Sin states, walking
over to the stovetop. He grabs a plate and starts putting eggs on it.

I walk around the island, my back to the counters so I can keep
an eye on my dad and fall into a chair, watching him walk over to
the table as well. He takes the seat farthest away from me at the
opposite end, sitting at the head of the table.

Sin comes over and sets a plate down with a fork and a bottle
of water. Leaning over, he kisses my forehead and then sits down
to my right, facing the entrance of the kitchen. "Eat up. You need
the energy."

An awkward silence falls over the room as I drop my eyes to
look over the eggs, bacon, and piece of toast. "I'm not hungry," I
whisper.

"Elli—"

"Why is he here?" I drop the fork to the table, listening to it
clank, and look at Sin, interrupting my father. "Why are you
here?" I growl, getting to my feet, irritation building. "Why are you
both in my house?"

"There's a lot we need to talk about," Sin states, his eyes
showing he's getting irritated as well that I won't just give up. Like
I don't deserve to know the truth.

I let him fuck me senseless this morning but that's sex. He
knows it's a weakness of mine. That doesn't mean I won't be levelheaded afterward. "Let's start with you." I place my hands on my
hips. "Hmm? What the fuck are you doing here?"

"The truth," he gets to his feet, the chair scraping across the
floor in the process, and turns to face me, "is that Gunner called

and told me you were at a party getting fucked up. As usual." He steps closer to me, and I swallow. "And asked what I wanted him to do. I told him to drag you out of that party if necessary. When he called me back, he had found you in a bedroom, by yourself. Unconscious and vomiting."

I narrow my eyes up at him as he takes another step closer, my back now pressed against the counter. "I was fine..."

"You were overdosing!" he shouts. "Holland lied to you. Mack didn't give you ecstasy. It was fentanyl. Gavin had to give you Narcan which led to withdrawals once it wore off. You could have died, Elli. Why did you do it?"

I can't answer. That would show him just how weak I am.

"Tell me! Why did you take something from someone not knowing what it was?" he demands.

"Easton..." My father stands from the table. "Calm down. She—"

"No," Sin interrupts him, eyes glaring down at me. "She wants to know what's going on. I want to know what the fuck she was thinking."

"Why the fuck do you care what I do anyway?" I snap, trying to deflect. "You're marrying Amelia. I'm marrying Chance. It's over for us. Go home to your soon-to-be wife, Sin." Giving him my back, I go to storm out of the kitchen.

"You're my wife, Elli."

I stop dead in my tracks and turn to face him. I expect him to laugh. Or to say sike. That it's another sick joke he's playing on me. But instead, he walks over to me, his look growing heated in a way that makes me think he's going to wrap his hand around my throat and choke me out. If my father wasn't present, I'd beg for it.

"Till death do us part, Elli."

## FIFTY-ONE

## SIN

Ice-blue eyes so round stare up at me. It reminds me of how she looked at me after I caught her seeing me kill James. The shock written all over her face. Her plump lips close and her throat works, swallowing. "I ... I don't believe you," she mumbles.

It's the same thing she said to me when I told her I didn't love her in the bathroom at the house of Lords when she came barging in demanding that I tell her the truth. That I wasn't just using her. She was right. I had been lying to her. She was more to me than a fuck. She was my wife. "I'm not lying to you."

Shaking her head, she takes a step back. Those wide eyes go over to her father, but he has no clue what I've done. If he did, he'd probably try and throw me out of this house. He'd have to kill me first, and by the looks of him, I'm not worried about it.

"I'm marrying Chance," she whispers, licking her lips.

"You *were* going to marry Chance because I told him to. He was doing me a favor."

Her dark brows scrunch together. "No," she growls, getting angry. "You and I didn't have a wedding..."

"You don't need a wedding to marry someone," I state, and her eyes widen once again. "All you need is a marriage license signed by two people. And an officiate to sign off on it."

"But I didn't—"

"You did," I interrupt her. "I slid it into the stack for you to sign when we closed on this house. You signed it. Not even bothering to read it."

She gasps.

"We've been married ever since."

She frowns, her eyes falling to her bare feet after a long second. She then looks up at me and I bite back a smile at the angry look in her eyes. *There's my little demon.* She shoves my chest, but I don't budge. "So what about Chance? You were going to make me think I was actually married to him?"

"I needed it to look real," I say defensively.

I knew her mother would make a big fuss about it. Hundreds of Lords were supposed to be there. A couple of them were already aware she is my wife, but the ones that mattered didn't. It was going to be my best-kept secret.

"For your own sick pleasure?" she barks out. "Another way to make me look like an idiot?"

"No," I snap. "To set up Linc."

"You manipulated me! But why? Were you going to let him fuck me?"

"Fuck no!" I shout, the thought making my blood boil.

He'll never get near her again, let alone touch her. Chance and I had a plan. He was going to bring her back to her house and have Linc meet them here. I was going to be waiting on them. And the moment he went to touch her, I was going to intervene. I had proof that he had already forced her to her knees for him in her bedroom before the engagement party, and she was already my wife. I never wanted him to touch her, but I saw that too late, otherwise I would have stopped it before that had even happened. Consequences be damned.

"The moment Linc got near you, I was going to step in. It's a crime in the Lords' eyes to fuck someone else's Lady without her Lord's permission."

She throws her head back, giving a rough laugh. "I forgot a Lady can't get dick anywhere else, except from her Lord, but he can fuck whoever he wants." She places her hands on her hips. "Just like you've been fucking Amelia this entire time we've been married. So instead of being your sidepiece, I'm going to be the one you come home to after you're done fucking them." She gives another rough laugh. "You've made my dreams come true, Sin."

I suck in a deep breath at her words and step into her. "You're the one who has spread her legs for others." She gasps. "I, however, haven't fucked anyone other than you."

"Well, I don't believe you." She places her hands on her hips and pops one out. "I saw you."

*The video my sister had mentioned.* "I can explain that…"

"Of course, you can. I'm sure it'll just be another lie that I won't be able to prove. But I'll be honest with you, I sucked Linc's cock."

She tries to make it sound like she wanted it. As if he didn't blackmail her into it. I get it. She wants to hurt me like I hurt her. But she has no clue what I have and haven't done.

"How's that make you feel?" she barks out at my silence.

I step into her, pushing her back into the counter, and she sucks in a breath when I cup her face. "I watched you on your knees in your bedroom for him, Elli." Tears start to fill her eyes at my confession, her lips beginning to tremble. "I know he forced your hand. And I know you did it for me." Sighing, I add, "I'm sorry but I saw it after the fact. I'll never forgive myself for not being able to protect you."

Her teary eyes narrow on mine, and then she reaches up, slapping me across the face. "You son a bitch—"

"ENOUGH!" her father shouts, making her jump. I think she

forgot he was present. I didn't. I just don't give a fuck if he knows or not. She's mine. No one can take her from me.

She takes in a deep breath and her eyes meet mine, that first tear finally falling down her cheek. "I hate you," she manages to say through gritted teeth.

The words mean nothing to me because it doesn't matter. "Hate me all you want, I'm still your husband and no one can change that. Not even you."

## ELLINGTON

*MARRIAGE?*

I'm Mrs. Easton Sinnett?

He watched me suck Linc off in my bedroom? How?

My heart is pounding at his betrayal. At this point, I can't tell what's a truth or a lie.

"I think we need to sit." My father breaks the silence and Sin takes a step back from me, giving me some breathing room, and I run a hand through my hair.

Following them into the living room, I sit on the couch, making sure there's plenty of room between me and Sin. My mind yells at me that I should be pissed but it also says *I told you he wasn't done with you.* I knew everything he said to me was a lie in his bathroom at the house of Lords. I was more to him than just a fuck. Wife never crossed my mind, though.

I'm married to Easton Bradley Sinnett. I wish I could scream it to the world. But it's obvious we have to keep it a secret. I hope not forever.

Sin is the first to break the silence. "I spoke to Chance earlier. He's calling off the wedding."

I want to ignore him, but I can't help but ask, "Why? You said we needed it to happen. Look believable." My voice is soft.

Shaking hands folded in my lap. I'm trying to calm my nerves. I want to slap him and fuck him right now. I've never been this confused in my life and that's saying a lot.

"We did," he answers. "But that was before your father was dropped off at *our* door."

I look over at my father sitting across from us and he's already staring at me. I drop my eyes, still not ready to tackle that situation. I tend to think I can handle a lot, but one thing at a time.

"Well, once I stopped Linc, I was going to make it a big scene, but things have changed." He relaxes into the couch and jealousy makes my body heat rise at how calm he is right now after what we both revealed to one another in the kitchen. "A Lord is taught to show the world our power. That's why we have confessionals at the cathedral. We string up those that do us wrong in front of our fellow Lords. And that was my plan for Linc, but now that's no longer an option. We've got to do it quietly."

When my father doesn't say anything, I ask again, "Why?"

"Because to the world, your father is dead. We have to keep him hidden and make sure no one knows except the ones we want to know."

"Which is no one," my father states.

Sin frowns at him in question.

My father leans forward, elbows on his knees. "There were only two people who knew my brother existed and could have set up my death."

"Who are they?" Sin asks.

"I'd rather not say just yet," my father answers and Sin shifts, no longer comfortable.

"Are you serious?" he asks.

My father nods. "It would ruin several lives if I'm wrong."

"Several lives have already been ruined," I state, getting to my feet. Why is he here if he's not going to help us? Who knows if he was even where he says he was for the last nine years. Who knows what he's been doing? We may never know the truth.

"Elli?" Sin sighs my name.

"Forget it, Sin." I wave him off. "He's not going to help us. So whatever you did to get him out wasn't worth it."

My father jumps to his feet too. "Ellington," he growls my name. "You don't know what's going on."

"I know enough!" I shout at him. "I'm so fucking tired of the lies, the secrets. The Lords do nothing but fuck up everything. And all you guys do is make excuses and cover for them." Turning my back on them, I head to the master suite. I slam the door shut and lock it. Not like it's going to keep Sin out. If he wanted to, he'd kick it down.

Placing my forehead on the cool wood, I take in a deep breath and realize he didn't follow me.

# FIFTY-TWO

# SIN

I stay where I am, not done with my conversation with Nicholas, standing in the middle of the living room.

"Why did you trick her into marrying you?" he asks, not sounding mad like any caring father would.

I glare at him but don't respond. See how he likes the silent treatment.

"Easton, things aren't always what they seem. Especially with the Lords," he says defensively as to why he wouldn't answer my questions.

"You think I don't know that?" I give a rough laugh. We're not supposed to question them. Ever. We get assignments, we follow out the orders, and then we move on.

"They'll test her," he goes on. "A Lady has to be initiated."

"They already have," I inform him. "She passed."

He bows his head, shaking it as if he can't believe what's going on right now. But he doesn't bother asking what they required her to do in order to be my wife.

My phone starts to ring, and I pull it out of my back pocket.

Seeing it's Chance, I hit answer and walk over to the floor-to-ceiling windows. "Yeah?"

"It's canceled. But just giving you a heads-up, Linc and Laura aren't happy."

"Of course not. They think you were their only option for her."

"Yeah, well, just wanted to let you know."

I can tell he's still pissed at me. I hope he can tell that I don't give a fuck how he feels about his situation involving my wife. "Thanks," I say dryly and hang up. Turning around, I see Nicholas standing by the couch, holding a picture in his hand.

Sliding my cell into my back pocket, I stuff my hand into it as well and realize that he's holding the picture I had of Elli that I found in the box in my father's office. I rush over and yank it from his hand. It must have slipped out when I removed my phone. I've always got it on me, not wanting Elli to find it.

Nicholas looks at me. "Why the fuck do you have that?" His eyes narrow in suspicion.

"I found it." I dodge the question. If he's not going to give me all the information I need, why would I give it to him? I'm still not one hundred percent sure how he ended up at Carnage. For all I know, it was some assignment with the Lords, and he was 'forgotten.' It's happened before. I'm sure it will with others in the future. And of course, there's the other option—the Spade brothers set him free only to keep an eye on me and Elli. I sure as fuck don't trust anything about them.

He runs his hand down his face and then looks at me. "I need to go somewhere. Will you take me?"

I pause, the thought of taking him somewhere makes my suspicions grow. Where the fuck would he need to go? He's been dead for nine years. But curiosity gets the best of me. I need answers. Maybe this will get me some. "Sure."

"Give me ten minutes. Get Elli, she needs to come with us as well."

My shoulders straighten at that. I open my mouth to tell him no. That he's not going to tell me what she needs to do. He doesn't know her. But maybe he's right. She does need to come with us. Be with me. Chance called off the wedding. I wouldn't be surprised if Linc were to show here within the next hour demanding to know what the fuck she's done for Chance to not want her anymore. After all, they had an agreement that he got her on their wedding night.

Finally, I nod. She's safer with me than here alone. "Ten minutes."

## ELLINGTON

I SIT IN THE BACK OF MY CAR WHILE SIN DRIVES AND MY father is in the passenger seat. He said he needed to go somewhere, and I was given ten minutes to get dressed and in the car. I can tell they're not getting along.

We've been in the car for over thirty minutes, and they haven't said a word to one another.

"Next right, up here around the corner," my father finally speaks, pointing out of the windshield.

I look over to Sin who has one wrist draped over the steering wheel. He's relaxed in the seat, but I can tell by his hard jaw that he's not happy. I'm not sure what they said to one another after I left the living room, but it obviously wasn't friendly. Or maybe it's me he's mad at, which I couldn't care less about. If anyone should be mad, it's me.

"Right here," my father speaks once more, pointing to what looks like a driveway.

Sin slows the car and makes the turn. We're on a gravel road, grass overgrown on either side. Some coming up in places through the gravel.

A house comes into view. It's gorgeous, or at least once was. One story and the front nothing but glass windows, the little siding it has is black with matching trim. You can tell it's older. Long forgotten by the flower beds out front left to die and taken over by weeds.

My father turns around and looks at me. "Does this look familiar?"

I frown at his odd question but it's Sin who speaks first. "Why the fuck would this look familiar to her?"

My father continues to look at me, ignoring Sin as he brings the car to a stop in front of the house. I shake my head, knowing he's expecting me to answer. "No."

"Nicholas," Sin growls, getting out and slamming the driver side door shut.

I crawl out from the back as my father holds the front seat forward for me. "Just curious," he answers vaguely.

I frown, so over this. I always imagined what it would be like to have my father. But the him before I thought he committed suicide. He's different now. I can tell by the way he walks, carries himself. I don't see it being a good thing.

We make our way up the three stone steps and my father bends down, picking up a once black flowerpot but over time the sun has turned it an ugly shade of gray. He removes a key and unlocks the front door.

It squeaks as we enter. The house smells musty and stale. Like it's been abandoned for years. It's sad, really. I bet it was gorgeous back in its prime.

"Last chance, Nicholas. Why the fuck are we here?" Sin demands. My eyes drop down to the back of his shirt as he stands in front of me, and I see the outline of his gun tucked into his jeans.

My cheeks flush, remembering what he did to me with it back when he was the masked man that I wanted to stalk me for the rest of my life. Now he's my husband. Funny how dreams come true in ways you never could have imagined. Too bad I want to punch him in the face now.

"I want to see something," he answers and walks through the house. Going over to a door off of a hallway, he pushes it open and there's a set of stairs to a basement.

My father goes first and then Sin grabs my hand, pushing me to go next, and then he goes behind me, leaving the door open at the top of the stairs for extra light.

Making the last step, I wrap my arms around myself and run my hands up and down my body to create friction. "It's cold in here."

Sin comes up behind me and wraps his arms around me from behind, his chin resting on top of my head, but I feel how stiff his body is. He doesn't trust my father. He's not trying to warm me up, he's trying to protect me from the unknown. My father has obviously been here before and I'm not sure we should trust him. Who knows why he brought us here.

"Do you recognize anything, Elli?" my father asks again, and I hear Sin growl in annoyance.

I frown but look around the room. It's nothing special. An old dingy white sheet covers something in the middle of the room. Other than that, there's nothing else in here that I see could be important. "No."

Sin drops his arms from my chest, and I instantly miss the heat from him. He steps around me. "Nicholas—"

"What about you, Easton? Do you recognize anything?" My father interrupts whatever he was about to say.

Sin tilts his head, his dark brows pulling down at the odd question. "Why? Should I?"

Instead of answering, my father walks over to the white sheet and yanks it off to reveal an old dingy twin mattress. It's got stains all over it. I'm guessing sweat and blood. Some look dark brown like pop but I guess that could be blood too. Not sure. "I don't understand," I say and look over at Sin.

His body is rigid, eyes staring straight ahead, jaw clenched, and hands fisted by his sides. "Sin?" I ask, but he doesn't even blink. Stepping closer, I place my hand on his shoulder and he jumps back from me. "Sin, what's wrong?" I ask, eyes searching his wide ones. I don't understand. "What am I missing?" I ask no one in particular.

Sin reaches out, grabs my arm, and yanks me behind him while pulling out his gun and pointing it at my father.

# FIFTY-THREE

## SIN

"How the fuck did you know to bring us here?" I demand, the same gun I used to kill James and fuck his daughter with is pointed right at his head.

"Sin?" Elli's hands grip the back of my shirt. "What's going on?"

We both ignore her. Nicholas places his hands in his front pockets, not caring that I'm about to shoot him between the eyes. I guess when you've been dead to the world for nine years, death doesn't really matter.

"I used to come here. A lot, actually," he answers, looking around. "I hate to admit this, but I would bring women here. Not down here particularly, but to this house."

"You cheated on Mom?" she asks, letting go of me. Elli goes to walk around me, but I push her behind me again, my gun still trained on him. "How could you do that? I thought you loved her?"

He gives her a sympathetic look. "The Lords are all about appearances, Elli. While out in public, but behind closed doors, things are different." Then his eyes go back to mine. "I recognized it right away when I saw the photo you had of Ellington that fell out of your back pocket."

"What photo?" she demands, but we still pay her no attention.

"Get to the point," I demand. "This is your place, right? After you died, James found it and would bring her here." That's the only thing I can think of. He had documents of this place where he brought his whores back at their home and James used this place to his advantage. Laura probably had no clue it exists.

"What are you talking about, Sin? I've never been here," she argues.

"Yes, you have," he informs Elli, his eyes going to hers. I feel her body stiffen against my back.

"No—"

"I've seen the picture," he goes on with a nod. "I spent enough time here to recognize what I saw in it."

I feel her hands slide into both of my back pockets and I'm not fast enough to stop her. Spinning around, she already has the picture in her hands, staring down at it. The gun drops to hang at my thigh as silence fills the room.

She lifts her eyes to look at mine through her dark lashes. They're filled with tears.

I step toward her. "Elli—"

She steps back, sniffing. "Why do you have this?"

I run a hand through my hair, letting out a long breath. "I needed to find out who the second guy in the photo is," I answer honestly.

"I know who it is," her father speaks.

I turn to face him, and demand, "Who?"

"The owner of this house," he states through gritted teeth.

"Which is?" I snap. I need him to get to the fucking point.

"Your father."

## ELLINGTON

ANOTHER SILENCE FALLS OVER THE COLD ROOM AND I TRY not to let the first tear fall. How long has Sin had this picture of me? How many more are there? Where did he get it?

I remember James taking pictures of me. He would tell me that I was too pretty to not capture the moment. Or that he wanted something to look at later when he was alone. I couldn't stop him from taking them. He would wait until I was tied up and unable to fight it. I would close my eyes most of the time due to the shame I felt over the fact that I enjoyed what he did to me, but I never stopped to think where they went. Or who he showed them to.

Sin turns to face me once again. "Did my father rape you?" he commands.

I flinch at his bluntness. My already racing heart skipping a beat. "No," I whisper.

"How do you know?" he goes on, pointing down at the picture that's in my hand. "You're blindfolded." His body stiffens and his wide eyes meet mine, making my breath catch. "Just like when I fucked you and you thought I was David," he whispers more to himself than me, and I watch him readjust his gun in his hand. His fingers flexing before his fist tightens on the grip.

The tears spill over my bottom lashes, unable to hold them back any longer. "I've never been here," I whisper to myself, refusing to believe that I've slept with his father.

He reaches out, ripping the picture from my hand and holds it up over the dingy bed. It's the same one. I can't deny that. It just doesn't look as old as it does now. Then he points to the wall where a mirror hangs at my refusal to acknowledge it's the same. The glass shattered in the upper right-hand corner looking like a spiderweb.

"It's this very room, Elli!" he shouts.

I wrap my arms around myself. I've never felt so dirty in my life. After everything that I let James do to me, then Sin when I thought he was the masked stranger—hell, even David didn't make me feel this way. Sin's father? If James let him fuck me, how many more were there that I don't know about?

I started doing drugs at sixteen, so it wouldn't have been hard for James to wait until I was fucked up, take me from the house to a remote location, and let others fuck me. Then take me back home so I woke in my bed the next morning. "I ... I don't know," I say truthfully through the knot in my throat.

"Sin," comes my father's soft voice.

"What?" he snaps, his chest heaving.

"Your father and my wife were the only two who knew my brother existed."

# FIFTY-FOUR

# SIN

"**W**here did you get these?" I ask barely over a whisper. "I got these in the mail one day. Anonymously."

I'm seeing fucking red. He lied to me. Why didn't I fucking question him? The Lords have taught us that it's never what it seems. But I'm the idiot that believed every-fucking-thing he said. Why else would he have had those pictures of her?

I take the curves faster than I should, my gun sitting on top of the center console. The headlights of her car shining on the two-lane road. She's passed out in the back seat, and her father sits quietly in the passenger seat.

"You think my father framed you?" I ask, tightening my grip on the steering wheel.

"That's been my thought for the last nine years. Of course, I've been wrong about things before," he states, looking out the window. "I just don't think Laura could have pulled it off herself."

"I'm not saying my father wasn't involved but could James have been in on it too?" I ask.

"Your guess is as good as mine." He looks over his shoulder

into the back seat to see she's asleep before looking at me. "Elli had mentioned that you were going to marry a woman named Amelia?"

I snort. "That was my father's plan. Not mine." Giving him a quick look, I ask, "Why?"

"Because..." He pauses. "We had a different plan." I give him a quick look when he continues, "You and Ellington were to marry."

"Wait. You and my father had agreed for me and her to get married?" I make sure I heard him right.

"Yeah," he nods. "She was to be your chosen and then you'd get married."

A rough laugh escapes my lips that I can't stop. "Fucking perfect."

"What is?"

"I begged him to do whatever it took to make her my chosen and he said *you* didn't want her involved with the Lords in any way. Her mother too."

"You're born into this life. You don't get to choose to leave when you want." He looks back at her again. "Remember that when you two have kids." A soft smile spreads across his face. "God, how I wish I could be there to see that day." Bowing his head, he runs his hand over his hair. "I missed so much. She's lucky she has you."

I flinch at his words. "Don't say that. You don't know what I've done to get us to where we're at." I've lied to her and manipulated her so much that I'm not sure she'll ever trust me. I mean, she's still been letting me fuck her even thinking that I was cheating on her with Amelia while engaged to marry her. How far would I have to go for her to turn her back on me? I hope I never find out.

"Why would he lie to me?" I question out loud. "Why push me on to Amelia when you two had agreed we'd marry?"

"Money," he answers.

"How would keeping me from her equal money from them?

Elli gets access to her trust fund at twenty-five, but no one can touch that. I mean, I guess they could if they somehow deemed her unfit. But that'd have to include an institute of some sort." Parents have done it before. I've seen it among the Lords. When money gets involved, people go feral. Even the ones that are already set for life. They do it out of spite. "But again, it doesn't make sense—I would think he'd want her to be my wife because he would want access to her money through me if I was her husband." I'd never let that happen.

"Asher Corp," he states, sitting up straighter in his seat.

"What about it?"

He looks over at me. "The stipulation was you marry Elli and Asher Corp was to be hers. Of course, you would help her run it. If there's no wedding, Laura can hand it over to anyone she wants. Including your father."

Asher Corp is the largest gun and ammo manufacturer in the world. Nicholas's great-great-grandfather started it and it's been passed down ever since. Elli was the first daughter to be born to the Asher family in over two centuries. That I know of, anyway.

It's not unheard of for the Lords to 'sell' their daughters after they were born. They didn't add to the Lord army they were trying to achieve. Men meant power. Women meant nothing. But that was back before my parents' time. I think along the way the Lords realized that they need the women to produce the children. They were cutting off their own noses to spite their faces. Now, I can't say that the Lords aren't still doing that today, some don't like change and will do anything in order to achieve what they want. But you'd have to be a sick son of a bitch to sell your child on the black market just because she can't carry on your name.

I lay Elli in our bed and she rolls over, turning her back to me but still asleep. I enter the living room, heading to the kitchen for some water, when my cell rings. "Hey, man, now's not a good time," I greet Prickett.

"Bad day?" he asks.

"Something like that." I'm still shaking at the thought of my father taking advantage of her. How many times did he see her in that position? How many of those pictures in that box did he take? She doesn't remember my father ever being involved. Did James want it that way, or was that something my father wanted? She grew up around my family, knew he was her father's best friend. So it would make sense that he didn't want her knowing his involvement.

"Well, let me make it better for you." He chuckles at himself and my teeth grind. "I just walked into Blackout and guess who I see?" He doesn't let me answer. "Holland."

"I'm on my way." His growing laughter fills my ear as I hang up. "I'm leaving. Can you stay here with her?" I ask Nicholas, entering the kitchen.

He nods, sitting at the island with a bottle of bourbon in front of him. "I have nowhere else to go." I notice that he's still wearing the same clothes that he was dropped off in three days ago. I'll get him some new ones but right now, I don't have time to worry about it. At least they let him wear something. The guy in the straitjacket comes to mind, reminding me it could be worse.

Turning around, I go to the spare room and open the safe I have. Pulling out a gun, I secure the safe and then find Nicholas now in the living room. That same bottle of bourbon now on the coffee table. "Can I trust you?" I ask, holding it out to him.

He glares at me, offended by my question. "To be alone with my daughter? Of course."

I hand him the gun. "Shoot anyone that tries to enter this house." If I'm being honest with myself, I do trust him with Elli. I think Nicholas had some enemies who pretended to be friends and fucked him over for greed.

"You think Linc will come after her?" He reads my mind.

"I think anything is possible, and if I'm not here, I can't protect her. So I need you to do it."

He nods, taking the gun and relaxing back into the couch. "You have my word. Anyone other than you walks into this house, they're dead."

It'll have to do for now. I pull my cell out of my pocket and call Tyson.

"Hello?" he answers on the third ring.

He said he wanted me to let him know when I was going to do something stupid over pussy. This is that time. "Heads-up. I'm coming to Blackout to kill a motherfucker," I state, walking back toward the master suite.

"Sin—"

"You told me to give you a heads-up. This is it."

He sighs heavily. "Who is it?"

"Holland." I step inside the room to tell my wife goodbye, but I see she's no longer in our bed.

"I'll get the basement ready for you," Tyson tells me.

Looking around, I see the bathroom door cracked. Entering, I find her sitting in the shower, back against the tiled wall and head down on her knees.

"Sin?" he questions at my silence.

"Never mind," I interrupt him, hanging up. I send a quick text to Prickett, telling him I'll take a rain check but thanks for the heads-up.

Placing my cell on the counter, I remove my shirt and kick off my shoes before I pull off my socks and get out of my jeans. The thought of beating the shit out of Holland sounded good. It was exactly what I needed. But as I see my wife upset and softly crying in the shower alone, he can wait. He doesn't deserve a moment of my time. She does.

He already took her from me for the two days she went through withdrawals, and I hated every second of it. There was nothing I could do to make it better. But right here, right now, I can do something for her. Show her what no one else has ever done—that she comes first.

Opening the glass door, I step inside and bend down in front of her. "Elli?" Reaching out, I push the wet strands that cover her legs while her head is down. "Ellington?" I say more assertively when she chooses to ignore me. Sighing, I push my hand between her face and knee, and force her to look up at me. Watery ice-blue eyes avoid meeting mine.

"I'm sorry," she whispers.

I grab her arms and yank her to stand.

"Sin. Stop." She sniffs, trying to push me away, but I pin her back to the tiled wall and wrap my hand around her throat, pushing my body into hers, holding her in place.

"Don't fucking apologize to me, Elli."

She swallows. "If I hadn't—"

"It's not your fault," I interrupt her. "You hear me? None of it was your fault." Letting out a long breath, I lean in and gently kiss her forehead. "I'm the one that's sorry." Pulling back, my hand around her throat moves to cup her face while my thumb runs over her bottom lip. "I should have been there for you. I promise you that my father will pay for what he's done. And everyone else who has ever laid their hands on you. Do you understand me?" I can't guarantee that I'll be the one to kill the fucking bastards, but I will make sure it's done.

Raising her arms, she drapes them around my neck, pushing her naked body flush with mine. "No, Sin. Don't do anything. Please. I don't want you in trouble with the Lords."

I snort. They're why she's had the life she'd had. "I'm not

afraid of them." I've already promised myself to Carnage. The Lords can't do shit to me.

"I just want to move on." She licks her wet lips. "And have a life with you." Lowering her voice, she adds, "That's all I've ever wanted."

I flinch at her words and hope that she doesn't notice. "I'm not going anywhere, little demon," I lie to her. The last thing I need is for her to think I'm leaving. That I've made a deal that I can't go back on. It's for her. Everything I do is for her, but she won't understand that.

She reaches up, pressing her lips to mine and I slide my hand into her hair, tilting her head back, devouring her. She moans into mine; I growl into hers. Lifting her leg, she wraps it around my hip, and I drop my free hand to it, digging my fingers into her soft skin.

I pull away and she looks up at me through her watery lashes. "I need you." Pulling her leg free from my grip, she falls to her knees in the middle of the shower and looks up at me. Eyes heavy and lips swollen. "Fuck me, Sin. Please." She runs her hands up and down her thighs, her knees opening and closing.

Reaching up, she grabs my hand and places my thumb in her mouth, sucking on it.

I groan, pulling it free of her lips, and her eyes fall to my cock to see it's hard for her. I always am. "Stay on your knees," I command, exiting the shower. Grabbing the belt from my jeans, I join her once again. "Hands behind your back," I order, stepping behind her.

She bows her head, her heavy breathing able to be heard over the sound of the shower running. Bringing her arms behind her back, I take the leather belt and wrap it tightly around her upper arms, pulling her shoulders back and pushing her chest out. She whimpers when I buckle it in place. I grip her wet hair and yank her head back, forcing her to look up at me. Bending at the waist, I lean over her from behind, capturing her lips with an upside-down kiss while my free hand drops between her legs. She wiggles her hips, and I swallow her whimper. Running my hand up her stomach and to her breast, her hips pick up, begging me to play with her pussy again.

I deny her.

Slowing down the kiss, I pull my lips from hers and she sucks in a deep breath. My fingers pinch her pierced nipple, making her whimper before I wrap it around her neck. "Keep your mouth open."

She nods the best she can with my other hand still wrapped in her hair. I spit into her mouth and watch it run down her tongue to the back of her throat. "Good girl," I praise her when she doesn't gag.

I'm enabling her. She needs a sexual fix just like she needs to get high. I may have burned her drugs, but sex? Fuck, I'll give her all the fucking sex she wants. I'll mark her as much as I can before this is over. I want her lying in bed alone and her pussy wet just thinking of the things I've done to her, knowing no other man will be able to satisfy her like I could. Letting go of her neck, I keep my hand in her hair, twisting it tighter as I move to stand in front of her.

She's panting, knees spread wide, tongue still out, the warm water spraying at her back.

I slap her pretty face, loving the way that she gasps while she pushes her chest farther out and the way her pierced nipples harden. Taking my cock in my hand, I slide into her willing mouth. Her cheeks hollow, sucking me in deeper.

Throwing my head back, I groan. "Goddammit." She's always been good at sucking dick. Lowering my head, I watch her bob her head up and down as I fuck her mouth. "You want me to use you?"

She pulls back, my cock popping free of her lips. "Yes," she pants. "Please—"

I drag her by her hair over to where the bench is, pushing her back into it. She sits on her ass on the floor, legs out in front of her. My hand fisting in her hair yanks her head back, resting her neck against the sharp edge of the bench and she cries out. I take advantage of it and push inside of her again. Holding her pinned in place against the bench.

My free hand comes up to the wall and I raise my right foot onto the bench by her head, and I slam my cock down her tight fucking throat, making her gag at this angle. "Fuck, little demon. That's what I want to hear from you." Her watery eyes stare up at me while her gagging and slurping fill the hot shower. "Fuck, Elli." I groan when she swallows with my cock at the back of her throat, creating a vacuum sensation around my dick.

Adjusting myself, I lower my foot to the floor of the shower. Bending my knees up against the side of the bench, I slide both hands into her wet hair, pulling her neck from the bench and controlling her head while I fuck her mouth.

I'm gasping, balls tightening, and I want to come down her throat so bad, but I take what little will power I have and pull out. Spit flies from her mouth as I pull her to her feet. Turning her away from me, I push her down face-first to the hard tile bench.

I slap her ass, making her yelp, and order, "Place your left knee on the bench." It's not deep enough where I can bend her over it, so we've got to go at an angle.

She does as she's told, and I do the same, pinning it up against the wall. Her face, chest, and stomach lying down on it. Her right leg hanging off the side and on the floor.

I use my right foot on the floor to spread her wide open for me. I slide my cock into her tight cunt and start fucking her while her cries and whimpers fill the shower. "I'm only coming in this cunt from now on, Elli." She's going to get pregnant, even if it kills me.

She's gasping, her body sliding back and forth on the wet bench. My free hand reaches out, wrapping around the buckle of the belt that ties her arms together, and grabs a hold of it.

Her pussy clenches on my cock and her voice rings out with my name as she comes all over me. I slam into her a few more times before my dick pulses inside of her.

Pulling out, I let go of her to open the shower door and grab a towel. I turn off the water and dry her off, then myself. Wrapping a hand around her upper arm, I pull her into the bedroom and over to the bed. "On your stomach," I order her.

She crawls onto the bed, lying flat. I slap her thigh. "Ass up in the air, legs spread. I want to see my cum dripping out of you, Elli."

Pulling her legs up underneath her, she spreads them wide. No shame at opening herself up for me. I shove two fingers into her, and she pushes against them, wanting more. Pulling them out, I run them up her ass and she wiggles it back and forth. "Stay still," I command, pushing my thumb into it and making her bury her face into the bed, crying out. "Don't worry, little demon. I'll fuck that too."

---

I REACH UP, KNOCK ON THE DOOR, AND QUICKLY SEND A text.

> Call me.

Placing the cell in my pocket, I take in a deep, calming breath. I can't lose my shit. Not like I want to. Not yet.

"Come in," I hear my father call out from the other side of the door.

Opening it up, I enter his study at my parents' house. "Do you have a minute?" I ask him.

"Easton," he growls my name, his hands going to his hips. "Sit." Barking at me, he points to a chair across from his desk.

Grinding my teeth, I do as I'm told. "Where the hell have you been?"

"Busy," I answer vaguely.

He snorts. "Amelia hasn't been able to get a hold of you. I've tried calling you and your phone goes straight to voicemail." Walking around his desk, he leans back up against it. "Does this have to do with Elli?"

Just the sound of her name coming from his mouth makes my blood boil. I say nothing.

Sighing, his jaw sharpens. "Linc called me. Said that Chance called off the wedding."

"Amelia told me," I inform him, which is true. But it also tells him that I've spoken to her. He doesn't have to know I didn't respond.

His lips crack a smile at my half lie. "Linc said that Laura can't get a hold of her. They think she's on a drug binge in someone's basement."

I laugh at how close they are to their assumption. She is in someone's basement all right—ours. But she's sober as can be. I've had two days with my wife. Nonstop sex. My time with her is limited and I'm more determined than ever to knock her up. Once I'm gone, there's no chance for her to have my child.

"What's so funny?" he barks.

"She's been on drugs for years and Linc cares now where she's at and what she's doing." I shrug. "Maybe if he would have cared sooner, she wouldn't be on them."

He runs a hand through his dark hair. "Doubtful. The woman is an addict. Sex, drugs, alcohol. I mean, no one can blame her." He pretends to care about her. "After what James put that poor girl through, but she needs help."

I tilt my head to the side. "What kind of help?" I question.

He doesn't answer and it tells me all I need to know—he doesn't trust me. If he tells me too much, he thinks I'll go and warn her what they have planned for her. It could be a rehab facility to something worse where they help feed her, her addiction by keeping her medicated. I don't put it past them to lock her up, that way they have access to her whenever they want.

Pushing off the desk, he walks around to sit in his chair.

"I spoke to Kira yesterday and she was over at Elli's. Said she was pretty messed up," I lie.

"See," he sighs. "Someone is just going to find her dead one day."

I flinch at his words because I've thought the same thing, more times than I can count. I don't believe my wife to be suicidal, but does she put herself in situations that are very fucking stupid? Yes. Case in point, Holland the other night at the party. I don't even want to think of what my father or Linc could do to her if given the opportunity.

My cell rings and I hide my smile as I lift my hips to dig it out of my pocket. "Hey, baby." I answer when I see it's Amelia. Perfect timing.

"Hey, where have you been, Sin?" she rushes out.

"I was on an assignment." Another lie and my father looks concerned. Like he hasn't thought to ask me how I'm doing with the Lords. Of course, he's too focused on my wife.

"Oh." She sounds surprised. "I miss you. Can I see you tonight?"

"I was thinking ... want to get away? Corbin and my sister are up at his parents' cabin for the next few days. He invited me yesterday, but I haven't had the chance to ask you." I'm the one that suggested he take her there. I need Kira as far away from Elli right now as possible since I'm hiding her dead father out at our house. Corbin was more than willing to take my sister away for an uninterrupted weekend. Might as well use their relationship to my advantage.

"Of course." She squeals. "I can be ready in an hour."

"No rush. I've got a few things to take care of before we can leave." My wife being the most important thing on my list. "I'll pick you up at seven tonight." I hang up the call before she can tell me she loves me. Every time she says it, it makes me want to vomit.

"I didn't realize you were on an assignment," my father speaks once I pocket my cell.

"It was nothing." I wave him off, getting to my feet. "I'm going to get away for a few days. I think it's what me and Amelia need. Some time alone."

He nods. "I'm proud of you, son. I know it's hard, but Amelia is the right one for you."

I want to slit his fucking throat and watch him bleed out. "I think so too." The lie gives me a bad taste in my mouth. "I'll call you when I get back into town."

## ELLINGTON

I SIT AT THE KITCHEN ISLAND IN SIN'S AND MY HOUSE. IT'S getting late, the sun set a couple of hours ago. I've got a shot glass and bottle of wine in front of me. I could just drink from the bottle, but I feel like counting the number of shots it takes me to drink all the wine.

I'm not drinking to get fucked up. No, I'm drinking to numb my body. I'm in pain, but in the best way.

Sin has fucked me so hard and rough for the last couple of days. Today was the first day I've seen daylight since I kneeled for him in the shower. He's had me locked down in the basement. I needed him to remind me that I'm his. The need to please him is so strong. To hear him call me good girl. Fuck, it makes me weak in my knees. I'd do anything for him.

Anyone else, I'd be embarrassed or ashamed, but not with Sin. He praises me for being his whore.

I hear a noise and look up from the island. "Hello?" I call out but am met with silence. My father left this afternoon. He called a cab and said he needed to go get a few things.

Taking another shot, I hear the front door open, and I smile. Getting to my feet, I exit the kitchen and head toward the living room to greet my husband but come to a stop when I see who is here. Swallowing the lump in my throat, I narrow my eyes on Linc. "What the fuck are you doing here?" I demand.

He places his hands in his pockets as the door opens and another man enters my house. My breath catches and it takes everything in me to not drop my eyes to the floor. He has no clue that I've seen the picture he took of me.

I've known Linc is a fucking bastard, but Sin's father? Not being able to remember if we did anything makes me feel dirty. Like the filthiest fucking whore.

"Hello, Elli," Linc speaks, making the hairs on the back of my neck rise.

"You need to leave," I whisper, not acknowledging Liam.

The door slams shut, and I flinch.

"We just thought we'd stop by and see how you're doing." Linc is the one who speaks. "I figured you'd be heartbroken after Chance called off your wedding."

I can't help but snort. "He was a piece of shit. Why would I care that he no longer wants me?"

Linc steps farther into the room and I take a step back. "Because he was your last chance at a normal life."

It's a threat. "You think your husband loaning you out to be used by other Lords is a normal life?" I ask. "You're more fucked up than I thought."

He laughs. "I was just doing that for your mother. She wanted you to settle down." Shaking his head, he frowns. "She's so disappointed in you, Elli."

My shoulders fall and I try to swallow the knot in my throat. I hate that I know he's right. But she was disappointed in me long before I started feeding my body poison and sex. "So she sent you to, what? Bring me back home?"

"Something like that." He smirks and reaches down, undoing his cufflinks before he starts to roll up the sleeves to his white button-up.

I take a step back from them, needing to get to the kitchen. "I'm not going anywhere with you." My heart races at the fact that this might not work. That I'm in over my head. I didn't expect both of them to show.

"Who said we were taking you anywhere?" Sin's father finally speaks, and I whimper at the sound of his voice.

I hate the unknown with him. What he's done to me. Hell, I thought I knew everything I did with Linc, but what if that first time in James's office wasn't the first time? How many others were there?

Linc reaches down now that both sleeves are rolled up and unbuckles his belt before pulling it through the belt loops of his slacks.

I turn and run toward the kitchen, my chest is pounding and pulse racing. I enter the kitchen, yank the hand towel up off the countertop and pick up the gun I had waiting. I spin around and face the archway as they both come strolling in as if I invited them. Not a care in the world. They know I have nowhere to go.

Linc laughs as he sees the gun pointed at him, and Liam just snorts. "What are you going to do with that, Elli?" Linc is the one who asks.

"Kill you with it." I lift my chin, but my hands are shaking.

"I have a better idea." He rubs his chin. "How about you give it to me, and I'll fuck you with it."

My stomach drops and I can't catch my breath. "No," I manage to get out. He had said he'd been watching Sin sneak into my room at my parents' and get me off. He knows what I've let Sin do to me. What I like. The gun lowers to my side because my hands are shaking so badly.

"That's a good girl." Linc smiles at me.

"I like that idea." Sin's father nods. "With the safety on, of course. We already know the whore likes it, don't want her to get too excited and accidently kill herself."

"Of course," Linc agrees, taking a step toward me.

Swallowing, I lift my chin, taking in a deep breath. "Like my father killed himself."

They both stiffen, looking back and forth between each other. "What happened to your father was—"

"You murdered him," I growl through gritted teeth, interrupting Linc.

"This bitch is crazier than I thought." Sin's father laughs at me.

But Linc? He looks happy about what I said. Proud, even. "Your father was too weak of a man to get the job done." Linc steps closer to me, farther into the kitchen. "Just like you're a weak, pathetic cunt. But don't worry, we'll finish you off as well."

He truly thinks my father is dead, which tells me he didn't know he had a twin. I lift the gun, pointing it at Linc once more, tightening my sweaty hands around it. "My father isn't dead."

Linc throws his head back and the sound of his laugh fills the kitchen, but Sin's father just stares at me. "Fuck, what are you on right now?" Linc asks, still cackling at the fact that he thinks I'm crazy. "It must be some good shit."

"Tell him, Liam." I look to Sin's father. "Tell Linc that my father isn't dead."

Linc turns to face him, and his laughter starts to die down. "What the fuck is she rambling on about?" he demands when he sees Liam glaring at me.

"She's an addict." He finally looks away from me to face Linc. "A fucking whore who spreads her legs for dick and drugs. She's delusional." His voice rises. "Making shit up. He's been dead for nine years. She's a bitch with daddy issues."

Linc turns back to me. "Is that the problem, Elli? Huh? Do you miss having a daddy?"

By the way he said *daddy,* I know he means James. I swallow the bile that rises at the thought of him. At what I allowed James and Linc to do to me in his office that day.

"Hand me the gun." Linc reaches out to me, getting tired of our conversation. "Get on your fucking knees and open that mouth. I want to see you choke on the gun before you come all over it." Stepping forward, he closes the space between us, and I pull the trigger back.

**Bang.**

"FUCK!" he screams, grabbing his right arm.

My ears ring and my heart is now pounding as I watch him stumble back. I meant to shoot him in the face, but I missed. The only experience I have with a gun was when Sin used it on me. Sucking in a deep breath, I step back even farther into the kitchen to put more distance between us now.

Blood soaks into his white rolled-up sleeve and down his arm onto the floor. "You're not touching me," I say, my voice shaky. "Not this time. Not anymore."

# FIFTY-FIVE

# SIN

I walk up behind my father and Linc, my gun raised at the back of my father's head. "Hello, Dad."

He spins around, face turning white when his eyes meet mine. "Easton—what the hell are you doing?"

"Protecting my wife."

His jaw sharpens. "What the fuck is going on?"

"We set you up," I say honestly, getting to the point of his visit. "Today in your study. Our conversation, my plans with Amelia. All a lie." Well, my phone call with Amelia was real. I called her and canceled last minute this evening. She hung up on me. I hope that means she gives up on us being together.

"What?" Linc cries, his hand still on his bleeding arm, and he kicks out a barstool to sit down. "I don't understand."

Looking over at my wife, I see her still holding the gun at Linc. It shakes in her hands, but she's watching him like a hawk. I wasn't one hundred percent on board with this idea. I felt too much could go wrong, but her father reminded me that we'd both be here watching over her. I figured my father would call and warn Linc of my plans for tonight, leaving Elli alone and vulnerable, but I didn't expect my father to come with him. Two for one.

"What do you mean your wife?" my father snaps, as if his brain is slow at processing the situation he's found himself in.

"We've been married for weeks," Elli states, lifting her chin. I've never been prouder of her.

Linc softly cries, "Shit."

"Shit is right, you son of a bitch." I push the end of my barrel into the back of his head. "You fucked my wife in her bedroom. And you know what happens to a Lord who touches a Lady that doesn't belong to him?"

He whimpers and I smile.

"Just wait..." my father snaps. "Just wait a second. I didn't sign off on you marrying this fucking whore."

I slam the gun into the side of his head, knocking him to his knees. "I didn't need your permission," I growl.

"Laura wanted her to marry him," Linc states, watching my father get to his feet, blood now running down his face. "You said no."

"I didn't want him marrying her," he snaps at Linc.

"Because you wanted her," I add.

My father turns to face me, eyes narrowed. "Why would I fucking want that trash?" He points over at my wife and I hit him again, knocking him back into the side of the counter. "Fuck, Easton—"

"I know about your house," I inform him. "The one you and James took her to."

His face pales and I hit him again. "Did you rape my wife?"

"No." He spits out blood onto the white marble countertop.

"Don't fucking lie to me." I hit him again and he stumbles back. "Tell me the truth!" I'm screaming, blood rushing in my ears, heart pounding. I know the answer, but I want to hear the bastard admit it.

Hitting him once more, he falls to his knees. I walk up to him, grab his hair with my bloody knuckles, and yank his head back, making him look at her as she stands by the island, gun still in her hand down at her side. I hold mine to his head, pressed into his temple. "Tell me the fucking truth," I demand.

He sucks in a deep breath before spitting out blood. "The truth?" he growls. "The truth is that she had the tightest fucking cunt—"

I slam his head into the edge of the counter while watching him fall to the floor, now coughing up blood. I kick him in the stomach, making him curl up into the fetal position. I stomp on his side.

"Easton?"

"What?" I shout, turning to see my father-in-law now standing in the kitchen. Linc stares at Nicholas wide-eyed as if he's seen a ghost.

"What the fuck is going on?" Linc whispers to himself. We both ignore him.

"Elli," he says softly, nodding behind me.

I turn to see her sitting on the kitchen floor, arms wrapped around her legs, staring at my father while tears run down her face. Walking away from my father to let hers deal with him, I go to my wife.

I drop to my knees in front of her and she lets go of the gun as it clanks to the floor. She lunges for me, wrapping her arms around my neck, and I pull her into my lap to where her legs wrap around my waist. I grab the back of her head and wrap the other around her waist and begin to rock her back and forth while her cries fill the kitchen.

"I'm ... so sorry." She sobs into my neck.

I hold her, my chest tightening. I needed to know. I wanted him to confess, but I never thought what it would do to her. Was she better off not knowing? Maybe, maybe not.

"I'm so sorry," she goes on.

"Shh." I run my hand down the back of her head. "You have nothing to be sorry for, Elli," I remind her. "You did good, little demon." I kiss her hair. "So good." I'm glad it's over. There's only one more person that we need to take care of and then I can spend a couple of days with my wife before I have to leave her for good.

## ELLINGTON

I stand in my parents' house, staring up at the balcony where I found my father nine years ago. There are no flowers, or candles lit today. Just a cold chill. There's been one ever since that day. I'm not sure if it's in my head or if it's real but it still lingers.

I stare at the man hanging from the second-story balcony. He's not dead. Not yet anyway. His feet barely touch the chair that's underneath him. His arms are tied behind his back, a rope around his neck.

Looking up at Linc, I feel a sense of calmness wash over me. After Sin forced his father to confess an hour ago, I cried. Sobbed my eyes out on the kitchen floor in my husband's lap. It was therapeutic. I understand I can't change the past, but I'm also very thankful that it doesn't change his love for me.

I belong to him. Now and forever. No matter what has or will happen, I'm his wife—a Lady.

"Elli, what are you ...?" My mother's shrill scream doesn't even make me flinch. I've been expecting her.

"Mother," I say calmly, turning to face her.

Her hands are up covering her face, eyes wide as she stares at her husband hanging from the balcony. "I thought it seemed fitting," I say, turning to look at Linc again.

Blood has dripped from the bullet wound in his arm where I

shot him. Now I'm glad I missed. This is much more dramatic. I wanted to prove a point and I think this did it.

"Laura—"

"What—" she gasps, interrupting him. "What have you done?" Her wide watery eyes meet mine. "Let him down. Right now."

"I did it."

She spins around and her legs give out before she stumbles backwards into the round table, knocking it over and shattering the glass top on the bloody floor. "No..." She reaches up, covering her face as if that will make my father disappear.

"Hello, Laura," he says, coming to stand next to me.

"What have you done?" my mother screams at me before looking at my father. She turns to run out of the room but comes to a quick stop when she sees Sin leaning up against the door, arms crossed over his chest. His father lies at his feet, barely conscious from the beating Sin gave him earlier at our house.

I'm surprised he's still breathing. We loaded them both into the car and brought them over here. We had one more person we needed to take care of. One more that knows my father isn't really dead. I wanted to see the look on her face when she realized she was caught. It did not disappoint.

"Why?" I ask, stepping toward her but my father grabs my arm, stopping me from getting too close. "Why did you do it?"

She turns to face me, makeup now smeared from her tears. They're not sadness, or regret, it's anger. She's been caught. Her fate sealed. Reaching into the back pocket of her skinny jeans, she removes her cell.

I charge her, knocking my body into hers and we both go crashing to the floor. She's screaming at me, hands slapping at my face as I'm yanked off of her. Sin wraps an arm around my waist, keeping my back to his front while my father grabs my mother.

"How could you do this?" I shout, fighting Sin to let me go. "How could you do this to us. To me?"

"To you?" She screams as my father holds her to him as well. "To you?" She repeats. "Nothing was done to you, Elli. Your father was worth more dead than alive."

He shoves her forward and she falls to her knees. Looking up at me through her lashes, she gives me a cold smile. "You, however, were worth more alive."

Sin let's go of me and steps into her. "What the fuck does that mean?" He demands.

Her injected lips thin, refusing to speak and Sin wraps his hands around her throat, squeezing while lifting her to her feet.

"What the fuck did that mean?" He let's go and she drops to her knees once more coughing, rubbing her redden neck.

"Asher Corp."

It's Linc who speaks, lifting his head trying to relieve the pressure of the rope wrapped around his neck.

"Shut...up." My mother's voice is hoarse, and she rubs her throat.

Sin walks over to the chair; he grabs the back of it acting like he's about to push it over when Linc speaks quickly. "With Nick dead, Asher Corp needed a CEO." He swallows, wiggling his shoulders. "Liam took it over. He requested if through the Lords and they approved. They didn't see an issue with it since he and Nick were best friend. Laura vouched for him."

"What's that have to do with my wife?" Sin demands.

"Laura was re-gifted to marry James. He found out that Laura had Liam kill Nicholas." His eyes drop to look at my father still confused how he's alive. "He threatened to go to the Lords, but Laura offered up Elli to him."

"You bitch." My mother gets to her feet and runs toward Lincoln, but Sin let's go of the chair to turn and grab a hold of her before she can get to her husband.

Sin spins her around, wrapping his arm around her neck,

holding her back to his front. "Keep talking Linc." He commands, choking her out.

He licks his lips. "Laura went to Liam and told him what happened and how she gave up Elli to him. Your father wanted in on the action. So he blackmailed James, forcing him to let him have a piece of Elli. It worked for a while. But James wanted Asher Corp and your father refused to hand it over. So James threatened to go to you. Show you the videos and pictures that had proved your father had been fucking the one you were supposed to marry."

My mother's eyes roll back into her head and Sin let's her go; she falls to the floor unconscious. "So my father had him killed." Sin sighs, his eyes on mine. "That part was true." He nods to himself.

I'm shaking. My breathing erratic. I take a few steps backwards needing some space. She sold me for a company? My innocence meant nothing to her. *You, however, were worth more alive.*

"You fucking ruined it."

We all look over to the Liam on the floor, getting to his feet. His eyes narrowing on his son as he wipes the blood from his face. "The Lords were supposed to find the pictures of Elli on his phone. Not only was she a slut, but she was also an addict. They would have deemed her unfit to be a Lady." His eyes meet mine. "She would have been tainted. Nothing more than a whore for us to use."

"So she couldn't inherit my business." My father adds. "Leaving it to you to run and control." He takes a step closer to Liam. "You knew I wanted Easton and Elli to marry. You knew I wanted Easton to help Ellington take over Asher Corp."

"He didn't fucking deserve it." Liam shouts.

"We had a deal." My father growls.

"Deal?" Liam gives a rough laugh. "I was supposed to be your partner and you cut me out of everything."

My father's jaw sharpens. "You wouldn't have known that until after I *died*."

"How did Nathaniel get involved?" Sin wonders.

"Who is that?" Linc asks and no one answers him.

"He had reached out to Laura. Needed money. Knew you wouldn't help him out because you'd been bailing him out for years. It was the perfect opportunity." Liam spits blood out onto the floor. "She slipped something in his drink, and I strung him up." he smiles proud of himself.

My mother starts to come to, groaning and rolling around on the floor. Sin walks over to her, grabs her by the hair yanking her to her feet and making her face her husband. "Say goodbye." He tells her.

"No. No." Linc begins to panic stomping on the chair and my mom starts crying.

Sin nods to my father who walks over to Linc and kicks the chair out from underneath him while we stand around and watch.

# FIFTY-SIX

# SIN

I walk into the man's office, and he looks up to see me. "Have a seat, Easton." He points to the chair across from his desk.

Doing as I'm told, he sets a stack of papers on the surface and slides them toward me and then hands me a pen. Looking over them, I sign my name where the yellow tabs are placed.

"I have to ask, Sin," he calls me by my nickname, "is everything okay?"

I turn the page and sign the last one and then place the pen on the paper. "Everything's fine," I lie as I stand and exit his office.

Entering our house twenty minutes later, I make my way straight to the master suite. The sun hasn't even started to rise yet. My meeting this morning was off the books. It needed to be done but draw as little attention as possible. The less who know, the less can ask questions.

Pushing the bedroom door open, I find her still lying in our bed, sound asleep. I shut the door and lean back against it, crossing my arms over my chest and just listening to her soft snoring fill the room.

My chest is heavy, everything she has been through was due to my family. My father started all of this. Her mother helped, but I never thought to ask why or how. Now it's too late. The damage is done. I don't mean my little demon. Although I hate what she went through, I'd never change who she is. I love her. Every crooked piece, every sharp edge. She is the frame to a picture. She is what holds me together. I just wish I could have been the same for her.

Pushing off the door, I pull my T-shirt up and over my head while kicking off my shoes. Then I'm undoing my jeans and shoving them down my legs along with my boxers. Pulling the covers back, I crawl in bed next to her. Wrapping my arm around her body, I pull her into me. She's so warm, like a fucking oven.

She shifts, burying her head into my chest. I love it.

I kiss her hair and slide my hand down her bare back. Whenever we're in bed together, we're both naked. Always. I want to see and touch what's mine.

My hand slides between our bodies and I find her pussy, running my fingers over it. She lets out a moan, her hips pushing against my hand.

I kiss her hair again, inhaling her scent while pushing a finger inside of her. Her breath catches and I push her onto her back, adjusting myself to sit between her parted legs.

"Sin," she sighs my name, her hands coming up to run through her hair while she arches her back.

I lean over, my free hand wrapping around her chin to hold it in place, and press my lips to hers. "I love you, Ellington."

Her eyes open and she looks up at me, and they're filled with concern. I never call her by her full name other than when she pisses me off. "You okay?" she asks, wrapping her arms around my neck. Goose bumps spread across my body as her fingers softly run through my hair.

I'm going to miss this. Her hands on me, hearing her voice, seeing those beautiful eyes every morning when she wakes up. I give her a soft smile, but don't answer. She will be okay. I've made sure of it. But me? I've had a clock ticking since I made my deal with the Spade brothers. And I don't regret it.

"Sin." She goes to sit up, but I continue to hold her down with my hand around her chin and press my lips to hers.

I kiss her passionately, trying to tell her I'm sorry without having to say the words. Hoping that she can feel how much I love her. Need her.

Pulling away, she opens her heavy eyes and looks up at me. "I love you, Sin."

Now I can die a happy man.

Letting go of her, I sit up and reach over to open the top drawer of the nightstand. Pulling out what I want, I take her left hand and slide the Harry Winston halo wedding ring onto my wife's finger.

She gasps, holding it up to get a look at it. Eyes wide with excitement and surprise.

"I hope you like it."

Her eyes look over at the nightstand and then back to mine. "How? How long have you had this?"

"A while." I admit shamelessly. "I always knew I'd make you my wife, Elli."

Her hands grab at my face, and she pulls my lips down to her. "Yes," whispers against them.

I laugh. "It wasn't a question." Nothing would have stopped me from making her my wife.

# FIFTY-SEVEN

# SIN

I spent the last two days locked away with Elli in our basement. I fucked her like there's no tomorrow. In a way, there isn't. It was my last chance to get her pregnant. To leave her with something of mine. She has my last name, but I wanted to give her a child. I didn't give her a choice, not like she cared. She lay there, bound and gagged, letting me have my way with her. She was too exhausted to even try and stop me. Her cunt dripping wet and my cock so hard it hurt. I used every second to my advantage.

Nicholas has been staying at his old house. I don't know how he's been torturing her mother and my father, and I don't care either. I did my part. Spent more time on them than I wanted to. Now was my time to be with my wife, so I made the best out of it. This morning after I was done with her, I carried her to our bed, and when I walked out the front door, I noticed her mother's SUV in our driveway, and I was glad that Nicholas was back. I didn't want her waking up this morning home alone.

"Guess I can't talk you out of this?" Tyson asks, breaking the silence.

"You of all people should know why I'm doing it," I say, looking out the windshield of his car, the clock on the dash of his Bentley shows it's now almost six in the morning. The sun is just starting to rise above the tree line.

"Why is that?" he wonders.

"You gave up your future for love."

He snorts. "I gave up mine for revenge. They are not the same. One is power, the other a weakness."

"If giving her a future that she deserves makes me weak, then so be it."

He gives a rough laugh. "You seriously think she wants a life without you?"

"I think she deserves a dad." Pulling my cell out, I look down at the cameras in our bedroom. She's cuddled up to my pillow, sound asleep. "I'm doing the right thing." I'm not sure if I'm trying to convince him or myself. I would never give Elli her father just to take him away after a week. Even I'm not that cruel of a person. She's finally starting to warm up to him.

"People don't go to Carnage to die, Easton." He growls, going on, "For fuck's sake. Look at Nicholas. Years they have kept him alive. They are about torture, not death."

"Everyone pays for their sins," I mumble. None of us are untouchable, no matter if we want to think we are or not.

His hand tightens on the steering wheel but thankfully he falls silent for the rest of the thirty-minute drive.

---

He pulls up to the circle drive and gets out of the car. I smirk, trying to lighten the mood. "You don't have to walk me in." I remove my cell and drop it into the car next to the journal I brought with me. "Make sure she gets that." I didn't want her to find it before Tyson returned. I remove my Lords ring and toss that into the seat as well. Won't be needing that.

Placing his forearms on the roof of the car, he speaks, "You know she won't forgive you, right?"

My jaw clenches.

"You really think she wants you here?" He taps his finger on the roof. Sunglasses covering his eyes. I can't see them, but I can feel them glaring at mine. "You think she'll find someone else? Love someone else?" He shakes his head. "I mean, she's going to fuck other men, sure."

"Tyson," I growl. I've already had this conversation with myself a hundred times. Somehow it sounds worse hearing it out loud.

"But she loves you, Easton. And you're doing what everyone else has always done, turn their back on her."

I grind my teeth. "I'm protecting her."

"By turning yourself in?" he snaps, pushing off the car. "For fuck's sake, Sin. Use your fucking head."

"Gentlemen, something we can do for you?"

I turn around to see all three brothers standing at the top of the stairs.

I slam my door shut and walk toward them, holding my arms out wide.

The one with the snake tattoos smiles. "You're early, Sin. Sure you don't want your two extra days of freedom?"

With fists clenched, I walk past them and into the open door, not bothering to look back. I follow the one I'm guessing is the leader down a hallway while the other two walk behind me.

We get into an elevator and my breathing picks up. Not because of what I'm doing, but because of what Tyson said to me. I hope that the pain is so unbearable that I never think of her with another man.

The elevator dings before the door opens. Freezing cold air

fills the metal box before we can even step out. My breath now a cloud in front of my face. I smell blood. Fresh and old. There's a haunting feeling in the air. Almost like souls trapped down here.

We walk down a narrow hallway and he pushes open a door, moving to the side to allow me to enter first.

Stepping inside, I come to a stop when I get a look at the room.

The guy with the gagged nun tattoo slaps me on the back, giving a dark chuckle. "We've never had someone willingly give themselves up. It won't be as fun knowing you won't put up a fight."

Taking in a deep breath, I square my shoulders. This is what I agreed to. For her. She deserves this. I deserve this. We are not forgiven of our sins just because we are Lords. In the real world, Lords are gods. Here at Carnage, you're nothing. Long gone, a forgotten soul. I'm not sure what my wife will say to the world when asked how I died. And honestly, it doesn't matter. Eventually no one will know that I ever existed.

"Remove your shirt," One orders.

Reaching up, I grab the back of my collar and rip it up and over my head, tossing it to the corner.

A hand hits my bare back, shoving me forward toward the center of the room. Spun around, I'm pushed up against a wooden post. The smell of blood is even stronger in here. And judging by the drains placed throughout the concrete floor, I'm guessing a lot is spilled. Hoses even hang from the ceiling. I count at least three. Easy to wash a body off. You want a quick and easy cleanup after taking a life.

My arms are yanked in front of me, handcuffs placed around each wrist, tightened to the point it pinches my skin and makes me hiss in a breath. Fuck, my hands will be numb in no time.

I see the other one walk behind me with something hanging from his hand that gets my attention, but it's too dark for me to see. The next second, a rubber ball gag is shoved into my mouth, prying it wide open. I feel him fastening it in place behind my head.

"This is so you don't bite off your tongue," he whispers darkly in my ear. "We like to hear the screams. It would be a shame to make you a mute so quickly."

Another leather belt is wrapped around my neck, pinning it to the post, before tightening to the point it restricts my air but not rendering me completely breathless. I try to slow my racing heart and breathe deeply through my nose.

The guy in front of me pulls a chain down from a spool on the ceiling. The sound echoing through the concrete room. A link is attached to the end that he places around the chain connecting the cuffs, linking them together. He pulls sharply to unlock the chain and lets go, yanking my arms above my head in the process. The position pins my already immobile head between my arms. The pinch the cuffs cause to my wrists makes me bite into the gag.

My legs are kicked wide open, and each pant leg shoved up to my calves where I feel a cuff wrap around each one, just as tight as my wrists, before they're shackled to the floor. A third belt is wrapped around my hips, pinning them to the post as well.

I'm unable to move a muscle. Hell, I can barely breathe.

The door opens and I get a glimpse of an older man pushing a cart with him. It looks like medical instruments on it. My breathing is rapid, and my heart is pounding as drool starts to run out of the corner of my lips.

The guy comes to a stop in front of me and pulls on a pair of gloves. Then he takes the stethoscope around his neck and places it to my chest. He listens silently and then looks to one of the brothers and nods. A cold chill runs up my spine when the guy with the snake tattoos around his neck smiles at me.

The doctor grabs a syringe and pushes the tip into a vial, extracting some of the liquid, and then turns to face me.

My body involuntary fights the restraints as he places his

fingers on my chest. I feel my skin tear around my wrists from the cuffs before the blood starts to run down my arms.

"You're going to feel a pinch." He plunges the needle into my chest, making the room fill with my gagged scream.

# ELLINGTON

I WAKE TO FIND MYSELF ALONE IN BED, MY BODY IS SO SORE. Sin acted like the world was coming to an end. I mean, he's always been rough, but he wasn't holding anything back over the last two days. Hell, this past week for that matter.

I make my way to the kitchen to get a drink and see my dad already sitting at the table. "Have you seen Sin?" I ask him.

"No." He frowns. "But I just woke up."

"Sin?" I call out, entering the living room. I yelp in surprise when I see Tyson sitting on the couch, arms out across the back of the cushion. "You scared me." I smile but it drops when he doesn't return it. "Where's Sin?" I ask, looking around as my father enters as well.

"He's gone," Tyson answers, his eyes going to my father then back to mine.

"What do you mean gone? When will he be back?" Maybe he had to go to the house of Lords for something.

"He's not coming back." Tyson stands and holds out a journal I hadn't seen sitting next to him until now. Then he sets a Lords ring on the coffee table next to what I recognize is Sin's cell phone. It starts to vibrate, and I see it light up with a text.

My breath hitches as the hairs on the back of my neck stand up. He'd never leave his phone behind. I pick it up, noticing there's no longer a lock on it and open up the message to read it out loud.

UNKNOWN: Nicholas, enjoy your
freedom.

"Fuck," my father hisses, yanking the phone from my hand.

"What's going on?" I demand. "What does it mean by
*freedom*?" Why is it unknown? Why would they text it to Sin and
not Tyson? I would wonder why they didn't text my father if it was
directed to him, but he doesn't have a phone that I know of.

"Tyson, may I speak to you for a second?" My father ignores
my questions and doesn't wait for an answer from Tyson. Instead,
he walks out of the house and onto the back porch. I open up the
journal to the first page.

*Little demon,*

*I'm sitting here next to you in our bed watching you
sleep. It's taking everything in me to not wake you up and
tell you goodbye. To see those gorgeous blue eyes look at
me one more time. To hear your sweet voice whisper you
love me. I won't do that to you. I've already put you
through enough.*

*So I decided to write you a letter. It's better this
way, I promise.*

*First, let me just say, I am in love with you, Elli. I
have been for as long as I can remember. I'm selfish, I
know that. But I also know that you were always meant
to be mine, and me yours. No matter what I've done or
said to you, please believe me when I say it was always
you. You are it for me.*

*I had to make a choice. And I know it was the
correct one. I hope one day you will wake up and agree*

with me. You deserve your father. My family took him from you, it's my responsibility to give him back. Nicholas can protect you from everything that is bad in our world. I failed you more than once and for that I'm sorry. I should have been there for you, and I wasn't. Not when it mattered.

I tricked you into marrying me. I'm not sorry about that, though. I went to an attorney yesterday and had divorce papers drawn up, but I couldn't bring myself to sign them. I can't let you go. Although, I will no longer exist to the world, I will still be alive. For how long, I don't know. But I promise you this, Elli, you will be my wife until I take my last breath. I did, however, make sure that you are taken care of. Tyson has the paperwork you'll need. I left you everything that I have. I know you don't need it, but you deserve it. You've always owned me so it felt wrong to not give you what was left of me.

This is where I'm supposed to tell you that I hope you find someone to make you happy. That you settle down with a good man that isn't involved with the Lords, have kids, and grow old with him. But I can't do that either. If that makes me a horrible person, then so be it. You know who I am, and I'm the guy that can't imagine you with anyone other than me. That will never change.

Lastly—don't lose yourself in your own mind, Elli. Don't let yourself drown trying to save someone who refuses to swim. Stay clear-headed. Don't fog your brain with drugs or doubt. You are stronger than that. Know *that you are loved by a man that wanted the world for you, even if he wasn't able to deliver.*

*Please know that you'll always be in my thoughts, and that you will remain my little demon forever.*

*Love, your devil*

"WHERE THE FUCK IS HE?" I HEAR MY FATHER DEMAND AND I look up through my watery eyes to see him enter the house. He yanks the journal from my hands.

I feel dizzy, my hands grab at my chest, pulling on my shirt.

Tyson walks over to me. "Breathe, Elli," he orders, gripping my face, forcing me to look up at him. "Fucking breathe. Before you pass out."

"Goddammit." My father hisses, throwing the journal to the floor.

"W-why would he do this?" I'm gasping, trying to catch my breath. I don't understand. The letter didn't answer any of my questions, it just gave me more.

"Because he's an idiot." My father is the one who answers. "Tyson, we need to leave."

"Where are we going?" he asks, confused.

"My old house. Now." My father starts gathering his things. "Does the cathedral still have a triage set up?"

"Yeah." Tyson nods.

"Good. Call Gavin. Have him meet us at the cathedral. We're going to need him."

I REFUSED TO STAY BACK AT THE HOUSE AFTER READING THE note that Sin left me. If he is going to choose to leave me, he'll say it to my motherfucking face. After everything we've been through, and he thinks he can just walk out on me? I won't accept that from him. He's never been a coward; I won't let him be one now.

I sit in the back seat of my mother's Cadillac Escalade. Looking over the seat, I see my mother and Sin's father both hog-tied, lying side by side in the back. We went and picked them up at my parents' house.

My father and Tyson have been talking nonstop. I'm trying to keep up with their conversation but half the words I don't even understand. The other times I'm too busy crying, wondering why Sin would do this to me. Why can't I have them both? Him and my father? Is that too much to ask? Just when I thought I was going to get what I want, what I deserve, the world takes it from me.

Tyson pulls into a driveway and stops at a gate. He punches in a code and the gate opens. We come to a circle drive, and I jump out of the SUV, my hands sweating as I look over the building. It looks like an old castle. One you would see sitting on a cliff where a monster would live. The dark clouds that cover the sky just add to the haunting feeling.

Tyson grabs my mother and my father grabs Sin's. I follow after them on shaky legs and up the stairs. Tyson shoves both front doors open, and we enter the grand foyer. Two staircases are on either side that lead up to a second-story balcony. The smell makes me gag. It looks just as threatening on the inside as the outside.

"Well, well, well. We love when company shows up unannounced, don't we, brothers?" a man's voice echoes before he comes into view from a hallway off to the right.

"Surprise," Tyson states dryly, dropping my mother to the floor. She sobs around the tape over her mouth. I should feel bad for her, but I don't. Not after I found out everything that she had done.

THE SINNER

Two more enter the room and they're all covered in blood. From their hands to their shirts and their jeans. One guy even leaves bloody shoe prints with his black boots as he walks to stand in front of us. I gag again, getting the attention of one of them. He looks me up and down, smirking. "If you brought the girl to beg for Romeo, it won't work."

My watery eyes go to Tyson, but he keeps his eyes ahead on the three men who stand before us.

"I'm here for a trade." It's my father who speaks to them. "Two for one." He then drops Sin's father to the floor at the men's feet.

"What am I going to do with them?" one asks, kicking Sin's father in the chest, making him cry out into his gag.

"Whatever the fuck you want." My father shrugs carelessly. "I'm sure you can come up with something."

"I say we keep the kid and let her come visit him." The same one from before steps closer to me. His blood-covered shirt almost touching mine. "We'll let him watch us fuck her. I bet they'd both get off on that. I know I would." He takes another step closer and my breathing stops. "Starve a man for a few days, he'll eat anything. We'll each take our turns, filling your cunt with our cum, then lay you out for him like a feast. He'll eat every drop of us out of you."

Tyson grabs me and yanks me behind him, and I try to swallow the bile that rises.

"Enough." The first one who entered sighs heavily, sounding bored. "Jessie?" he then calls out, making me jump, and the one that was speaking to me laughs at my unease.

A man appears dressed in an all-black tuxedo. "Yes, sir?"

"Take these two to be prepared for initiation," the one guy orders with a wave of his hand.

That one guy who was talking to me steps closer to Tyson, and he notices. "She's not for you," he tells the bloodied man.

"I'm just having fun, Tyson. Of all people, you should know

475

what it's like to have a piece of something that doesn't belong to you."

If Tyson is irritated, he doesn't show it.

The one who called for Jessie gives us his back and the other two follow. Tyson takes my hand and drags me down a hallway on shaky legs and to an elevator. I cling to his side, staring straight ahead, ignoring the eyes that are on me. I want to ask if they're taking us to Sin but bite my tongue instead. Where else would we be going?

The door opens and a shiver runs down my spine at the freezing cold air that hits me. Tyson steps out, yanking me with him. Down another hallway and to a door. One of the brothers opens it and Tyson steps in, but then spins around, stopping.

I run into him and ask nervously, "What?" I look up at him with wide eyes and I catch his jaw working as he clenches it.

Tyson looks down at me and commands, "Stay out here."

"What?" I shriek. "No—"

"Leave her with me," one of the brothers says from behind me, and I notice it's the voice of the one that was fucking with me in the entrance upstairs. "I'll take good care of her."

Tyson's eyes narrow on his before they drop to mine and soften. "Keep it together," he mumbles, and I frown. Confused about what he means by that.

I nod quickly, swallowing the knot in my throat and trying to calm my breathing. Tyson turns to the room, pulling me inside.

I gasp, my heart stopping at what I see once we enter. Sin is in the center of the room, strung up. His arms cuffed above his head, his ankles spread wide and shackled to the floor. A gag in his mouth, drool running from his lips. His eyes are closed, a belt around his neck and hips tying him to a post. Bile rises when I see a piece of skin on the floor in front of him. It's the Lords' crest, they cut it off of him. 666 has been branded into him where the Lords' crest once was. Blood, there's so much of it. Now I understand where all the blood came from that was on the brothers—it's Sin's.

I don't realize I'm sobbing until Tyson grabs my hand, yanking me into his side. "Get him down," he barks, making me jump.

One of the guys reaches up, grabs a chain and pulls on it, releasing Sin's cuffed wrists from above his head.

Tyson lets go of me and walks over to remove the gag and belts holding him up while another one of the brothers releases his ankles. The cuffs around his wrists are undone and Tyson throws one of Sin's arms over his shoulder while my father helps him out by grabbing the other.

My heart races at the silence in the room. He hasn't made a single noise. Why isn't he in pain? Is he even breathing?

"Out," Tyson snaps at me as they start to drag Sin across the room toward the door.

I spin around to exit, my hair slapping my tear-streaked face, only to find that one guy standing in the doorway, blocking it. His eyes run along my body, making me shiver in fear. "It's amazing what a man will do for a cunt." He tilts his head to side in thought. "Makes me want to see what's so special about it." He steps toward me.

"Get the fuck out of the goddamn way," Tyson shouts, still behind me.

The guy licks his lips "Maybe another time." He steps back and I run out of the room into the hallway and then lead the guys out the way we came in.

Making it outside, Tyson hollers at me. "Open the hatch. Then lay the back seats down. We're going to have to lay him flat." I do as I'm told and he and my father load Sin inside the SUV.

My father jumps into the back, making it to Sin's head, and grabs him underneath his arms, pulling him up while Tyson pushes his legs. I jump in and kneel next to Sin. Tyson shuts the hatch. "I'm going to make this quick. So hold on back there," he tells us once he jumps into the driver's seat.

My father nods, removing his shirt. He rips it down the middle, and then into a few more pieces. "Wrap this around his wrist. Make it tight. We have to stop the bleeding." He hands it to me.

I sniff, snot and tears running down my face, and do as I'm told, seeing the indentions that the cuffs left. They cut deep. Too deep. It looks like he took a knife to the inside of his wrists and cut them himself horizontally.

Then my father is undoing Sin's belt. He wraps it around Sin's forearm. "This should provide a little extra help. At this point, it can't hurt." He then removes his own and does the same thing to Sin's other arm.

"Why isn't he awake?" I cry, my now bloody hands shaking while I place my hand on his chest, trying to feel his heartbeat. He can't be dead. I don't believe it.

"You don't want him to be awake. Trust me, it's better he's out." Tyson is the one who answers me.

# FIFTY-EIGHT

# ELLINGTON

W e pull up to what I heard my father call a cathedral. I've never been here before so I'm not sure why we are here now, but it's exactly what I expected to be. Old and haunting with its rosette window in the center, two towers on either side. There's an out-of-place cross that hangs upside down.

The hatch opens and I jump out, stepping to the side so they can get Sin out of the back. I follow them inside because I don't know where they're going.

I follow them down a set of stairs to what looks to be a basement where the doctor from our house waits for us. He helps them get Sin onto a hospital bed. It's like a surgical center down here. Like one of those triage centers you see in a war zone movie.

"What did they do to him?" I finally manage to ask. I wasn't sure I wanted to know, but now I need to know. I don't understand. His letter made it sound like he wanted to leave me. Why would he willingly let them do this to him?

"Adrenaline." Tyson is the one who answers.

"Wh-at?" my voice wavers.

"They gave him a shot of adrenaline. Straight to the heart. They do that so he wouldn't pass out. It lasts about twenty minutes. They remove the Lords' crest by cutting it off. And to keep him from bleeding out, they cauterize it with their own. Three sixes. One for each brother."

My hands come up to cover my face. Fresh tears spill down my cheeks. "Why would they do this to him?"

Tyson's eyes soften on mine. "They do it to everyone, Elli. It's their initiation. It may vary from person to person, because not everyone who enters Carnage wears the Lords' crest, but everyone gets branded."

My eyes shoot to my dad who stands next to them, and I look at his chest. He had removed his shirt to use it for Sin. Sure enough, I see the three sixes on his chest. They're healed but you can't miss the hack job they did.

"Once the adrenaline wears off, they come down and crash pretty hard," Gavin adds,

My eyes go to him, and I see he's already started an IV and is administering something into it.

"What is that?"

"I've sedated him. I've got to clean the wound and do an auto-graft," Gavin responds. Tyson hands him a pair of scissors and Gavin starts to cut down Sin's thigh, shredding his bloody jeans to expose his leg to the room.

My eyes go to Tyson, needing more of an explanation.

"It's a type of skin graft. He's going to take a piece of skin from Sin's thigh, brand it with the Lords' crest and then reattach it over the brand the brothers gave him."

"Use mine," I all but shout, stepping forward, knowing that I can be of help.

They both frown at me. "Elli," my father starts, but stops when my shaking hands go to my jeans. I undo them and shove the material down my legs. Gripping my inner thigh, I turn my leg the best I can to show them my brand. "Take it."

All three look at one another and then back at me. "This is what you need, right? Use it."

Gavin frowns. "Where did you get that?"

Before I can answer, Tyson speaks, "He branded her with his ring."

"Goddammit." My father sighs.

"But you can use it, right? Don't cut him." I'm trembling. I don't want to see him suffer anymore. What skin will replace the piece that Gavin removes? It sounds like a vicious cycle that doesn't have a good ending. They can take it from me, and he'll be whole. A quicker recovery.

Tyson walks over to me, yanks up my jeans, and catches my shaking hands in his.

"This is important, Elli." He speaks slowly, calmly. *How can he be this calm right now?* "The Lords can't find out that Sin was ever at Carnage."

"What if they do?" I ask wide-eyed. My eyes go to Sin, and it breaks my heart to see him lying there. I've never seen him look so vulnerable. I want to protect him. Any way that I can. He's covered in blood. Some is dried to his skin; other parts are still fresh. There aren't any visible bruises or cuts other than the three sixes and the cuts around his wrists that are still wrapped in pieces of my father's shirt.

"They won't," Tyson assures me, getting my attention, but I don't believe him. How will they not know? They know everything.

"Although you have the Lords' crest, it's too small. The one we wear is much larger in size. I'm sorry but we can't use it. We're going to have to make a new one."

Gavin gets my attention again as he tilts Sin's head back and begins to feed a tube down his throat. "Why are you doing that?" I go to walk over to the side of the bed, but Tyson grabs my shoulders, stopping me, and pushes me into my dad. He wraps his hands around my upper arms, keeping me in place as Tyson walks back over to stand next to Sin and Gavin.

"I'm intubating him, so his body doesn't have to work so hard to breathe while he's sedated." His eyes meet mine for a quick second. "He deserves the break."

## SIN

I OPEN MY EYES TO A SOFTLY LIT ROOM. THE FIRST THING I realize is I'm lying on my back because I'm staring up at a ceiling. The second thing I realize is that I can't feel much. Why do I feel numb? The tips of my fingers tingle and so do my toes. Swallowing, I flinch at the soreness in my throat. A groan escapes my lips when I try to roll over onto my side.

"Hold on." A hand touches my shoulder and I reach out to shove it away. "Easton, relax. It's me."

I blink, looking up at a face hovering over mine. "Ty-son?"

"You're fine. But I need you to stay on your back." He removes his hand from my shoulder, and I relax into the bed.

"What—why are you here?" I ask, my voice rough. Why the fuck would he be at Carnage?

"Here, drink this." He places a straw in front of my mouth and I take a sip, not caring that I need him to hold it for me.

Pulling away, I nod, and he places it next to me.

"Nicholas, Elli, and I went to Carnage—"

"What?" I snap, making myself flinch. Using my heavy arms, I push myself into a sitting position as Tyson curses under his breath. My heart is racing and I'm breathing heavily once I'm sitting upright. My feet dangling over the side of what I realize is a hospital bed. "Why the fuck would you bring her here?" I demand. "She has to go." I go to push myself to stand but he places his hands on my shoulders, keeping me sitting on the edge. I grind my teeth that I'm not strong enough to fight him.

"Sin—"

"What were you thinking?" I ask through gritted teeth. "Where is she? I want to see her."

"You're not at Carnage. We're at the cathedral," he says slowly, as if I'm hard of hearing. When he understands that I can't beat him, he takes a step back, shoving his hands into the pockets of his bloody jeans. I don't even bother asking whose it is. It doesn't look to be his. Nodding behind me, I turn to look over my shoulder and see her cuddled up on a hospital bed. A blanket pulled up to her neck, sound asleep. I let out a deep breath.

"She passed out about thirty minutes ago. She fought it for as long as she could," Tyson goes on.

I look over at him. "What in the fuck happened? How did we get here?"

"She got your letter. Cried. A lot. Thought she was going to pass out after she read it. Your phone got a text, it was to Nicholas from the Spade brothers telling him he was free. He got pissed. We rounded up her mother and your dad and went to Carnage. We made a trade, you for them. We brought you to the cathedral. Gavin was already here waiting for us."

I sigh, lifting my hand to run down my face but I see a bandage wrapped around my wrist. Looking to the other, I see the same thing. "How bad was it?" I ask. I remember them removing my brand and giving me their own. It was hell. But other than that, my head is foggy. Even now, the soft lights are hurting my sensitive eyes. My body is sluggish and although I don't feel much pain, I do feel light-headed.

"It wasn't good," he answers. Stepping back, he rests his back against the counter and crosses his arms over his chest. "Pretty sure she thought you were dead. Then she offered up her brand when Gavin explained you needed a skin graft."

My hand runs up my bare stomach and to my chest, I flinch when I feel the bandage over where my original Lords brand was. "Please tell me he didn't—"

"No." He shakes his head. "He took it from your thigh."

"Thank God." I sigh, closing my eyes. They're growing heavy.

"What you did was stupid, Sin," he growls. Leave it to Tyson to tell you you're an idiot. "We found you unconscious. Who knows how long they would have left you bleeding out and hanging in that room. You could be dead right now."

Cracking my eyes open, I stare at him, and he arches a brow, expecting me to say something. Instead, I look over at Elli cuddled up in the other bed and a smile tugs at my lips. "We all do stupid shit for love, Tyson." Then I close my eyes again and let whatever drugs Gavin has me on swallow me up into the darkness.

---

WHEN I OPEN MY EYES AGAIN, I SIT UP AND THE ROOM STARTS to spin, making me dizzy. "Take it easy." A hand gently touches my shoulder and I look over to see Tyson.

Fuck, I thought I had dreamed that conversation with him earlier. Looking around, I find what I'm looking for. Elli—my little demon—lying on the hospital bed next to mine. Where she was earlier. I throw off the blanket and get to my feet as Tyson sighs. I ignore the way my body protests at the smallest movement. I've always enjoyed pain. It means you're not dead. And believe me, you'd be surprised what your body can endure.

Walking over to her bed, I reach out and run my dried-up bloody knuckles down the side of her cool cheek. "Is she okay?" I ask, my fingers going to her neck to check her pulse.

"She's fine." I look over to see her father sitting in a chair, arms crossed over his chest and one ankle on his other knee, glaring at me. "Can't say the same about you." He looks me up and down, lingering on the bandage covering my chest.

I look down to see my jeans have been removed but I've still got my boxer briefs on and there's another bandage on my thigh. "Don't start," I mumble, turning back to her and lifting the blanket to cover her shoulders, tucking it underneath her neck.

"Don't start?" he repeats, getting to his feet. "Do you—"

"I was trying to give her what she deserved," I growl, interrupting him. I'm not in the mood for this shit right now. I may be alive, but I feel like I've been through hell.

"A dead husband?" he snaps, stepping over toward me.

"A father," I growl.

Jesus, why is it so hard for them to see what I was doing? That I did it because I love her. That I think she deserved a better life than what she's had since he *died*. A part of me was trying to make up for what she's been through in the past. I love my little demon just the way she is, but I hate what she went through. How many times had there been signs that I chose to ignore or just didn't catch on to?

"That's not your job." He punches himself in the chest. "I had a chance to make it right and you ruined it."

"Oh, I ruined it?" I scoff. "What were you going to do? Go back to Carnage? Act like you *did* die all those years ago? That you didn't come back into her life only to leave her again?"

"Exactly," he snaps, and she stirs. He lowers his voice and runs his hands through his hair. "I've spent nine years at Carnage." His blue eyes drop to her, and his face softens. "I don't know how to live here."

"I get that, but don't you want to try?" I ask. I'm not saying it's going to be easy for either one of them but she's worth trying for.

"I can't be who I was." He shakes his head. "I'm not a Lord,

I'm not a husband. Hell, I handed her mother over to them. I have nothing to offer her."

"Offer her?" My brow furrows, confused by his words. "All she ever wanted was you. Her dad. All you have to do is show up." I point to him. "You think she gives a shit about the Lords?" I shake my head. "And her mother was a fucking worthless cunt who betrayed her." My voice grows louder. "You get a second chance at life, Nick. It may not be the life you had before, but it's something that you can share with her."

The door opens and I look over to see Gavin enter. He comes to a stop when his eyes land on me. "You shouldn't be up walking around."

"I'm fine," I say through gritted teeth.

"I'll be the judge of that."

# FIFTY-NINE

# ELLINGTON

I hear voices off in the distance as I start to wake from my nap.

"How do you feel?" I recognize Gavin.

"Like you gave me too many drugs." I hear Sin's voice and I don't know if I should cry or scream. I bring my hand up underneath the blanket and cover my mouth to keep myself from doing both.

"It was either immense pain or drug-induced bliss," Tyson growls. "We chose for you."

"Well, I'm awake now and I choose no more drugs," Sin states. "Is there something that I can sign to make sure that doesn't happen?"

I open my eyes and pull the covers down just enough to peek out into the room. I'm lying on my side, facing Sin's hospital bed. He's sitting up, legs dangling off the side with his back toward me. Gavin and Tyson both stand in front of him. My father off to the side.

"How do you feel?" Gavin asks him.

"Fine," comes his clipped voice.

"You should..." Tyson trails off as his eyes meet mine.

I've been caught. Sitting up, I let the blanket fall to my waist.

"What?" Sin asks Tyson while turning to look at me over his shoulder.

"We'll give you a two a minute alone," Gavin states. He and my father walk over to the door, but Tyson doesn't follow them out. Not sure if he's staying for my benefit or Sin's.

"Elli." Sin turns on the bed and I watch the way his jaw sharpens at the pain he's in. He's not one hundred percent himself yet but he's going to pretend as much as he can.

That also pisses me off. Now that I see him, I want to slap the shit out of him. Does that make me a bad person? Probably. Do I care? Absolutely not. "What in the fuck were you thinking?"

His eyes narrow on mine. "Elli—"

"Because your letter sounded like you were leaving me. Then once I saw you, I realized it was more of a suicide note."

"I just went through this with your father," he mumbles, and then speaks louder, "I was doing what was right."

His words make my blood boil. How dare he decide what's right for me. "You had divorce papers written up."

"I didn't sign them," he says through gritted teeth. "They were shredded."

I get to my feet. "You tricked me into marrying you, then you want to just throw me away. How fucking dare you, Easton." Turning my back to him, I head to the door but stop and spin back to face him. "You don't get to decide when *we're* done!" I shout. "I get to decide that." Storming over to him, I watch a smirk lift the corner of his lips. He thinks this is a game. That I'm joking. "Have me served with divorce papers, Sin, and see what I fucking do with them. I'll shove them so far down your throat, you'll fucking choke on them." With that, I spin back around and run out of the room, making sure to slam the door shut behind me to further the point that I'm pissed at him in case he didn't already get the hint.

I run out of the cathedral, thankful I don't run into my father or Gavin, and to the parking lot to my mother's Escalade. Tyson had given me the keys when he and my father were removing Sin from the back. I had stuffed them in my pocket.

Getting in and starting it up, I drive to my parents' house. I'm so pissed at Sin that I need space to breathe right now. The fact that he left me after everything we went through makes me so angry with him. Why would he put me through more? Did he seriously think that I could lose him and be okay? Go on with my day-to-day life? Forget moving on and loving someone. I'd be miserable for the rest of my life.

Reaching over, I turn up the volume to drown out my own thoughts as "DARKSIDE" by Neoni fills the car while I watch the headlights illuminate the two-lane road as I speed down it.

Not much longer, I'm pulling up to my parents'. It's weird being here knowing that my mother is gone. The thought hits me that she's got the same brand that Sin has now. Well, the same one that he had before I watched Gavin cover it up with a new one. A part of me hopes it hurts her. That it feels like hell.

I thought my father and Sin were going to take care of her, make her pay for ruining our lives, but after what I saw at Carnage, she deserves whatever they have planned for her. And I hope she lives for years there. At least nine, anyway.

Entering the house, I look around and get a cold chill. It's empty. Sin sent the staff home before we brought in Linc and Liam days ago. We haven't discussed it, but I'm not sure what we're going to do with this house.

I would say my father will move in but why would he want to? His twin brother was killed here. My mother has shared this home with two other men, even having one of the wedding receptions here. As far as I know, my father has to stay hidden from the Lords. They think he's dead and I'm not sure it has to stay that way or not. I just know he can't become a Lord again. That part of his life is over.

Making my way up to my bedroom, I grab a suitcase out of my closet. I've only got a few dresser drawers full of clothes at Sin's and my house. I didn't feel like going there just yet. I'd rather be here alone than there, knowing he's at the cathedral. Who knows how long before he can come home. The way he was moving around, I'd say he's going to push himself more than he should too soon.

I'm shoving clothes into my suitcase and grabbing things from underneath my sink when I hear something. "Hello?" I ask, stepping into my bedroom from the adjoining bathroom. Nothing but silence follows.

I walk over to my Bluetooth speaker on my desk and connect it to my cell, pulling up "Pray" by Xana, before blasting it.

Walking into my closet, I grab my belts, carrying them back into my room to where my suitcase is open and on the floor. I come to a stop when I see a man standing in my bedroom, over by the door, blocking it.

He wears black jeans, a matching hoodie, and a mask over his face. It's a simple black mask with mesh over the eyes and white stitching where the lips should be. I place my hands on my hips, pushing one out. "Shouldn't you be resting?" I shout over the music. He must have run out right after me. I'm guessing Tyson brought him here.

He just stands there, not moving or saying anything that I can hear. "I'm not doing this, Sin," I shout once more and spin around. Going back into the closet, I start grabbing some scarves this time. Exiting, he's still there. I drop them into my suitcase. "Knock it off. I'm not in the mood." The song is interrupted when my phone begins to ring.

Rolling my eyes, I walk over to my desk and look down at my screen. **Sin** lights up on it and I spin around quickly to look at the guy standing in the doorway to my room. There's no phone in his hand.

My father had it on him after he got the text. As far as I know, he gave it to Sin at the cathedral. So it's him calling me. "How are you doing that?" I ask, taking a nervous step back. Maybe he hit call and then shoved it in his pocket. Sin is always thinking of ways to trick me. "Knock it off," I repeat, my pulse racing.

He steps inside my room as my phone stops ringing and the song begins to play again. "I don't want to play your stupid game right now, Sin. I mean it." The music stops almost immediately, and the ringing fills the room. Blood rushes in my ears when I realize both of his hands are by his sides. *It's not Sin.*

Spinning around, I go to exit the French double doors to the balcony, but they burst open. So hard, they hit the interior wall and one shatters. I try to scream but nothing comes out when I see another guy dressed the exact same.

Turning back, I see the one by the door has stepped farther into my room and all I can think of are the guys from Carnage. How many of them were there? Two? No, there were three. That means there's one more here. They've followed us. Want to make me pay for helping free him. How would they have found me? My mom. She's thrown me to the wolves before. This wouldn't be any different. Especially if she gave me up in exchange for her freedom. That's what she'd do.

The guy by the open bedroom door steps to the side and I take advantage of the situation and run out of my room. I don't look back, my heart hammering in my chest. I take the stairs, running down them, trying not to trip while telling myself to breathe. It's not working.

I'm halfway down when I see a figure jump in front of the bottom of the stairs—the third brother? All I see is black clothes and another mask. I jump the last three, throwing my shoulder into the body as hard as I can.

I knew it was them. The brothers. They want to drag Sin back and torture him. I won't let them take him. I won't let him turn himself over because of me. Or anyone else. If they plan on using me for bait, it's not going to work. I'll make them kill me first.

I hit the body so hard that I shove them into the opposite wall where there's a rectangular table with a crystal vase and mirror above it. We fall to the floor, and I curl up into the fetal position to protect my face when I feel the shattered glass fall down on top of us. The table making a loud crashing sound as it hits the floor as well.

Rolling onto my back, I whimper at the burn in my side. My shaky hands reach down, and I feel blood. I cut myself on something but thankfully there's no glass sticking out of my body.

Rolling back over to my stomach, I come face-to-face with the person I hit and it's that same mask as the other two in my bedroom.

A moan escapes their mask-covered face, and they move faster than I expected for being thrown around like a rag doll because my body is slow as fuck right now.

Moving, they jump on top of me, straddling my hips. I reach up, trying to shove them off, but their leather-covered hands manage to wrap around my throat. I arch my back and thrust my hips, shoving theirs farther up my body but not knocking them off completely. I raise my hand above my head and bring my elbow down hard, managing to knock their right hand free and I suck in a deep breath as I roll over just enough to reach a piece of glass lying on the floor next to me. Grabbing a hold of it, I feel it dig into my palm. Before they can choke me again, I stab it into the bottom of their mask, right at the neck.

I yank it out and blood squirts everywhere, splattering on my face, neck, and arms.

I grab a hold of it in both of my hands, lift them above my head, and scream as I shove it into the black hoodie, over and over, making more blood splatter until the body falls off of me and onto the floor.

My arms fall to my side while I try to catch my breath and my eyes fall shut, needing to take a second, but a hand grips my hair, yanking me to my feet and making me cry out. My fall and fight gave the other two upstairs in my room the chance to catch up with me. I'm kicking and screaming as he drags me to the family room where I'm shoved to my knees.

A knee is shoved into my back, holding me facedown into the floor, and I scream at the top of my lungs as my arms are yanked behind my back. I feel the familiar rough material of a zip tie wrap around them before I hear the zipper being pulled tight, pinching my skin. I'm picked up and thrown onto the couch, lying on top of my now tied arms. I breathe heavily, staring up at the two men through my watery lashes.

"Sin is going to kill you both," I shout angrily, knowing he will do whatever it takes to save me. After all, the devil thrives in hell.

The one that dragged me in here by my hair slaps me across the face. So hard it knocks me onto my side. The glove making my cheek sting and my ears ring. Grabbing my shoulders, he rolls me onto my back and jumps on top of me, pinning me down and making it hard to breathe with his heavy weight.

He grips my cheeks, and my eyes begin to water at how rough he is. "Sin can't save you, baby." His voice is a low growl, making me shiver. "He's dead."

"No." I manage to mumble through my squished cheeks. *They killed him?* Why would they let him go only to kill him? Did they follow me here from the cathedral? What about my father and Tyson?

The mask nods once before lowering his face to my ear and whispering, "He's gone, Elli. You're ours now. Forever." Pulling back, he squeezes my cheeks, forcing my mouth wide open while shoving my head back, making me arch my neck. I look up to see the other one standing at the end of the couch.

He drops something into my open mouth and before I can spit it out, the one straddling me lets go of my cheeks to place his gloved-covered hand over my mouth. My body convulses as I choke on whatever it is. The taste of chalk makes me gag.

"Swallow them." The one standing by the couch orders and tears fall from the corners of my eyes. *Them?* What did they give me? How many are there?

He kneels down, reaches around the guy that's still straddling my waist, and slides his hand through the collar of my shirt, stretching it out. His hand dips inside of my bra and pinches my pierced nipple, making me scream into the other guy's glove that's still covering my mouth.

The fresh tears blur my vision when I feel the pills finally slip down the back of my throat, and I can't fight the sob that shakes my shoulders "That's a good girl," the one playing with my breast praises me. He removes his hand from my shirt and speaks, "Now we wait. You'll be begging to swallow our cocks in no time."

## SIN

I THROW MY PHONE DOWN AND BEGIN TO PACE. "SHE'S ignoring me."

"You need to take it easy," Tyson urges.

I snort. "We've been branded before."

Gavin scoffs. "That's more than a brand. Hell, it looked like you slit your wrists in a suicide attempt."

Picking up my cell, I grit my teeth to not give them the satisfaction of being right. It rings in my hand, and I immediately answer it. "Elli—"

"Hello, Sin."

A cold chill runs up my spine at the voice I recognize. I hoped to never hear it again. Pulling the phone from my ear, I see **UNKNOWN** written on it and place it on speaker. I turn toward Tyson so he can hear. "What the fuck do you want?"

A dark chuckle carries through the room. "That's no way to talk to a man who gave you freedom."

"You didn't give me anything. A soul for a soul," I grind out.

"How's your girl?"

I stiffen and I hear Nick curse under his breath as he begins to pace. "What the fuck did you just say?" I grip the phone tighter.

"Ellington. It would be a shame for something to happen to your wife," he says, sounding bored as fuck. Like he's sitting in a chair, feet propped up on a desk while staring at a drink in his hand.

"You son of a bitch!" I shout, and Tyson pries the cell from my grip. "Let me speak to her," I demand.

Tyson raises his hand to me, putting the phone to his mouth. "Where is she?" he asks, sounding much calmer than me. He doesn't care what happens to her. He doesn't love her.

The guy laughs again. "Since when did you become the father of the younger Lords, Ty?" he asks. "You gave up your title to babysit. Sounds beneath you, if you ask me. You had so much potential"

Tyson's jaw flexes but he refuses to acknowledge that. "You have no use for her."

"Oh, I could think of a lot of ways to make her useful..."

"I'll fucking kill you!" I rush Tyson to grab the phone, but Nick pulls me back while Tyson moves out of the way at the same time. My teeth grind at the pain I feel in my chest while Nick's hands pull my skin, taking my breath away for a split second.

"Does the kid not track his pet?" He makes a tsking sound. "Ty, man, you're disappointing us. You need to teach these younger Lords how to handle their whores."

Tyson looks at me, arching a brow, and I nod quickly. Shrugging my shoulders, Nick lets go of me and I raise my hands, letting him know I'm not about to tackle Tyson to the floor. I need to know where she is first.

Stepping over to Tyson, he hands me the phone and I don't hang up, but back out of the call to go to the app that I track her phone on. "It's turned off," I growl. She must have shut it off after I called her.

"I suggest *if* you get her back, that you place a tracker inside of her," he goes on. "Phones can be manipulated."

"Where the fuck is she?" I'm screaming so loud, my throat hurts. My entire body is shaking. Or that could be the adrenaline. I feel like I'm back at Carnage in the room, tied up, and needing to fight but unable to.

The thought of getting her back with 666 branded into her skin makes me want to vomit. I'll have Gavin knock her out while I remove it... My head snaps up to Tyson as a thought hits me and I stiffen.

"What?" he mouths.

All I can do is stare at him. *I branded her.* The Lords' crest on her thigh. They'll remove it. Cut her open like a fish while she hangs there in the cold room. I can't let that happen to her. Swallowing what little pride I have left, I say, "What do you want?" They wouldn't have called me. Otherwise, they would have just taken her.

*Click.*

"MOTHERFUCKER!"

"Let's go." Tyson snaps into action and all I can think is that I did this to her. It's my fault. "Easton?" he barks my name, hand on my shoulder. "Do you have trackers on anything else?"

"No..." I trail off, trying to think. "But I've got cameras in our house." I pull them up, only to find no activity on them.

"Her parents' house. Don't you have cameras on it?" he goes on.

I pull up the camera in her bedroom. It's the only place in the house that I have them. "Nothing," I growl, my hands shaking while holding my cell. I go to exit out of it but pause. Squinting, I look down and see her phone sitting on her desk. "Wait." I open up a new angle and see the French doors open, glass on the floor. "She was there," I call out.

Rewinding the recording, I turn up the volume for everyone in the room to hear what I'm seeing.

"How many?" Tyson asks when she runs out and they chase after her, causing the sound to go silent again.

"Two." Her father is the one who answers next to me, watching it over my shoulder.

I don't wait for any of them, I turn and rush to the door, up the stairs, and out into the cold night.

"I'll drive," Gavin offers, and I look behind me to see he brought a bag with him. That after he heard what I saw, he thinks she's going to need him for medical help. Looking around, I notice that his car is the only one in the parking lot so I'm not sure how we got here. Or what she left in.

"Sin, I'm going to need you to stay back. You can't be tearing stiches open," Gavin says once we're all loaded in his car.

"I'm fine."

"You have limits right now." It's Nick who sits beside me in the back that speaks.

"I can recover after we find her," I growl, watching the live feed on my phone. She's nowhere to be seen. Neither are the two masked men. I stare at it, heart pounding waiting to see the worst—them drag her back into her room kicking and screaming where they'll rape her, beat her, kill her.

At least at her parents' house, I have some sort of advantage against them. If they get her to Carnage, she's as good as dead. I can't bring her back from there, but I will make sure they kill me. I'll walk right through their fucking front doors, guns raised and ready. It'll be a suicide mission, but I won't live without her. Not anymore.

"Anyone have guns on them?" Tyson changes the subject. "Not like we were prepared. And we don't have time to stop by Blackout."

I barely have clothes on. Nicholas was able to find me a T-shirt and sweatpants after she left. He grabbed them from a closet in an office at the cathedral. Pretty sure they once belonged to a dead guy that was killed during Confession. That's when a Lord brings in someone they want to make an example of in front of the congregation.

"I've got two in the glove box." Gavin nods to it. "Another in the center console. You guys take them. I'll tend to her."

I flinch at his words. My mind going through a million different scenarios. One being the fact that I might find her hanging from the second-story balcony where her father's murder was staged. They'd be sick enough to display her like that just to prove a point.

Tyson opens the glove box, releases the magazine, checking to see if there are any rounds, and then hands it to me over his shoulder. "The safety isn't on," he warns.

I take the gun and rest it on my thigh, bouncing my knees. My entire body is vibrating right now with anger, pain, regret. If I don't die tonight, I'm going to need a week of rest after this. They were right, my body will shut down eventually. It just has to hold on until I know she's safe in my arms and every one of those motherfuckers is dead.

# SIXTY

# SIN

We pull up to her parents' house, not even bothering to hide. Gavin brings the car to a stop right at the front door and I jump out of the back. Looking over the driveway, the only car I see is her mother's SUV.

"Sin!" Tyson shouts. "Wait." He rushes in front of me, taking the stairs two at a time. "Let me go in first, at least." His eyes drop to my shirt. "Christ, you're bleeding."

"I'm fine." I shove the door open, gun raised. Tyson steps in behind me, followed by her father and then Gavin. We all stand in the grand foyer, listening for any kind of noise, but are met with nothing. "They've got to be here," I say to no one in particular. Why else would they call me? They wanted me here. Whatever they have planned, they want an audience.

Nicholas steps to the left and out of sight, only to come back. He nods for us to follow him. Walking around the corner, we see a body lying on the floor at the foot of the stairs. Shattered glass everywhere and blood smeared along the floor. I see two different sets of boot prints that step through it and then track toward the formal family room. There are small handprints that I'm assuming are Elli's and you can tell by the smeared blood that they dragged her away from here.

I bend down, grab the black mask, and yank it off the face.

"That's ... not what I expected." Tyson is the one who speaks.

"Who the hell is that?" Nicholas asks.

I reach out to check for a pulse and there is none. Standing, I look down into the set of dead eyes and smile. *My wife did that.* "Amelia," I finally answer.

"Who the fuck is she?" Nicholas goes on.

"She was who my father tried to get me to marry."

"Why would the Spade brothers get her involved?" Tyson wonders out loud.

I shrug. "Who the hell knows. Come on. They're in the house. Follow the blood trail." A part of me knows that not all of that belongs to Amelia. There was a struggle by the obvious broken glass and turned over table. I just pray that she's not bleeding out somewhere.

I raise my gun as the blood-stained boot prints start to fade. Stepping into the family room, I see Elli lying on one of the couches. I lower my gun and rush over to her. "Elli!" She lies on her back, arms underneath her and head tilted toward the cushions. "Elli." I grab her chin and force her to look up at me. Her eyes are closed so I open them up to see they're dilated. "Fuck," I hiss.

Grabbing her shoulders, I pull her to a sitting position and her head falls forward into my chest. I hold her as Tyson comes up to the couch. He removes a knife from his pocket and cuts her bound wrists free.

"What's wrong with her?" Nicholas asks.

"Drugs." I look at Gavin. "Can you do anything about it?"

He sighs. "Depends on what they've given her."

My eyes go to Tyson as I nod behind him. "There's a bedroom at the end of that hallway. Check it. If it's clear, I want her in there." He nods and takes off in that direction.

I don't know where the Spade brothers are or why they left her here alone. But I want her out of this room when they return, before the bullets start flying.

Lying her back down, I yank my shirt up and over my head and start to wipe off her bloody hands and arms. It's on her neck and cheeks. I smear it anywhere I see it to make sure it's not hers. But as I get to her thigh, I see she's been cut. It's not deep or life-threatening, but it looks to still be bleeding. I apply pressure to it with the shirt.

"Elli?" I cup her face. "Wake up for me. Look at me, Elli."

Her dark lashes flutter open and her dazed ice-blue eyes meet mine, but I know she's not seeing me. "That's it. Elli, this is impor-tant, what did they give you?"

Looking away from me, her lashes flutter before her eyes fall closed and then open again but she doesn't respond.

"Maybe a sedative?" Gavin offers.

Tyson re-enters the family room and nods his head. "It's empty."

I stand, pick her up off the couch, and follow after him. Entering one of the many the spare bedrooms, I place her on the bed and look at Gavin. "Stay in here with her. No matter what you hear out there, do not leave her in here alone."

"I'll stay with them," Nicholas offers, lifting his gun. "I'll protect them."

Tyson follows me out and he closes the door behind him. It won't stop the brothers from getting in, but it may give Nicholas one extra second to shoot their fucking heads off.

Making our way back down the hallway, I hear voices. We pause, pressing our backs into the wall, both nodding to one another in understanding.

"Dude, where the fuck did she go?" one barks out.

"She was right here," another states.

"She couldn't have gone far. She was tied up, for Christ's sake." The first one laughs.

"You only secured her wrists. I told you we should have hog-tied her. There's no chance of movement in that position."

"Come on," the first guy growls, growing irritated. "She's around here somewhere."

I readjust my grip on the gun and hold it down in front of me, listening to the sound of their boots growing closer and closer. I hold in my breath so they won't notice us as they pass by the end of the hallway. Once the second one passes, Tyson nods to me and we both step out. I slam the butt of the gun down on the back of his neck. He drops like a rock instantly.

The second guy turns around, hearing the commotion. "What the—?"

Tyson hits him across his mask-covered face with his gun and he too drops. Bending down, I yank off the guy's mask just as Tyson does the other. We both stand and look at each other.

"What the actual fuck is going on?" he asks me, sounding as confused as I feel.

"No fucking clue," is the only answer I can think to give him. "But let's find out."

## ELLINGTON

*"Now we wait. You'll be begging to swallow our cocks in no time."*

*My heart sinks at his words and I pray to God it's not true. "What did you give me?" My voice shakes. But I need to know. Am I going to die? Or just wish I was dead?*

*"Ecstasy," the one who dropped the pills in my mouth answers.*

*The other guy shoves him back a step.*

"What?" he asks, placing his hands out wide. "Not like she can fight it. She'll be fucked up soon."

The guy gets up off my chest and I'm finally able to take in a deep breath. I roll onto my side, to relieve the pressure of my arms underneath me, but it doesn't help. They've gone numb. And soon my mind will do the same.

The one that had placed his hand down my shirt and gave me the pills, kneels down beside the couch, getting eye level with me but I still don't know which brother he is. The mesh part of the mask that covers the eyes keeps you from seeing them. "You've been such a dirty whore, Elli."

I whimper.

"It's amazing how much you'll believe. How much you allowed him to manipulate you."

I frown. How long have the brothers been part of our lives? I know my father's been there for nine years. Have they been watching us for that long? I never pretended to not be stupid for Sin. That man made me an idiot. But I kept crawling back, asking for more.

"FUCK."

The other one shouts from the bottom of the stairs.

"She dead?" the one next to me asks.

He doesn't answer. Instead, he kicks the body a few times.

"She?" My wide eyes go to the masked guy in front of me. "Who ... who is she?"

He gives a dark chuckle, pulling out his cell phone from his hoodie pocket. He then holds it up to my face. "Remember this video that Amelia showed you?"

I see Sin sitting on his bed at the house of Lords. Closing my eyes tightly, I turn my face away from him, but he grips my cheeks, forcing me to face him. "Watch the fucking video!" he shouts, making me flinch.

*Opening my eyes, I notice the way my body starts to tingle as it relaxes into the couch. "I've seen it," I whisper.*

*"Just watch. All of it." He goes on, holding it right in front of my face. The light on the screen making me squint it's so bright.*

*Amelia walks in, gets naked. She lies on the bed, and he ties her arms above her head. Then he turns to open the nightstand. This is where I slapped it out of her hand. He opens the top drawer, grabs a blindfold and then slips it over her eyes.*

*Spreading her legs wide open, she arches her back while lifting her hips. "Sin—" He shoves something into her mouth, and she starts mumbling around it before he places tape over her lips so she can't spit it out.*

*Then he walks over to his bathroom door, opens it up, and out steps Chance. My eyes blink as I watch him undress then crawl onto the bed and begin to fuck her while Sin leans up against the wall, crossing his arms over his chest and watches them.*

*I want to be mad. To get angry at myself. But I can't. My mind won't let me. It's foggy, my eyes growing heavy.*

*He laughs, putting his cell back in his pocket. "Let it swallow you under, Elli." Running his hand down my face, I try to pull away, but I can't. It dips inside of my shirt once again and he roughly grabs at my breasts, the material pinching my neck as he stretches it out. "Once you're good and ready, we'll get this party started." Removing his hand, he stands and walks out of the room with the other guy, leaving me alone.*

*The last thing on my mind is what Sin said to me when I brought up the tape with Amelia to him.* "I can explain that..."

*Now, I wish I would have at least let him try.*

# SIXTY-ONE

# SIN

I slap the guy that I've tied to the chair. His head snaps to the right before popping up. He blinks, green eyes looking around aimlessly before they land on mine. "What—" He jerks on the rope that ties his hands to the back of the chair and his ankles to the legs.

I slap him again just because I can.

"Fuck," he cries, looking up at me. His eyes go large, and he gasps. Sitting rigid, he looks from me to Tyson, who stands beside me, Turning back to me, his face drains of color. "Sin ... you're dead."

"You wish." I punch him in the face so hard this time it knocks the chair back, pinning his arms behind it.

His screams fill the large room and I walk over to him. Pressing my shoe into his stomach, I hold him down. And just to add more weight, I lean my body into it, placing my forearm on my thigh.

"St-op." He's gasping. "Please."

"Where are the Spade brothers?" I ignore him. I'm still trying to figure out what the fuck is going on. They called me. But when we arrived, Amelia is dead wearing a mask and we find the other two masked men to be Chance and Holland—shit's not adding up.

"Who?" He grits his teeth, tilting this head back and screaming once again. His body fighting the position it's in with no such luck.

"I'm going to slit your fucking throat and watch you drown in your own blood if you don't start talking," I warn, pressing my foot farther into his stomach, smashing his arms underneath the chair. I hope I fucking break them. "Tyson." I reach out my free hand and he hands me an open pocketknife.

I reach across Chance's chest, placing the tip of the blade into his neck right below his ear and get about an inch before he's screaming.

"Stop. Stop. Stop. Please. Okay. Okay." He's crying.

I smile when I see the small trail of blood running down the side of his neck to the carpet beneath him. "Where are the Spade brothers?" Let's start with something easy. I should have known that wasn't them when we stepped out of the hallway. The brothers aren't that fucking stupid.

"I don't know who that is." He's sobbing, spit flying from his mouth, only to land on his face. "I ... swear."

I look up at Tyson and he shrugs. A quick look at Holland and he's still out of it. His face busted up pretty good from Tyson's gun to his face.

"Okay, let's try this." I push off his stomach and he takes in a deep breath before sobbing at the heavy weight now gone. "Why the fuck is Amelia dead at the bottom of the stairs?"

"Elli killed her." He confirms what I already thought.

"Did you have something to do with that?" Otherwise, why would that bitch fucking be here.

He nods.

"Explain it to me," I demand.

Chance swallows. "Your father came to me. Demanded I make sure that you don't pursue Elli."

"Was this before or after you made a deal with me?" I wonder.

Closing his eyes tightly, he lets out a soft sob. "Before."

"So that's why you came to me." I nod, giving a rough laugh. "You made a deal with my father and pretended to help me out."

"I was always supposed to marry her," he rushes out. "Back when James was alive. Him and Linc would bring me in ... make me watch."

"What the fuck do you mean *make you watch?*" I shout. Something tells me he had no problem watching her do anything.

"James would wait until she got fucked up. He'd order her around. Make her a fucking slave and she'd do anything he wanted. They had me watch because Linc said he was training her for me."

I take a few steps, closing the small space between us, and kick him in the fucking face like I'm a kicker for an NFL team and this game depends on me.

His head snaps to the side, blood splattering across the floor. He begins to choke on it, body convulsing.

Reaching down, I pick up the chair and bring it upright. I grip his busted face, pinching his bloody skin and demand, "Keep going." The one thing that I'm glad I kept a secret was that me and Elli were married. I called her my wife a few times here and there to him, but he never seemed to have taken it seriously. Now I know why. He thought all along he was going to get my girl. "Talk." I shake his face and he spits blood out of his split lip.

"Me ... and Amelia set you and Elli up," deep breath, "at Blackout that night. I gave her the video she needed to confront Elli with in the bathroom. I needed Elli pissed at you. If so, she'd throw herself at someone else. Therefore, pissing you off in return." He cries softly. "She wasn't going to walk away from you. I needed you to walk away from her."

I think about his words for a second. "My sister mentioned the video." He fucking whimpers. "I even asked you what she meant about James and Linc, and you said you didn't know."

"I'm sorry." He sobs, body shaking uncontrollably.

"I know." Letting go of his face, I slap his chest. "But why here? Why tonight? You said you thought I was dead." I rub my chin.

He nods, sniffling. "I got a message that you were dead..."

"Who the fuck from?" I demand, making him jump.

"It was an unknown number." He cries. "I thought it was the Lords."

"And?"

"And I called Holland, wondering if he was the one who sent it." He stops to take a breath. "He said no but that he owed Elli for what you did to Marcus because of her. And since you were dead..." Trailing off, he doesn't finish that sentence. But I can connect the dots.

I take the pocketknife in my hand and stab him in the thigh. He throws his head back, screaming. "Focus, Chance." I slap his bloody face enough to get his attention. "Pay attention."

His bloodshot eyes meet mine, drool running from his busted lips while he bares his teeth at the pain. I remove the knife, making him sob. "Then what? How did you know she was here?"

"We've been waiting for her to return home for over an hour. Me and Holland were here. Amelia was at the other house. We knew once she was notified you were dead, she'd return home to one of them." Sucking in a deep breath, he hangs his head.

I look at Tyson, who has remained silent as I get the information I needed, and he finally speaks, "What is she on right now?'

"Ec-stasy," comes his shaky voice.

"Did you lace it with anything?" I ask through gritted teeth. I don't want her going through another two days of hell like the last time she went out. That was torture for her and for me, not being able to help her. Being helpless to the one you love is a different kind of hell.

"No." He looks up at me through his wet lashes and I arch a brow. "I promise. We just wanted her..."

"Wanted her what?" Tyson snaps, ready to get this over with.

"Begging." He hangs his head. "Not dead."

"Tyson." I nod to Chance, and he walks behind him.

Chance's head snaps up, wide eyes on mine. "I didn't know," he rushes out. "You were dead."

"Yet here I am." I hold my arms out wide.

Tyson grabs a hold of Chance's hair and yanks his head back. I run the tip of the blade slowly across his neck, doing exactly what I told him I'd do. Stepping back, I watch the bastard bleed out onto the floor with a smile on my face.

## SIXTY-TWO

## SIN

I get her back to our house and carry her into the kitchen. The only light that's on is over the stove, giving me just enough to see the island and to set her down on a barstool. "Sit right here," I tell her, turning to the fridge and grabbing her a water.

Turning back to her, I see she's now bent over, chest and face lying on the marble island, arms fanned out in front of her. Sitting the bottle down, I go over and flip on the light, only to turn back and freeze when I see a man sitting at the head of the table, and it's not her father. "What the fuck do you want?" I growl.

He taps his fingers on the table, tilting his head to the side. His blue eyes drop to Elli, and I step in front of the island to block his view of her, and he smirks. "I don't believe in love," he states and I snort. "Something so pure can't survive in hell. But I do believe in revenge."

"Why are you here?" I've had all the riddles I can take tonight. I'm fucking sore as shit and exhausted. I just want to clean both of us off and crawl into bed with my wife, knowing she's safe and sound.

"Do you know why I called Tyson and told him to bring you back after your first meeting with us at Carnage?"

"No." I didn't care.

"Me and my brothers didn't run Carnage when Nicholas was brought in. Not until later on. But we found it strange that all those nine years he'd been there no one ever asked about him. Until after you showed up."

I frown, stepping closer to the table. "What do you mean?"

"We hadn't asked who you wanted because it didn't matter. We don't hand anyone over. No one gets a pass. But you..." He sits up straighter. "You show up with Tyson, demanding to see our roster, and when we tell you no, you leave. That very next day we get a phone call. Someone checking on a Lord. Do you know how often we get calls from people wanting to know the status of someone at Carnage?"

"How many?"

"Never."

"Who was it?" I wonder, looking over my shoulder to see her still lying on the island. I quickly scan the room to make sure the other two aren't here as well. I'm here alone right now. Gavin dropped me and Elli off and her father stayed back at the house with Tyson to clean up the mess of dead bodies we made.

"Your father," he answers, getting my attention once more.

I look at him and frown. "How did he...?" Of course. I asked him about Carnage. If he knew about them, but I never told him who or what I wanted. Thank God for that. He could have beat me to Nick and made sure he was dead for real somehow. Making sure we never found out the truth of what my father did to put him away.

"I don't believe in coincidences," he goes on. "So we called you back for a meeting, and wouldn't you know, you wanted the same Lord that he called about." Crossing his tattooed arms over his chest, he sits back in the chair. "We decided we'd hand him over in exchange for you. Honestly, we didn't think you'd do it." Tilting his head to the side, he asks, "How do you feel, by the way?" his eyes drop to my bloody shirt.

I don't answer, making him give a dark chuckle. "Yeah, it hurts like a bitch. That's what it's supposed to feel like."

"What do you want?" I'd rather not rehash this situation. And he came here for another reason other than why they let me make a deal to release Nicholas.

"The only reason you're free to fuck your cunt," he nods to Elli, "is because her father offered up yours."

My hands fist. "Get to the point," I demand. This is not news to me.

"Your father hasn't been able to keep his mouth shut since he's been dropped off. Went on and out about his partner."

*Partner?* What the fuck is he talking about? Who else is out there that I have to hunt down and kill to make sure my wife stays safe?

"We thought he meant your mother at first, but he started dropping names. Guess who was one of them?"

Elli moans and I look over my shoulder to see her run her hands through her hair to push it off her face. But her eyes remain closed. "Who?" I ask, ready to get this over with.

"Chance."

My spine straightens and he taps his tatted knuckles on the table. "So I planted a bug."

"What do you mean by planted a bug?"

"I made sure he got word that you had passed away." He gives me a smile, showing off his white teeth. They're a stark contrast to the black ink that wraps up around his neck to his jawline.

"You what?" I snap, stepping closer to the table. That's why Chance's face turned white when he saw me and said I was dead. He was so sure that I had died. "Why would you..." My voice trails off and I suck in a deep breath. "You wanted him to go after Elli." He used her as bait. "You son of a bitch..."

"It worked, didn't it?" He looks over at her still passed out.

"He could have killed her." I point to her.

"She looks alive to me. A little out of it," he shrugs carelessly. "But breathing nonetheless."

"He could have. Fuck. He drugged her. Who knows what he would have done to her had I not got to her in time." I'm screaming, throat burning. Fuck him for playing this game with me. My wife is off-limits.

"I made sure you were aware of the situation..."

"Situation? You didn't tell me where she was. I thought you guys had her, for fuck's sake."

He snorts at that. "If we were going to take your wife, the last thing we'd do is let you know. She'd just ... vanish."

My chest tightens at that thought and I step back, getting closer to her once again.

"What happened to Nicholas was unfortunate. And we don't like being made to look like fools." His eyes go to my wife as she makes another noise that sounds more like a whimper. "And Elli really was an innocent." They return back to mine. "I'm all for brutal revenge, but not when it's not deserved. So..." He stands from the head of the table. "Take it as the peace offering it is. She has her father and you. Not to mention, I brought to your attention an enemy that you didn't know existed. Now you've killed every person that has harmed or planned to harm your wife. I'll say our business is done." Walking over to me, he holds out a black box I hadn't noticed he had with him. "Here, you'll want this."

"What is this?" I'm so tired of surprises.

"It's your father's phone. There's some interesting content on it." He walks past Elli, not even bothering to look at her, and goes to exit the kitchen.

"My father and her mother?" I ask, needing to know.

He pauses, wanting a second to decide if he wants to tell me or not. "They're both still alive. For now. But don't worry, you have my word they won't ever leave Carnage. The guys have already found her mother to be useful, and they enjoy the way your father begs." He smiles. "Now enjoy your wife, I know I would." He turns and exits the kitchen. I hear the front door open and close seconds later.

I slide my father's phone into a kitchen drawer; I'll come back and get it later. Walking over to Elli, I grab a hold of her shoulders, pulling her face and chest up off the island. Picking her up in my arms and grabbing her water, I carry her into the master suite bathroom.

I sit on the edge of the corner Jacuzzi tub and hold on to her with one arm while the other turns on the faucet. Once the water is where I know she'll like it, I stand and set her on the edge.

Her head falls forward, and I cup her cheeks, holding it in place. "Elli, I need you to help me out a little, okay?"

Heavy eyes open and look around aimlessly. "Sin?"

"You need a bath, Elli. Okay. I've got to clean you off." Reaching the hem of her shirt, I pull it up and over her head. Then I unfasten her bra and toss it to the floor. I lift her up and hold her with one arm while the other undoes her jeans. I manage to get them down her legs and pick her up before placing her in the tub. I'm going to get her clean and put her in our bed. Then I'll shower and wash myself off before joining her because I'm having problems keeping my eyes open. I'm crashing hard. I'm so done with this day. Hopefully tomorrow is better.

# ELLINGTON

I OPEN MY EYES, A LITTLE CONFUSED, BUT IT ONLY TAKES ME a second to realize that I'm back at home. Morning light filters through the window. I look over to my right and see Sin on his stomach, arms up under the pillow, sound asleep. I remember bits and pieces of last night. Like in the bathtub—him washing me clean and me crying, confused why he was there. I was told he was dead. He just kept reassuring me that he wasn't going anywhere and that I was safe while I hugged him tightly. I was afraid to let him go. That he'd disappear.

I've got a slight headache but other than that, I feel okay. Reaching under the covers, I run my hands over my body to find myself naked and I wonder if we had sex last night. If so, I don't remember. My body feels tight, muscles ache. That could have been the drugs or a really good fuck.

The thought has me lowering my hand between my legs. I run my fingers over my pussy and I'm wet. Like soaking wet. My pussy begging to be fucked. To get off. Pushing one finger inside of myself, I'm disappointed when I don't feel sore there. That my husband didn't take advantage of me last night while I was fucked up. Probably because he was too tired. Or maybe he was hurting. He went through so much while at Carnage.

Looking at him once again, I bite my lip. I don't want to wake him up. He's got to be exhausted. Rolling over the opposite direction, I open up the top drawer of my nightstand and pull out my silver bullet. I want a fucking jackhammer right now but this'll do.

Lying on my back, I shove it under the covers and between my legs, turning it on. A moan escapes my lips, and I throw my free hand over my mouth, taking a quick look at Sin. But he hasn't moved, thankfully.

I close my legs, trying to smother the vibrating sound. It works a little, but you can still hear the powerful thing. I rub it back and forth over my hood piercing. I don't need an earth-shattering orgasm, just something to hold me over for a few days, maybe a week. However long it takes him to recover from the Spade brothers. I wonder if he killed them—

I push that thought out of my mind and take a deep breath. *Concentrate, Elli. Think of Sin, tying you up in the basement.* My clit pulses. That's it. *Forcing his cock down my throat.* I swallow at the thought, imagining drool running out of the corners of my lips while he tells me I'm his good girl and how well I take it.

I arch my back, my hand moving the bullet faster. My fingers digging deeper into my cheeks to keep me quiet.

My breath hitches and my body stiffens. I come, biting my tongue, and then sink into the bed. I stay staring up at the ceiling for a second, the bullet still in my hand but now off. Reaching over, I place it on the nightstand and close my eyes. Rolling to my other side, I sigh, getting comfortable, and open my eyes.

I gasp, looking into a set of blue eyes. I bite my lip nervously, knowing he probably just watched me get myself off. "Good morning," I say. "How do you feel?"

He reaches out, grabbing the back of my neck and shoves me onto my stomach before I can react. My body too sluggish at the moment. The ecstasy is still lingering, not to mention the orgasm I just had. His knees effortlessly spread my legs wide open, forcing my ass up in the air. "Sin—"

He slaps my ass. "I watched you get yourself off, little demon."

I whimper, my fingers digging into the fitted sheet.

"That won't be happening again." His knuckles run over my exposed pussy, coating his fingers with my cum. Then they're gone and I hear him sucking on them a second later. "I love the taste of my wife for breakfast," he mumbles, making me moan. "You want to come, Elli? I'll make you come. Ask me nicely." He slaps my cunt, making me cry out, and I try to move away from him, but his hand wrapped around the back of my neck keeps me pinned in place.

"Pl-ease?" I suck in a deep breath.

"Again." He slaps my pussy once more.

I'm gasping. "Please ... make me come."

He slides two fingers deep inside of me and I push against them as he adds another, spreading my cunt open. "You know I watched you tie yourself up and get off once before."

"Oh, God." I rock back and forth against his fingers at his words, making my pussy clench around them.

"I wanted so bad to hold you down and fuck that mouth of yours. To punish you for touching what's mine." Removing his fingers, I tense, thinking he's going to slap me again, but instead I feel his cock against my pussy before he pushes into me, making my breath hitch. Leaning forward, he places his weight against my body, his mouth by my ear, and he lets out a moan as he slides balls deep, stretching me wide to accommodate his large size. He whispers, "From here on out, you get yourself off, you will be punished, Elli. Do you understand?" He pulls back and slams his cock into my pussy.

"Yes," I cry out.

"I own this cunt, this ass, and this mouth." He pulls his hips back and thrusts forward again, making the bed hit the wall. "Say it," he commands, gathering my hair in one of his hands and fisting it tightly, making me whimper. "Say *I'm yours, Sin*."

"I'm ... yours, Sin." I gasp, licking my lips. "Please, make me come," I add, that feeling building once more.

He gently kisses the side of my face as his free hand slides underneath me and wraps around my throat. "You're going to come all right, little demon." I whimper. "On my cock, then my fingers, and lastly on my face." His hand tightens, taking away what little air I had. "We're going to spend all day in this bed and I'm going to make sure that you never forget that you're mine."

## SIXTY-THREE

## SIN

I'm in my father's study back at my parents' house. His cell phone on the desk, paused on a video of my wife. It's the fifth video I've watched so far. All the same. Some James sent my father. Some he recorded himself. Another has Linc in it.

The one in particular I've got open is one that I never even thought to think of. It's Chance. He's sitting in James's office and my wife is bent over his desk. James fucking her cunt while Lincoln's cock is down her throat.

I never asked Elli about what my sister meant when she barged into my bedroom and she spoke about Amelia saying I told her about James and Linc both fucking her. When I turned to ask Chance about it, he pretended to know nothing. But he did. The fucking bastard was there. Recording it. The thing was, Elli never told me how or when Linc fucked her. I never asked her to give me details and she never offered them.

When they're done with her, they toss her to the floor where she lies there, naked from the waist down, barely conscious. *She's fucked up.*

The video ends and I drop my head, running my hands

through my hair, my body shaking with fury. It's over. But knowing that isn't enough. There's so much that she doesn't even remember, how much is there that we'll never know?

Jumping to my feet, I shove everything off his desk and watch it crash to the floor. Picking up a paperweight, I throw it across the room and break a framed picture he has of our family. It was after my first year at Barrington. Who knew how long he had been sleeping with Elli by then. How many times he had seen her naked and used.

Storming over to it, I yank it off the wall and bang it against the desk, until it is nothing but shattered glass and splintered wood. I remove the picture from the remains and rip it to shreds. Then I turn and grab his golf clubs, slamming them into the wall. Over and over, enjoying the holes it leaves.

Throwing it across the room, I go over to his safe and punch in the code, hoping he hadn't changed it since last time. It pops open and I grab the box that contains naked pictures of my wife. I throw his cell in the box and go to storm out of the study, when the door opens, bringing me to a stop.

Wide blue eyes search the destroyed room before they land on mine. "Sin—" Her eyes drop to the floor, and I realize a picture had fallen from the box. She goes to pick it up and I step on it, covering up a naked Elli from her view. Taking a step back, her watery eyes meet mine once again. "Mom told me," my sister whispers. "I've tried calling Elli..." She trails off and I don't have anything to say to that.

A lot has come to light in the last week, and it'll take time to move on. She knows how I feel about my father, but Elli still feels ashamed. Didn't know how my mother and sister would feel about my father raping her and as far as they all know, I killed him. The last thing I want is for them to find out about the Spade brothers.

"Will you tell her to call me?" she asks. "That I'm here for her. Whatever she needs."

I bend down, pick up the picture, and toss it into the box. "Yeah." I walk past her toward the door to exit, but she speaks again.

"Sin?" I turn to face her but say nothing. "I hope you made him pay for what he did to her."

Without another word, I turn and leave the house, heading home to my wife. We're going to have a bonfire with this box of pictures and destroy this phone.

———

I STAND IN THE LIVING ROOM, HANDS TUCKED INTO MY SLACKS as I watch my wife stand out on the balcony of our cabin. We wanted a weekend away from everything. Just the two of us. Things have been so hectic for so long. It's weird now, even though things have yet to calm down. It's just a different kind of chaos now.

I've stepped in and taken over at Asher Corp. It wasn't what I was supposed to do, but it's what I want. Me, Elli, and Nicholas sat down and discussed the options for the company. Like I figured, Elli doesn't want anything to do with it. She wants to follow in her mother's footsteps as a sex therapist. I wasn't sure how I felt about that at first, but she explained to me that she wished she had someone to talk to all those years and I couldn't deny that I wished she had that too.

My eyes run up over her red six-inch high heels and over her exposed legs up to the hem of her black cocktail dress. We've got dinner reservations in an hour. I had taken a call, only to find her standing out of the balcony, looking over the town lights at the bottom of the hill. My cock hardens at the fact that her matching thong is soaked with my cum dripping out of her cunt. I love my wife and I would do anything for her, but I will always remind her that I own her. That no other man can bring her to her knees like I can. Make her beg like I can.

Life isn't normal but I think it's as close as it will ever be for us. She's returned to Barrington; she's even attending her psychology of human sexuality class. There is a new professor since I killed David, and I accompany her and sit in her seat every time she's up there reading off what everyone thinks is an imaginary scene. It's the biggest turn-on I've ever experienced. Knowing that the journal entries are about me and her. It's like our little secret that no one gets to be a part of.

I also like to go to make Mack uncomfortable. Remind him to not fuck with my wife. I beat the shit out of him a few weeks ago. Went over to his house and broke his nose along with his jaw. He deserved to be reminded that what he did to her will not be allowed. I know Holland was the one who wanted to make her suffer because of me but Mack had an opportunity to warn her what she was really taking that night at the party, and he didn't. That deserved consequences.

A cell rings and I pull mine out, expecting it to be another business call, only to realize it's hers. Looking up, I see her remove it from her clutch. "Hey, Dad."

"Hey, princess. What are you up to?" I hear him on speakerphone.

"About to go to dinner," she states. "Everything okay?"

"Yeah, yeah. I'm sorry. I didn't mean to interrupt your vacation..."

"You're okay," she assures him, sticking her ass out while she leans against the railing.

I lick my lips, thinking about dropping to my knees behind her and burying my face into her cum-dripping cunt.

"What's going on?" Elli asks him.

"Me and Tamara are on our way to Paris," he answers.

I let him borrow my father's jet. Not like he'll need it anymore.

Her mother had sold Nicholas's jet after she helped set up his death. I figured it was the least I could do for him.

"I was wondering..." He clears his throat, sounding nervous all of a sudden. "If you and Easton would like to have dinner with us when we return?"

She's been wanting to meet his girlfriend, but she hasn't been sure if he wanted them to meet or not. His girlfriend has no idea that he was a Lord, or that we even exist for that matter. After we made sure every threat was taken care of, I got him a new identity. Jenkins Lancaster is just an average man who works his ass off every day at Asher Corp, chasing the American dream. I fired everyone that was employed at Asher Corp that knew or could recognize him, including anyone on the board of directors. Jenkins stays behind the scenes for the most part, but you can never be too careful. I thought about giving him his brother's identity, but he deserved a fresh start. A new name that wasn't tainted with a past record and debt.

"Yeah." Her voice cracks and she clears her throat, recovering. "That would be great."

"Okay, we'll be back on Sunday. We're about to take off, Elli. Tell Easton I said hi and I'll see you when we get back. I love you."

She goes to tell him she loves him too, but he's already hung up. Placing her phone back in her clutch, I hear mine beep, signaling a message.

I pull it out to read the text.

UNKNOWN: We need to talk.

I frown, reading over it.

"Everything okay?"

I place the cell back in my pocket without responding. *He can wait.* "Yeah," I answer, seeing she has turned around now, facing me but still on the balcony. "Everything is great."

Smiling, she pushes off the railing and walks through the open sliding glass doors. I stay where I'm at, letting her come to me. My eyes dropping over the V-cut in her dress that shows off her amazing tits. They're still pierced. She loves when I play with them. Especially lately. They've been extra sensitive.

Coming up to me, she tosses her clutch onto the white leather couch to my left before wrapping her arms around my neck. "My father called."

"I heard."

"Listening to my conversations, huh?" She arches a dark brow.

"Yes." I nod, reaching up and pushing her bleach-blond hair from her shoulders to fall down her back so I have a clear view of her gorgeous face.

"I want to tell him." She speaks softly as if I'm going to tell her that's a bad idea. *I'm not.*

"You know what I want?" I ask.

She tilts her head to the side, brow furrowing at my question. "What?"

I reach down, grab her soft thighs, and pick her up, the dress riding up to show off her ass as her legs wrap around my hips.

"Sin," she breathes as I lay her on the bed to my right. She spreads her legs for me as I kneel between them and push her dress up her body to expose her growing belly. Most wouldn't notice it yet, but I do.

Leaning down, I gently kiss it and she runs her hands through my hair, arching her back. "Sin—"

"I'm going to take my pregnant wife to dinner, but first you're going to ride my face until you're coming all over it. I want you to be what I taste when we're sitting at the table."

She whimpers.

"How's that sound, little demon?" I trail my lips lower to her thong and I pull it to the side, exposing her wet pussy to me.

"Amazing." Her hips buck, and I smile.

"Beg me, Elli," I command softly, giving her inner thigh a gentle kiss, knowing it'll drive her nuts. My wife likes to be fucked, taken, owned. "Beg me to get you off."

"Please." She's gasping, hips bucking while her fingers dig into my scalp, trying to force my lips where she wants them.

# EPILOGUE

## SIN

I drive down the two-lane road, my windshield wipers working overtime to try and keep up with the storm that decided to hit us out of nowhere today. My left wrist is causally laying across the top of the steering wheel, my right hand in my wife's lap holding hers while "Battle Born" by Five Finger Death Punch softly fills the car.

Giving her a quick look, I see her sitting in the passenger seat, eyes straight ahead and she's nibbling on her bottom lip nervously. "Talk to me." I say giving her hand a gentle squeeze.

She sighs and removes her hand from mine sitting up straighter. "I don't understand why they want to see you."

"It's nothing serious." I try and downplay it.

"Obviously it is, or they would have just called you." She argues.

"Hey," Reaching back over, I grab her hand once again and bring it to my lips while keeping my eyes on the road, kissing her wedding ring. "I wouldn't be bringing you with me if I thought you were in any danger."

She snorts, yanking her hand free of mine this time and crossing her arms over her chest. "I'm not worried about me, Sin."

Readjusting myself in the driver seat, I slow down coming up to our exit. I pull to a stop and roll down my window, the rain instantly soaking myself and the seat as I press in the code for the gate. They open up to allow me entrance and we drive up to Carnage. I got a text over the weekend while we were away on a vacation. All it said was *we need to talk.*

Well, I had put the Spade brothers off until we returned yesterday when I got another one telling we needed to be here— me and my wife.

Putting the car in park, I pull my hood up to keep from getting wet and exit the car. Elli's already getting out by the time I make it around to her. I grab her hand and drag her up the stairs and into the double doors where I shake off my hoodie and she pushes her hood off her dry hair.

"This place gives me the creeps." She whispers, her eyes shooting to the staircase and then to the balcony. "It smells like death."

"Mr. and Mrs. Sinnett. Please follow me." their butler enters the grand foyer.

"Sin—"

"We're fine, Elli," I interrupt pulling her after me and following him down a hallway. I was given their word that they would not touch her when one appeared in our kitchen the night I saved Elli from Chance and Holland. Otherwise, I would have made her stay home with her father.

Following after him, he leads us to what I remember is their office the first time I came here with Tyson. He opens the door and I place my hand on her lower back to usher her in.

"The Spade brothers will be right with you." The guy speaks backing out, closing the doors.

Elli looks around, walking over to the desk that sits in front of three floor to ceiling windows showcasing the downpour. I plop down in the leather couch, my eyes watching my wife. Whatever it is they want better be good. Because I had planned on spending the day with my wife in bed.

She picks up a framed picture off the corner of the desk and frowns looking over it.

"What is it?" I ask.

"I—"

The doors creak as they open, and she places it back where she found it and looks up to watch the three brothers enter the room. I stand.

"Sin," The one with the snake tattoos nods to me while the one with the nun tattoo smirks at me, the third is staring at my wife. I still don't know their names and I don't give a fuck to. That's not important.

"What are we doing here?" I get to the point. I know they don't fuck around, and I can think of something else I could be doing with my time right now.

"We've got a ...situation." He says crossing his tatted arms over his chest.

"Not sure how anything involving you three could be a *we* situation." Elli speaks.

He ignores her which just pisses her off more.

"Well, we're here. So fill us in." The last thing I want to do is put her in a situation that I've got to kill our way out of.

"We need to show you." He says and walks toward the door.

I look over at my wife who is glaring at him, and I wait for her to walk over to me. Placing my hand on her lower back, I guide her out of the door and into the hallway placing myself between the brothers and her. "Lead the way." I gesture out in front of me.

We all remain silent as they take us down a hallway, to an elevator and to a basement. She clings to my side, her fingers digging into my arms through my hoodie. Not sure if she's afraid or pissed. Probably both at this point. I can hear her heavy breathing fill the tight space.

We come to a stop and enter a large rectangular room that has a glass wall. It reminds me of something you'd see if you were about to choose someone out of a lineup.

"Have a look." The one with the neck tattoos points to the glass.

She steps up to it first and I step up behind her placing me between them once again. I look through what I'm guessing is a two-way mirror and see her mother lying in what looks like a hospital bed. Her arms down by her side, leather cuffs around each wrist, tying them down. Her legs spread wide also leather cuffs around the ankles. She's thrashing in the bed, yanking on the restraints. You can see her mouth moving while she screams but you can't hear her in the room we're in. She's dressed in an all-black jumpsuit that zips from the crotch to her neck. There's blood on her face from a gash above her eye and her lip is also bleeding. Her hair matted and oily. Obviously, she hasn't been bathed since god knows when.

"Why are we here?" Elli asks, stepping to the side and turning to face the brothers who stand behind us. I do the same. "Want me to feel sorry for her or something?"

"Not at all." He shakes his head. "But we wanted to give you the choice."

"Choice to what?" I'm the one who speaks this time.

Leaning back against the far wall, he crosses his arms over his chest. Nun tattoo guy shoves his hands into the pockets of his ripped jeans, pulling his shoulders back. The other just stands there—it's always the quiet ones you need to worry about. "She's in the same current situation as your wife." his eyes drop to her hoodie, and I don't like the way his lips curve upwards. Or the fact that he knows anything about my wife for that matter.

I feel Elli's body stiffen against mine. "What do you mean *situation?*" She asks softly.

"No." I shake my head. "Not possible." I know exactly what they're referring to and they're wrong.

He tilts his head to the side. "What makes you think you know better than us?"

"My father—" I stop mid-sentence thinking how fucking stupid that sounds to say out loud after everything that bastard has lied to me. Looking down at Elli, I sigh. "How far?" I ask instead.

"Not sure on specifics. Wanted to speak to you on how to proceed."

"What the fuck are you guys talking about?" Elli barks stepping in front of me, her pretty blue eyes glaring up into mine.

"Your mother is pregnant." I announce. Then I look up to the brothers. "I was told she had a hysterectomy after Elli was born. How did you find out?" I'm not even going to ask how they know my wife is pregnant. I mean, a Lord is to reproduce so it makes sense that I would knock my wife up as soon as possible.

"We have our own way of doing things here." His eyes drop to my chest, and I know he's referring to their initiation. "Men and women aren't that far off but women are required to undergo a hysterectomy."

"You can't be serious!" Elli barks at them.

He looks at her. "Carnage is no place for a child." He sounds like he's speaking from experience. "We don't kill the innocent, but we will take precautions to prevent pregnancy."

"Unfuckingbelievable." She mumbles to herself.

His attention returns to me. "She was given a test. It came back positive. When we confronted her about it, she freaked the fuck out. Tried to throw herself down a set of stairs. Promised us that she would not be giving birth to a child here at Carnage."

I look at my wife and she's moved to stand at the glass, her eyes on her mother. She's not even listening to us anymore.

"I told you that we were even." His eyes go to the back of Elli's head then meet mine once again. "This is another curtesy we're offering you. Like I said, Carnage is no place for a child."

"We want the baby." My wife rushes out, spinning around to face the room. "We'll take them both."

"Whoa. Whoa." He pushes off the wall uncrossing his arms. "Your mother is ours. She's not going anywhere."

"You have her strapped to a bed." She steps forward but I grab her hoodie and yank her backwards toward me when I see the quiet one step toward her. "She's pregnant. You can't keep her hear as a prisoner, tied down, abuse her, and expect her to give birth to a healthy child." Her voice grows.

"Did we go easy on her when she arrived? No. But we haven't touched her since we found out she was pregnant. And the marks she has right now, are self-inflicted."

"If you're not willing to hand over Laura, what are you offering?" I ask. They've already got a plan in place, and they need to get to the point.

"What are you going to do to her?" Elli demands before he can answer me. "Place her in a drug induced coma and keep her strapped to a bed."

"Women in comas carry children to full term all the time." The one with the nun tattoo shrugs.

Snake tattoos dismisses them both speaking to me. "We've got a hospital here—fully staffed of course." Elli snorts at that as if their doctors aren't equipped to care for a pregnant woman. "Doctors to monitor her. But..." he looks at Elli who looks like she wants to shoot him if she was given the chance. "We'll give you full access to our facility. Bring in Gavin as often as you want. We'll grant him access as well to whatever he needs. But Laura does not leave Carnage. The moment Gavin delivers the baby, you take the child home with you. And she remains here."

"He's not an OBGYN." She snaps referring to Gavin.

"Take it or leave it." He shrugs carelessly.

"You can't—"

"We'll take it." I interrupt her.

She spins around yanking my hand free of her hoodie. Her wide eyes shoot to the glass behind me, and tears start to fill them. "Sin—"

"I want to see my father." I don't give her a chance to speak. She'll have plenty of time for that while on the car ride home. Right now, she needs to take what they're offering and vent to me later about it.

The guy in the ripped jeans throws his head back laughing. "Why would we allow that?"

I ignore him and keep my stare on the one I know is in charge. After a long second, he nods. "You may see your father." He agrees.

---

WE WALK INTO A ROOM AT THE OTHER END OF THE BASEMENT holding onto my wife's hand. The brothers enter behind us. It smells of piss and blood.

My father sits in the far corner, back to the wall. He lifts his head as we enter a smile on his busted lips when he sees us. The sound of his laughter echoing off the concrete walls makes the hairs on the back of my neck stand up.

"Didn't know I'd be allowed conjugal visits." His eyes go to Elli, and I hold out my hand placing it on her chest to stop her coming further into the room. Of course, the bastard has to make a dig at raping my wife.

"Horny, Liam? I can get someone in here to fuck you if you'd like." The one jokes with the nun tattoo. I watch my father shiver at that thought. "For someone with a dick you're shitty at sucking one." He hangs his head, his heavy breathing filling the cold room and the Spade brother laughs at him. "Don't worry we'll teach you how to take a cock like a good boy."

"I'll make this quick." I say, shoving my hands into the front pocket of my hoodie, moving on from that conversation. I don't care what they do here. To him or to others. As long as my wife isn't one of them. "Found out that Laura's pregnant." He remains silent staring at the floor. "Which is funny considering you told me she had a hysterectomy." Still nothing.

He raises his head, his eyes going to Elli and lingering on her longer than I'd like before they meet mine once again but still remains silent.

"I find it funny how you told me Lincoln wanted an Asher heir, yet he knocked up Laura in no time of them getting married."

"She was nothing before Nicholas." He says softly.

True, Elli's mother came from a Lord, but her family wasn't powerful. Not like an Asher. "I just wish we wouldn't have hung the bastard, so he'd know me, and my wife are going to raise his child as our own." I turn, grab Elli's hand and go to exit the room when his laughter makes me pause and turn back to look at him.

"You think you know the Lords." He shakes his head. "You know what they want you to know. What they want you to see. What they want you to hear. They manipulate you just as you do your wife." I feel her body stiffen against mine and my jaw clenches. "Why do you think they gave Laura to Lincoln for her third husband?" He doesn't even give me a chance to guess. "Because they were both nothing. And a Lord that's nothing can't reproduce. At some point you just have to cut them off."

I frown and Elli whispers. "Cut them off?"

"He's talking about a vasectomy." The Spade brother in charge steps forward. "I've been told that the Lords felt they needed to thin out the ones that didn't have enough power to help rule as they saw fit, so they gave them vasectomies so the families would eventually die off."

"But…" Eli trails off and my father's eyes meet mine. They're colder than I've ever seen. The smile tugging at his lips tells me all I need to know. His eyes go to my wife, and I step in front of her blocking his view, my hands reach out behind me to keep her shielded.

"Remove my wife from the room."

"What?" Comes a shrill scream. "Sin?"

"Now." I bark and I turn placing her hand in the Spade brothers with the snake tattoos on his neck. He pulls her out by it and shuts the door leaving me with the other two and my father. I trust him with her. The others not so much. But I needed a second alone with him.

Stepping forward, he slowly gets to his feet. I'm not sure if that's lack of strength from being here or if he just doesn't give a shit. Holding his hands out wide, his smile just grows. "Like mother like daughter. But I don't have to tell you, son, the younger cunt was better."

I swing, my fist connecting with his face, knocking him into the wall behind him. Reaching out I grab the black jumpsuit that he wears just like Laura had on and yank him to me, bringing my face down into his. My forehead making contact with his nose, giving me an instant headache but worth it. Blood drips from his face and a strangled moan comes from his lips. Bending over, I place my arm across his back, holding him place while I bring my knee up to his chest. He falls to the floor while he wheezes. I kick his shoulder pushing him on his back.

I crouch down next to him, hands on my jean-clad thighs. "I'm going to come back and visit you from time to time. I'm going to watch the Spade brothers make you the best 'good boy' they've ever had." I stand and turn to exit to see the one with the nun tattoo smiling at me proudly. "He's all yours." I say walking toward the door.

Yanking it open I see my wife and the brother in charge having a staring contest. My wife wanting to kick him in the balls and him keeping a good distance. "We'll be back with Gavin." I say and grab her hand.

"What the fuck was that Easton?" She demands as I drag her out the front double doors and into the pouring rain. Neither one of us bother to pull our hoodies up.

Opening the car door I place her in it, slamming it shut. The moment I get in, she turns on me.

"What the fuck?" she reaches over, and her fists slam into my arm.

Turning in the seat, I face her the best I can and grab both of her wrists to keep them making contact. "Elli—"

"Don't fucking Elli me." her large ice-blue eyes scan my face. I know I'm bleeding I can feel it running down the side of my head. My knuckles bruised and I'm shaking. I'm so fucking pissed that I want to go back in there and kill my father. But we had a deal. He belongs to Carnage. Not to me. All I can do is keep reminding myself that they will make him pay. Over and over for years to come.

"What was so important, huh?" She demands, her shoulders starting to shake as tears fill her eyes once again. "What did you need to say to him that was so secretive that I couldn't know?"

My chest tightens at what I'm about to tell her. That it's just one more thing to add to her long list of fucked up shit in her life. "Liam is the father."

She pauses, her body softening into the seat, and she frowns. "I don't understand."

"My dad was sleeping with your mother. She's pregnant with my father's child." That's what he meant by Linc couldn't get her pregnant and him having them both. Who knows how long he's been fucking her mother. Hell, maybe that's another reason why she helped plan Nicholas's fake suicide.

Elli's hands loosen their grip on my arms, and she falls back into her seat, staring straight ahead out into the storm. Her wet bleach-blonde hair plastered to her gorgeous face. "The baby will be our brother and sister?" She whispers.

"Yes."

Looking back over at me I see the first tear run down her face. I reach out and wipe it away, pushing the wet hair behind her ear. "I hate them." She whispers, her body shaking. "I hate then so much." Placing her hands in her face, she let's out a sob and I reach across pulling her into me.

"It'll be all right." I assure her rubbing her back.

She pulls away and looks up at me. "All they do is ruin everything. Everyone. I won't let them ruin this child's life."

"I know." I cup her face.

"We have to save them." Her bottom lip trembles at her words.

"We will."

"Call Gavin. See if he can meet us here. Tell him we'll wait." She slowly sits back into her seat and bows her head staring down at her hands in her lap and I pull my cell out of my pocket knowing we're about to be spending most of our time here at Carnage until my son or daughter is born. Along with my brother or sister. Because they're going to arrive around the same time.

## ELLINGTON

IT'S BEEN A MONTH SINCE WE TOOK OUR VACATION. WE'VE been going nonstop since we returned. But I wouldn't have it any other way. Smiling, I look down at my wedding ring. Sin will always be my devil. And I'll forever by his little demon who will choose to burn with him. It's who we are.

A hand runs up and down my thigh and I smile, looking over at Sin who sits next to me. We invited my father over for lunch. He sits across from us at our kitchen table.

"I don't understand." He shakes his head, reading over the paperwork in front of him.

"I sold it," I explain. "Sin has wired the money to your account." My husband slides the receipt from the transfer across the table to him. "It's all yours," I add.

My father looks up at me, then over to Sin. His blue eyes start to water, and it makes my chest tighten. "Why would you do that?" he asks softly.

"It was your house," I answer simply. He bought that mansion when my mother was pregnant with me. I came home to that house, so many good things happened there but it was never the same after his brother was murdered. So many evil things took place there. I have no use for it, and I know he wouldn't either. Sin and I decided this is what we wanted to do with it.

"You deserve a fresh start," Sin tells him. "You and Tamara."

My father is in love. We met her a few weeks back and she's great. He tells us that he's planning on marrying her. I hope that she can make him happy. That she can be the wife that he deserves.

He picks up the receipt and sighs heavily. He had paid cash for that house. It was a long time ago, but still in the millions then. Sin's mother was able to sell it for more than the asking price, which was over what my father paid for it all those years ago. He's no longer a Lord and with that comes a different life for him. One he doesn't deserve. We want to help him out as much as possible.

"I ... I don't know what to say," he whispers.

"Say that you'll remain in Pennsylvania." That's my biggest fear. That he'll leave and I won't get to see him as often as I want. I know that's selfish of me, but I want him to be part of our lives and our children's. I want my family to have the life I wish I had. Surrounded with lots of love and support.

He gets up from his seat and walks around the table. I stand and he pulls me into a big hug. "I'm not leaving, Elli," he says roughly, and I feel tears sting my eyes. His arms hug me tighter. "I'm not going anywhere." Letting me go, he steps over to Sin, and they share a man hug.

I feel the first tear run down my face while I smile. This is what I always wanted. To be loved and feel safe.

# EPILOGUE TWO

## SIN

*Eighteen years later*

I exit the bedroom to find my wife in the kitchen. "Good morning, little demon," I whisper in her ear as I step up behind her. My arms going around her waist. Burying my face into her neck, she lets it fall to the side to give me better access. I groan, my left hand coming up to grip her chin. "I'm so—"

The front door opening and slamming shut cuts me off and I pull away. "Who the fuck is here this early?" I mumble. When you've got two teenagers, kids are always coming and going all hours of the day and night.

My wife and I both walk into the living room in time to see our daughter running up the staircase.

"Where have you been?" I demand.

Annaleigh stops midway, throws her head back and sighs before turning to face me. "We went to get coffee."

"Who is we? And shouldn't you be getting ready for school?"

A bleach blonde pops her head over the second story balcony. "Hey, Mr. and Mrs. S." Her best friend waves down to us.

"I'm ready." Our daughter gestures to her sweatpants that look three sizes too big and a T-shirt. Neither look like hers. I've never seen them before. I'm the kind of dad most kids hate. I'm very active in my kids' lives whether they want me to be or not. I notice everything and am always asking questions.

I've never believed in God. But if I had, I'd tell him to go fuck himself. Those days spent with Elli in the basement trying to knock her up worked. I'm forever in my father-in-law's and Tyson's debt for coming and dragging me out of Carnage. But God laughed and said watch this. He gave me a daughter that's just like me. Hardheaded, stubborn, and a pain in my ass. Then to make it worse, he said let's make her look just like her mother.

"Hurry along. I don't want you to be late." Elli shoos them away.

Heading back to the kitchen, I follow her. "If she went to get coffee, where was it?" I ask my wife.

She gives me a pointed look. "Calm down. You worry too much."

"She's eighteen," I point out. About to graduate high school. I don't trust the boys she hangs out with.

She pats my chest. "It's fine."

"Mornin'."

My wife pulls away to look at our son. His eyes are barely open, he's got red marks down the side of his face where he's been sleeping. His hair a messy mop on top of his head and hanging in his eyes. "This is what a teenager is supposed to look like in the morning," I point out.

Our kids couldn't be more different in every way. People who don't know our family think they're twins. But what do you expect when they're the same age?

By the time they were old enough to talk, they'd tell people they were twins. We never corrected them. They know the truth, but to them they are brother and sister. Elli is Mom and I'm Dad and anyone who can't understand or accept that can go fuck themselves.

"Hungry?" she asks him.

"Starving," Brexton answers through a yawn.

"Up late?" I wonder.

"Yeah, was studying for a final." Laying his face down on the countertop, he closes his blue eyes.

I hear the front door open and close again, and seconds later my father-in-law enters the kitchen. "Good morning." He greets everyone with a bright smile.

"Dad, what are you doing here?" Elli asks, giving him a hug.

"Thought I'd drive you to work," he offers. "We're still doing lunch today, right?"

Elli's been a licensed sex therapist since the kids were five. I told her she didn't have to work but she wanted to. She chose to have a practice outside of the house. She didn't want patients coming in and out for sessions. I understood and supported that.

"Of course," she answers him.

Annaleigh enters with her friend and hits her brother on the back of the head. "Wake up."

He sits up, rubbing the spot and narrowing his eyes on hers. "Some of us actually care about our grades and study."

She laughs him off but doesn't argue.

"Brex, want to do some shooting after school today?" Nicholas asks him.

"Sure," he answers with a shrug.

"What about you Anna? Want to join us?" he asks her.

"No thanks. I've got plans."

"What are you doing?" I wonder.

"Study group," she responds without even looking up from her cell while typing away. "Graduation is in three weeks. Have to prep for finals." Her brother snorts as if he doesn't believe her.

I have to agree with him, but my wife speaks before I can. "With whom?"

"Ryann."

At least I can confirm that. All it'll take is a text. I'm quite close with a few Lords that I wasn't back when attending Barrington. That's what happens when you have kids the same age who go to school together.

"She's not a senior," Brexton argues.

"She's in advanced classes." Annaleigh rolls her eyes at him and adds, "You should let her help you. She'd probably teach you a few things."

His face hardens. He opens his mouth like he's going to say something that'll just piss her off even more but decides against it. Picking up his cell, he walks out of the kitchen.

"You didn't eat your breakfast," Elli calls out, but he doesn't respond. "Anna—"

"What?" She grabs a piece of bacon from her brother's plate. "It's no secret he has a crush on her. I'm just trying to help him out." The smile she gives her mother says something entirely different. "If he's going to be a Lord, he needs to grow some balls."

"Annaleigh!" her mother scolds her.

She ignores her mother's tone and turns to her grandfather. "I'm free tomorrow, though. I need to practice on throwing my knives."

Like I said. She's my twin. I'm not sure Brexton could shoot anyone unless his life depended on it. But Annaleigh? I have no doubt she'd stab someone multiple times if you try and tell her how to drive. Then she'd hide the body while setting up a search party.

"Absolutely," Nicholas tells her with a proud smile.

"We're off to school." She then turns and rushes out of the kitchen. Her friend quickly following, waving bye.

"I'll wait for you in the car," Nicholas tells my wife. "Easton, I'll see you at work." He nods and leaves us alone.

"Finally." I reach out and pull her into me. Cupping her face, I lower my lips to hers and kiss her, needing her taste to get me through the day. I'd love to drag her downstairs and keep her tied up in our basement until tomorrow, but I know that won't be happening.

She pulls away and opens her ice-blue eyes to look up at me. "I know what you're doing, and I don't have time."

"I'll be quick."

She gives a rough laugh. "Yeah, right. We both know that's a lie." Wrapping her arms around my neck, she presses her chest into mine. "But the kids won't be home this weekend. They're going on their senior year camping trip. You know what that means?"

I groan. "Means I'm going to have you to myself." The thoughts of what I'll do to her are endless. "We're going to spend the entire weekend down in the basement." I will forever love my wife, but she'll always be my little demon that loves to be used. And I will always be her devil that will give her whatever she wants.

## THE END

Thank you for taking the time to read *THE SINNER*. Did you enjoy it? See where it all began with *The Ritual*.

Want to discuss *TS* with other readers? Be sure to join the spoiler room on Facebook. **Shantel Tessier's Spoiler Room.** Please note that I have one spoiler room for all books, and you may come across spoilers from book(s) you have not had the chance to read yet. You must answer both questions in order to be approved. *Join spoiler room*

Keep on reading to get a sneak peek of *The Sacrifice*.

Want to know more about Tyson? Continue on to read a sneak peek of *The Sacrifice* (Tyson's book)

# THE SACRIFICE

USA TODAY & WALL STREET JOURNAL BESTSELLING AUTHOR

# SHANTEL TESSIER

## LAIKYN

Your wedding day is supposed to be one of the most exciting days of your life. Just like my mother, I'm about to marry a man I didn't choose and who I don't love. I actually despise him and everything he represents—money, greed, and power are just a few of them.

My mother hates my father, but there was nothing either one of them could do. Their fate was decided, their destiny sealed. Same as mine. Same as my children's. And my grandchildren's. We are bred for the sole purpose of power. Control in numbers.

*Fuck that!*

Women in my world—the secret society of the Lords—should not reproduce. I don't want children. The cycle will end with me. It has to. The Lords will only find a way to use its members. They marry us off to ensure we add to their army. The next generation of Lords and Ladies will help them take over the world.

I stand in the middle of the room, overlooking the white dress in the mirrored wall, running my hand down the mulberry silk—some of the finest silk available in the world. I take in a deep breath. It cost a whopping two million. Two million dollars for a fucking dress? My soon-to-be husband had it custom-made by a designer in France. I know this because my mother reminds me every chance she gets.

Why would I get to pick out something so important in my life? That's insane, right? To think I should have any say in what I wear on the day I give my life to another.

It's as if she thinks his wealth will impress me. It's blood money. I know this because it's the same fortune I grew up with. I never did want the finer things in life. I know a poor person would roll their eyes at that statement, but it's true. Give me a beer, a cheap hoodie, and a hat to hide my three-day old mop of bleach-blond hair, and I'm happy.

But no. That's unacceptable. The one percent aren't allowed to look anything less than perfect. Not in public anyway. I'm surprised they even let us speak. We as women might as well walk around with duct tape over our mouths dressed in nothing but chains.

A Lord needs a Lady but not because of the reasons you may think. It's a way to hide who he really is. He'll have fucks all over the world, but we're expected to cook, clean, and spread our legs for him when he's home. Worship him like he's God himself and birth his children.

I've never been religious, and I'm not going to fall to my knees and start worshipping a man now.

My brother comes up behind me, his eyes scanning over my dress in the mirror. "At least he has good taste."

I roll my eyes. "As if that matters."

"Just pop out some kids and get fat." He shrugs. "Then he'll screw anyone but you. Oh! Hire a hot, much younger nanny." He nods to himself. "Let me try her out first, though. Make sure she's good enough."

His words just prove that all Lords are the same. He's been a

Lord for years but has yet to marry. He has the privilege of fucking his way around the world while I'm forced to sign my life away.

A cell rings, and he pulls it out of his tuxedo jacket to answer. "Hello?"

Sighing, I pick up the dress and walk over to the stained glass window. You can't see shit out of it. This place is ancient. The Cathedral is to a Lord as a church is to a religion—their sanctum. It holds a hundred years of secrets like a sarcophagus encloses a mummy.

It was handed down to them years ago—a place to perform their sick and twisted rituals. There's nothing fancy or special about it, if you ask me. I could be walking down the aisle in blue jeans and a T-shirt or lingerie. Doesn't matter.

Not all Lords and Ladies are required to wed here. But it's where my future husband picked. Our parents wanted it to be as traditional as possible. It's a bullshit reason. They just want to make a spectacle of handing me over to him. We might as well be standing in a courtroom with a judge sentencing me to life in prison without the chance of parole for a crime I didn't commit.

I place my hand on the cold glass, listening to the rain fall. It's been storming for the past two days. It's like the world knows I've been destined for a lifetime of servitude to a man I'd rather kill than kneel and suck his dick.

I blame my mother. She raised me to be strong-willed and determined. But now, I'm just supposed to turn it off and believe that I'm to devote my life to a man that will neglect me during the day but demand I spread my legs at night.

I won't accept that. I deserve more. I want more.

My brother ends his call, getting my attention, and looks at me. "We have a problem," he states.

*My whole life is a fucking problem.* "What?"

"Luke is missing."

I snort. "Don't toy with me like that." That's not a problem; that's a prayer answered.

"I'm serious." He swallows, looking around the large room nervously as if Luke's going to appear out of thin air. "He's not here. He never arrived. He's also not at his house. He's missing. No one has seen him."

"I'm not sure why that's a problem." I don't want to marry the sick bastard. Luke Cabot is the highest-ranking Lord you can come by, which just makes this even worse. Lords are like anything else in this world. You have some at the bottom, and others at the top. There are different tiers. But honestly, it doesn't matter; they're all sick fucking bastards who will kill anyone to get to where they are. Even the bottom feeders will destroy anything to get a chance at serving.

He steps over to me. "Laikyn ..."

The door opens, and my father enters with my mother. I cross my arms over my chest. "I'm guessing this good fortune has nothing to do with you two?"

My mother's injected lips seem to thin a tad at my comment. She's told me a million times that this is just the life we live. That it's a "tradition" and I just have to accept it. That as far as Lord and Lady goes, we're royalty. Bull-fucking-shit. I'd rather be someone's bitch than a Lord's Lady.

My father, however, stares at the floor while running a hand through his dark hair. "Daddy?" I step over to him, holding my dress in my hands so I don't step on the hem. "What's going on?"

His throat works, swallowing before his eyes find mine. There's a look of regret in them, and hope fills my chest. Maybe he's realized that I don't want this life.

He clears his throat. "I just received a call ..."

"Please tell me you did this—called off my wedding?" I rush out, my words hopeful.

"I'm sorry, Laikyn, but the wedding is still on." He sighs.

And what little hope I had is now smothered. "But Miller said Luke's missing." I point at my brother. Had my father received the same phone call that my brother did? Or was it someone else?

"You are no longer to wed Luke." He yanks on the collar of his tux.

Picking up the dress so I don't trip over it in my six-inch hooker heels—that my soon-to-be husband also picked out—I take a step back, my heart picking up speed. This is good news. Why does he look so concerned? "I don't understand. If he's not here—"

"A new Lord has chosen you," he interrupts me.

My mother places her hand over her mouth, trying to quiet a sob.

"No," I argue. "That can't be." It was decided that Luke would be my husband when I was eighteen—three years ago. Things like this aren't just changed at the last minute. I've lived the past few years preparing for this day. To be his wife. What he wanted. A Lord can't choose to marry me, not when I'm already promised to another.

"Who?" my brother demands. "Who in the hell would make this change?" He fists his hands at his sides.

I reach up and grab the pearls my mother gave me. She thought they would give me some kind of comfort, and I laughed, but now I hold on to them as if they're an anchor to a lifeline.

"I—" The door swings open once again, this time hitting the interior wall and making me jump.

A set of baby-blue eyes meet mine, and my stomach drops. The wind knocked out of me. I haven't seen them in years, but they've haunted my dreams ever since.

"Tyson," my brother growls, shoving me to the side and pulling me out of that memory, and steps in front of me. "What are you ...?"

Ryat, Tyson's best friend, slams the door shut just as hard as he opened it.

I take a step back, tripping over the dress, but thankfully, the stained glass stops me from falling to my ass.

"How?" my father demands, turning to face him.

Tyson just gives him an evil smile that reminds me of how fucked up he really is. "Leave us," he orders.

Just the sound of his voice makes my legs want to buckle, but I manage to stay standing.

"I will not!" My father sidesteps to block their view of me.

Tyson takes the steps to close the small space between them and leans in, whispering in my father's ear. His cold, baby-blue eyes are on mine, and even if he were screaming at my father, I wouldn't be able to hear him over the pounding in my chest and the blood rushing in my ears. Sweat instantly beads across my forehead, and I'm having trouble catching my breath at the sight of him. Suddenly, the extravagant dress is too tight. The expensive material an anchor, pulling me down into a bottomless sea.

My father grabs my mother's hand and pulls her from the room, leaving me. My brother goes to step out, but Ryat grabs his tuxedo jacket, yanking him back into the room. "You may stay," Ryat tells him.

"Get the fuck out!" my brother yells at them. "Or I'll call security."

"Go ahead." Tyson shrugs. "I replaced your guards with my own."

I raise my sweaty hands. "What ... what are you doing here?" Luke would never invite them to our wedding. He hates Tyson. I'm not sure how he feels about Ryat, though. But I can almost guarantee he's not a fan due to the fact that he's Tyson's best friend. It's that guilty by association thing.

"Ryat." Tyson snaps his fingers at his best friend, who reaches into his tux and pulls out a folded piece of paper. He slaps it to my brother's chest.

Letting out a huff, my brother opens it up and his eyes scan the paper, his body stiffening, and my breathing picks up. "What?" I ask nervously, my sweaty hand gripping the pearls around my neck.

"No," he growls, shaking his head quickly.

"What is it?" I step forward, and Tyson moves in front of me, his large frame towering over mine. I try to step away, but the glass is at my back again.

My brother's face pales, and he whispers, "You are to marry Tyson."

"Wh-at?" My legs threaten to buckle, my heart stopping altogether. "No. There must be—"

Tyson's hand wraps around my neck, and he pins me to the cold glass. My hands shoot up, my nails digging into the sleeve of his black tux. I try to kick him away, but he's standing on the skirt of the dress, restricting my movements.

"Laikyn!" My brother drops the paper and runs for me, but Ryat grabs his hair, yanking him back while kicking the back of his knees and forcing him to kneel. Reaching into his pocket, Ryat pulls out a pocketknife and flips it open. The sound of the click makes my breath catch before he holds it to my brother's throat.

"No!" I shout at Ryat, and my eyes find Tyson's blue ones. They're cold. I'm not even sure if the man feels anything. He's as bad as they come in the Lords. Most of the Lords are placed strategically out into the world to fit in while they take what they want. But not Tyson. No, he openly runs the underworld for them. "What do you want, you fucking bastard?" I demand. My body twists under his grip.

"Just you. Forever," he answers simply.

My teeth grind and I lift my chin. "You sick fuck! You really think I'll marry you?" He's the reason my sister is dead. All Lords are evil, but something about him has always been off. "Over my dead body."

A smile spreads across his face, telling me he expected this. He knows how I feel about him and that I'd never willingly give myself to him. I'd marry Luke a thousand times over before giving myself to Tyson. "Either your brother walks you down the aisle and gives you away to me, or Ryat slits his throat, and he hands you over to me himself with Miller's blood on them."

"Don't do it," my brother growls at me, and Ryat yanks his head back, forcing him to look up at the ceiling. Bringing the blade across his neck, he pushes the tip into my brother's skin as if he's about to slice it open.

"Don't," I cry out, knowing that he'll kill him right here in front of me. I don't know Ryat personally, but I know enough to know that he's not the joking kind. He's here for Tyson and will do whatever he tells him just to prove a point. I wasn't able to save my sister, but I'll do anything to save my brother. "I'll ... do it." My chest tightens on the words, making it hard to get them out. I just signed my death warrant. But I will not lie down and give him the satisfaction of accepting it. He may run the Lords' hell, but I will make sure I burn it down with me.

"That's a good girl," Tyson praises, running his free hand down the side of my face. He gently caresses me as if he thinks it'll give me some sort of security. It's all a fucking lie. I know how the Lords work. I've seen my father manipulate my mother over the years. But she allowed it. I, however, won't. "Ryat, let our guests know we'll be ready in ten minutes." He steps away, releasing me, and I rub my sore neck where the pearls were digging into my sensitive skin.

Ryat exits the room, dragging my brother with him and leaving me alone with the monster who ruined my life.

# ALSO PART OF THE LORD'S WORLD

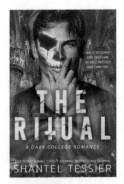
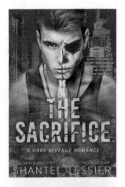

# CONTACT ME

**Facebook Reader Group:** Shantel's Sinful Side

**Goodreads:** Shantel Tessier

**Instagram:** shantel_tessierauthor

**Website:** Shanteltessier.com

**Facebook Page:** Shantel Tessier Author

**TikTok:** shantel_tessier_author

**Store:** shanteltessierstore.com

**Email:** shanteltessierassistant@gmail.com OR darkangelcreationsllc@gmail.com

**Shantel Tessier's Spoiler Room.** Please note that I have one spoiler room for all books, and you may come across spoilers from book(s) you have not had the chance to read yet. You must answer both questions in order to be approved.

Printed in the USA
CPSIA information can be obtained
at www.ICGtesting.com
LVHW020252290124
770172LV00002B/266